I0706068

WOLF AND BARE IT

WOLF BROTHERS BOOK #2

ANNE MARSH

COPYRIGHT

This book is a work of fiction. Names, characters, places, rants, facts, contrivances, and incidents are either the product of the author's questionable imagination or are used factitiously. Any resemblance to actual persons, living or dead or undead, events, locales is entirely coincidental if not somewhat disturbing/concerning.

Made in the United States of America

Print Edition

ISBN: 978-1-959097-94-5

CHAPTER
ONE

"I might be forgiven for having no magic, but I have no beauty, either. I am curvy where I should be thin and my hair is dark instead of blonde. I do not look like the other Fae maidens . . ."

— EVANGELINE ANDERSON, *THE THRONE OF SHADOWS*

Dicks were trouble.

The long, fat stalk? Red flag. The plump head? Also a red flag.

Misfortune or fault, the mushroom at my feet resembled a very puffy phallus.

Why not pick it? That was my thought when I reached out with grabby hands.

And then suddenly I was somersaulting downhill, betrayed by my fungi lust. Betrayed by a dick. AGAIN.

The world blurred in a haze of green ferns and brown dirt. Grounding was therapeutic, but right now I was *too* connected to the mountainside.

Landing was even more painful.

Looking back, maybe I should have planned my day off better.

The forest was a place where my kind, those with certain supernatural gifts, came to recharge. Replenish the magical well. Get away from the humans, get away from ourselves and the masks we have to wear to fit into your world.

1

Sick and tired of wearing that magical mask, I'd temporarily traded the glitz of my TV-star life for alone time with Mother Nature. Trees! Fungus! Epiphytes hitching rides on other plants! At first I thought Tennessee had the best woods ever. Awesome decision!

But now, I was starting to rethink my choices. For example: these woods were *not* well marked. Was there an EXIT sign?

Well, no. This was compounded by my sad failure to grab a trail map when I'd decided to stop for a hike instead of pushing straight on to my rental cabin. "Unexpected detours are so much fun," I'd enthused to the barista who'd told me about the trail. "I love surprises!"

Then I'd run out of the coffee shop before anyone could recognize me—ball caps were *the best*—and hopped in my rental car. In the parking lot, on the road, stopped for traffic lights, I'd got a few second looks. Some sideways glances. One lady snapped a picture with her phone before waving hesitantly.

I'd been happy to hit the trail and be alone. It was just me! No one else around! HEAVEN!

But now that I'd crash-landed at the bottom of a tricksy slope, I was rethinking my anti-people sentiment.

I took inventory. Winced.

I was . . . functional?

Multiple scratches, some missing and much mourned skin on my left elbow and right palm. Bruises, dirt, and bug bites. Was I otherwise in one piece? Yep. Was I looking forward to covering up the damage when I went back? Not at all.

People talked up personal glamour, but it came with a hefty price tag. It was like a plane: the farther you flew, the more gas it took. The more I changed my appearance, the more energy I expended. Let me tell you, my TV-star good looks and charm took *considerable* energy. My face was the gas-guzzler model.

The crunch of dry autumn leaves as I carefully rolled over almost but not quite drowned out the angry rumble of my stomach. I was hungry and grumpy. Grungry.

Keeping my feelings to myself was like staying silent during sex: unsatisfying, offputting, and sure to disappoint. I shared those feelings—loudly and liberally—with the forest floor.

"*Oye*, stupid, warty, spiny, oversized puffball. What the *pineapple*?"

Was the trail anywhere in sight? No.

Cell phone signal? Also a big, fat no.

Actually, both living creatures and bars of cell phone service had been absent ever since I'd left the trailhead to forage for mushrooms . . . which had landed me here. Somewhere in the dirt in the middle of nowhere, Tennessee. At least it was still daylight and would be for hours. Trust me, October days in this state did not end quickly and the sky was still blazingly, brightly hot.

Really, I'd die out here from dehydration and starvation. The epitaph on my gravestone would read: *No finding spell could help. Her sense of direction was so bad, even the trail mix was confused.*

Was I overdramatic? Was I letting my acting job bleed into my personal life? You betcha, but I still rechecked my phone like the essential lifeline it was. Perhaps a massive cell phone tower had sprouted in Moonlight Valley and this isolated, people-less corner of the fine state of Tennessee miraculously had cell phone reception and Google Maps.

Nada.

I'd just have to find the trailhead and my stupid, stick-shift car on my own . . . or maybe I'd try a finding spell if I had the energy. It had rained recently, and the ferns taunted me as I climbed back up, a layer of delicious green frosting on mud pie. Moss, more ferns, unattractive dead branches, a sprinkling of lichens, and ooh . . . *sparkle.*

Quartz crystals, my brain supplied. Black, slightly glassy, just a hint of sparkle. *Field diamond*, my ever-hopeful heart whispered back. *DIAMOND.*

It was nestled amongst the dirt and leaves, as if it had been placed there just for me. It was luck. An unexpected gift to find something so precious where it shouldn't be. No digging, no searching—it was simply *there*. Waiting.

I tucked the rock into my pocket.

That bit of hope motivated me up the ravine, although I faceplanted in the muddy dirt more than once. *Stupid mushroom hunting, making me walk miles. I'll eat you for dinner!*

A distant, tuneless whistling tugged on my attention as I clambered back onto the path. There was a sort-of melody to the off-key sound, a cheerful but terrible warble that heralded a fellow hiker having a good day. Or an untalented bird with powerful lungs.

Did birds have lungs? I made a note to research that after I returned to civilization and the land of working internet. And showers . . .

I was covered in dirt and leaves. My hair stuck out in a dozen different directions, all unflattering. The last thing I needed was pictures of me imitating a crone from Shakespeare's *Macbeth* all over the internet. Or worse, pictures of unglamoured me.

Trust me. There would be questions if anyone saw my real face.

The bad whistling morphed into an inexplicably peppy but recognizable rendition of the 1812 Overture. Booted feet crunched over the leaf-covered trail, coming closer.

Commencing evasive maneuvers.

I sucked in a breath, pressed a hand over my noisy stomach, and reached for the energy for a glamour. *Hi, unknown hiker! I'm just a random, unknown person you've met on the trail! You don't recognize me at all, but you'll point me in the direction of the parking lot? Awesome! Thanks SO much!*

Except . . . An unwelcome, far uglier thought popped into my head.

What if it wasn't picture-taking that he wanted? The universe was full of assholes —both human and supernatural—and I was a woman alone in the woods. Some-times, bears were safer.

Having read this story dozens of times on Yahoo, I fished my very unmagical but handy mace out of my bag and tucked it against my side.

I ducked behind a tulip poplar to put my glamour on. My new tree friend was a good hundred feet tall, papered with shaggy brown bark, and slimmer around than I was. The glamour was a simple magic, one I'd honed further with practice, and it changed how people perceived me, like magical makeup or a face mask. Glam-oured me was more confident, more empathetic, just *more*.

And also *less*.

Specifically: I was less supernatural.

People reacted badly to half-Fae, half-Chaneque women. The pitchforks came out. Threats were made. Ergo, I glamoured when I wasn't in private, letting the magic hide my eye color, smooth down the rough edges of my teeth and ears. And then I added a little *oomph* for good measure. Maybe it was unethical. Maybe that meant people didn't like me for myself. Maybe that was why my relationships sucked— but I was safe.

The product that kept my long, brown hair sleek and smooth had dried up or rubbed off, and now random waves and curls sproinged and sprouted. I'd donated my hair tie to the forest floor. Dry twigs and crunchy leaves poked out at random intervals. Given how much energy I was devoting to the glamour already, I'd live with the bad hair.

I snuck a peek around the tree trunk—was Whistling Dude flashing a camera or a phone in my direction? Was I in imminent danger of being filmed? Did Southern hikers do social media?

If a tree falls in the forest, and there's no one around to record it, does it make a sound?

I saw no phone, no camera, no drone.

The unbuttoned state of the black flannel that hugged Hiking Dude's frame was entirely due to his chest being too muscly for his shirt. Or possibly it was protesting the truly awful biology pun on said shirt: *DJ Enzyme breaks it down!* A boring pair of khaki-colored hiking pants stretched over a far more interesting, broader set of thighs. He had one hand shoved into a pocket, and a thick beard framed plush lips as he whistled badly but happily. Beneath an honest-to-God, beat-up black cowboy hat, his other hand gripped a Gandalf-worthy walking stick. Was it for beating off bears and other woodland creatures? He frowned up at the tree canopy as if the leaves had offended him.

BLESS YOU, FOREST SPIRITS.

I twisted my hair up on top of my head, anchoring it with the backup tie from my wrist, brushed the biggest clumps of dirt from the front of my sweatshirt, and exhaled. This was good. I didn't need my glamour dialed to maximum effect or a script—just the most basic of enchantments to hide my otherworldliness. We'd do the head-tip thing, he'd point me toward the way out, and boom! End of social interaction.

As I inched out from behind the tree and faced him, magic in place, his confident stride faltered. Surprise! You have company!

His eyes narrowed, and interest tempered his gaze. Ugh. *Showtime.* I turned my glamour up a notch, but it was as sluggish and shy as I was tired and hungry. Glamouring wasn't like flipping a light switch on or off. It was more like a dial that I turned up or eased back, a magical on-ramp rather than a sudden precipice. On set, I dialed it up to maximum.

Before I could wrap myself in the magic more securely, however, he'd recovered from his surprise and swaggered toward me. His arrogance was strangely cute and was paired with a crooked grin and a magnificent pair of dimples. Apparently, he found dirt and leaves amusing.

He gave up trying to hide his smile and outright grinned. "Afternoon, ma'am."

His voice was deep and rough, a dark chocolate burr that made me think of molasses and honey, whiskey and midnight promises. Dear Danu—the man could earn a fortune in Hollywood.

He tipped his head and then, surprisingly, hung back on the path. It took me precious seconds to figure out why.

OMG. He was a gentleman hiker.

He was trying not to scare me.

I was so relieved that I snort-laughed. Maybe it was nerves. Maybe that's why I made such a socially inappropriate noise. I wasn't in danger at all.

Mr. Lumberjack was a teddy bear with boundaries.

A giant, adorable, dimpled *teddy bear*. Six-foot something, hazel eyes with gold-green flecks the color of sunlight filtering through the spring fronds of *Onoclea sensibilis*, my favorite fern. A strong, chiseled jaw covered with a thick pelt of brown beard. Okay, so he wasn't precisely cuddly. In fact, he was built along the lines of a very sexy bouncer or a professional wrestler.

Fortunately, five years of Hollywood living had inoculated me against male hotness. His good looks barely registered. His attractiveness flitted through my brain the same way I'd have noticed a cute dog someone had snuck into the coffee shop or a darling mug in the window of my favorite boutique. *La, la, la, la, that's adorable, too freaking cute, but I don't need it and it's NOT coming home with me.*

Hot men were the cute coffee cups of relationships—you never needed one more because you already had more in your life than you could use. Plus, they tended to be shallow, fragile, and require special treatment.

Early in my showbiz career, I'd leveraged my star appeal to date pretty actors—muscled and lean, dark and grouchy, sunshine and flirty, or all-round attractive—I'd dated them all. Naïve, young Sonnet's motto had been: why stop at one chocolate in the sexy box?

Older, wiser, and far more cynical, I had come to understand that too many chocolate-box men gave me a stomachache.

Firstly: hot guys dated hot women.

Secondly: the hot guy ran the hotness dictionary and decided who was hot—or not. This meant he wrote the script, and I said the lines he wanted me to say. I was expected to remake myself into whatever he thought was hot for a woman. As I liked maintaining creative control, this did not work for me. Also, it was a lot of work tweaking my glamour to charm someone into believing I'd been poured into the dream woman package.

Thirdly: I couldn't afford to waste time on dating.

Being Sonnet Ruiz, *Smoky Spirits* TV star and successful novelist, consumed my time. My planner had no empty square for dinner out or couple time on my sofa. As my manager and sister, Elena, reminded me constantly, success required putting my job first.

Time available for hot guys: zilch.

No, scratch that.

Time available for ANY guys: zilch.

My life was a guy-free zone.

And sure, this hiker was an attractive stranger guy, but he was also (I hoped) a man-sized EXIT sign who would point me toward my way out. I was sweaty and damp, muddy and miserable. And not that I wasn't always sexy, but right now I might be actually, seriously lost and solving that problem was far more important than any future orgasm.

Ergo, I tipped my head once at the hot hiker's polite greeting, shoving my tangled curls out of my face. "Greetings, fellow hiker."

Noooo. Cut! That terrible line was a stinker that I'd have ruthlessly revised in edits. I did not do well in real time—I needed my laptop and twenty minutes to arrive at a decent opening line. But as I really did need his sense of direction, I hoped he was a smart hot guy. Or at least equipped with an excellent personal compass and a working cell phone.

His lips quirked. Parted. He seemed unsure of his next line in our scene.

How to interpret his interesting silence?

Sometimes people got weird when they met me. They'd ask me to reenact their favorite scenes. Strangely enough, these were not always the kissing scenes. They'd also ask me to sign stuff: napkins, coffee cup sleeves, ball caps, forearms, and other, more personal, body parts. I'd decline the reenactment requests and scrawl my signature on whatever non-animate objects they produced. It was part of the job. But right now, I'd fallen down the mountain. I was covered in dirt. I was grouchy and hungry, and he was way too freaking adorable.

But instead of holding out an arm for me to sign or mansplaining the plot holes in my latest novel where a curvy half-Fae astronaut had crash-landed on a planet of alien orcs with monster dicks, this man cleared his throat, pushing his cowboy hat back with one scarred and battered finger.

"Ma'am, do you need assistance?"

The expression on his handsome face conveyed his belief that this was a rhetorical question.

"Possibly." I rushed across the path and latched onto his (very muscled, unsigned) arm. Hot or not, he was human, and I was lost in this mountain of green, trees, and rocks. His gaze dropped to my hands, clutching his flannel-covered forearm with obvious need. "Okay. Yes. Please. I fell down a giant hill, and I've lost the trailhead. I don't know where I am in relation to the exit. My car is somewhere that is very much *not here*. Plus, it's a stick shift, and it's sentient and hates me. And I'm hungry, my phone is dead, and I don't have time to learn how to trap a poor, defenseless rabbit and barbecue its fuzzy ass just so I don't starve to death. You are perfect and currently meeting all my needs. Don't leave me here."

"Are you okay?" His forehead puckered slightly as he leaned toward me, concern filling his eyes. His eyes narrowed. "You have a bruise."

A big, warm paw of a hand reached out to me. Did I want him to touch me? I would never know because he caught himself short. My stomach growled, in a hungry and combative mood.

He drew back, offered me a small smile as he shoved his hand into his pocket. "Sorry."

His hand emerged, covered mine briefly, and then retreated again. It was a huge and warm. In fact, it felt so unexpectedly good that I almost grabbed it except that—

He'd handed me a chocolate bar.

I'd never taken candy from a stranger before, nor had a hot guy ever given me a present. As a curvy gal, most people were more inclined to "helpfully" point out that I should consume carrots instead of refined sugars.

This guy was *not* most people.

His kindness was as unexpected as the gift of chocolate itself.

"Where do you need to go?" he asked gently.

Stranger danger, my mami's voice shrieked in my head. *Hija! You do NOT tell him where you live.*

Mami had a point, but this man might have a map. Or, at the very least, directions. He definitely had chocolate.

Faced with the possibility of spending the rest of my (short) life lost on a Tennessee mountain, I discarded her sensible advice.

"Phantom Falls. I'm willing to consider selling my soul or making a deal with the devil to get there too." This was said around a mouthful of chocolate.

He frowned. "Phantom Falls? You live up there?"

"Not yet. I just got here today. A friend, Wyatt Reynolds, has a rental with a view of the waterfall that he's leasing to me for a few months and I'm on my way to pick up the keys."

"Wyatt? You know Wyatt?"

"Yes, sir. We were college roommates."

The adorable pucker in my lumberjack-cowboy's brow deepened. The cutest pink flush colored his cheeks. "You don't need to call me *sir*, ma'am."

And you're calling me ma'am. I bit back a smile.

"Do you have an alternate name? Mr. White Knight in Khaki Pants?"

The dimple in his cheek deepened. "You can call me Maverick, ma'am."

Oh, my Goddess. I couldn't *even* with his old-school manners and his sexy Southern accent.

"Your name is Maverick?"

Danger. That was either a hot-guy name or a stripper name. And since I didn't see a stripper pole or a dancing conga line of guys with toolbelts, I needed to be careful.

He nodded. "My daddy was a big fan of trucks."

"Uh, sure?" I said.

"And so he named my brothers and me after his favorite vehicles." My new friend Maverick lifted one big, flannel-covered shoulder. Clearly, he was as flummoxed by his daddy's naming choices as I was.

He was charming. Friendly and self-deprecating. It was downright adorable. The orcs I wrote about in my very popular paranormal romance novels were all swash-buckle and confidence. They were apex predators, giants of sexiness who swaggered around until they met their fated human mates. But when my heroes got near their heroines . . . BAM. They *knew*. She was their one and only. They didn't even have to see their ladies; they had magical love-proximity radar.

I was a big fan of fated mates.

Because, in my experience, real-life hot guys did not date normal-looking women . . . and they certainly weren't interested in supernatural me. My Hollywood boyfriends had asked me out under the influence of the glamour that made me look one-hundred-percent human.

"Where did you leave your car?" Maverick asked.

"The trailhead." I whipped out my phone and showed him a picture of my rental car surrounded by trees. I guess I'd thought it was like the airport, where you took a photo of where your parked car was so you could find it again after you staggered off a red-eye, sleep-deprived and grungry. Unfortunately, the pull-off where I'd parked was smaller and less obvious than an entire parking structure. I'd also come to realize that one tree pretty much looked like any other tree.

Nevertheless, Maverick nodded and pointed back down the trail he'd come up. "You go down this trail until you spot the white blaze on the dead tulip poplar. Take the left fork, go two miles, take a right, then right again, it's maybe four miles from here and—"

That was too much information.

Also: FOUR MILES?

Maverick blinked impossibly long lashes. Possibly, he was telepathic? "On the other hand, my truck's a half mile away."

Then he hesitated.

He appeared to be performing complex social calculus. Or correctly interpreting the look of desperate despair on my face and weighing the not-so-remote possibility that he would have to carry my perishing but not slight body down the mountain to my car.

"Or—" he said. Then stopped. Blinked.

I gave him an encouraging smile, hoping I didn't have chocolate smeared on my teeth. Should I up the wattage on my glamour? Strangely, I didn't want to.

"There are twelve thousand different species of ferns," I volunteered when he didn't finish his sentence.

"Excuse me?"

Maverick blinked again. It was likely Morse code for *Help, I'm trapped on the mountain with a socially inept person—please rescue me!*

I was blurting out fern fun facts. Dear Danu. That meant Maverick made me nervous. Which was inexplicable because my last boyfriend had vaccinated me against hot guys.

It's a miracle.

Or a curse.

My money was on curse. I should not have snagged the last doughnut at the coffee shop when a half-dozen hungry witches were waiting in line behind me.

"Or we could go in my truck. To your cabin. For today, maybe it's easier if I give you a ride, and I'll have someone pick your car up later."

His eyes moved over my very ordinary face as he said this, still warm and interested. I double-checked but my glamour was still dialed down. I was just me, a little smoother, a whole lot less Fae. Maverick stared at me. I stared back. This was . . .

A hawk screeched overhead.

The ferns beside the trail rustled.

Maverick kept right on looking at me.

The way he focused on me, interested and intent, made me reconsider my conclusion that he hadn't recognized me.

Perhaps he was a superfan of my TV show or my mushroom- and magic-focused Gremlincore accounts? Maybe he was a voracious reader of orc romance, defying the statistics that proclaimed my core reader to be female and an average age of forty-two. Maybe he was starstruck at meeting someone famous.

Whatever the reason for this stare-fest, I needed him to take charge and get us out of this wilderness and back to civilization. I had to pee and his chocolate, no matter how delicious, was small.

"Yes," I blurted out.

Maverick blinked and his brain rebooted. He turned, placing a big paw on my shoulder, and turning me with him so that I faced an entirely different direction. Then he promptly removed his hand and gestured toward my old nemesis, the ferns. "This way."

"Are you sure?" It looked like an optimal direction in which to lure me and then stash my lifeless body. You know. If the rugged take on Prince Charming was just a super clever ploy.

"Very." His mouth quirked up.

Huh. The direction he was indicating looked suspiciously like the direction from which I'd just come. Revisiting my Waterloo (aka the deceptively steep slope of fiddlehead ferns that had tripped me up so badly) seemed unwise. Nevertheless, faced with the choice of remaining out here alone or tromping along after my flannel-covered rescuer, I opted to tromp.

"Here." He paused and held out his Gandalf stick. "For balance."

I took it, then looked down at the front of my sweatshirt, which displayed unmistakable evidence of balance issues.

"Water," he finished, holding out a canteen.

He was a one-man rescue group.

Maverick turned around and started effortlessly breaking a path through the ferns. He seemed to know exactly where he was going. In fact, he was entirely *too* comfortable out here. Was *he* human?

Not having a supernatural woodland species guide to consult (not to mention having a bursting bladder and an empty stomach), I decided to take my chances.

I followed along behind him, after a token protest. "I can't take all of your stuff, Maverick."

"You seem like you've had a rough day." He stopped—I hoped it wasn't because he was lost too—and gave me another thoughtful once-over with his eyes. "If you're tired, I could carry you."

He patted his ridiculously broad, flannel-covered, lust-worthy back.

I shook my head automatically, then kicked myself. Not that he should have to carry me down a mountain when I had two functioning legs that had got me into this mess in the first place, but . . . holy research opportunity, Batman.

Pink colored his cheeks again. "Right. Down the mountain it is."

He turned and started forward again, holding back ferns and branches with one big arm so that I was not further assaulted by the wilderness. His thoughtfulness caught me off guard.

I had never met a hot guy who was empathetic. Most were orc-like with beastly manners.

It made no earthly sense.

Or I had met all the wrong people.

Possibly, the hot, Hollywood types were a different, more bright-light-loving species than their Southern counterparts. They throve in the spotlight, turning their faces up to the sun. Sometimes beautiful plants had shallow roots—and sometimes, like my mystery gentleman, they were shyer, more mysterious, and hid in the shade.

I thought about that for the next twenty minutes while we twisted and turned our way down the mountain. Once, he came to an abrupt halt and stared with adorable concentration as a slender ribbon of neon green snake peered at us from a tangle of vines.

"Rough green snake," he shared as I snapped a picture. "Probably looking for lunch," Maverick added.

I gave him a look.

"Insects," he clarified, with a grin. "Spiders. Miscellaneous invertebrates."

Well, whew. I had a backbone, even if it didn't always function.

"That's not a snake. That's a tiny nope rope," I told him.

This earned me another grin. We continued on our way, unmolested by the snake.

"So." He held out a hand to help me over a giant fallen tree. "What brings you to these parts?"

Magic. Magic, and an opportunity to forage for spell ingredients.

Most people didn't believe in the supernatural or magic because the only people who were witches were (they thought oh-so-wrongly) the colorful, free-spirited, nature, granola types. Or they remembered *Macbeth*'s Weïrd Sisters and decided all witches were cackling crones with cauldrons, and that wasn't how I rolled, thank you very much.

I laughed to myself, imagining Maverick's face if I told him the truth.

That I was magical and searching for ingredients for a spell.

But I wouldn't—*couldn't*—do that. I was in town to do a job, and probably this was the moment where I should have mentioned *Smoky Spirits*, my TV show. The plethora of people waiting for me to show up, just in case he was the world's most gorgeous, flannel-wearing serial killer.

Instead, I went for the joke.

I grabbed his hand. "Mushrooms."

He was solid and bracing. I had a feeling that I could throw myself off the top of the fallen tree, and he would simply catch me. My imagination embroidered on this possibility, adding some pair skater lifts and delicious twirling. He was large enough to handle my substantial weight.

He nodded. "What kind of mushrooms?"

The jokester kind.

"Big ones. I love to eat enormous mushrooms, and you guys have a reputation for having the largest, tastiest ones in the fine state of Tennessee."

"Mushrooms." He choked. I was so riveted by his lumberjack good looks that I didn't miss the faint pink flush now painting his cheekbones. Oh my GOD. He was a blusher. This would be so much fun.

"*Sí, claro que sí.*" I rested against him ever so briefly. He was my gentleman rescuer. I wouldn't tease. Much. "Mushrooms are delicious. I could eat them every night. I love a nice, thick stalk with a fat head. Plump, juicy tips on massive clubs. There's a buffet of choices in your fine state."

My words came out a little too playful to seem serious. Still, he thought about my buffet for a moment. And then he gave a moment to the mushroom selection. I hoped I hadn't given him a heart attack or performance anxiety. We were not yet to the parking lot or civilization.

Eventually, a small smile quirked the corners of his mouth. "So, you're not interested in a tiny frill of a mushroom?"

He was *playing* with me.

Can I keep you? I had to clear my throat. "Big mushrooms are the best."

After we'd exhausted the dirty mushroom puns, we mostly walked. He pointed out the occasional tree or bird, while I snapped pictures of ferns and moss for my social media. It was so nice that I was startled when we popped unexpectedly out of the woods and into a neatly cleared rectangle of dirt parallel to a road. An over-sized, mud-covered pickup truck the color of a rusty Halloween pumpkin was perfectly parked in a space outlined by pieces of deadwood. My suspicions about his humanity grew: no one could parallel park with that degree of accuracy.

He strode over to the passenger side of his truck and opened the door. He hadn't locked it, proving either that Maverick was the trusting sort or that we truly were in the middle of nowhere. Now he waited, a playful smile playing over his plush lips. The quirk of his mouth was happy and flirty. His eyes warmed as he looked me over, moving up and then down my body.

He likes what he sees.

I tripped over an invisible boulder because something unexpected and quite unusual was happening in disused regions south of my brain. My heart gave a curious flutter in my rib cage, tapping out an SOS. My breath caught.

I liked him right back, in a purely visual way. The long lashes on his stunning eyes. The stern slope of his nose. His shy grin framed by all that beard. He was big and beardy—absolutely perfect for woodland rescues—but most of all he was sweet. Gentlemen lumberjacks were the *best*. He'd done his best to give me space, even though I'd been alone on this mountain long enough (really, it felt like years) that I'd been willing to sacrifice my boundaries in the excellent cause of returning to civilization. For some reason, I regretted his polite insistence on keeping some distance between us, and also felt a teensy bit like leaping across that space and wrapping myself around him like a monkey. It was perplexing. Even more discombobulating was the way in which he truly seemed to see me.

Me.

Really? Does he? Because he would be the first. After all, my previous men friends had all asked out Sonnet the Star. Which meant . . .

This was either Stockholm syndrome or a strong survival instinct combined with my legitimate fear of starving to death in the wilderness. I knew exactly what my mother would say:

Hija, I told you! You do NOT get in a truck with a strange man!

I hesitated. He removed his wallet from his back pocket and pulled out two cards, holding them up so I could read them.

"My driver's license and my college ID. I teach at the local community college."

I tried and failed to imagine him in a tweed jacket and a rumpled button-up.

My rescuer waited patiently by the door. I got the feeling he'd wait a week if that was what it took—and he wouldn't complain.

"Perhaps you'd feel better if you told me your name?" he asked.

Hold on . . .

I peered suspiciously at Dr. Maverick Lincoln Boone. "You don't know who I am?"

"I'm a snake expert, not a mind reader. Can I have a hint?" He tipped his chin at me, that mischievous smile lighting up his face once more.

"Uh-huh," I answered. How, exactly, did I announce I was a famous TV star and therefore almost never anonymous?

It was a conundrum.

Nevertheless, I climbed into his truck. While I considered future car retrieval logistics, he went around, got in, and then waited for me to buckle up before he started the engine and drove us away. Presumably toward Wyatt's rental property, but possibly toward the Outer Hebrides or his secret lair.

Not that he seemed like a secret-lair kind of guy.

I thought about that for a good ten minutes.

I had so many questions.

I slouched against the window, folding my arms over my sweatshirt as I tried to hold the questions in. Eleven minutes into our drive, I gave up and asked, "You really don't know my name?"

Professor Mav's smile faded.

He slowed the truck, braking carefully, as the light up ahead of us on the sloping road switched to yellow. Then he set the parking brake out of an abundance of caution. His eyes examined my face, anxiety coloring his.

"Were you one of my students?" he asked warily.

He doesn't watch TV? Can I be myself? Drop the glamour? I stared, forcing down the bubble of hope that wanted to float up from my stomach, travel through my esophagus, and emerge as a proposition.

When was the last time I'd started out with a social blank slate with someone? I was covered in dirt, angry, and needy. So why—

Slowly, the clues presented themselves to me.

The flirtatious grins, the hot eyes, the white-knighting with chocolate—Professor Mav was attracted to me.

Me.

He'd been testing the waters in the Sea of Attraction and flirting with *me*.

Not Sonnet Ruiz, the famous author, television star, millionaire, award-winner, everybody's best friend, and fun sidekick.

Just me.

Danu's beard! I hadn't gone unrecognized in years. I had an instant to process the relief and joy that his bafflement gave me before the anxiety painting his handsome face erased my pleasure in his ignorance.

Judging by how his forehead crinkled and his big hands beat out a nervous rhythm on the steering wheel, he was worried about the whole student thing. Perhaps he thought he'd graded my performance, and I hadn't taken it well. Perhaps he worried that there had been some flirtation—or more—in this putative teacher-student relationship and he'd forgotten all of it.

This was when I realized that I knew exactly what type of hot guy he was. He was the bad boy, the always moving on, never calling again hot guy, which was the deadly polar bear of dating bears. Because that kind of hot guy was funny and charming, so nice that you didn't see the teeth until it was too late.

They were fun until they ate you for dinner.

And then, being bears of voracious appetite, they moved on and had some other lady for dinner. Lots and lots of ladies. Serial meals.

I didn't begrudge Professor Mav his hot ladies. Even a year ago, I might have gone out with him for a night or two. It would have been fun. Sexual enjoyment would have been had by all. But seeing as how I'd given up dating for the greater good of my career, losing my heart to a serial dater was also not part of my life plan.

He frowned at the road as the light changed, and he released the brake, looking fierce and anxious and so very large. I couldn't help myself, I really couldn't.

"No, I was not one of your students." I burst out laughing.

CHAPTER
TWO

MAVERICK

"People always fall in love quickly on folktales. Do you know any stories where the couple take a few years to know each other?"

— BRANDIE JUNE, *GOLD SPUN*

I had zero game left.

Instead of texting me her contact info—or even sharing her name—my pretty hiker was laughing at me. I'd made her completely lose it, and not for sexy reasons.

Use it or lose it, my wolf growled. **I warned you to get some love practice in.**

I ignored the commentary. Mostly. My wolf was a randy bastard and arrogant, even by lupine standards. Her laughter was amazing, a belly laugh that seemed too large even for her delicious curves. It was beautiful, the way she went all in, not holding back, and I just had to laugh along with her.

"You're too much." She swiped at her eyes; she'd laughed so hard that she cried. It was hard to look away. Her lashes were thick and lush, framing brown eyes, and for the first time in my life I wished I'd been an English professor. I knew how bats mated and where hognose snakes laid their eggs. What I did not know, however, was how to describe my companion's eyes. Beautiful, yes. Warm and brown and . . .

My wolf groaned. **You are so not a poet.**

That was not untrue.

Damn it.

Oblivious to my poetic shortcomings, she reached over and patted me on the arm. "You are too cute. I could eat you up."

I'd prefer to eat her, but I could settle for reciprocity. Or taking turns.

Stupid modern century, my wolf opined. **Let's take her home with us. She'll taste so good.**

It wasn't a bad plan.

Do it. Now. Before another wolf snaps her up.

I gripped the steering wheel, alarmed by this unexpected feeling of optimism. I'd deliberately spent the last five years *not* having sex. So, I was not entirely certain what these feelings meant.

Why was I flirting? Why now, and why with this woman?

I'd spoken with beautiful women in my 1,825 days of self-imposed celibacy, and I'd never had the urge to do . . . things. With them. To them. Or hell, even in their general vicinity.

BIG mistake, my wolf snapped. **We need to make up for lost time. Lean over and kiss the girl. We are not "cute."**

I tried not to grimace. My wolf and I were in agreement about her poor adjectival choice.

"You've got a real great laugh," I said instead of taking umbrage, because that was a truth I could get behind. Also, she had great socks. Her right foot sported a pink-and-yellow-striped sock, while her left foot had a green sock with white polka dots.

The rest of her was less colorful: black leggings, a short black skirt whose purpose was either purely decorative or to demarcate where the lush curve of her bottom ended and her thighs began, and a black sweatshirt with white lace on the cuffs and *Ferns: Nature's Little Hugs* embroidered across her amazing chest. Despite being covered in a greenish-brown layer of mud and leaves, she looked great.

She grinned. "That's not what people usually notice about me."

She has amazing tits, my wolf prompted. **And her ass is spectacular. Imagine what she—**

I shut him down. It was not okay to be thinking lascivious thoughts about my passenger. She was trusting me to get her to her destination safely.

"Those people are missing out on the most amazing parts, if all they concentrate on is how breathtakingly beautiful you are," I remarked. "And you are." I let myself drink in the profile of her face, before turning back to the road.

It wasn't just her laughter. It was her happiness, the joy she had. It was contagious. Special. She might have been dressed like a Goth elf in head-to-toe black and lace, but I could not look away. She possessed a magnetic quality, that intangible *something*. I'd bet people always noticed when she walked into a room and regretted when she left.

This earned me another snort of laughter.

"Oh sure," she muttered, toying with the lace on the cuff of her sweatshirt. When I snuck a peek at her face, she was focused on the road unspooling in front of us. "I'm lucky you picked today to go hiking. Otherwise, I'd have been taking up permanent residence on that mountain. It would have taken me a decade to find my way down, unless I made a bargain with a wood dryad or a leprechaun."

I cleared my throat, not certain if she was serious about the dryads. We had werewolves in abundance in our small town of Moonlight Valley, but that was it for the supernatural. There were rumors of a vampire over in Knoxville, though, and the occasional witch showed up in the federal park, collecting ingredients for spells.

It was likely a mundane joke.

We weren't all that far from Wyatt's rental at Phantom Falls. Moonlight Valley was a small place and everything was close by, including the haunted waterfall and several other paranormal hotspots. I'd have her to her doorstep in minutes.

Keep going, my wolf suggested. **We can drive to Canada. Elope.**

I couldn't lie. I was tempted. But even though five years ago I'd sworn off sex, stealing cars, and doing bad things that hurt other people, this woman tempted me. She was exactly my type.

Long, dark hair, a brown-eyed beauty, all gorgeous curves and not a hard line to her. Her mouth was even softer, with the most kissable pair of lips I'd ever seen. My fantasy woman was riding shotgun, and that was more tempting than shifting into my wolf at full moon.

And yet she still hadn't told me her name. Her reticence, given my instinctive response to her, wasn't a bad thing. I'd have been all over her in the front seat of my truck if she'd given me the green light.

I didn't know what to say. Around her I was nervous and on edge. I hadn't felt this thrill of nerves since I'd come face-to-face with the local sheriff from two towns over when I'd been out in wolf form on illegal business for the Iron Wolves. She'd been a real pretty woman, strong and bold. But she'd also been armed, and my wolf had surprised her.

A wolf that was now whining like a pup to find out my curvy hiker's name.

Because she's OURS!

"Would you like the grand tour of Moonlight Valley?" I drawled. "I know this place real well. I even do fun facts."

My wolf groaned. **Your pickup lines are not improving.**

"That way you'll know where you are, and you won't get lost anymore. Although I'm at your service if you need another rescue."

"Right now?" From the way she dropped those two words into our conversation, my wolf wasn't the only one who thought my charm was rusty.

"It won't take long." I shrugged. "This isn't a big place."

"Fast, quick, and small." She winked at me. "You know how to sell yourself. Usually, I wouldn't hesitate to take you up on that kind offer, but I'm starving, so if we could head straight to Wyatt's, that would be great."

I forced myself not to grin. She was funny. Funny and charming. And gorgeous. Of course, she could recite the fifty states and their capitals, and I'd be just as riveted.

"If Wyatt hasn't stocked the kitchen, I've got emergency snacks behind your seat." I slowed and signaled to turn off onto the dirt road that led to the waterfall and Wyatt's house.

"I already stole your chocolate," she protested. "I can't take your emergency snacks too."

When her stomach growled again, I reached behind the seat and rummaged one-handed in the cooler I kept back there. My sandwich wasn't five-star gourmet cuisine, but I liked the thought of taking care of her, of meeting her needs. And no, I wasn't just thinking about her sexual needs, although they weren't entirely out of my mind, either.

She took the sandwich and dug in. Satisfaction flared through me. She ate in silence—and with gusto—while I tried to hold my horses. Not bother the lady. Magically find some game.

We made it ten minutes down the road before I caved and blurted out the first thing that came to mind.

"Since you're eating my sandwich, perhaps we should be on a first-name basis?"

Lame, my wolf whined.

"It's Suzette." Her words were muffled by a mouthful of my brother Ranger's famous faux chicken salad. It had tofu in it—much to my wolf's disgust—along with raisins, apples, and a top-secret sauce Ranger refused to disclose the ingredients of. After the fifth time I'd asked, he'd claimed it contained *love and other sweet things* and I'd stopped asking. Love was not a protein source, and it was not on my menu.

"Suzette? I'm pleased to meet you, Suzette." I pulled up in front of Wyatt's rental cabin.

"No, it's—" She dragged her attention away from my sandwich and stared at the enormous architectural monstrosity in front of us. "Wow. Is this it?"

"Wyatt's rental? Yeah." The place had started life as an unpretentious cabin in the woods, but Wyatt had gone overboard with improvements after he'd written that erotic book that had been more successful than striking oil in the backyard. Now it looked like something from an *Architectural Digest* magazine, all glass and steel. You could also see straight through it, which was not a feature in my opinion, but tourists loved it.

Her gaze bounced back and forth between Wyatt's McMansion and my face while she worked out what she wanted to say. "I didn't give you the address. Do you just know where everyone lives? And where his rental house is? Is this one of those freakish small-town things where everyone knows everyone? How do you know Wyatt? Are there any secrets here?"

Boy is she in for a surprise, my wolf said.

I had to agree. We kept plenty of secrets here, starting with the werewolf population.

I picked the safe option. "Everyone in Moonlight Valley knows that Wyatt owns the two ugliest, gaudiest, and largest places in town. You should see his primary residence."

Compensating, my wolf growled. **Because he's nowhere near as awesome or as hung as we are.**

I tried to banish the unwelcome thought about Wyatt's personal equipment. Terrible architectural choices aside, everyone in Moonlight Valley did know Wyatt Reynolds—even before he'd published that super explicit werewolf romance that had brought him so much attention (the town book club had had a real good time reading it and trying to figure out who was who in real life).

For instance, everybody knew he'd got himself a PhD in English from Harvard after his daddy had suggested going into the plumbing trade, and then he'd written That Book and come home to open an erotic bookshop smack in the middle of downtown Moonlight Valley. Add to that his penchant for forest bathing in the nude on hot summer days (and as a wolf on cold ones) and his general lack of fucks to give, and you had Wyatt.

It was hard not to know him—or not to know that his parents found him an embarrassment.

It was the same way that everybody knew me, Maverick Boone, and my five younger brothers, my Miss Tennessee beauty-queen sister, my no-good, disappearing daddy, and the wonderful woman who had been my momma and who had also disappeared the previous year. Besides the big werewolf secret (which half the town was in on), about the only unknown in Moonlight Valley was what had really happened to Momma.

So, yes, I knew Wyatt, both in his two-legged and his four-legged form. He and my younger brother Atticus were best friends. Wyatt, Atticus, and I often ran together at full moon. Also, I'd stolen a souped-up Dodge Charger from Wyatt's daddy when I was sixteen. And then later a BMW. Wyatt's daddy had always had more cars than manners.

More recently, after I'd turned over my new, sober, and sexually celibate leaf, Wyatt and I had gone into the book business together. He'd turned an empty storefront into The Pink Parts, his erotic bookstore, right after he'd hit a big bestseller list and sold the movie rights to That Book. I'd done the renovations and generally kept the place looking both pink and perfect as my contribution to our silent partnership. I'd built a stage for his book readings, installed a pastry case for snacks, and reupholstered the armchairs. On select Friday nights, Wyatt would read out loud from his current work in progress.

I had not attended any of those readings, but they were legendary.

"It is a big place," she said thoughtfully, still taking in the magnificent, glassy splendor that she'd apparently rented sight unseen. "Although it seems a trifle exposed."

I shrugged. "To be fair, no one has much privacy in a town this small."

She made a face.

"But to answer your question about my acquaintance with Wyatt, he and I go way back. We all used to strip down and go skinny-dipping in a plastic pool in my momma's backyard."

Let's take her to the waterfall for swimming! She's hot. It would be downright charitable of us. Or, y'all have that giant waterslide going to waste up at the house.

She grinned, her eyes dancing.

"He argued that the pond behind our dorm was a swimsuit-optional beach." I laughed. "He's not a fan of clothing, that's for sure."

When he wasn't in his furry form, he was often buck naked (see forest bathing). I'd seen more of Wyatt than I cared to recollect.

"He runs an adult romance bookstore, right?" she asked, the easy acceptance and lack of judgment in her voice surprising me. Most folks either poked fun at what Wyatt wrote or dismissed it outright. Getting sex right was hard, though, no pun intended.

"You bet." I wondered what she liked to read, which fantasies were her favorites. "The Pink Parts."

In my experience, there were three kinds of people: those that read erotic books, those that wrote them, and those who couldn't understand why on earth someone would write down a private fantasy for other people to share. I wondered if she would write one of hers down for me, and if I could write her back. We could be a special kind of pen pal.

"Professor, are you wondering if I like to read?"

I answered her grin with one of my own and shrugged. "I could make some recommendations if you're in need of reading material."

"I'm always looking for my next book." Her voice dropped, throatier, huskier. Her mouth curved up in a wicked grin, more naughty and less polite. "I also love to write."

My brain short-circuited, my pulse kicking up. I could just imagine how she *loved.* There were so many thoughts running riot in my head that I lost my verbal brakes.

"Do you? Would you like to workshop a scene with me?"

"In public?"

"I'm open to suggestions." I nodded thoughtfully, willing her to continue.

"Are you a unicorn?"

What?

As if, my wolf grumped. **Those horned horse wannabes are VIRGINS. We've workshopped the heck out of this town.**

This was truer than I cared to admit and a key reason I'd been celibate for the last five years. I had a lot of careless behavior to make up for. On the other hand, I could hardly tell her that I was a werewolf. She'd either dismiss me as delusional or freak out.

Also, I wasn't entirely sure how unicorns and workshopping were connected.

"I'm not sure I take your meaning," I said. "Do you believe in unicorns?"

She twinkled at me. "Actual unicorns, no. Nor was I referring to the dating practice. I was alluding to that mythical man who's willing to take direction."

Her eyes dropped to my mouth, a change in direction that was a pretty clear indicator of what she was thinking.

My muscles tightened, the blood evacuating from my brain and rushing south. God, she was beautiful. It was hard to focus on our conversation and keeping up my end of it when she sat this close to me. I'd spent years mastering my beast, and she'd undone all that hard work in under an hour.

"I could be convinced. Are you good at giving directions?"

She shook her head vigorously, sending her long, brown hair tumbling around her shoulders and clinging to her cheeks and the soft swell of her breasts, framing the curves of her. She mouthed, *I take them*, as if those three words were the best and dirtiest line in one of Wyatt's books.

I was on fire.

Well, son of a bee sting.

She was good.

Real good at this.

Having once been a top-notch flirt myself, I recognized a kindred spirit. My hiker was a charmer. I was more surprised by this than by the stunning harmonica solo that Mr. Allerbee had played with the fancy string orchestra one memorable Fourth of July because her disheveled and genuinely upset appearance back up there on the mountain had been endearing. Had it all been a ruse?

She peeped up at me through thick, dark lashes. A mischievous grin lit up her face, hinting at a pair of naughty dimples. Her eyes darkened from the sunlit gold-brown of forest branches to the twinkling green of late-autumn leaves . . . I was still no poet, but I was a wolf who knew and loved my twigs and berries.

This was a game I loved, and I waited to see what she'd do next. It was her move, and she was a master player. Yeah, my hiker understood the assignment.

Her grin grew, turning into a smile and then a full-blown laugh. "You are too much. This is the best."

"What is?"

"Flirting with a professor."

The corner of my mouth tugged up. Her honesty was a joy. Perhaps her upset up on the mountain hadn't been a ruse after all.

Shut the front door, you LIKE this girl.

"Are we flirting, Miss Suzette?" All that liking had her name coming out in a low growl, making it sound like a bedroom word.

She gave me a playful chiding look and undid her seat belt. "I'm pleading the Fifth, Maverick. You fill in the blanks. Plus, I have to go raid the pantry because otherwise I might start eating everything in sight."

That was not a problem.

Picnic for two coming up, my wolf growled. **She'll taste so sweet.**

Reciprocity *was* important. I chewed on that for a moment too long because Suzette popped her door open and peered down. I was a gentleman wolf, so I opened my door, jumped down, and got myself around the truck before she'd got her feet on the ground. I grabbed her door with one hand and offered her my other.

She didn't budge.

"I don't need help."

I nodded. "Noted."

"Alrighty then."

The slide of her bare fingers against my own larger, callused ones drove my response right out of my head.

We'd touched on the mountain, and it had been perfectly pleasant. Perhaps our flirting spell had turned up the heat, or perhaps it was our forced proximity in my truck—or my five-year sexual dry spell—but an unexpected shock of heat shot up my arm as her palm slid against mine.

She didn't seem to notice. I, on the other hand, was entirely too aware.

Our hands were two tectonic plates meeting, sliding past each other, my body and my heart buckling at the impact.

When I tightened my grip on her hand, holding on rather than letting go, she looked startled. "What's up?"

I looked into her eyes, searching. She didn't seem aware of that pulse of claiming, so I reluctantly let go.

My wolf snarled inside me, demanding I let him out. **FOOL. You're gonna lose the girl.**

"Nothing." I cleared my throat. I did not need or want this logjam of unexpected feelings. "Let's get you inside. Wyatt keeps a key for the guests in a frog. Also, if you would trust me with your car keys, I'll make sure your vehicle gets back to you."

I moved past her toward the front door. I did not know what had just happened. I did not *need* to know what had just happened.

The buzzing of my phone was a welcome distraction. With an apologetic tip of my head, I stepped to the side, pulled it out, and accepted the call. "Afternoon, Ranger."

"Maverick," Ranger intoned in his usual monotone. He could have been reading off the next item on his grocery list, except that I knew he cared. Although Ranger was the third-born in our family, he'd inherited the lion's share of the brains, along with an outsized portion of oddness. You never knew what was going on in his head, but you'd be a fool to disrespect it. "You need to head over to The Pink Parts lickety-split."

"Are you sure?" I checked the time on my phone briefly; it was just gone four, which made it almost closing time at the bookshop and far too late for the coffee drinks it sold. I'd be up all night for the wrong reasons. "What do you all need me to do?"

"Sanye needs rescuing."

My happy lust fog cleared up faster than fast.

If I pushed it, I could be at The Pink Parts in ten minutes. Sanye Jansen-Webster had been the wife of my best friend. Now after Evan's death in a tank rollover, she was his widow, and it was my responsibility and pleasure to be there for her whenever and however she needed. Evan would have done the same for anyone I'd left behind. I'd cleaned up my act and gotten honest, thanks to her, because I would not let either of them down.

"Sanye is a DIY woman," I reminded my brother. Suzette and she had that in common.

Wolf. That woman is ALL wolf.

Technically, that was the truth, seeing as how she was a shifter. It was also true that Sanye did not need or particularly want my rescuing. As much as I wanted to be there for her after we'd lost Evan, she had her own thoughts about how her unexpectedly solo life should unfold. The first year, she had humored me but—more and more—I had to admit (if only to myself) that she saw my efforts on her behalf as meddling and overprotective. I did not want her to get hurt. Or to feel lonely, tired, anxious, or otherwise crapped on by life.

She let me handle her home repairs and improvements, but that was where she'd drawn a line the width and depth of the Grand Canyon. I was not to interfere in her life. It was a well-known fact that she was more wolverine than wolf, and a wise man did not stand in her way.

These days she mostly handed me a beer, let me change her fuses or haul her trash to the dump, and then she sent me on my way.

"Well, she has a project that she cannot handle on her own."

I groaned, staring at the cabin's wide-open front door. My impish, mysterious Suzette had tossed me her car keys, ransacked Wyatt's key frog, and marched on in. "Use your words."

"Come to The Pink Parts," Ranger intoned dramatically and then hung up on me.

Damn it. I glared at my phone, but there was no point in calling back. Ranger would not answer. He was not big on phones, phone calls, or sharing basic information. I'd had occasion to wonder if he was a foreign spy because he treated everything as top secret. Mostly, the need-to-know basis on which he operated was just plain funny, but today it irritated the heck out of me.

My plans to flirt with Suzette would have to wait.

"Are you coming?" Suzette poked her head out the door and looked up at me. Her regard sent a warm feeling blossoming through my chest. It was looking like she'd become the sun in my universe all right, and I was a needy, needy seed.

I put those thoughts aside to examine later. Hooking my thumbs in my belt, I reluctantly called an end to our shenanigans. "No, ma'am."

"No?" Her forehead got the cutest little pucker as she mulled over my answer. "That's not the next line in this game, sir. I've found the food, and now I'm inviting you in for dinner."

I cursed Ranger and his poor timing, and then I cursed my new, reformed self. "I have to get back on the road."

She made a face, looking some shade of disappointed. She might not be begging me to stay, but she wasn't thrilled to see me go, either. I'd take it.

"Can I make it up to you later?" I stepped closer, bending my head to inhale her scent.

OURS, my wolf caroled. **Gonna make her ours, ours, OURS.** Something about her made it hard to disagree with my beast. Suzette felt right, and I did not want to leave her.

She flashed me a grin. "Sounds like a plan."

I tipped my hat. "It's been a pleasure, Miss Suzette. You have a good night now."

Her eyes rounded ever so slightly. "What a gentleman."

My grin grew, my eyes crinkling up and making promises to her. I might be out of practice with flirting and dating, but I would give her my best.

But before I could head back to my truck, she stepped into me and rested a hand on my arm. Leaning up on tiptoe, she brushed her lips over my cheek. Her breasts pressed against my arm—not to tease but because she had a generous bosom—and my body surged to life. Five years of celibate living flew straight out the window. My dick had never been so hard. She smelled of herbs and pine—free, wild, and delicious.

Her lips hovered near my cheek; her body balanced against mine. Without pulling away, she peeked up at me through her long lashes and whispered, "*Gracias*, my white knight."

I swallowed roughly, heat surging through me, more incendiary than before, volcanic. My control slipped through my fingers like water over a streambed, stirring up old emotions and my wolf. **NOW.**

"Always," I gritted roughly, fighting the urge to give in, to do as my wolf urged and wrap myself around her and kiss the living daylights out of her. Her lips on my cheek were a prelude, and I was about to launch into the main piece when she stepped back.

My eyes locked on hers, and I watched her reestablish the distance between us. She bothered me. And by bothered I meant hot and bothered, desperate to press my kisses against each of her lush curves.

She beamed at me, and I stared, lost, until she told me to get lost. "Goodbye, Maverick."

This was not how my dates had ended in my long-distant past. Of course, this wasn't exactly a date, it being more of a rescue mission or search-and-retrieval.

Lyft, my wolf snapped, **seeing as how you're the driver and this appears to be the end of the road.**

I reminded myself that I had changed. That I did not do casual relationships, or even casual kissing. I was reformed and I had important boundaries.

Still, my jaw tightened and I pasted a smile on my face because growling and going wolf on her would not win this game we were playing. I had always been the flirt and the charmer. I was the one who walked away and left my date wanting more.

Turnabout sucks, my wolf growled.

He was not wrong. I walked back to my truck in a daze, boundaries intact but feeling that I'd missed out on something—some*one*—important. The door shut behind me, followed by the unmistakable click of the lock. Suzette was safe and tucked in for the night. That was good.

Never mind that I was on the wrong side of that door.

Or that I had a whole stew of feelings brewing in me that packed more punch than the moonshine Ranger brewed in our tub.

My hiker . . . she was a hell of a woman.

And I was plumb crazy for her.

CHAPTER

THREE

"Down the hill I went, and then,

I forgot the ways of men,

For night-scents, heady and damp and cool

Wakened ecstasy."

— SARA TEASDALE, *FLAME AND SHADOW*

Sanye did not need my white knight services.

No sirree. Turned out, I was the one in need of a rescue.

"HAPPY BOOK BIRTHDAY!" chorused at me from every direction, people popping out from behind the bookcases and the counter in The Pink Parts. What felt like every werewolf in town bounded toward me, making my hackles rise.

Also hollered, mostly by my brothers: "A star is born, asshole!"

Given the amber sheen I could feel sheeting over my eyes, the pictures of my surprise entrance would be hilarious. Ranger was an oversharer, so I'd likely find my shocked mug projected onto the side of our house in our annual Christmas light display come November (Ranger believed in starting the holiday season early). Not to be outdone, my youngest brother, Rebel, would make the photos into cushions for us to sit on at the local ball games. There might be fridge magnets.

33

After Wyatt's last book launch, I'd sworn that the only way he'd get me to attend another literary event was if he tied me up and dragged me into the bookstore bodily; clearly, he'd taken my threat to heart.

Given the mountain of embargoed stock he'd signed in the back room these last two weeks, I should have predicted the sneak party. In my defense, meeting Suzette had knocked the stuffing clear out of my brain. If I'd remembered that today was release day for Wyatt's latest book, I would have made him a bourbon cake, dropped it off on his doorstep, and stayed far, far away.

Now I was good and trapped, so I decided to have a laugh and figure out why my brothers were snort-laughing so hard. Their glee did not bode well for my dignity.

Ranger and Sanye wandered out of the crowd of Moonlight Valleyers surrounding Wyatt. He'd whipped out a gold fountain pen and was scrawling his name on a stack of glossy paperback books. Sanye looked happy to see me. Ranger, on the other hand, looked smug. His selfie stick was pointed plumb at me.

Sanye threw her arms around me, squeezing me tight. "You've been holding out on me! Congratulations!"

"I have?" I knew Wyatt struggled with the whole notion of a *silent* partnership, but I had trusted him not to spill the beans about our business dealings.

"Wyatt said you're the inspiration for his new book," she replied ominously. "He *dedicated* it to you."

Seeing as how Wyatt wrote erotic werewolf romance, I had questions. Before I could ask her to explain herself, Ranger poked me in the side with his finger. "You are an inspiration."

Wyatt smirked at me from behind his wall of books as he signed a frontispiece with a flourish.

He cheated, my wolf said sulkily. **This is not a fair fight.**

I shrugged. "Seeing as how I have not yet read Wyatt's book, I don't have an opinion on that. This comes as a big surprise."

Based on the smirks aimed my way by my friends and neighbors, I needed to skim the book. Fast.

Ranger waited until the nice lady at the post office, my first-grade teacher, and the preacher's wife walked by us, Wyatt's new book clutched in their hands as they gave me assessing up-and-down glances, before he addressed my surprise. "You know I do not like to spoil the ending of a book."

"It would have been prudent of Maverick to get his hands on an advanced reader copy. He does like a happy ending." Sanye patted my arm. She sounded like she was trying not to laugh.

Ranger shot her a confused glare. "He did not attend the book club meeting this month, and thus he missed my hot takes on werewolf romance. To barb or not to barb! That is a very important question."

I was not going to think about that.

No barbs, my wolf said grumpily. **Have you considered a penis piercing?**

Knox, the second oldest of my brothers, stomped up to the edge of our threesome, slapping a copy of Wyatt's book against his palm. Knox always looked sour in my vicinity, but his imitation of a storm cloud did not put off other people. Women frequently cited him as the best looking of the Boone bunch. Objectively, he had won the genetic lottery.

He'd been eavesdropping all right because he rolled the icy, bright blue eyes that he'd got from our daddy and growled something under his breath. Amber flickered in his gaze.

"Do you have an opinion on the sexual imagery in Wyatt's book, Knox, that you'd like to share with the class?" Ranger turned his selfie stick on Knox, who scowled back.

Knox wore a fancy two-piece suit, which was casual wear for him. Needless to say, his presence was a surprise. Firstly, he believed that eighty-hour workweeks were both healthy and an excellent training regimen for climbing the corporate ladder.

And secondly, he hated me.

No joke.

I experienced the usual suite of regrets: regret that I had done a poor job as his older brother, regret that I had not protected my momma from our daddy's abuse, and even more regret that Knox had done what I didn't and had stepped up to take the beatings for all of us.

Younger me was best described as an asshole and the worst kind of animal.

Since regrets were just painful wishes and entirely unactionable, however, I mostly regretted that the bookshop did not stock whiskey. I would not have minded backsliding an inch or two—in delicious, brown bourbon—on my new, sober, and upright life.

Knox shot an irritated glance Ranger's way, giving the selfie stick with Ranger's phone a one-finger salute.

"I do not have an opinion." Dislike and anger sharpened Knox's voice. Then, realizing that Sanye was standing with us, he gave her a tight smile, as if he had some unpleasant regrets of his own. His voice softened as he asked, "Can I get you a coffee, Sanye?"

Sanye lowered her eyes, not quite ready to challenge an alpha wolf. "I'm good, thanks."

He tipped his head in acknowledgment, his eyes lingering briefly on her face. Then his gaze met mine, and he frowned as I refused to drop my eyes. I would not show him my throat. Scowling, he spun on his heel and strode away.

"That brother of ours is so rude," Ranger said, watching him disappear into the crowd of book-buying, laughing werewolves. "What if I wanted a coffee?"

"He's okay." Sanye frowned down at her hands, inspecting her manicure. She had a white Pomeranian painted on the pink polish of her thumb. "He just thinks that he hates Maverick, but he's wrong. Sooner or later, he'll figure that out."

Sanye's words pierced me through and through. Sure, I'd had the same thought myself, and not even two minutes ago, but hearing the words said out loud *hurt*.

There was truth to those words, no matter how much I wanted to deny it.

"Maverick is not the problem here," Ranger contradicted her. They engaged in some kind of silent eyeball-to-eyeball communication while I was forced to sign Jennie Dean's momma's book. She hugged me after I reluctantly complied, squeezing my bicep with her book-free hand.

"Your momma loved you, Maverick." Mrs. Dean waved her book for emphasis. "She really, truly did. Don't you forget that."

I nodded down at her, realizing that I had one more regret to add to my growing collection. I had not been a good son, what with joining the Iron Wolves and stealing cars, and I had stubbornly stuck to that bad path until the last three years of her life.

"I won't, ma'am. Thank you for coming out for Wyatt's book party."

"That Wyatt Reynolds made you out to be a hero." She squeezed my arm again, beaming widely.

I broke out my aw-shucks grin. "Well now, Mrs. Dean, I don't rightly know what's in that book of his."

"He based it on your life." She looked around and then leaned up to whisper in my ear. "On your *love* life. It was all quite impressive."

Then her gaze dropped south and her cheeks pinkened.

Jesus, take the wheel.

Fortunately, Jesus listened because Mrs. Dean rapidly dropped my arm and scurried off. I was starting to have a good idea of what my business partner had done: he'd made me the hero in those ridiculous sex scenes he wrote, and now half the town—or more—was convinced that it was either straight up biography or a sexual menu they could order from.

A low rumble followed by a smattering of enthusiastic applause had me turning toward the small stage. It was more of a low platform, to be honest, furnished with an ostentatious reading light and a leather armchair. Wyatt had settled himself there with a glass of water and his damned book.

"Time to bring your fantasies to life." Ranger tipped his chin in the direction of the stage. "I am taking audience questions for Wyatt, and then Sanye is reciting some dirty limericks. You are on your own."

"I'll manage."

"If you get lonely . . ." Ranger dimpled mischievously. "I would suggest you look for the Relyae twins."

I froze in dismay. "Excuse me?"

"I invited them," Ranger said.

"Along with Daisy March. And Liesel Sturm," Sanye added. She was grinning broadly.

"Did you invite all of my former girlfriends?" I gritted out.

Sanye giggled uncontrollably while Ranger answered, "I was not aware that you had girlfriends. Did you date one of these lovely women exclusively?"

Dating is for losers, my wolf snarled. **Fun was had. Orgasms were shared. Our sexual reputation is *impeccable.***

As *impeccable* came from the Latin word *impeccabilis,* or to sin not, my wolf had it wrong. I was sinner central.

"You know I did not," I gritted out. "Explain yourself."

"Ohmigod, I'm going to laugh-pee." Sanye clutched Ranger's arm. Laughter shook her frame.

Get the lady a bucket, my wolf growled. He was still snappish at the implication that we'd failed to satisfy any of my former ladies.

Ranger nodded his head as though I'd asked a question and not made a demand. "Maverick, I merely revisited certain aspects of your sexual past."

"God help me," I groaned.

"You are a literary man. Think of this as *A Christmas Carol* reenactment but with sexual specters rather than crotchety old Englishmen. This is your chance to consider your failings in bed."

"Kill me. There will be payback. It will be a bitch." I stabbed a finger at them.

Onstage, Wyatt began to read. He had a rich, posh voice like an audiobook narrator. Unfortunately, his perfect diction made it very easy to understand his words. His werewolf hero was rogering the heroine. At great length and in questionably public circumstances. It was unclear to me whether fur was involved or not.

Around me, people whispered and jostled. They slid sidelong glances at me.

Let's make a run for it.

My instincts agreed with my wolf. Forget about supporting Wyatt—I needed to sprint for the door. The bookstore was packed. Childhood friends, neighbors, my momma's book club, my brothers, people I'd worked with . . .

And apparently a decade's worth of former girlfriends.

Five years ago, before I'd turned over my new leaf, I would have run for the door. I'd have straddled my bike, put pedal to the metal, and gone away.

But I was no longer that person who left without a destination in mind and who never stopped to think about how his absence affected the people who stayed behind. I'd had sex and then I'd gone about my life, and I had not bothered calling or so much as sending a card or a text.

I'd just run.

And then I'd run some more.

Even tonight, I realized most folks did not expect me to stay. They were waiting for me to bolt.

So I stayed, pasting a grim smile on my face as Wyatt read and read—and read some more. He was giving so much milk away that no one would buy the cow. Book. Whatever.

After the first ten minutes, I zoned out, trying not to make eye contact with anyone. Wyatt's hero had a legendary dick, and I could feel the town's assessing gaze on me. Or, more precisely, on a region south of my belt.

When Mackenzie, my only sister, bounded up to me, I threw my arms around her. She was number four and the smallest wolf in our pack of seven, but there was no overlooking her vibrant presence. She was as pretty on the outside as she was on the inside, not to mention smart as a whip. She'd gone to nursing school. Deelie Sue had pressed her into entering our state beauty pageants for the scholarship money, and all of us Boone boys had bought tickets and attended the final show to holler and applaud whenever our girl came out. And sure, I might have been biased as Mack's brother, but there was no better woman in the world. She deserved all the tiaras life had to offer.

Plus, if I stood close enough to her, no mistakes from my checkered past could sneak up on me. I squeezed her tighter.

"Mav?"

"What?"

"I can't breathe," she complained.

"You're talking," I pointed out. "That means air is making it in. You're my wingman tonight."

"Scaredy wolf." She stuck her tongue out at me.

In the grand scheme of things, having my sister on my arm wouldn't keep people away, but I still clung to the idea. Unless I could convince Suzette to take a chance on me, I was a retired charmer.

Eventually, the reading ended—thank you, sweet baby Jesus—and people milled around the store, fanning their faces and paging through books. More than one interested face turned my way, but I skipped my gaze over the female faces like a stone skimming the surface of a Tennessee lake.

"Who?"

I quirked a brow. "Was that a complete sentence?"

"Who. Are. You. Looking. For?" Mack enunciated each word with unwarranted glee. She knew me too well.

Truth be told, I planned on having a word with Wyatt. Now that I had Mack to run interference with any former (or future) flames who might be lurking in the crowd, I wanted intel. Wyatt had to know more about Suzette.

I had only reformed so much.

Which would be not at all.

I ignored my wolf's unwelcome truth. I might have vowed never to date or hurt the people in my life again, nor steal their cars, but my Suzette wasn't just another date.

It was far too soon to be certain, yet somehow, instinctively, I knew. Suzette was unique and special.

Sure, she was beautiful, with that naughty dimple and the smile that lit her up from within. She was all glorious curves and wild curls, dark-eyed and playful, and she fit in my arms as if she were the missing piece of my life.

I couldn't put my finger on it, but there was something about her. A mystery waiting to be solved or maybe the best kind of puzzle. When I thought about her, I wanted to spout stupid pickup lines about how *heaven was missing an angel.*

Don't, my wolf groaned. **For fuck's sake, you need help. There's got to be a dating book in here somewhere. Buy it. Steal it. Annotate it, please. Reenact Wyatt's stuff if you must.**

I did need help. Suzette was refreshingly blunt, but I got the sense that I might not really know where I stood with her. Was it her open love of bad puns? Her easy charm and playful flirting?

I wasn't interested in falling back into bad habits, moving from one bedroom (or truck cab) to the next, never giving myself the chance to care or know more. My relationships to date had been truck stops, quick pull-ins and even quicker pull-outs. There was a whole lot of mileage on me, and I'd earned it going nowhere important. That wasn't the man—or wolf—that I was anymore. It wasn't who I chose to be.

I'd barely met Suzette, but I wanted to know more about her.

I wanted everything with her.

Love at first sight? Not a chance, my wolf scoffed. **Blue balls and a pretty woman, that's what I'm thinking. She's not our mate.**

He didn't sound sure, though.

He sounded as scared and off-balance as I felt.

"Tell me," Mack demanded. "Why are you making that face?"

"Because I'm apparently Wyatt's muse?"

Mack pursed her lips. "A valid point."

I grimaced, and she giggled. Spotting Wyatt standing by the cash register and chatting with the town sheriff, I laid a course for my business partner and nemesis. Mack let me draw her along, acknowledging the greetings and questions from the crowd with a brief head tip and no more. I was not getting waylaid.

"Where are we going? Are we drawing some personal boundaries with Wyatt?" Mack waited to ask her question until we'd gotten past the worst of the crowd. Who knew that so many people in Moonlight Valley enjoyed reading?

I shook my head. That wolf was out of the bag.

"I've got questions for Wyatt. I dropped someone off at his place in Phantom Falls, and I want to know more about her."

Mack wouldn't share my secret. She did not believe in blackmail or holding past misdeeds over my head, like my brothers did.

Sure enough, she was all in on helping me out. "We can grill him like a steak, but first I need caffeine. Let's coffee up and then go after him."

"I'll buy you the world's best espresso machine if you stick to me tonight."

"Make it a Velvetiser and you've got a deal."

She had herself a deal. I pulled up in front of Wyatt and the sheriff, mentally prepping my list of questions. Alphabetical order, by theme, in order of importance? I was not sure what my best approach would be, but then I heard what the sheriff was saying.

". . . and most of the television crew has arrived. They'll start filming next week, so the nondisclosure isn't necessary anymore. You can let folks know. The producers are all up at those cabins by Phantom Falls, and the production crew is coming in. They'll be at the motel."

Wyatt nodded along, clearly not surprised by any of this information. His gaze snagged on Mack standing by my side. The corner of his mouth quirked up. "Mackenzie. I had no idea you'd come out tonight."

He stepped around the sheriff, arms coming up for a hug as he reached for Mack.

I stepped into his arms and winked at him. "You give the best hugs. It's been so long since we saw each other."

I might trust Wyatt Reynolds with my money, but I did not believe for one hot second that he deserved my little sister.

He shoved me away, scowling. Too damned bad. He could come and ask the Boones how we all felt about him stepping out with Mack. I was just one of six overprotective men and their wolves who would have an opinion, and even then, she'd already made her choice. She'd picked Rue Ansel. And Rue was six foot five of muscled, grim scientist.

"Wyatt. It's been an age." Mack held out her right hand like a queen. She also did not trust him one bit.

She's got good instincts.

Wyatt frowned—as Mack out-mannered him—and she turned to the sheriff. "What are y'all chatting about?"

Sheriff Jacob scratched at the stubble on his jaw. Being hairy and rough around the edges was one of the disadvantages of being a werewolf. "We have us some out-of-towners. They're shooting some episodes for a television show out at Phantom Falls and hereabouts. There will be an open call going out for extras next week."

Mack clapped her hands. "Who's in it? Anyone famous?"

"No idea." Sheriff Jacob shrugged. "But then I don't subscribe to all those services you all have today. I'm not paying to watch television."

"Luke Hensley was the male lead last season and it looks like he's reprising his role in some form." Wyatt counted off names on his fingers. "Then you've got Zach Quick, Nick Swift, Marlene Kerrigan, and Sonnet Ruiz. Those are definitely headliners."

"Wow." Mack's mouth fell open, and she looked vaguely stunned. "Sonnet Ruiz? *And* Luke Hensley? Sweet sassy molassey."

Wyatt grinned. "Sweet sassy molassey?"

"Whisper to the stars and make them sigh," Mack continued her made-up rhyme, babbling nonsense in her glee at the possibility of all these visitors descending on our corner of Tennessee.

"Should I know who these people are?" Their names were not familiar.

"Sonnet Ruiz writes really funny books and one of them is the basis for my favorite TV show. She plays the lead in it and it's had multiple seasons already. I think she's also super into Gremlincore on her social media, although she mostly keeps that stuff private. She's not the usual Hollywood type, but the show is really good and having her *and* Luke on the same set will be explosive."

That was a whole lot of information. "Why is this Luke a problem?"

"He was briefly Sonnet's boyfriend, and he's had a hard time getting new parts since they broke up and he became the *ex*-boyfriend."

"And you know this how?"

"*Everyone* knows." She waved her hands. "It's all over social media and the internet. Even those tabloid magazines by the checkout in the supermarket know."

Those same magazines assured me weekly that Bigfoot had been sighted and that aliens had crash-landed on the lawn of the White House. I did not trust Mack's sources.

"I'm going to agree with Mackenzie." Wyatt nodded. "None of this is news to me."

"Well, it is to me." The sheriff shot me a look. He was under the mistaken impression that our shared ignorance was one of many things we had in common. "I'm gonna go and update the rest of our fine town."

I watched him go and inadvertently met the gaze of one of Wyatt's female readers. Hastily, I turned to Mack, giving the lady my back.

"You are too funny, Mav." Mackenzie looked downright gleeful. "You don't actually think Ranger invited your lady friends, do you? He was pulling your leg with that crack."

"For real?" Not having considered the possibility, I stared at her stupidly for a moment too long. *Click.* My slack-jawed gape would be immortalized for all posterity on Ranger's phone.

Wyatt bellowed with laughter. "You believe anything, Maverick. Ranger has been planning tonight's little joke for ages. He did not invite the Relyae twins. They ain't here."

Mack nudged my shoulder with hers. "You're a big chicken when it comes to the ladies."

"Not all ladies," I clarified. "Just the ones I've dated and never called back."

"Have you not-called any ladies in the last five years?" This was Wyatt asking, and that wolf had done more writing about sex than having it.

"I have called no one and dated no one. My life has been a dating desert. I have made zero overtures."

"As far as you recall." Mack laughed harder.

This did not make me seem like a reformed man or even a semi-decent person. "Y'all make me seem like a heartless charmer. I am reformed."

"You got around." Wyatt shrugged. "But not anymore. You charm no one and nothing, not deliberately at any rate."

Before I could protest, Mack cut in, "You can't help being a himbo."

Wyatt nodded vigorously. "People think you can't possibly be smart, looking the way you do. Cute is not a dating plus."

A . . . *himbo*?

I looked the definition up on my phone and had questions. I was not an attractive, stupid man. Or at least, I was not both of those qualities at the same time.

"I am not cute," I growled. "Or a *himbo*. I am a wolf. That's the antithesis of cute and stupid."

"Furry. Fluffy. Super friendly. You're a total teddy bear." Mack ticked these points off on her fingers.

Canis lupus. Not Ursidae.

"And flirtatious," Wyatt said dryly, reaching over to tap Mack's fourth finger. "Don't forget that. You and Atticus get that trait from your daddy. When either of you walk into a room, the rest of us might as well be wearing an invisibility cloak."

Once upon a time, I would have loved hearing how I took after my sire. Now I knew better.

Any comparison to Darrell Boone was a negative, and I'd spent the last five years proving I was better than that.

Given the note of bitterness in Wyatt's voice, however, I suspected that he'd had a recent personal run-in with Atticus, because Atticus was the very definition of *not celibate*. My brother enjoyed having sex, and he enjoyed having it often.

This was my cue to change the subject rather than raise Wyatt's hackles. I still needed information about my Suzette.

"I met your newest tenant earlier today," I said.

Wyatt frowned then bristled. "My tenant?"

"Suzette," I prompted. "Short, curvy, dresses like a witch on Halloween?"

"Suzette." He gave nothing away.

"She said she was renting at your cabin on Phantom Falls and that she knew you from your college days."

Amber sheeted over his eyes. He knew who I meant alright. "You met her?"

"Hiking around in the mountains. She'd fallen down a hill and got turned around, so I drove her up to the falls and your cabin."

"Right." He fiddled with the fancy fountain pen he used to sign his blasted books. I did not point out that he'd drawn a streak of gold ink across his thumb pad.

From the way he was prevaricating, the less interested I sounded, the better. Apparently, he either thought Suzette was too good for me (true) or he was interested in her himself (**the better wolf is gonna win**).

"Anyhow, I'm just letting you know that I took her over to Phantom Falls. Ford is picking up her vehicle and delivering it."

He nodded. "Great."

I waited, but he did not elaborate further. He also did not acknowledge that personal vehicle delivery was not a service All-Purpose Animal Services provided and that I was not an Uber driver.

He sucks, my wolf opined. **That's our girl. Let's bite him.**

It was tempting, but I'd spent too long trying to be a better person (**WOLF**) to lose it now.

I flashed my teeth at Wyatt and said, "Great." Turning to my sister, I held out my arm at a perfect ninety degrees. If I was going to be dismissed as a gentleman, I'd be the best gentleman ever. "Milady? Coffee?"

Mack tucked her hand into the crook of my arm. "You betcha."

I guided her away from the ever-annoying Wyatt and toward the coffee bar in the back of the bookstore, greeting the other wolves we met with polite thanks and my very best aw-shucks manners.

My temporary literary fame was no big deal. I was the same wolf I'd always been: in control, affable, laidback.

Suzette had seemed interested in me, or so I'd believed. But I was also a rusty dater. My flirting skills had grown moss from disuse. Maybe I had been mistaken. Maybe she was just a charmer or someone nice. Maybe she had merely been polite.

Clearly, I needed to practice my social skills.

Suzette's being Wyatt's lady love was good, right? There was no room in my life for a mate, and I had sworn off casual fun.

CHASE THE GIRL. DO IT.

No chasing, I vowed. *We keep our hands and paws to ourselves.*

FOUR

"'Look, it's easy to outsmart a werewolf or a vampire,' Jace said. 'They're no smarter than anyone else. But faeries live for hundreds of years and they're as cunning as snakes. They can't lie, but they love to engage in creative truth-telling. They'll find out whatever it is you want most in the world and give it to you—with a sting in the tail of the gift that will make you regret you ever wanted it in the first place.'

He sighed. 'They're not really about helping people. More about harm disguised as help.'"

— CASSANDRA CLARE, *CITY OF ASHES*

Moonlight Valley was wonderfully, suspiciously, *preternaturally* cheerful. Where Hollywood dazzled with toothy smiles, this place felt genuine.

I suspected spells. Charms. Possibly, Macbeth's three crones stirring up trouble in their cauldrons.

On the surface of things, this small town surrounded by some of the world's oldest forest should be my jam. My plant magic might be weak, but I loved snails and frogs, mushrooms and the sweet decaying scent of forest loam. I wore black almost constantly (it was important to stay in character), although I did accessorize with colorful socks.

Cute socks were mission critical.

"You have a real nice day now!" My new friend caroled this parting shot as she handed over my cup.

I didn't do mind magic. I swear that I had not charmed her.

She was simply nice.

It was unfathomable and not what I'd expected. As no spell in the world could make me do an early call time without caffeinated sugar, I'd snuck out of Wyatt's poorly stocked cabin and walked a mile downhill at near-dawn to Moonlight Valley's single main street.

The diner was euphemistically named the Peaches and Cream Parlor. Someone had painted the clapboard exterior pale green and then gone all in with white gingerbread trim, tin cans of red geraniums, and Adirondack chairs with pink-and-green ticking cushions. When I looked back through the diner's door, the coffee lady beamed at me.

Something twisted in my chest.

Heartburn. Or cuteness overload. Exhaustion from being up at the crack of dawn.

You don't belong here, I reminded myself. *You're passing through. This place is just selling coffee, not putting out the welcome mat, coffee lady notwithstanding.*

I clutched my cup like the lifeline it was. Moonlight Valley did not have its own Starbucks. It did not even have a dedicated, small business coffee shop, the kind that sold curated knickknacks and nine-dollar chocolate bars to go with seasonal coffee drinks. The Pink Parts had a coffee bar, but as the bookshop was closed until civilized hours, my only option had been the diner. Which served black coffee, black tea, and—I peeked into my brand-new *Someone in Moonlight Valley* ♥ *you!* reusable plastic to-go cup—frozen pink Frappuccinos with sprinkles and whipped cream.

SO MUCH SUGAR. I WOULD NEVER MANAGE.

. . . just joking. It had been half gone by the time I'd reached the diner's door and the obnoxiously cheerful bell jingled to announce my dramatic departure.

Now I plopped myself down on a conveniently placed bench and considered my next steps as I drew an octopus man on the cup with a Sharpie from my ginormous, flower-covered crochet tote bag. Highly pink, fluffy beverages might be delicious, but doodling focused my mind. Plus, everything was better with tentacles. Ergo, I added appendages. My mollusk was giant and abundant! Then I gave him a beard and a mollusk friend because even bearded mermen-octopi monsters deserve love too.

Speaking of which, a large, red-headed, red-bearded man had returned my rental car and keys yesterday.

I'd spied on him from inside Wyatt's house, where I'd been recovering from my near-death moment with Mother Nature. I should send him a thank-you fruit bouquet. Or maybe I could try one of my sister's patented blessings and prosperity spells? He'd earned a good turn.

Moonlight Valley was full of people who overachieved in the categories of both personal niceness and holidays. Maybe I'd spent too long on the road, working. I had a great job and a fabulous team, but I couldn't exactly relax and let my guard down. Maybe that was why I could imagine myself staying put in this town.

Just for a little while.

Maybe for Halloween?

It was only a few weeks away and would be a hoot. Fun, even. Moonlight Valley was a welcoming kind of place, the sort of spot that always had room for one more.

A flotilla of perfectly perpendicular brooms flew across the window of the hard-ware store, a flock of black construction paper birds hovering above them. Stacks of orange pumpkins alternated with white-and-black-striped pumpkins in front of a very sparkly, pink shop called Vanity Fur Salon.

Drawn by the sparkle, I was trying to decide if the stripy ones were painted or some kind of monstruous hybrid when my phone buzzed. *Supreme Commander and Gal Friday* flashed across the screen. Elena was calling.

I'd texted my sister earlier explaining that Moonlight Valley was the Bermuda Triangle of cell phone reception and not to expect hourly updates from me, although I'd failed to mention the (not so) near-death experience on the mountain that could have left me permanently out of touch. There was no point in worrying her.

"Hi?"

"Sonnet? Dear Danu! We have been freaking out. Why did you ditch your security detail at the airport? Why aren't you traveling with the rest of the crew? Someone could have bespelled you. *Kidnapped* you."

Elena's business acumen came with a side of paranoia like eggs with hashbrowns. My sister was convinced that I was one spell away from paranormal doom and an unhappy ending. My brother, Victor, a trapeze artist and software engineer in New York City, was the only member of my family more convinced that evil lurked in every shadow.

Elena was my part-time manager and a full-time worrywart. Usually I was deeply grateful for her help. But over the last few years, things had become tense.

I had told her repeatedly that I needed to take a break. I was tired. Run-down. Sick of always acting and having to keep my glamour up. Her answer had been to wait until after we'd filmed just one more season of the TV show. She'd said this every season so far, her voice drowning mine out as she spelled out the many, many benefits of my career.

"*Dios mío*, I'm twenty-five. I am capable of operating a motor vehicle." *Although I do have bad taste in footwear and can't estimate a slope to save my life.* "And who is this *we* you speak of?"

"I texted Mami and Papi."

This was epically bad.

My mami was a wonderful person who I loved to the moon and back, but she believed I'd be spirited away if she so much as blinked.

More to the point, I'd grown up in a Chaneque witch family. Latin American folklore believed Chaneques were super short, mischievous sprites who delighted in leading people astray. Everyone in my family—myself included—was short.

We were also witches.

And most importantly: we were masters of misdirection.

You never, under any circumstances, asked for directions in our hometown in Baja California because you would end up in Siberia or Antarctica. Any place, really, that was not the spot you'd been aiming for. I was fortunate that Professor Hottie had not been Chaneque.

The misdirection was all in good humor, of course. We accessorized our petite stature with an impish sense of fun. My cousins were happily employed as airport information desk guides, software support engineers, and municipal employees. They got paid to send people down rabbit holes.

I was only half Chaneque, however, and had an uncharacteristically bad sense of direction to go with some seriously underdeveloped witchcraft. I'd also been dropped on Mami's doorstep as a baby.

The baby-abandonment reasons were unclear, although possibly one of my fellow Chaneques had misled the dropper about the location of the fire station with its baby safe box, but the note pinned to my onesie had claimed I was half Fae, half Chaneque.

I certainly did not look like the tall, pale, impossibly svelte fairy folk who had tricolored irises and powerful magic.

I was short, fat, and dark, and my only magical talent was my glamour.

I thought sometimes about whoever had left me because my life could have gone in another direction.

It was weird and impossible to shake, those thoughts about what might have been. Did they feel the same connection to the natural world? Love ferns and mismatched socks and things that sparkled? Why had they chosen to walk away from me?

Sometimes, I felt the loss keenly, but not everything that sparkled was either a diamond or valuable. That had been a different ending, and I loved my found family. *They* were the true gems.

Mami claimed it was the best of fortunes that had delivered me to her; she worried constantly that some Fae would come back and spirit me off to the Otherland.

We don't want them realizing what a mistake it was to give you away, my mami would say. *You do not go near the Fae, hija, because they will kidnap you and drag you off to one of their fairy mounds.*

Professor Hottie did not seem Fae, however. He was too big, too burly, and too flannel covered. The Fae I'd met tended toward Gucci and Prada.

"Please tell me our mami did not call the local police."

"She did not."

Thank you, sweet baby Jesús.

"She called your editor."

I wondered if it was too late to relocate to another continent and sell crafts on Etsy for a living, someplace where Allegra, the editor in question, could never, ever track me down.

"Allegra told Mami that she was still expecting the first ten chapters of your new book even if you were dead and in hell. They then had a loud philosophical discussion about Allegra's Western religious worldview, and Mami hung up on her."

My editor was an amazing woman who was outstanding at her job. But like any great editor, her DNA was fused with shark genes. If I were dead, she would not waste any time mourning me. She'd just hire a medium and raise me from wherever it was I'd gone to because death was no excuse for missing a deadline. Then she'd probably use my reincarnation to promote the bejeezus out of the book.

"Ergo, Allegra called me," Elena continued. She typed something with the precision and speed of a laser-guided missile. "I am supposed to send her a health update and your chapters today. I emailed and texted you this information at 8:00 a.m. yesterday and hourly thereafter."

I pressed my forehead against the cool glass of the store window. "I was busy falling down a mountain. I'm also living in the middle of nowhere. Did you not get my text?"

She ignored my question. "You did not answer your phone."

"Did you know that it's possible to have negative bars of cell phone service?"

"Do not exaggerate. You know a dozen communication spells. Scry. Find a puddle, a bucket of water, or a penny-filled fountain. Do you need rain? I'll send it."

Had I mentioned that Elena was also a very talented weather witch?

She'd taught me what she could, but I was not the best of students.

"There is a distinct lack of herbs on the mountainside," I grumbled. "And I didn't have any thread."

"We have discussed being prepared," she said severely. "There are supermarkets. Amazon. A kitchen garden. *Pockets.* You are in Tennessee—not on the moon. I have comments on your last book proposal and two potential projects for you to pitch. You have not read your email in hours. I need to know whether or not you are attending the overseas premiere for *Smoky Spirits.* If you are, I need the name of your escort so the organizers can schedule your red-carpet arrival. I need your travel dates if you would like to travel by plane rather than swim or try to hang onto a broomstick for eight hours over the Atlantic Ocean. It's cold this time of year, so I strongly recommend business class or a private plane charter. You need to approve the social media posts for October. *Cosmo* sent over the final text of your 'What's in My Bag?' interview. There is product placement for—"

My stomach cramped. The sprinkles I'd consumed churned. My belly was the Atlantic Ocean in hurricane season and Elena's to-do list was a massive wall of water sweeping toward me.

I ground out a few feeble words. "Time out. Stop."

It was a start. Next, name three things, I reminded myself. Three things, three sounds, three touches. That was the nonmagical incantation for reducing my anxiety.

Gourds.

A bale of past-its-prime straw.

Orange pumpkins.

Moonlight Valley's Main Street clamored for my attention so three sounds was easy. The sound of a diesel engine in a pickup truck. The annoying bell over the diner's door. Elena's voice listing all of the many, many things I had to do.

Abracadabra. Sí, claro que sí.

Sadly, there was no magic incantation to drive away anxiety or make my to-do list shrink. No matter how far away from Elena I got, she could find me and remind me of what I hadn't done yet.

"These things can wait," I said (semi) firmly. "I told you that I wanted to step away to write. I told you that I need a break."

I'd told her, but she hadn't listened. Was there a spell to make her pay attention?

"You could not possibly have meant that."

"I could have. I did."

"You always say that you're going to go away and write in one of those overwater bungalows in the Indian Ocean or in a snowbound cabin in the Blue Ridge Mountains. This is Pinterest fodder. It is not reality. You do not do this."

I slurped up the last of my pink unicorn caffeine fix. "I have always meant it. It's go time."

"Sonnet, *conejita.*" Elena paused. Knowing her, she was probably compiling a slide deck of her arguments. "*Hermanita,* listen. You know I want you to succeed. I love you."

"I love you too." And I did. Elena was my older sister by ten years. She'd earned an MFA from one of the best creative writing programs in the US and had worked in a coffee shop while she wrote her first novel. Just before I'd sold to my publisher, she'd placed a short story with a literary fiction magazine. She'd walked away from the literary circuit to manage my writing career.

"You are hot. You have tremendous reader engagement. They are BUYING YOUR BOOKS. The third season of *Smoky Spirits* is a huge hit in the US and now we're debuting it overseas. You're shooting a new season and there will be at least one more. Now is absolutely not the time to step back. You will lose your momentum. And then all the amazing things you've done, the money you've made, the ceilings you've smashed for Latinas and women writers and actresses will go *poof* like a bad spell. You will be the bad kind of invisible. You will have to START OVER."

She yelled those last two words into the phone, making me jump.

She was not wrong, but I was so very tired of being told to check my numbers every ninety seconds.

So, so many numbers.

There were the number of words I'd written, the book sale numbers, social media post numbers, advance numbers, print copy numbers, viewer numbers . . . I was tired of them.

In fact, I was just plain tired. In addition to writing the script for and starring in every season of *Smoky Spirits*, I'd written six paranormal romantic comedies in three years and was working on getting one of them optioned for a movie. At some point, surely it had to be enough? *I* had to be enough.

Once upon a time, I'd loved writing, sharing my stories, making people feel happy and romantic. *Loved.* Most days, I still loved my job, but it was a job now, and I desperately needed a vacation.

"I need some time off." I sounded whiny, as if I didn't appreciate my success and the people who loved my stories. I did. Of course I did. "I just want to read someone else's books and wear a onesie on a walk without someone snapping a picture and claiming I'm gestating Big Foot or recovering from a food addiction."

In one recent but memorable moment in my life, the jumbo-sized package of toilet paper I'd been photographed carrying had inspired a wealth of punchy headlines: "From Red Carpets to White Rolls!" "VIP Wipe Out!" and "Potty-Couture!"

Reporters had speculated that I had resorted to diuretics to slim my curvy shape down with unfortunate consequences; an anonymous source whispered that I'd thrown a fit when my last set hadn't stocked my favorite brand of TP.

It was way too much attention.

"*Conejita.*" Elena's voice warmed. "You'll get those things. I promise. I'll schedule a vacation for you next year."

It was always next year and never now.

I glared ungratefully at the gourd display. "I want beaches. And fish. And a snorkel tube. Possibly a super unflattering life jacket and the chance to waddle like a neoprene duck in fins without someone photographing me. Please tell me this vacation won't actually be a book or promotional tour."

"Noooo. Well. Maybe, not mostly. We can discuss it. But right now, you need to accept that you're not on vacation. You need to get out there and post something on social media that's not about mushrooms. You have the new season of *Smoky Spirits* to film. We need people to interact with you. And if you're interacting, your security team needs to be there."

There had been incidents in the past. Uninvited people showing up at my house, my property vandalized because a fan spray-painted her love for me in ten-foot letters, folks who squeezed harder than a boa constrictor because who didn't want to be hugged by total strangers?

"Understood. I'll get my address to the team. They can stay here with me at Phantom Falls—the place I'm renting is enormous."

"I'll let them know," Elena said. I imagined her checking a box on that pesky to-do list: *Get Sonnet to toe the line.* "You take care now."

I still didn't have my beach vacation, but I said my goodbyes and we ended our call.

I did not feel excited or energized by the thought of moving my security team into my new home away from home. I would need to work up some enthusiasm because the guys would already be salty about my abandoning them for solo time in Moonlight Valley. To be fair, I understood that they had one job: sticking to me and safeguarding my person. Also, to be fair: I was desperately in need of alone time.

And to be the fairest of the fair: I got to star in a TV series and stay in a palatial rental. I had nothing to complain about.

An obnoxious honk startled me out of my inner pep talk. I turned around as a gigantic stretch Humvee glided to a halt next to me.

The Humvee was a monster, big, crow-colored, and far too pristine. Maverick's pickup truck had been crying out for a trip to the local car wash. Mud, leaves, and other natural souvenirs had decorated its wheel wells. This new vehicle was its manscaped, Brazilian-waxed, high-maintenance counterpart.

A familiar voice bellowed out the rolled-down window. "Sonnet?"

I grinned at my landlord/college bestie. Wyatt was always so loud. The man did not do whispers or subtle, although he buried a heart of gold beneath his obnoxious bravado. "I was waiting for my handsome prince to come along, *cariño*. Please move along so that there's room for him."

"You don't wait around." His rough hoot of laughter was welcome, although his decision to stop in the middle of the road seemed questionable.

He leaned out the driver-side window, grinning at me. Despite the October weather —a less than balmy fifty degrees Fahrenheit—he wore a fitted Army-green T-shirt that clung lovingly to his pecs. Hunter casual? Lumberjack/mountain man casual? His dark hair was freshly cropped, and a pair of mirror sunglasses shielded his eyes from the glare of the rising sun. The smile that lit up his typically reserved face made him seem wickedly handsome.

"Ten minutes," I said solemnly. "I gave him ten minutes, and he's stood me up. I'll have to move on."

"Ten?" he repeated. It was a small number, and Wyatt preferred to think big.

"Yeah. How long would you wait for your fairy tale?"

Out of the corner of my eye, I spotted Eric, arms folded over his broad chest as he leaned against a building. My security team had found me.

Wyatt had to think about his answer for an alarming amount of time, long enough for two pickups and an ancient sedan to pile up behind him in the road.

Eventually, he stated the obvious. "I'm not good at waiting. I don't have to wait. Lovers flock to me."

"Uh-huh. I could offer you feedback. Ten tricks to up your wooing game. Some love magic."

"Magic doesn't exist." Wyatt fired finger guns at me for reasons known only to him.

While I'd stumbled onto the truth about Wyatt's werewolfism during our college days, he did not know about my own supernatural abilities. He believed I was the daughter of Mexicans who had immigrated to the United States when I was a baby, gotten their citizenship, and successfully chased after the American dream. He had no idea that I was half Chaneque, or that I was a practicing witch. If he'd ever seen me without my glamour fully on, he'd have run screaming.

Someone tooted their horn. Wyatt waved a big, friendly paw in the air and inched his monster vehicle closer to me.

"Do you need a ride up to the set?"

"I have a rental car." I gestured vaguely in the direction I'd come from. "Up at the cabin. A noble and trustworthy steed. I have dubbed her Eleanor. Like Eleanors around the world, she is stubborn, gritty, and quite set in her ways."

She was also a stick shift, which was something I had never mastered.

Wyatt grinned. "I'll take you."

As he promptly shoved open the passenger-side door (thus blocking the entire street), I skipped around his Humvee and climbed in.

"It's good to see you." He pulled me into his side, turning to wrap me up in a bear hug.

"You too." I hugged him back, leaning happily into him. Wyatt was the best hugger: dependable, rock-hard, and unshakeable. He'd hold me for as long as I wanted, and fuck traffic, the world, and our adult obligations. He did not demand anything or, Danu forbid, talk. He was just there for me.

Eventually, I went back to being an independent adult and let go of him. He waited until I'd waved to Eric (who would undoubtedly follow me), clicked my seat belt, and then got us on the road.

I blinked, and we were out of Moonlight Valley.

Yes, it really was that small.

"Why didn't you tell me when your flight got in? I could have picked you up at the airport."

"I rebooked onto an earlier flight. My mami wanted me to meet someone, so I needed to get out of Los Angeles."

A line appeared between his thick eyebrows. "She's still doing that thing?"

"The one where she tries to match me up with all her friends' single sons? Yup. She thinks I need a guy to keep me happy, so she orders them like spring bulbs from the garden supply center."

He smirked. "She wants you to have sex and make grandbabies."

"I have siblings," I pointed out. "Plus, she's convinced the world's full of predators. She's certain that one of these days I'll be one of those sensational Yahoo stories, where everyone dies in a spectacularly gruesome fashion."

"The cuckoo guy is going to get you?"

"El Coco," I corrected, "and maybe. He'll pop up in my bedroom some night with the sack he uses to steal misbehaving children, and it'll be all over for me. He's not the only bogeyman running around Central America, either."

Wyatt grimaced. "Your momma is one superstitious lady."

I curled up in the seat. My left sock today was white with purple thistles; my right had a girl hugging her pony in a field of white flowers. "Are you saying that you, oh hairy one, do not believe in the supernatural?"

He slid me a skeptical glance. "Have any paranormal creatures shown up in your bedroom recently?"

"There has been no one at all in my bedroom lately, paranormal or human," I groused. "I live in a sexual Sahara."

I waited for Wyatt to make his usual jokes about my unfortunate celibacy, but he just stared at the road in front of us with studied calm.

The lack of paved surfaces, street signs, and other markers of civilization was concerning—there was nothing but pines, pines, and more green leafy things surrounding our vehicle—but it was not like Wyatt to miss an opportunity to give me shit.

Awkward silence spooled out between us.

"About that." He cleared his throat.

"My sad sojourn in the dating desert?"

"Yeah." More throat clearing. The truck sped forward at a speed that seemed unsafe given the branches scraping at the top of the cab. "I ran into Mav, the guy who helped you get up to my place. He said he gave you a ride after you had hiking issues."

"Ah-ha! The sexy professor!" I grinned out the windshield, recalling how much fun the end of my hike had been.

I'd flirted up a storm with the professor. Too bad he was so stinking cute.

In hindsight, I might've been interested if he had been just a little bit less hot. It would have been interesting to give him a kissing pop quiz, see what he knew and if he was any good at it. And if he'd passed that test, then I might've shared my number with him for . . . an epilogue.

One of those bonus scenes with a little happily-ever-after, if you took my meaning. Wink, wink.

Wyatt frowned.

"I did not touch your friend. His honor is intact."

The frown deepened.

"Although there is nothing wrong with consensual touching."

Sometimes I was in the mood for sex. Sometimes I wasn't. Either mood was perfectly fine. And although I had not planned on sexy moods while I was in Tennessee, I could have deviated from the plan and given my number to the hot professor.

"Did he flirt with you?"

"*Sí, claro.* Yes, he did." I replayed the end of the hike in my head just to be sure. Our banter had for sure been amorous. "He was a charming guy. That kind of skill does not come naturally to most people."

"Maverick flirts with absolutely everyone," Wyatt muttered, driving faster than was strictly necessary.

I wrapped my hand around the oh-shit handle above the window. "Slow down. If he flirts with everyone, why did you need to ask if he flirted with me?"

Wyatt slowed down. Amber sheeted over his eyes as he muttered something I did not catch.

"Do not go wolf on me," I reminded him. "Not inside a MOVING VEHICLE."

Wyatt's response was a rough growl. He was not enjoying our conversation. "Fine. Maverick doesn't flirt with absolutely everyone. Or at least, he doesn't mean to do so. But he's a charmer, Sonnet. He makes people like him just by . . ." Wyatt muttered some words that did not flatter Maverick's ancestry.

"Charm," I stated flatly. "Natural, Goddess-given charm?"

Wyatt nodded vigorously, his fingers squeezing the wheel. "His daddy was the ultimate con man. A sweet-talking criminal. Maverick takes after him."

"He's a felon? No way." This made me laugh outright. Professor Boone was no lawbreaker. He did not seem like the kind of person who cut corners and cheated to his own advantage. On the contrary, he'd proved he was a white knight when he'd rescued me. Though, the heated glances he'd directed my way indicated that he was more the Lancelot type of knight, interested in debauching my Guinevere. My muscled, burly professor was more than a bit of an animal beneath his flannel shirt and cowboy hat.

"Once upon a time he was. He did turn over a new leaf, got a doctorate in biology. But before that, he was the town's blackest sheep. If a car went missing, you knew he'd taken it."

"My professor was a professional car thief? He's spent time in state prison?" I waved my hand around, accidentally smacking it against the window. He drove so much more responsibly than I'd have expected from a stealer of cars.

And also . . . PLOT TWIST. Maverick seemed like a nice guy, a Southern gentleman, a giant, bearded teddy bear of man. This man of whom Wyatt spoke was a bad boy and the whiff of danger was . . . *chef's kiss*. He wasn't perfect, anymore than I was, and I liked that about him. He'd lived, he'd made choices, and he had unsuspected depths.

Did I have questions? Sure.

Was I even more intrigued? You betcha. There was a whole person underneath that good-looking, bearded veneer.

Wyatt shrugged. "I mean, no one ever *caught* him. There were a couple of arrests, but the charges were always dropped. He never had a trial, but everyone *knew*."

"And no one ran him out of town or . . ."

My knowledge of small-town vigilante justice was limited to Yahoo articles, but those had confirmed that people were creative. More to the point, they hated feeling stupid or ripped off. If Maverick had been convicted in the court of public opinion, someone would have done something.

"He never stole a car from someone who needed it." Wyatt did not look comfortable explaining that his friend and my lumberjack rescuer was some kind of unethical Robin Hood. "Mostly he ripped off tourists rather than locals. He did take my father's new BMW. Twice. The second time, I bribed him to hide a largemouth bass under the driver's seat."

A hit, a palpable hit. I had not been pleased to make the acquaintance of Wyatt's dad. He was rude, arrogant, and an unmitigated asshole with a narrow-minded, bigoted worldview—and that was on his good days. He'd assumed my parents were here in the United States illegally (not true) and that I was a hot-tempered Latina who was out to sink her hooks in his baby boy for a green card (goes without saying: not true). I would have put more than a stinky fish in his car.

"So, he was working for the greater good? Doing the wrong thing for the right reason?" I allowed myself a moment to imagine a teenaged, leaner, softer Maverick imitating Robin Hood.

"Not at all." Wyatt turned us off the main road and onto what looked suspiciously like a deer trail. It was a wooded dirt track that led away from civilization and toward a tremendous number of trees. "He was working for the local biker gang, the Iron Wolves. They had a chop shop that moved stolen cars, and Maverick topped up their inventory whenever they ran low."

I considered the implications of this as we drove steadily farther and farther into the woods. "So, you're saying that Maverick was an incredibly successful thief who did not get busted ever? Why would he stop?"

In my experience, people did not stop doing things that they were good at—and could get away with—if it made them money.

"He had a come-to-Jesus moment." Wyatt slowed down, aiming for a thinner patch of trees ahead of us. If I squinted, I could just see a blue and gray streak that was likely water. "If Jesus was named Rue Ansel. Rue headed up the Department of Wildlife Management at the state university, and he was not pleased when Maverick made off with his truck. Of course, he shouldn't have left it running by the side of the road while he hopped out to chase after some snake or other, but"—he shrugged—"he did, and Maverick took advantage, and then they had themselves a conversation about life choices."

"A conversation, huh?" I could see trailers now, along with tents, cameras, and many people milling about. A tiny, charmingly run-down, one-street town filled up the rest of the available, non-wooded space.

"More gestures than words. Possibly someone got the stuffing knocked out of him." Wyatt looked suspiciously pleased at this mental image. I, on the other hand, was questioning this information dump. Its timing was suspect. "But whatever happened between those two did not end up with Rue pressing charges. Instead, Maverick left the Iron Wolves and enrolled in college. Then he tore through graduate school at record pace. The two of them have a grant to spy on hognose snakes and report back on their mating habits."

Reptilian voyeurism? Professor Hottie just got more interesting.

I needed this drive to take at least another half hour so I could learn more about Professor Boone's scandalous and intriguing personal history.

Or I needed to change the topic and stop this 411 because it was not my business if Maverick had been the town bad boy back in his high school days.

He was a grown man, and I would judge him on how he behaved now.

Wyatt, however, was not done with his overshare. "But I think it was Evan Webster who tipped that scale."

I promptly consigned my moral scruples about gossiping to a fiery end. "Who is Evan Webster?"

"Evan and Maverick were best friends. They more or less grew up together, but Evan had ethics from the moment he popped out of his momma's womb. He had words for Maverick about the car stealing and the plethora of girlfriends, but none of them stuck. He went off and died fighting for our country, and only then did Maverick start thinking that maybe there was a better way to live the life *he* still had." Wyatt parked by the edge of the set, at the end of a row of SUVs and trucks. "Mav takes care of Evan's widow."

I painted the picture in my head, something Thomas Kinkade–like, sweetly pastoral, all soft colors and blurred lighting. A darling house, a woman who was his last connection to his closest friend. A second chance to protect what was left, to make a difference, to remember. Was he holding on to what was left of Evan?

"Is that a euphemism?" This sounded like one of the soap operas my aunties loved, particularly if Maverick was standing in for his dead friend in the bedroom. I was, I admitted to myself, jealous. It made no sense whatsoever. Maverick wasn't mine and he could date or not date as he chose, but part of me was deeply unhappy about it nonetheless.

Wyatt shrugged. "You know, he does the home improvement projects, re-gravels her driveway, wields a chainsaw when she needs it. He's the man of the house when she needs one."

"Man of the house?" I raised a mocking eyebrow, downplaying the awe I felt at how Maverick had turned his life around. I might act as if I was outraged by having just time-traveled back to the 1950s, but Maverick—

He—

I—

God, he was amazing.

I was interested in playing house with him in any century, I realized, so I rearranged my features into a red herring of a scowl.

Wyatt gave me a look that I interpreted just fine. It said that he saw through my frowny face and had noted my feminist amusement at his patriarchal role-playing. "Man of the house. Maverick is a traditional guy. He likes to take care of the people he cares about, and he cares about Sanye. Plus, we wolves look after—"

Wyatt stopped, finally looking chagrined, but the world flipped. Stood on its head. Yelled CLUE at the top of its lungs. I could finish that sentence. *We all look after . . . each other. Our fellow Moonlight Valleyers. Other wolves.*

My paranormal radar went off, an entire symphony of WHOOP-WHOOP in my head.

There was more to my Maverick than met the eye.

"Wyatt Reynolds, are you telling me you're not the only werewolf in town?"

Wyatt looked guilty.

This was not an unusual state for him—Wyatt was what my mami called a *cizañero*, a shit-stirrer—but he looked more perturbed than usual.

Apparently it was okay to out his friend as a former felon, but not so fine to reveal that he went lupine in his spare time.

"Well—"

I crossed my arms over my chest and glared at him. "Do NOT lie to me. Am I in a town full of werewolves or am I not?"

"You are." Wyatt looked ever so slightly chagrined. Mostly, however, he looked calculating. I wondered if his *slip* was really such an accident—and if it wasn't, why had he wanted me to warn me about Maverick's paranormal side?

"And you didn't think to alert me? You can take all this time to hint that my rental car could be at risk if Maverick backslides, but not tell me that he goes *furry*?"

"Shapeshifting is a secret," he countered. "It's not as if we've put up a sign on the edge of town that says, *Welcome to Moonlight Valley! Werewolf population: 127.*"

Honestly, they should have picked a more discreet name for their ridiculous small town. Did Specter Springs come with specters?

And what about Phantom Falls? Were there wolves *and* a ghost population?

I really needed to be here for Halloween.

"So Maverick Boone is a car-boosting werewolf who runs around growling and protecting the people he considers pack." Called it! *Totally* knew he wasn't human! "He's big and protective and he looks out for others. I should have realized from that beard of his that he turns furry. He's all muscles and hair."

Wyatt was super easy to tease when it came to his werewolf. If I wanted to get him going, I'd call him a beast. Mind you, I didn't personally think of Wyatt as a beast. He was one of the most disciplined, focused, workaholic, literary-minded beings that I'd ever met. Plus (although I'd obviously never told him this), I'd actually met a few creatures that slavered and had vicious teeth. There was no competition.

But he was fun to poke, like a big brother or an annoying cousin.

He gave the cutest little growl, and I bit back a smile. "Fine, so there's more to werewolves than amazing hair and big teeth. I won't pick on your full-moon rampages, your anger management techniques, or your carnivorous diet."

"Noted." He killed the engine and slid a glance at me. "Then I won't call you out for hiding all my socks or doing that spell thing you do."

Well, pumpkins and pixies. He knew. *No mola.* It was not cool.

He patted my shoulder. "You don't do the spell thing on me, do you?"

"If—" I stopped myself before I outright confessed. Then I cleared my throat and started again, "If there was any magic involved, it started and stopped on the day of our roommate interview."

As the glamour I wore to make me look fully human wasn't specifically aimed at him, I decided it didn't count. It wasn't my *like me* glamour, the magic that charmed people into being friends.

He kept his fur hidden, and it was really the same thing. You didn't walk around in public in your supernatural underpants.

"And don't do it to Maverick either," he added.

"Even if he's a former felon."

"Yeah." Wyatt frowned at his steering wheel. I'll bet it was scared. "No. I shouldn't have said all that."

You think?

1. It was Maverick's personal information, not something I could Google.
2. It was part of his past. The wolf stuff could affect me now if he went

furry, but I was in no danger of losing my car to him. Only my panties and certain body parts were at risk here.

"So give me a reason why?"

Wyatt met my gaze. "Let me get back to you on that. I don't think I can explain, not really. You ever say stuff you know you shouldn't but you choose not to hold back? And there are probably complicated reasons for that you should be working out in therapy or at least acknowledging?"

I spoke far too many things out loud. So I nodded.

"I apologize," Wyatt said, and I thought he meant it. "But I think we'd both be more comfortable if we left it at that."

Truthfully? There were a lot of awkward, uncomfortable emotions underlying his apology and I very much did not want to dig deeper.

I'd wondered once or twice if Wyatt's feelings for me were more than friendly, but he was such an important friend and such a constant in my life that I did not want to probe further.

Did that make me a bad friend? It might.

Fortunately, Wyatt switched gears, redirecting our conversation away from awkward emotional reveals and back to Maverick.

"Maverick's had a rough year. His momma just up and disappeared. Sheriff Jacob dredged the lake thinking she must have run off the road in her car because no way, no how, she'd have left those boys of hers. They never did find her body."

Wyatt's info dump about Maverick's bad-boy past took a tragic turn. My heart broke, just a little. It shattered for the man who'd held me, rescued me, and then intrigued me.

My eyeballs wanted to join the sympathy train. I rubbed them hard, putting them in their place.

There would be no unsolicited moisture. I would not cry.

It was just that I loved my mami and could not imagine losing her. She was the locus of my life, an anchoring presence. No matter how far away I traveled, I knew I could always come home to her. "*Ay, pobrecito.* That's . . ."

I had no words.

Just feelings. Far, far too many feelings.

"And his daddy was an asshole, plus he has five brothers."

"He has five uncles?" They would need an enormous table at Thanksgiving.

"No. Maverick has five brothers: Knox and Ranger, then the twins, Atticus and Ford, then Rebel. There's also a sister, Mackenzie. Maverick is the oldest of the bunch."

I shook my head. "My books aren't this complex. His life is a telenovela. I could serialize it and make a fortune. Why is his daddy such bad news?"

I should not be asking nosy questions, but now I really wanted Professor Maverick to get his happy ending. Life had not dealt him a good hand.

"It's a long story." Wyatt looked doubtful about his ability to abridge what appeared to an epic Boone family history. It was true that I was due on set shortly. Still, Wyatt was an overachiever, and he gave it a shot. "Darrell Boone, Maverick's daddy, got Kate Pemberwell with child when she was in high school. She had Maverick before she got her diploma. She came from some money, though, and her daddy—"

This was *War and Peace*, Southern style.

"Condense," I suggested. "Give me the PowerPoint bullets."

"Darrell cheated on his wife, treated her like dirt up to and including beating on her, and chose to make a career for himself in the Iron Wolves."

"That's the local biker gang?"

"Sure is. And after Darrell worked his way up, he pulled Maverick in. Made it the family business. Maverick spent the first twenty-five years of his life shifting with the Iron Wolves and doing their dirty work because it made his old man proud."

"How old is Maverick?" I wished I'd snapped a picture of him, but all I had were my memories, and they definitely painted my white knight in a glowing light. He was big and fit, his skin bronzed from his time outdoors. He had fine lines around his eyes that I'd chalked up to spending all that time outside in the sun. Happy, warm lines maybe from laughing too—or being charming. You did not see lines like that in Hollywood—actors Botoxed those suckers away like dry-erase markers on a whiteboard.

"He's thirty-one. You can add that to your list of reasons to avoid him: he's too old for you."

This made me feel weirdly defensive. "Luke is thirty-eight."

Luke Hensley, my current co-star, was the last man I'd dated. He'd also been under the (mistaken) impression that we were still sharing a luxury car on the road to matrimony and never mind that I'd stopped that car real quick, got out, and headed in a different direction.

It had not taken me long to learn that he needed constant reassurance about his looks, his life, and his lovemaking. I was no good at performance reviews or pep talks.

"Luke was too old for you, too," Wyatt announced.

It was none of Wyatt's business, but we were friends, and I appreciated his caring.

Despite the thirteen years he had on me, Luke had not been a mature adult. Or even a fully functioning one.

Partly, this was due to his being an honest-to-God Fae prince who had never quite adjusted to life outside the fairy courts. Mostly, though, it was due to his self-centeredness.

He was a tall, lean, underwear-ad-gorgeous, well-groomed, and entirely helpless man-child. The only area he'd been remotely competent in had been the bedroom, and even there I'd been forced to be the director and give him his lines.

Professor Maverick, on the other hand, was a mere six years older than me, but light-years more mature. I enjoyed being silly and unserious. I wiggled my feet, admiring my socks.

I'd bet Maverick had a drawerful of neatly paired black hiking socks.

"So, now Maverick looks after lonely widows. Is he sweet on his best friend's lady?"

My palms were unbecomingly moist. Crawling back into my borrowed bed at Wyatt's house suddenly seemed like the best idea ever. Disappointment sucked.

"Not really, no." Wyatt looked at me. "If Maverick wanted to date Sanye, he'd have asked her out by now. I think he just likes being there for her. In fact, I think he'd like to be there for lots of people. It's his thing."

"Then why can't I flirt with your reformed buddy? Is it impossible that I put down roots right here in Monstrous Valley? I could be his wolfy friend. We could make beautiful pups. I hope they have his gorgeous beard and my eyes."

Wyatt bit back a smile at my facetiousness. "First of all, it's Moonlight Valley, not Monstrous Valley. And second, I'm not warning you off Mav for your sake. I want you to stay away from him for *his* sake."

This was . . .

Hurtful.

Qué chingados?

I'd thought Wyatt was secretly jealous of Maverick, but it turned out that the problem was me. Somehow, I wasn't enough—and Wyatt knew me better than most people did. He'd judged me not good enough for his best friend.

Wyatt gave me a look. "You are not a settling down kind of person, or has that changed?"

"I do not settle. That implies settling. Compromise. I never plan on compromising."

"And as a result, you move from one guy to the next, leaving a trail of broken hearts behind you." Wyatt had known me for years and he was not wrong. "This is because you're so awesome with your dimples and your sexy curves and your amazing sense of humor. Only an idiot would not fall in love with you."

"You're sure it's not the werewolf thing? Like needing to stick to like?" I did not think so, but I was going to make Wyatt say it.

"It is not the werewolf thing." Wyatt shook his head. "It's that Mav has left enough pieces of his heart scattered over Moonlight Valley, what with his momma disappearing, Evan's untimely death, and his family issues. He may have been an excessive dater, but he's reformed now. Don't tempt him to relapse."

"You make me sound like a fate worse than death," I groused.

I'd been called fat and loud, too career-focused and not focused enough. I'd been dismissed as a hack actress, a bad writer, and no good at a positively encyclopedic list of things. I'd grown a genuinely thick skin and it wasn't made from magic, either.

It was easier and less painful to joke about Wyatt's criticism and add another layer to my shell.

Wyatt ignored me, opening his door. "No matter how much of a bad boy Mav was before, he's one of the good guys now. You chew cinnamon roll men up and spit them out."

"Do not tempt me with delicious pastry," I grumbled.

I wasn't here to date men anyhow. There wasn't room in my life for real romance —only the fictional, on-screen kind. So what if Maverick Boone was a best-selling nonfiction book? I only had time to shop in the fiction aisle of the bookstore. Man store. Whatever.

I stepped out of the truck, shaking off my feelings of hurt and disappointment. I was a duck and emotions were water. Boom. They rolled right off me.

It was surprisingly chilly, but that was October in the Tennessee mountains for you. The remnants of early morning fog still wrapped around the trees and the familiar smell of wet, composting leaves filled the air. My inner witch stretched, grounding herself in all that lovely earth as I ratcheted up my glamour, preparing to go on set.

"Maverick is off-limits," Wyatt called as I headed toward the set.

I waved a hand in the air. Sure, he was. No dating for me, and certainly not for Moonlight Valley's handsome, reformed professor.

It was all over before it began—and never mind that the more I was denied something, the more I wanted it.

FIVE

"'Men,' said he, steadily turning upon the crew, as the mate handed him the things he had demanded, 'my men, the thunder turned old Ahab's needles; but out of this bit of steel Ahab can make one of his own, that will point as true as any.'

Abashed glances of servile wonder were exchanged by the sailors, as this was said; and with fascinated eyes they awaited whatever magic might follow . . ."

— HERMAN MELVILLE, *MOBY-DICK*

Have you ever cast a motivation spell?

Tucked sprigs of mint and thyme, basil and rosemary into a jar? Held it as you invited energy and clarity, courage and confidence into your life *right now if you could please hurry up, Universe, that would be great?*

And then five minutes pass. Followed by five hours, five days, five hundred years? And you're just as tired and unenergized as before?

Me, too!

After a week of shooting with no days off, I'd bailed on waiting around for the jar spell to work. I was pretty sure I would not be manifesting more energy any time soon, so instead I'd opted to sneak away before anyone could remind me of the billion things I needed to do before I was due on set later today.

It was hiking time!

Better yet, I'd done my sneaking so well that I'd shaken my security team. Now I was deep in the woods, phone out, ready for some mushroom foraging and social media content creation.

I was part woodland creature, was I not? Never mind that many of my followers liked me for my TV show and were a mushroom-optional crowd. This was for me.

I'd brought along the cutest wicker basket to hold my forest finds. I'd collected several deliciously fruity, late-growing chanterelle mushrooms, and then I'd started scanning tree trunks for *Laetiporus sulphureus*, the chicken of the woods.

It was a tasty fungus (that did indeed taste like chicken) and suitably ghoulish for October: it grew on the base of dying hardwood trees. I'd been mentally writing great Instagram captions for my corpse-eating mushroom when I realized that—yet AGAIN—I'd misplaced myself on the mountainside.

The woods were as delightful as always. Ferns and hardwoods with wonderfully floral names like Tulip Poplar and Eastern Redbud. I'd walked, collecting spell ingredients, wandering here, there, and most definitely off the path . . . which was a common theme in my life, wasn't it?

"Snickerdoodles and sunbeams!"

Thanks to my un-Chaneque-like (and all-round terrible) sense of direction, I usually stuck to well-marked paths. Something about Tennessee, however, had me making exceptions.

I squinted at the trail blaze painted on the tree trunk on my right. Maybe it was a trail blaze? Or had a red-bellied woodpecker taken an enormous dump on the bark?

I hated not knowing exactly where I was.

I blamed my mazeophobia on the vast quantity of unsupervised movie watching I'd done growing up.

The Chaneque side of my mother's family lived in a remote and mountainous part of Mexico. They had a big place there with enough space to house multiple generations of the family. Mami's *abuela* ran a day spa in Bernal, a colonial village at the foot of one of the world's largest monoliths, Peña de Bernal. Her *abuelo* took hikers rock climbing and headed up the local search and rescue. They put in a lot of hours and weren't often home, but they'd always dropped what they could during my summer visits.

I'd had a lot of alone hours, though, and my brother and sister had to step up and keep an eye on me. I'd helped them help me by learning how to turn on the TV. I'd loved stories even then, and the TV was my read-aloud buddy. I'd come home from my summer at the *abuelos* in love with my shows.

The first time I'd stumbled across a horror movie shot in the woods, I'd been hooked. I'd squeezed my eyes shut through the parts where innocent hikers were set upon by cannibalistic mountain men and mutant trees. I'd spent days wondering, *What kind of supernatural creature would do that? Eat people? And would we do the same thing?*

Spoiler: no.

Chaneques would get you lost.

Maybe we'd hide your socks or your car keys and giggle while we did it.

We were not the monsters I watched on TV. Papi had spent a weekend pruning tree branches back from the windows of our house after I'd seen *Poltergeist.* Presumably even my Fae relatives weren't into people-eating.

But right now, stomping through the Tennessee forest in the backend of nowhere, my imagination came up with a new scary backwoods script.

I was good and lost and it was not even my fault this time. I'd done all the due diligence. With Eric, the head of my security team, hovering in the background like a Miss America chaperone, Wyatt had driven me around the mountain throughout the week, pointing out trailheads.

I'd downloaded maps.

I'd bought honest-to-God paper maps—and I'd committed them to memory.

I had pictures of said maps on my cell phone.

I had my scrying mirror with me in case all else failed and I needed rescue.

I was READY.

Hiking outside by myself was a treat after a week working on my book from sunrise until after midnight. I'd answered emails, posted on social media, and paraded back and forth between Nashville, Memphis, and Knoxville because I needed to be visible and promote All The Things. And then I'd come back, and Wyatt's house was stuffed to the gills with my security team.

Who I couldn't call for help now because my phone was dead. AGAIN. It would have to be the mirror and that meant my sister, who would absolutely hold it over my head that I'd needed rescuing. It was in the big sister code.

Frustrated, I picked a random squiggle of dirt. It led downhill, and I was almost certain that the TV set was downhill, or downhill adjacent.

Twenty minutes later I discovered a crappy wooden lean-to built haphazardly by the side of my path. This proved that I was on a trail, which meant it had to be on my map, right?

Wrong.

So, so wrong. Neither the lean-to nor my trail was on my useless, out-of-date map.

Bonus: just below the lean-to, down a very steep slope, was a road. Seeing as how it lacked both street signs and asphalt, it did not help me determine where I was, although it was proof that this location was not entirely unknown to people.

It was lost and found spell time, and if that failed, *then* I'd resort to the mirror. Last chance, magic! Help me out here!

One of the things Mami had taught me was to ground myself. *You take your shoes and socks off,* hija. *Get your toes into the ground.*

Be ooooonnnnne with the earth, my snotty six-year-old self had teased. But it worked. I'd sighed, complained, and secretly acknowledged that *Mami* was a synonym for *right*.

I slipped off my shoes and socks and stood there with my feet planted on the earth. Wiggled my toes like worms on a hook. *Come here, magic. Here magic, magic, magicmagicmagic.*

Did I sound like I was calling an invisible pet? Sure, but it worked.

I imagined the charge running down my legs, through my ankles, and out my feet. There was a connection growing there between my feet and the earth. At first it was like a trickle of water dripping out of a leaky tap, but it grew.

I inhaled deliberately, filling my lungs with mountain air. My bladder waved hello, demanding attention. And was that an itch on my nose? And under my bra band?

The magic was pushing up through the ground and into me, filling me up, a warm, happy tingle that spread throughout my body as it took root.

"Bring back what's lost. That which was misplaced is now revealed."

I repeated the phrase over and over, concentrating on my car. The magic flowed through me, wrapped itself around my words, did its thing.

The car would come back to me. The path would open up.

I was finding my car.

It was finding me.

It was right—

The sound of an engine broke my concentration, and my eyes flew open. A familiar-looking orange truck trundled its way up the road at a nice, safe twenty-five miles per hour. There was a bemused smile on Professor Maverick's gorgeous face as he got out of the truck and spotted me barefoot and hovering overhead like an exotic bird in a tree.

Plot twist! the magic squealed gleefully.

Also, really? On the upside, sometimes it was fun to deviate from the plan.

His hazel eyes looked almost gold as they held mine, glowing with heat and interest. One large, battered finger reached up to tip his hat at me. He was every bit as hot and handsome as the first time we'd met on the mountain, but he was so much more than a pretty face and a pair of broad shoulders. This man had a backstory now, and I knew things about him. As if we were replaying that first meeting, he once again asked, "Ma'am, do you need assistance?"

Yes, yes, I did. Heat trickled down my throat, pooled in my belly, then rushed to my southern regions at the sound of his rough, growly voice. Wolfish. Alpha. Absolutely certain of himself. Despite the sexual warmth that was not part of my morning plans, I leaned over the edge for a better look. "Cupcakes and caterpillars," I blurted out. "Not another rescue."

Maverick folded his arms over his broad chest and tilted his head back to maintain our eye contact while he mulled over my oddball conversational reply.

"Gadzooks," he offered solemnly. "Galloping gadzooks."

A dimple dented one chiseled cheek. I was doomed.

"This is not what it looks like."

Which reminded me to check my glamour. Fortunately, it was still on and dialed up to everyday levels. What would he do if I dropped it? If he saw me as I really was, without the human skin? Would I still get dimples from him? The magic sighed as I put my shoes and socks back on.

He nodded. "From where I stand, it looks like a cute lady with an adorable laugh and a mischievous smile. One who is absolutely and indisputably not in need of any rescue. This is a rescue-free zone. DIY only."

I grinned down at him, unable to help myself. I appreciated a compliment as much as the next person, and he was good at it. He hadn't called out my face or my boobs. I did not want to hide in a sack and bemoan his creepy sexualization of my person. His words warmed me up better than cocoa, yet they seemed heartfelt.

Maverick was a sincere kind of person. Confident, as well. Maybe it was the wolf side he hadn't told me about, but he seemed at home out here in the woods in a way that I envied.

I flashed my own dimples and shamelessly dropped my eyes to his mouth because it merited a second look. It was too bad I couldn't admire those lips and stare into his beautiful eyes at the same time, because there was a whole lot of Professor Boone that was admiration worthy.

"So, you are not a white knight or a noble rescuer?"

He shifted on his feet, planting his boots more firmly on the ground. "Nor am I a volunteer firefighter or a caped hero. I have done no rescuing in years."

"Is there a lack of fair maidens in these parts?"

His eyes twinkled and his dimple almost gave him away. "There have been maidens. Just none that I'd like to rescue as much as I'd like to rescue you."

I snorted. "Are you up for some good, hard rescuing, Professor?"

"Rescue-free zone," he said solemnly. "I gave you my word. And please call me Mav."

"Not Professor?"

"Professor is not my name, Suzette."

Uncomfortable ethics moment, ahoy! Suzette was not *my* name.

The twinge of discomfort I'd felt at not correcting him when he'd misheard my name had grown into something large and even more uncomfortable.

He had not recognized me as a celebrity, and I had not enlightened him. Our miscommunication the other day had been an accident, but now I was outright lying to him.

I really was not a liar.

Before I could tell him the truth, however, he held up his arms to me. "Unless you are Rapunzel, can I interest you in coming down?"

Oh. His big, warm hands were rock solid, steady, and sure. He would not drop me. I was totally, one-hundred-percent safe with him, and so his gold-and-green eyes assured me.

I was not generally big on trusting people, and certainly not large men who had not signed iron-clad personal security contracts with my management team. And yet . . . I was somehow leaning forward, my hands fluttering in the air above his.

He flashed me an exceptional grin, one that made my long-dead romantic dreams explode like a phoenix from the ashes of my past relationships. "I must admit that I like hearing *Mav* from you. Seems a shame to waste our time together when you could be hollering my name instead."

He tipped his head at his upturned palms. I had no idea that hands could be so sexy. Why was his calm acceptance, his willingness to wait, so attractive?

"You could also say other things," he offered. "I would like to hear whatever you want to tell me, although I would prefer it if you include my name."

A kaleidoscope of butterflies landed in my stomach. They swarmed and fluttered, agitated by the low, sure rumble of Mav's voice.

Mustering my powers of concentration—which had been overwhelmed by his sexiness—I leaned down and set my hands on his. "You are the most charming flirt I've ever met."

"Am I?" His eyes warmed beneath the brim of his hat, his smile deepening. He did not seem to take any umbrage at the label.

"Yes. I am a world-class expert on flirts. I've lived in Hollywood, their natural breeding ground, and I've met tons. You could give a master class in charm, and I would happily leave you a five-star review. Thumbs up. I love it."

He stared at me for a long moment, during which I curled my fingers around his.

We were barely touching. It was entirely, unfortunately platonic.

I'd had airline stewards and drivers touch me like this, and yet he felt so good.

He was close enough for me to imagine the ways in which we could be even closer. All I would have to do was lean down, lean into this moment, and my dream would come true.

His eyes were a masterpiece. They twinkled up at me, full of good humor and heat. So. Warm. They invited me to come out to play, to respond to his sexual invitation. He'd gently hit the ball into my court, and I wanted to serve him so hard.

Biceps bunching, Maverick lifted his arms. My world tilted as he tugged. For a second—maybe two—I fell for him, and then his arms wrapped around me, steadying me.

Huge, warm hands settled on my hips. He spread his fingers, brushing a sliver of exposed skin where my shirt rode up. I held him back, planting my own hands on his thick, wide shoulders—balance was so important—and then I let go and simply trusted him to have me.

I landed on him and he caught me and held me up. My feminism card was one-hundred-percent revoked because, dear Lord in heaven, I felt dainty and feminine in his big, manly arms. His eyes sparkled at me, not backing down or looking away. He was here and present even as he gently, carefully set me down on the path.

He kept his hands on my curvy hips, and I wished he'd taken longer to put me on my feet. That I'd leaned in for just a moment more, taken shameless advantage of my chance to feel every hard inch of him.

Hazel eyes swept over my face, lingering on my mouth.

Yes, please.

It was deeply unfortunate that I was late for work. Clearly, the professor knew what he was doing. He might be a cinnamon roll of a man, but he totally owned his bakery.

And I was really, really hungry.

Nevertheless, I took a reluctant step back.

"I hate to fast forward through the part of the rescue where you literally sweep me off my feet and clutch me against your muscled chest, but I need to be at work soon. Can you help me with that?"

The corners of his mouth turned up in a devilish smile. He did not pout or protest at the space I'd put between us. Just accepted that our sexy rendezvous was over and done with. He was so . . . *mature.*

Maverick nodded, pulling his phone out of his back pocket. "Let me just text my lab."

Right. Wyatt had mentioned last week that Maverick had a federal research grant with Rue, a science hottie engaged to Maverick's sister, and who had single-hand-edly set Maverick back on the path of ethical uprightness and moral virtue.

While Maverick tapped out a small screenplay—or a novel—on his phone, I politely stared off into space.

Okay, busted. I stared at my hot professor friend.

I COULD NOT LOOK AWAY. *Who had laid a spell on whom?*

Any witch would have stared. He was hotter than Prince Charming dressed up as a lumberjack for Halloween. Thick lashes framed his eyes, and his dark beard was lush and imminently pettable. It framed his lips. *Come sit right here*, his beard crooned. It advertised a lovely, comfortable place to park my fanny.

He no longer felt like a stranger.

Probably because Wyatt had overshared about the guy's personal life. And yet, he didn't know the first thing about me, seeing as how he thought I was a Suzette and not a famous celebrity.

The anonymity was amazing.

Usually everyone I encountered was certain that we were best friends. Not only did my glamour predispose people to like me, but they were quite sure that they actually knew me—from my books, from my social media posts, from the quality time they'd spent staring at me on their screens. They snuck peeks at my life on their work breaks and when they were procrastinating. They told me how they felt about my writing and my outfits and whether or not I *really* should have gone into that dark basement when I'd been hunting vampires in season two of the TV show.

It had gone viral on TikTok. Check out #WhatWouldSonnetDo.

But back to my present.

This man had no idea who I was.

It was nice to be the one keeping secrets.

But knowing all those details about his life did not sit well. The stranger playing field was not level or even. It was not even fair. Knowing that he was a reformed bad boy and a family guy colored my thoughts and how I reacted to his actions. Worse, I'd gotten my information about him secondhand, and now I was proceeding as if that gossip were scientific fact.

Maverick's text exchange was nowhere near long enough for me to resolve my moral quandary. He tucked his phone back into his pocket before I'd gotten any further than WRONG.

"Where do you work?" he asked, turning us both around to face his truck. Normally I was not a fan of people steering me, but I could get used to having his hands on my body.

"Specter Springs." The springs were a natural area with a waterfall that spilled into a rocky, shallow creek. It got its name from a derelict mill where my character was investigating a haunting. In real life, it was one of many tiny springs that were found around the small town of Moonlight Valley.

He frowned. "Where they're shooting that TV thing?"

I should have been more specific with my spell. I started rewriting it in my head. *Bring back what's lost. That which was misplaced is now revealed but don't ask me any personal questions?* That did not have quite the right ring to it.

"Are you . . ." He took another inventory of my features, his eyes widening slightly. "You're an actress."

The hand pressed against my back dropped away.

Honey buns.

Feeling unexpectedly awkward, I prevaricated. "I'm a writer."

As soon as I said it, I regretted it. It wasn't a lie, but it wasn't the whole truth, either. Why, exactly, didn't I want to confess to who I was?

"Wow." Maverick opened the passenger-side door of his truck for me. He was looking at me with the sort of interest I reserved for rolled ice cream or a new book from my favorite author. "Did you write the script for this TV series? The one being shot here in Moonlight Valley?"

"Yes? I write TV scripts? And books that become TV scripts? It's a chicken-and-egg situation."

Which I was scrambling.

Nevertheless, Maverick looked impressed. Which, in this case, meant his wolfy eyes got all cute and round and his lips parted. This made me think of kissing, not scripts. Noooo. I should come clean, not debauch the man with my excellent imagination.

I chewed on that while I clambered into his enormous truck. Unlike last time, he did not wait around to offer me a hand or close my door. Those gestures had made me feel like a princess, and I was still not sure how I felt about that. I could get into a motor vehicle and close my own doors; I was not a member of the British royal family. Of course I didn't miss those little marks of his attention.

He slid his big, flannel-covered body into the driver's seat and looked over at me expectantly. "What made you want to become a writer?"

He picked up a charging cable that was neatly coiled on the center console. It looked like the iridescent green snake we'd met in the woods on my first day in Moonlight Valley. "For your phone."

I slipped the free end into my phone and clutched it like a lifeline while I considered my answer.

"I entered a contest my senior year of high school." This was not untrue, although it had been a shock to get the news that I was a finalist in the middle of gym class.

"What kind of contest? One for writing TV pilots?" Maverick positioned his own phone in the cupholder between us and started the truck.

"No. It was a playwriting contest. They flew the finalists to New York City and staged our plays with actual actors and actresses."

It had been an intense and fascinating experience. I'd stayed with an actress in her loft apartment, and I'd walked the handful of blocks—alone—to the theater. For the first time, I'd been peppered with questions about why my characters did and said what they did. I'd spent a not inconsiderable amount of time sitting alone in the hall outside the small rehearsal stage, rewriting lines. I had not won the contest and my play had not been chosen for the book they printed, but I had learned some things. The first was that theater acting could be financially limiting (the lead in my play had announced his intention to take a break and then audition for TV commercials because he was tired of being broke). The second was that I loved telling stories.

"You're a scriptwriter." He smiled at me. He had the best smile: warm and genuine, crinkling up the corners of his beautiful eyes. Given his werewolf side, especially the urge to shift at the full moon and what was undoubtedly a carnivorous bent, I was amazed at how laidback and nice he was. Plus, his teeth were straight, white, and not at all fang-like.

When I looked at him, I did not think about bloody steaks or lupine rampages or even my very favorite paranormal romance, where the heroine is chased by an entire pack of amorous wolves and falls happily into bed with all of them (as a writer, I was impressed by the author's ability to keep all those similar pronouns straight).

No, I thought of sweet things, of cocoa and cinnamon rolls, of cozy nights tucked up by a fireplace full of wood my man had chopped. Maverick would never, ever, buy fireplace logs at the grocery store.

I had to be upfront with him, but I did not want to give away my superstar secret. "Well, the contest was for teenagers. We wrote plays, things for off-Broadway, and angsty dystopian dramas. I dressed all in black and glowered everywhere. But it gave me the writing bug. And I had that taste of almost-success, and I wanted more. So I started submitting to agents, and things went from there."

This was all true, except I did not mention that my first book led to a bidding war between publishers and that it had spent a respectably long time on the bestseller lists. It had been optioned, and the TV network executives wanted me to play the witchy lead. They had been very insistent.

Not that I had wanted to refuse. I'd been a broke, unemployed English major. Starring in a TV series was a major step up from scanning leasing documentation for a bank (which had been my only other job offer). Picking staples versus speaking lines? *Yeaaaah, option number two, por favor.*

Maverick turned us back onto the main road, which had an actual street sign and all. He kept taking quick peeks at me, working up to asking another question. But I wasn't in a question-answering mood.

Why would a woman who was supposed to be laying it all out deflect?

I didn't want to say. There was no acceptable reason. There was my inexplicable interest in this man, interest involving his good looks and sweet nature and the way his broad shoulders filled out his flannel shirt. He was funny. And nice. And no one I should be thinking about romantically. Not because I was against casual sex, but because Wyatt had been very clear that Maverick was not the type to hook up outside of a relationship. Maverick would demand a commitment. He'd insist on getting to know *me*.

I was not a relationship star. In fact, I was learning right now that I was a big chicken and that *forthright and honest* also meant *vulnerable and might be rejected*. I redirected the conversation. "That was six years ago, and now here I am. Wandering around the Tennessee mountains while working on my next project."

"You need to watch out for the local wildlife." His smirk did wicked, wicked things to his dimples.

"I would hate to be eaten by a black bear. I could meet all sorts of animals. Mountain lions, cougars, so many choices." I patted his arm. God, it was muscled. My patting turned into stroking. "This neck of the woods is awash in people-eating critters."

"And wolves. We've got lots and lots of wolves in these parts."

Wow. He had gone there. I smirked at him. "Do y'all have a wolf problem?"

"Not a problem, no, but I'd be happy to eat you up myself."

Oh, I just bet you would. I rested my chin on my palm. Winked. Tried to ignore the spontaneous combustion happening in my nether regions. "Are you a bear?"

"No, ma'am." He grinned easily, flashing his dimple. "I am not an animal."

I leaned over and bumped his shoulder lightly with mine. "That's not what I've heard."

FYI, he had a beautiful shoulder. Hard. Warm. Mount Rushmore worthy. He bumped me right back, and for a moment it was more that we were leaning on each other. Such a small piece of skin, the shoulder, but the effect was incendiary.

But I had to draw the line. I could hardly tell him that I knew his little werewolf secret, plus he'd offered to give me a ride in his truck, not a ride on his dick. I reached for my phone, needing to hold something less manly and fun. "You are such a charmer. I feel like you could teach me tons."

"About being charming?" His voice was sort of growly now, the kind of mock-irritated tone you'd use when your cat has drunk out of your water glass.

"You bet. You could be a hero in a romance novel. You're tall and you've got great hair. In books everyone wants the hero to be a grumpy Gus who the heroine wins over to the sunny side. But in my stories—paranormal romantic comedy stuff— you guys get to be funny and charming. Cinnamon roll men that we just want to lick up."

Maverick wouldn't allow me to elaborate. The most adorable pink flush had crept up his cheekbones. He was horrified, or so I interpreted by the hand he held up. I knew a universal *stop right there* gesture when I saw one.

He shook his head. "I am not a pastry guy, although I am open to the idea of licking."

Laughing once more because I couldn't help it—this guy was *fun*—I curled up in my seat and looked him over. "I would not know where to start. You are a total buffet."

"I could make some suggestions." Now his grin was downright devilish. "Or, better yet, I could demonstrate on you."

His laugh started low, rumbling out of him. It was a very bear-like laugh, rough and warm, burly and delightful. It made me feel safe.

I loved this. LOVED. It.

I couldn't remember the last time I'd flirt-chatted with a guy who had no idea who I was. Usually, if the guy wasn't an actor, producer, or some other established Hollywood type, he had aspirations—and he thought that dating me would be a shortcut to achieving fame and fortune. My dating life had taught me several painful lessons about users.

Even if my date was already a celebrity, dating was hazardous and often competitive. Was I famous enough, pretty enough, liked by enough people that he could justify his interest in me? Or was there someone better that he could be seen with? I was an accessory, a prop. And even though those guys never knew about my glamour, they still asked me to change my appearance to suit their own brand and style.

Even before I'd sold my first book, I stuck to the dating slow lane. I did not open up quickly, nor was it easy for me to get to know a guy. Writing romance novels had been natural for me because I'd always been that girl who rehearsed her conversations before she made a call or went on a date. Really, all I'd had to do was write them down and add a sprinkling of orcs and Fae. BOOM. Ready-made books.

With Maverick, however, things felt easy. I did not know what he—or I—was going to say next. There was no script, no perfect lines. We definitely had moments of silence. And yet it was fun. I loved it, and I wanted an encore. This man was a forever man and a keeper.

Naturally, I could not keep that awkward thought to myself. Nope. I blurted it right out. "I've named our kids."

Not missing a beat, Maverick responded, "Did you read *Consumer Reports* too? Our daddy picked our names out of that magazine. Guess he didn't want to waste all the research he'd done on a new truck."

Despite the good-humored way he'd turned my admission into a cute personal revelation, I still felt weird. Why did I say these things? This was worse than the time on a press tour that I'd kissed the hotel manager's cheek when the poor guy had just been going in for a handshake.

This was awkward and I was awkward. I had zero social game. I was used to charming the people I met, making them feel important and seen. I doubt there was a magic eraser for conversations, but I wanted one. Or maybe a nice forgetfulness spell or a memory charm? Instead, I started rewriting our conversation in my head.

I'm so happy to see you.

It's like the universe is throwing us together!

Are you free for coffee?

"Is there a part for me?" Maverick eased the truck to a nice, slow stop for a red light.

"Excuse me? In what?" Had I missed something he'd said? Elena had compared the inside of my head to a soundproof vault on more than one occasion. Once I got to thinking, my ears shut off.

He shifted in his seat so he could face me, looking at me as if I weren't awkward, as if he still wanted to eat me up. "You're curled up in that seat, talking to yourself about something. I'd like to participate."

"Well . . ." I tweaked a line or two in my head, and then went off script. "I guess I decided that I'm the queen bee of awkward. After less than sixty minutes in your company, I've offered to have your babies. That's awkward."

He shrugged, unfazed by my reproductive urges. "It's not awkward. I'm excellent genetic material. Japanese crepe cake?"

I blinked. "Cake?"

He tipped his head to the right. "If we go right, we can hit up the bakery that does Japanese crepe cakes. They're the best. It'll take five minutes to get there. But Specter Springs is in the other direction, which means we must detour for cake. Do you have time for that?"

"Uh." The sudden topic shift had me off-balance. I had offered him heartfelt personal vulnerability, and his response had been to offer me dessert. On the other hand: cake. "I'm super late already." But would it hurt to be a few minutes later?

Maverick signaled to turn left.

"They stay open late. We could go later."

I nodded enthusiastically, my mind seesawing between cake and baby making. "Yes. Later."

"How about tonight?" he asked, his voice light.

"Tonight? You want to eat cake with me tonight?"

He was the king of confidence. And of plans. Surprises, too. Because I had *not* seen this coming and I didn't know what to say. I quickly reminded myself that I had work. Responsibilities. That I was not experiencing a delirious little bubble of joy because my wolfman had asked me out on a cake-eating date.

"Yeah. I could get you after you finish work and take you back to the house via the bakery. It wouldn't take any time at all."

I was pretty certain that time did not work that way, even if it did seem to stretch like bad taffy when I was stuck in the line at the DMV.

"Alright, it would take time, but it would be time well spent." The smile he shot me was soft and bright. "But I'd be saving time as well, seeing as how I would not have to chase you all over the mountain. If you let me drive you to and from the set, you'd be on time and not lost. And I wouldn't have to spend my time looking for you."

I bit my lip, trying to hold in the laughter. His cheesiness was endearing, and he got an A for effort. "I'm sure you have better things to do than drive me all over the fine state of Tennessee."

"There is nothing better than looking after the mother of my future children."

My face was on fire. It was the fiery color of a cardinal. "Can I convince you to forget that I said that?"

He chuckled, but it was a good-natured sound. I wasn't sure this man had a mean bone in his fine body. "Here's the deal. You let me take you back to Wyatt's place tonight and pick you up in the morning. If it takes too much of my time or you don't like it, we won't do it again. But if our driving arrangement pleases us both, then . . ."

Then what? I needed him to finish that sentence.

He did not. Le sigh.

"But what's in it for you?" I fanned my face, seeing as how I had already lost any chance of seeming glamorous and cool in front of him. "I get a free chauffeur. But I'll be in town for twelve weeks. Do you want to save me from the evil torments of my rental car and its stick shift by driving me hither and yon for that long?"

The glance he gave me was soft and playful. It warmed as his eyes moved over my face. The fire in my cheeks migrated lower.

I wished I could see myself through his eyes always.

His voice was rough when he said, "I will hither and yon you for as long as you will let me."

His next glance was less soft, and it got his . . . point . . . across just fine.

Maverick Boone had some sexy plans in mind for us.

And for once in my life, I was too awkward and caught off guard to say anything. I did not have the perfect line ready. I was not directing this scene. Because now I was thinking about going places with the good professor, and those sexy possibilities made me hot and bothered.

So, so hot.

I looked at him, saying nothing, because for once I was just going to let the next thing happen in my life without trying to script or plot it. The rest of the short drive to Specter Springs was quiet, but it wasn't awkward. It was tense. Erotically tense. The *I can't wait for tonight and can we skip all the daylight hours* tense.

My wolf was such a charmer.

CHAPTER
SIX

MAVERICK

"He looks every bit the handsome faerie prince, beloved by everyone and every-thing. Rabbits probably eat from his hands. Blue jays try to feed him worms meant for their own children."

— HOLLY BLACK, *THE STOLEN HEIR*

We need to write a movie.

Invite her for a sleepover.

We could bite her. Just a little.

My wolf whined quietly, anxious to touch Suzette and mark her.

Wolves kept their mating bite for their one and only.

Once you marked a woman as your mate, there was no going back. Not only might she become a shifter if she wasn't one already, but there would be a bond, an emotional tether, between the two mates.

If you were too far apart, you'd get stuck in your wolf form, too.

There was no biting someone *just a little.*

Still, a silly grin stretched my face. I did want to see more of Suzette.

A whole lot more.

Not being a kidnapper or a psychopath, however, I had not stopped her from getting out of my truck.

I'd opened the door for her and wished her good luck with her day.

I'd even ignored the territorial glances a large, muscled human male had shot my way.

She'd paused, staring up at me, the dimple in her cheek on full display. The smile she'd given me had been both bashful and alluring. Then she'd said, "*Muchísimas gracias,*" and disappeared into the organized chaos of the set.

Flirting was like riding a bike. My skills had been rusty, but I'd not forgotten how to charm a lady. Five years of alone time had not dried up my imagination, not one bit. Of course, it helped that she was not the only one who wrote scenes in their head.

I'd spent the whole week imagining what I would say to her when we met next.

Although I'd known where she was staying, I had not gone out to Wyatt's place. It would not have been appropriate without an invitation. Good, sweet baby Jesus, I was grateful for her poor navigational skills and mountain shenanigans. Now I got to have cake with her tonight after her shoot wrapped, and I'd see her again in the morning as her newly appointed chauffeur. With all those opportunities, I ought to be able to invite her out to dinner.

My smile did not fade as I pulled back onto the road and drove to campus.

Grabbing my samples, I noticed Suzette had left a to-go coffee cup and a small handheld mirror on the floorboard of the truck. Those were weird companions, but perhaps the mirror was a set prop? I tucked it inside my satchel, so I could clean it before I picked her up tonight, then banged my way inside the laboratory.

Rue was frowning at a scale that held a tangle of baby snakes. He grunted something that I took for a greeting but he did not look up.

That was fine with me. Baby snakes were escape artists, and you never knew exactly how many of them you'd started with.

Shelves of glass jars and specimen samples lined the walls. We had the usual assortment of metal tables, scales, and what I liked to call our resort facilities: a series of tanks where we temporarily housed the snakes I was nursing back to health.

It was downright shocking how many people thought they'd buy themselves a reptile for a pet and then were surprised by the upkeep involved. Plus, snakes were not fluffy, and their cuddling skills were frequently misunderstood.

You should have studied bovines, my wolf opined. **Steaks are delicious. Snakes have no meat.**

"What are you humming?"

I grabbed my lab jacket from its hook while I tried to come up with an answer. I was not musically inclined, being mostly tone deaf. Ranger had pointed out several times that as enthusiasm and volume did not compensate for skill, I should refrain from music making. "Nothing."

"Opera aria." Ranger popped up out of nowhere, scaring the bejeezus out of me. He gave me a disapproving frown. "You are far too bearded and bass for a Russian aria."

Rebel, my youngest brother, had his feet up on my desk in the corner. Why was I hosting a family reunion at my lab? I was not focused—my head was back in Specter Springs.

"And the song is 'I Love You, Olga.'" Rebel pronounced the girl's name like he actually knew how to speak Russian.

"Since when are you a Russian expert?" Ranger narrowed his eyes at our youngest brother and sipped what smelled like grass clippings and compost from my coffee mug that read: *Don't judge a lizard by its scales*.

We could take him.

"What the hell is that, Ranger?" The pungent odor wafted across the lab, stronger than the snake musk and the diluted Gatorade stink of Rue's culture cells.

"It's mushroom coffee with kale. I brought enough to share. It improves my concentration and reduces bloating." Ranger held the cup out to me.

"Ranger, you're twenty-seven. Bloating is not a problem you have." I crossed to the sinks at the back of the lab and retrieved Suzette's cup from my satchel to rinse it off. Someone had scrawled a tentacled figure on the polypropylene. It seemed to be embracing a smaller octopus.

Curiouser and curiouser.

"My midsection is just fine today, thank you for your concern. But bloating happens to everyone. And when it does, I will have taken the proper steps. Additionally, drinking this gives me something to add to conversations about being swimsuit ready for summer."

"I have never heard anyone discuss their swimsuit readiness." Cup clean, I turned my attention to the mirror. The dirt washed right off, but the surface underneath was foggy. I squinted at it. She needed a new one because I could almost imagine I saw someone squinting back at me.

"That's because you don't belong to my crochet club. If you crocheted, you'd talk about your upcoming vacation and your swimsuit readiness and know all about bikini line preparation and what is going on in Moonlight Valley bedrooms."

"I have no desire to hear about Moonlight Valley's bedroom activities."

"What I have not heard is that you like mirror sex. This is a new side of you." Ranger sounded impressed and surprised. "And why haven't you shared what you've learned with me? You know that I like to try new things in the bedroom."

Boy has a point. Let's do that! Didn't Marie Antoinette have mirrors in her bedroom? We could have French sex!

I was very happy not knowing how French aristocrats preferred their sex.

"I am not having mirror sex." I yanked the mirror out of the water and dried it off with a paper towel. I mean, I was certain that I'd prefer to look right at Suzette, but I guess if she wanted to try it, I would.

I was open to mirror sex with her.

Nevertheless, I did not want to explain to whom the mirror belonged because then Ranger would be thinking about Suzette and sex, and I would have to kill him. "Why are the two of you here anyway?"

Rue straightened, taking up most of the available space in our lab. "Rebel is working with me for the next three months."

Rue had mentioned his plans to introduce an intern into our laboratory. It made sense, given how Rebel had been accepted into a zoology program, for him to shadow Rue. As the department chair for the Department of Wildlife Management, Rue worked a lot with animals. In addition to the nest of snakes he was sorting out, he had a collection of orphaned chipmunks and two baby crows. We were both certified wildlife rehabilitators.

"And Ranger is here to help you." Rue pointed at my brother. "He volunteered himself."

I smelled a rat.

"Why do I need a volunteer? I do not need another research assistant."

"There's a snake thing. Or maybe it's more of a general wildlife thing." Rue frowned at me, then got busy with the scale. One of the baby worm snakes had escaped onto the table, and he gently lifted it back onto the scale. "We've had a request. But you'll need Ranger too."

Now we're screwed and not in the fun way.

I rubbed the mirror one last time, tucked it back into my bag, and wiped my hands on my lab coat. Hydie, our resident mama gecko, had nested in the cabinet under the sink where we kept the paper towels, and until her baby offspring were grown, there was no going in there and startling them. "What kind of snake thing is it?"

Rue frowned at the knot of tiny snakes wriggling around on the scale. He was a straight talker, so his silence concerned me.

Ranger slurped his lawn clippings. Loudly. I would need to run my coffee cup through the autoclave because the stench was downright offensive. Any bloat in his gut would vacate the premises in self-defense. His bright-eyed gaze bounced between Rue and me like a tennis ball at Wimbledon.

What with our grant and his teaching load, Rue was busy. He did not need more stress, so I'd handle whatever this new problem was. "Alright, don't tell me. I'll still do it. Sign me up."

"It's that TV crew," Rue growled, his face radiating mild disgust.

"They need a wildlife rehabilitation expert, and you've been nominated." Ranger toasted me with the coffee cup, slurping up the remnants. He looked happier than any man who'd just consumed grass for breakfast should.

"An expert? I thought they already had people for that, as part of their permitting process."

Rue had explained that *Smoky Spirits* had gone through a lengthy permitting and approval process to get permission to film on location on national park land. Most of the shooting would happen at Specter Springs and the gray bats, slender chub, and other protected species were not to be upset by the influx of TV people under any circumstances.

"They have a bat issue." Rue's tone was grumpy.

"Why would they send a guy who did not know how to handle bats?" Rebel asked the obvious question, waving his coffee cup around. He had not noticed the reptilian trespasser clinging to the lid, so he was in for a surprise. "That's downright ignorant."

"I got a call an hour ago about bats flying into the miller's cottage where they're shooting. They are living in the attic and flying through the scenes. That means someone needs to go and rescue the bats. And it can't be just All-Purpose Animal Services because the TV crew's contract states they must employ a wildlife expert if they relocate any critters. If I go, I'll be relocating the two-legged critters as the bats were there first."

Rue's grumpiness was legendary; he was not what was known as a "people person." He'd been compared to a grizzly bear, and the bear had come out ahead in the personality sweepstakes.

"Gotcha." I mentally rescheduled my research and classes for the week. This would put me behind on the article I was finishing up for *Science* magazine, but there was an upside. I would almost certainly be seeing Suzette before our date tonight. In fact, there would likely be Suzette spottings all week long.

And outdoor time, my wolf chimed in. **No doors, no walls, just you, me, and the wild!**

"Why do you look so happy about this?" Ranger sounded suspicious, but that was not new. Momma had claimed that he'd been born asking questions.

I ignored him. "So, I'll go on down there as the wildlife expert, and All-Purpose Animal Services is the muscle?"

Rue responded with the scantest of head tips; he had already refocused on his snakes.

"When?" I prodded.

"Now would be good. Take the new bat houses, and put them in a better neighborhood. Then convince the bats that they'd like to upgrade their lodgings."

Bat colonies could not be relocated for five months of the year when the bat pups were too young to fly on their own. Since we were into October, however, the bats would be preparing to settle down and hibernate. All I had to do was offer them a better alternative than a run-down if historical cabin.

Rue gave me a semi-sympathetic smile, then promptly marched out of the lab, Rebel hot on his heels.

"I think he means a neighborhood with no TV people." I chuckled because Rue was a hermit. The only person he willingly made room for in his life recently was my sister, Mackenzie. Still, he'd turned my life around even if he was not one for social back-and-forth.

He is a WISE MAN.

"Or we can all move." Ranger set my now-empty mug down in the sink beneath the faucet and added exactly enough soap and water to fill it to the brim. His beard had acquired a greenish tinge above his upper lip. "If these TV people are as annoying as Rue thinks they are, we should move somewhere else until they're gone. Moonlight Valley could be a Boone-free zone. Cancun is nice this time of year, seeing as it's almost past hurricane season. We could go on a yoga retreat."

* * *

Ranger was a big help. Not that I told my brother that.

No way. Keeping Ranger and his ego in check was a full-time job I did not want. He was scary smart, and boy did he know it.

Still, I would have had a hard time installing the bat houses on my own. I was master of bat houses, and usually put up several new ones each season as our Moonlight Valley bats liked to move in where they weren't wanted. Today's houses were Victorian-inspired and made from cedarwood. The outsides were painted pink and yellow, and I'd used a hot glue gun to attach white gingerbread trim. The bat houses were not heavy, but they were installed on fifteen-foot posts, and that work went easier with two people on the job. Plus, Ranger was good to have around, as long as he was not in a plotting mood. The problem was, Ranger was almost always conniving. He did not enjoy downtime, so he usually had some plan or other brewing.

Fortunately for me, today seemed to be a rest day for him, and we were able to share a truck cab and a workday without my needing to figure out what he was up to. He'd been complaining for the last three miles that Sanye had so far refused to be his sous chef at an upcoming barbecue competition. Knox had also declined to participate.

"You've tried blackmail?"

Ranger nodded. "Blackmail did not work on Knox, although it most certainly should have. That man is one hundred percent on Santa's naughty list."

"Did you try Rue?"

This earned me a Look. "I believe you are aware that blackmailing Rue Ansel would be an utter waste of my time. That man loves rules. He's as upright and law-abiding as Comet C/2022 E3 ZTF is old."

Getting to this point with Ranger—where we had a genuine conversation rather than taking shots at each other—had taken five years and no small amount of effort on my part. The damage I'd done during my years with the Iron Wolves had been considerable, so I appreciated moments like these.

The set was busy when we arrived, with the crew shooting a scene at the mill over by the water.

I snuck a few peeks, but did not spot Suzette in the crowd. I couldn't get a real good look, however, seeing as how I had to set up the bat houses a decent distance away from what a harried-looking production assistant told me was "Betty Rae Jenkin's haunted cottage."

The "cottage" was the miller's derelict nineteenth-century house. It had a shingled roof and gables; a weathered picket fence enclosed a yard filled with daylilies and ferns. It was about as far from today's scene as I could be without actually climbing back into my truck.

After the production assistant confirmed that where I planned to move the bats would not interfere with their shots (I spent an extra long time confirming exactly where those shots were happening and checking them out long range), Ranger and I set to work.

It took no time at all before we had the new houses up, during which time I continued to fail in my attempts to catch a glimpse of my girl. Fortunately, I'd have to come back at dusk, add some netting after the bats had flown out of the gables, turning their bat hole into a one-way exit. That would be another chance to see her and just the thought buoyed me up like a pontoon boat in a swamp.

"You're humming again," Ranger remarked as we climbed back into my truck and I gave one last, unsatisfied look around. Maybe writers stayed in the trailers? Could I come up with an excuse to check in there? "That grandiloquent Russian song about unrequited love and missed opportunities, the one Rebel can't pronounce because that man did not avail himself of foreign language opportunities when we were at school."

"I don't know how I picked it up." I started the truck, double-checking the rearview and side mirrors. And then once more, because I might be a werewolf, but I was not immortal and I liked my insurance rates as they were.

"Momma sang it when we were growing up. She had a record of the whole thing, and then we'd pretend that we were going to the opera."

"She did." The memory came back at his prompting, and I could see Momma now, too young to have so many of us storming through her big old house and making so much noise.

She and my grandmother had insisted on teaching us to be Southern gentlemen, polite and well-behaved. Obviously, only so much of those lessons had stuck. But I remembered pretending to file into a fancy-ass theater to listen to Russian opera with bath towels tied around our shoulders for opera capes and empty Quaker Oats containers on our heads for hats.

"It's a love song. *IA LIUBLIU TEBIA, IA LIUBLIU TEBIA, LIUBLIU TEBIA,*" Ranger belted out with operatic fervor. "*I LOVE YOU, LOVE YOU, LOOOOOOOOVE YOU!!!!*"

He sounds like a wolf howling.

Ranger's Russian sure sounded authentic to me, but to be fair, he could have been singing in Klingon for all I knew. He finished with an improvised cadenza as I pulled out onto the dirt road that would connect us back to the main highway.

There had been zero Suzette spottings, and I was unhappy.

Also disappointed. Blue-balled. Reaaaalllly frustrated.

"Why did you pick that song?"

"No idea." But that wasn't true. While I hoped I was less melodramatic than some Russian aristocrat bellowing about his feelings, I was thinking about Suzette and her brown eyes and pretty mouth. I'd felt happy and expectant when Momma played that song, and that was also how I felt thinking about seeing Suzette again.

"You do know." Ranger sounded irritated. He was doing that knuckle-cracking thing he did when he got anxious or upset, popping the joints in his hand one after the other like bubbles in a piece of bubble wrap. "But you have no intention of sharing with the class."

We don't need another wolf butting in.

That was true—but it was also true that Ranger was my brother. Sharing with him was more dangerous than getting arrested, seeing as how he absolutely would use anything I said against me.

Rue, however, had insisted that I needed to demonstrate to my brothers that I trusted them. He'd argued that it just good social mathematics: I invested in them, and then they'd invest back in me, in a tit-for-tat kind of situation.

If he hits us, we hit him back!

Ignoring this less than helpful advice from my wolf, I cleared my throat and confessed, "I met someone."

The cab was silent for a few seconds while Ranger processed that. "You met someone? Like a girl?"

I nodded and pretended to check my sideview mirror. Seeing as how our current speed was all of ten miles per hour on a dirt road, it was an unnecessary precaution. We were not going to hit traffic.

"And she has you whistling Russian love songs?" Ranger started in on the knuckles of his right hand. He was going to give himself arthritis by the time he was thirty.

"Maybe," I said. No. That was evasive, and the new and improved Maverick was open and trusting. Mostly I thought that was bullshit, but—"Yes. Yes, she does. She makes me want to whistle Russian love songs."

I figured this would give Ranger plenty of material to work with, but he surprised me by flashing a rare smile in my direction.

Danger.

"That's good." He nodded. "Real good. I'm pleased for you."

This was a passionate endorsement, coming from Ranger. My brother was sparing with his adverbs and adjectives. Hence, when he fired off his usual onslaught of questions, I gave him answers.

"What's her name?"

"Suzette."

He can call her OURS. Or Ms. Maverick.

That was too fast even for me. Probably.

When a wolf knows, he *knows*.

"And how did you meet?"

"She got lost hiking on the mountain and couldn't find her way back to Wyatt's place. I took her over there."

Ranger frowned. "She's staying with him?"

HELL no.

"No. She's staying in that cabin by the waterfall that he rents out to tourists."

"Is she here visiting?"

"She's a writer. She wrote the script for this TV series. I think it might be based on a book she wrote. Whatever." I shrugged. "She writes awesome things and gets paid to do so."

Ranger stopped his salvo of questions. When I glanced at him again, he was staring out the windshield. He looked confused.

"What's wrong?"

"Your writer girl's name is Suzette?"

"Yep."

"You are totally, one-hundred-percent certain? You are not experiencing premature hearing lost? *Suzette?*"

Can I bite him?

"Yes."

Thank FUCK, my wolf growled, rising to the surface.

I gently pushed him back down. I was not biting anyone today—or ever. My biting days were behind me.

"Did she give you a last name?"

"It did not come up." She hadn't given me her phone number, either.

Or a kiss, my wolf grumbled. **We should make a list.**

"Describe her?"

I frowned. "This had better not be some kinky game of yours."

Ranger widened his eyes innocently. "You know how much I love my TV series. I'm trying to figure out if I know her or have watched any of her shows."

"Fine. She's on the short side. Curvy. Dark hair, dark eyes, dimples for days. She got her start in a contest when she was in college."

Ranger tapped his chin with his forefinger. "A playwriting contest."

"Yeah. How'd you know?"

His eyes did not meet mine. "Playwriting is a good basis for screenwriting. There are similarities, so it makes sense. And you said she told you that she wrote the book this TV series is based on?"

"So you know who she is?" Ranger was the bane of my existence. His questions were driving me up the wall. My Suzette was prettier than anyone I'd ever met, with those laughing eyes of hers and the smiles . . . I loved her smiles. I loved that she was so happy and approached life with such glee. She threw herself into it like you would jump into a swimming hole on a Tennessee summer day. I wanted to discover all the things that made her smile. I wanted to learn all about *her*. She'd opened up and shared some stuff, but I wanted everything with her.

He jiggled his foot. "I do think I've heard of her. A couple of years ago, she wrote a book about a bunch of supernatural creatures that included orcs and Fae; it was real popular and made all kinds of money when it was turned into a TV series. Jump-started the lead actress's career. Ruiz is her name. She won an Emmy this year. She's a big-deal celebrity, has all sorts of social media endorsements. People love her."

"Huh," I said, in the face of all this new information. "Suzette didn't mention any TV show fame or career launching. She was downright modest about her book stuff." This just made me like her even more.

And she's got great—

I forced myself to concentrate on my driving.

Ranger jiggled his foot and stared out the windshield some more. Maybe he had finally run out of words—or questions. I took advantage of the silence to think up some questions of my own. I could look Suzette up when I got home, check IMDb or some such website. I'd find out facts that way, but I wasn't sure that facts were what I wanted.

Facts were only a small portion of who Suzette was. She had stories, likes and dislikes, and all sorts of characteristics. I liked hearing her talk, but more importantly, I wanted her to share with me. Looking her up on the internet did not feel like the right thing to do.

"You can meet her tonight," I said, mostly to fill the silence. It was downright unnatural, Ranger staying silent like this. "I'm picking her up at the end of the day. Be nice to her."

If not, THEN we'll bite him?

It was a definite possibility.

Ranger smoothed his fingers over a worn spot in his jeans. "If you're singing Russian love songs, you must really like her, huh?"

"I do." I put it right out there into the universe.

WE do.

"You're good with the ladies," Ranger said, mostly to himself. "And she's expressed an interest in you?"

I grinned. "She has."

His eyes flickered to mine before dancing away. "You haven't seen anyone in ages, Maverick. Not that I've been logging your dating hours, but I've noticed. You have not stepped out in over five years."

"You know why I haven't."

"I sure think I do." Ranger's voice was low and rough, a gentle burr that said my brother was trying. "It's just that you do try real hard. I know you think you've gotta make amends and that you owe us all something. What you do is appreciated."

This was not a conversation that should be conducted in the cab of a moving vehicle. It felt genuine but tenuous, as if it would vanish if I said the wrong word. I did not want to make light of Ranger's feelings, not ever.

"Thank you," I said carefully. "That means a lot to me. I have changed, and I'm not the wolf or the man I was five years ago. I'm better. I won't backslide. There's nothing much between me and this girl, not yet, but I wouldn't chase her if my intentions were dishonorable. I'm no longer in the business of hurting people."

Ranger looked frustrated. "I know that, you dingbat."

We were not big on talking about our feelings. Especially not as adults, for crying out loud. Mostly we shifted into our wolves and tussled some. I clenched my jaw, trying not to say anything embarrassing or sappy. "So what's wrong then?"

Ranger didn't answer. He sat there looking thoughtful and cracking his knuckles.

CHAPTER

SEVEN

SONNET

"Long ago, the High Fae had been our overlords—not gods. And they certainly hadn't been kind."

— SARAH J. MAAS, *A COURT OF THORNS AND ROSES*

I spent the day shooting scenes, going over last-minute rewrites, getting re-measured for a few costumes, and fending off flirtatious remarks from my co-star Luke, as well as "well-meaning" recommendations for an exercise and fasting app he used. I was this close to using Elena's patented banish him spell when the director called cut and released us for the day.

I should have been exhausted and over peopling for the day, but instead I was energized thanks to thinking about two equally delicious things: cake and Maverick.

He'd promised to pick me up at 7:00 p.m. in the same spot where he'd dropped me off this morning. I'd given Eric and my security team a heads-up about my travel arrangements, headed off their objections (while they headed off to do a background check), and then hustled outside, hoping that I was not about to be stood up.

Maverick turned out to be a man of his word.

Despite his timely arrival, he'd swapped his truck and brought someone else along.

103

So, no, this was very much *not* a date. Not that we'd agreed that it was. I had no business being even the teensiest bit disappointed.

I concentrated on his vehicle instead.

First of all, the new truck was enormous. ENORMOUS. It also wasn't a . . . truck?

Maybe trucks were different in the South? This one looked like the mechanic had dropped a black Volkswagen bug onto four oversized wheels. I would need a ladder to get up there, not to mention the climbing skills of a monkey.

Secondly, the bonus passenger was a shaggy-haired man-creature leaning against a person-sized monster wheel. He sported an All-Purpose Animal Services polo shirt, a flannel shirt, and an overgrown brown beard dense enough for a half-dozen bats to roost in. I was not prepared to ride next to the wild man of the woods. This was not shaping up to be the romantic truck ride of my dreams.

But then I looked past the weird-ass truck/car and the semi-feral bonus passenger, and there was Maverick.

He grinned at me, big and wide, which had me smiling back at him. It was impossible not to smile, because Maverick gave big, heated, happy smiles. Tonight's smile was wide and uncontained. He did not hold anything back. I'd let my glamour relax some, but I let it go further, keeping just enough to make me look one-hundred-percent human. It felt so good to slip the mask off, like taking off a pair of gorgeous heels that cost a fortune and looked beautiful but that also made your feet cramp and threaten mutiny.

I wiggled my fingers at him.

Gah. Was I fifteen?

He tipped his hat with a finger and returned my wave.

By Bigfoot's footprint, I felt like I'd been transported back to my high school years. My stomach quivered in happy anticipation.

I had no idea what the wild man's TV-viewing habits were. Would he recognize me? He might watch all the things or none. Be a big Buffy fan or into documentaries on the French Revolution. It wasn't possible to get a read on him, so I sucked in a calming breath, hitched up my crocheted tote bag, and headed for the truck.

As I got close, Maverick strode forward to meet me, lightly slapping the other man on the shoulder to get his attention. But the wild man didn't look up. He was focused on the screen of an iPad, disproving my barbarian cave beast theory.

A home renovation played on the screen, though, so my identity seemed safe.

"Hey there." Maverick's green-and-gold hazel eyes warmed up as he took me in. He sounded tired, his voice hoarser and rougher, as if he'd spent the day doing hard things. "You left your mirror and your cup in my truck this morning. I cleaned them up, and they're inside the Love Tank." He jerked his thumb at the Volkswagen/truck monstrosity behind him and reached for my bag, adding, "Let me get this for you."

"Thanks." I let him take the bag. It wasn't that I couldn't carry my own stuff, but it made me feel cared for. Plus, he looked really cute holding a flower-covered bag.

After a long day with Luke and the other actors and colossal ego monsters on set, Maverick felt refreshingly different. He was genuine and thoughtful. Not scripted and rehearsed. *Honest.*

He nudged the wild man. "This is Ranger, my brother."

Was he a werewolf, too? He certainly had the hair for it.

I held out my hand. "Nice to meet you, Ranger."

Ranger didn't look up as he wrapped an enormous paw around my hand for the briefest handshake in human history. "Pleased to meet you. Maverick mentioned that you had some trouble up on the mountain."

Since he addressed this comment to his iPad, I was not sure what the appropriate response would be. Maverick caught my eyes and rolled his, indicating that his brother was a fixer-upper and would require significant work.

I knew all about difficult family members, so I shot Maverick a commiserating smile as I addressed Ranger's last observation. "Yes. I got lost, and then I had some stick-shift issues. Your brother has been nice enough to help me out."

"I'm sure he wasn't expecting hardship pay," Ranger muttered under his breath. "So, you write?"

"I do."

"You wrote the screenplay for this TV series?"

"Ummm . . . yeah?" Upon closer inspection, Ranger's resemblance to the wild man of the woods was even stronger. His hands were big and strong, sun-bronzed, and covered with dozens of tiny nicks and scars. He had a thick mane of hair with odd curls that sprang out in random directions. I wondered if I could share my hair products with him. He looked much more werewolf-like than his brother. Still, although his hair was a wild halo around his head and broad shoulders, it was clean and well-conditioned. It was also much lighter than Maverick's dark brown, streaked with a warm honey color.

The sliver of his face that I could see was manly and square, too rough-hewn to be pretty or cute; nevertheless, there was a definite resemblance between the two brothers. They were roughly the same height, although Ranger was stockier and more muscled than the leaner, more chiseled Maverick.

"What happens in the episode you're shooting?" Ranger still did not look at me.

"Ranger!" Maverick sounded as if he were losing patience with his brother's unsociability.

"Well, we're shooting a series about a supernatural murder investigator. She's come to Smoky Spirits to check out a mysterious death, but it's challenging because she can see ghosts but won't admit it."

"And does she fall in love with a ghost?"

"*Out*," I said gleefully. Luke's cinematic stock was lower than low and although the producers had brought him back for the season we were shooting, he was headed for an exorcism. "Her love interest from the last season is a handsome but klutzy Civil War ghost, but she drops him for a local werewolf."

"Well, that's unexpected." Ranger chuckled, lifting his chin. This gave me a fuller view of his face. He had the same nose and chin as Maverick, but his eyes were rounder and bigger, framed by ridiculously lush, dark eyelashes.

I continued explaining the details of my script. "But she doesn't know that werewolves exist, so she's in denial about some important things."

"And her werewolf is certain she could never love a beast," he guessed.

"It's a popular trope." I looked at Maverick. Good humor lit up his face, and I had to bite back my own smile. What did he think about my being Team Werewolf?

I was wondering how much longer we'd be exchanging social chitchat when Maverick's brother lifted his eyes and looked at me. Actually, he pinned me with his stare, and he did not look happy.

He knew who I was.

My stomach pitched, the contents churning wildly. He knew that I knew that he knew who I was. He just hadn't decided what to do with his knowledge yet.

His stare was hard, irked, and entirely mistrustful.

He was not a fan, and he was not starstruck. He'd likely known who I was before I'd reached the truck, and maybe even before then. The quiver in my stomach was not pleasant.

"Remind me of your name?" Ranger asked flatly.

"I told you. She's Suzette. Let's get going." Maverick opened the cab door and gestured for Ranger to sit behind the driver's seat. I'd have his eyes boring into the back of my head for the duration of our drive.

Ranger shot me a narrow look, tucked his iPad under a flannel-covered arm, and climbed up. I guess he was willing to take direction from his brother. I swallowed hard and tried to act happy as Maverick guided me around the truck (sweet but unnecessary) and opened the passenger-side door (also sweet but unnecessary).

Ranger leaned forward before his brother could climb in. "Can you check the chipmunks in the back? I'm concerned that we didn't use enough tie-downs."

"Sure." Maverick nodded shortly, his attention focused on helping me clamber up into the cab. This I did need help with. It was also an excellent excuse to enjoy his hands on my waist and arm.

I would be fantasizing about his helpfulness later.

Unfortunately, his chipmunk checking left me shut in the cab with Ranger. Lovely. Still, I'd survived the hostile comments of internet fandom. I had this, right?

"I can—" I started, but he waved a hand, cutting me off.

"I don't know why you didn't share the truth with Maverick. But I haven't seen my brother this positive in a long time. Mind you, positive is not the same as happy. He's real good at making the best of a poor situation. I will give you this warning, though." Ranger paused, waiting for me to turn around and face him.

Joderrrr! I was in so much trouble.

"He's got five brothers and a sister, and all of us love him to the moon and back. We've got his back, and we won't sit back and let you play with him. So, either you fess up and tell him who you are, and do it real soon, or I will out you."

CHAPTER

EIGHT

"Far more often [than asking the question 'Is it true?'] they [children] have asked me: 'Was he good? Was he wicked?' That is, they were far more concerned to get the Right side and the Wrong side clear. For that is a question equally important in History and in Faerie."

— J.R.R. TOLKIEN, *TOLKIEN ON FAIRY-STORIES*

I had not magically found a way to confess my not-so-secret identity to Maverick by the time he dropped me off at my rental place with a box of Japanese cake. I was not going to just blurt out the truth: that I was not Suzette, and that I was actually a TV star. I liked the way Maverick looked at me too much, and I did not want to lose that. Maybe it wouldn't make a difference, but it might.

For a delicious, weak moment I even considered trying to glamour Ranger. Could I make him like me? I'd come by his dislike fairly, however, and somehow working my personal magic on him seemed like a betrayal of everything I liked about his brother. After all, he was hiding something, too.

Nevertheless, despite how exhilaratingly nonmagical it had been to be just a girl flirting with a hot guy, I promised myself that I would explain everything to Maverick the first time we were alone. Using words, not spells.

Unfortunately, Ranger rode along the next morning when Maverick picked me up at 5:00 a.m. for my six o'clock call time.

109

Maverick held the door for me, giving me a warm smile and offering his hand. "You left your kraken cup in the truck again last night, so I reckoned I'd get it filled back up. Frozen pink Frappuccino with sprinkles and whipped cream, right?"

He was good. He placed a protective hand over the top of the doorframe so that I wouldn't bump my head and then helped me up. His fingers were warm and callused, squeezing gently and sending hot tingles up my arm and through my chest before he let go.

The delicious twinkle in his eye was more of a flirty promise. Or maybe that was just his dimple getting in on the action?

I did not want to let go, watching him greedily as he strode around the truck with an easy, powerful stride. He would make a gorgeous wolf.

The less pleasant wolf that I was now trapped in the cab with growled my name, his hard voice pulling me out of my romantic daydreams.

"Morning," I returned, my happy glow fading.

"Did you tell Maverick?"

"When did I have a chance?" Maverick was almost around the truck.

"You have to tell him."

"I plan on it."

"When?"

"When we're *alone*," I hissed. "I don't need an audience. Why are you here?"

"Do it soon," he snarled. He shut up, however, when Maverick opened the door and climbed up into the truck.

Maverick gave me a friendly and sweetly concerned smile. "Is there enough whipped cream? Diner Dinah and I had a debate about the proper coffee-to-whipped-cream proportions."

"She hasn't had a chance to try your whipped cream," Ranger answered on my behalf, adding, "but she wants you to take her out tonight on a private date. Someplace that's not public so that the two of you can talk. In private."

"Don't say those things." Maverick glared at his brother in the rearview mirror. Even the way the faintest hint of amber rolled over his eyes said he was irritated and that Ranger was in danger of having to walk to set.

That was just fine with me.

In fact, just the thought of evicting the self-righteous, growly Ranger had me snort-laughing into my kraken coffee cup.

"Bless your heart, big brother. I reckon she's got a thing for your ugly mug even if she's cute as a button. And I know you feel the same, judging by how long you took in the bathroom this morning."

"Ranger!"

I was briefly worried that Maverick would go full-on wolf and lunge for his brother in the backseat.

"You were singing," Ranger said. "That Russian love song stuff again."

"Why do you do these things? Don't meddle. Don't talk. Ever. You should consider a vow of perpetual silence." Maverick looked at me sheepishly, sighing remorsefully. "I am so, so sorry. I should not have subjected you to him."

I set my hand on Maverick's bicep—his upper arm was rock-hard and deliciously firm—and patted him. Mostly, this was intended to ease his fears, although partly it was because I wanted to touch him, and both our audience and the amount of available space in the truck's cab did not allow for a full-body hug. A proper, deep hug would have been an excellent way of building trust, plus it would feel amazing. It was clear Maverick could benefit from an increased oxytocin level.

"It's true." I squeezed his bicep because, holy moly, it was more addictive than the squishable hedgehog my sister had given me for calming my nerves. "I do like your face."

Maverick bit back a smile; he was not ready to calm down yet. "I'm glad you're happy with what you see."

"Just *see* her," Ranger demanded. "She ain't busy tonight. You two go on out tonight."

Maverick uttered a rough sound that was *definitely* growly, but I spoke over him. "I am free tonight."

Ranger punched his brother lightly in the shoulder. "See? You have a date. You're welcome. I'm gonna take a nap back here until we get to the falls. If you two smitten kittens could keep it down up there, I'd be much obliged."

* * *

I had my second unfortunate encounter of the day at the craft table before we'd even started shooting. Craft services had gone all out with buttermilk biscuits and sausage gravy, plus cornbread with honey butter. Tomato, bacon, and cheddar pie with thick wedges of heirloom tomatoes and basil. And the ever-ubiquitous shredded pimiento cheese that looked like a pile of yellow straw with weird red bits (I was not a fan). There was even an entire hummingbird cake dotted with pecans that I intended to introduce myself to later.

I was filling my plate and debating whether cake counted as a breakfast food when Luke strode in looking like the golden prince he was.

Luke's glamour was a billion times better than mine, and he possessed far fewer ethics. His personal magic made it easy to imagine fairy-tale weddings, glass shoes, and heirloom diamond rings. I'd briefly succumbed to the romance he projected the first time we'd met, mesmerized by his good looks and sexy saunter.

Closer encounters had inoculated me and broken his spell. Now, he scowled at me, attracting attention from the other diners and our fellow actors.

"Why the prune face, Luke?" Marlene dug into her slice of pie. She'd been cast as Loretta Spellman, a sassy witch who ran a local herb shop and offered supernatural remedies for all sorts of social problems. "If it's a poop issue, you should up your fluid intake. Maybe add some chickpeas and lentils to your diet."

"I eat chia seeds and avocados." Luke was only momentarily distracted by one of his favorite subjects: his digestive health and its relationship to his current diet. "And I'm here for a word with Sonnet."

"Pull up a chair." Marlene stabbed her fork at the empty bench across from her.

Luke frowned. A few lovestruck crew members leaned in, sighing.

That was my cue. "I'll walk with you."

I hopped up and Luke smoldered at me with every ounce of charm he had. He was a sexy sun trying to blind me.

I blinked away the spots dancing in front of my eyes. "What's up?"

"Let's go to my trailer," he said huskily, leaning into me. "We can talk. We haven't had a chance to catch up in ages."

"We talked yesterday. We discussed your new weight loss regimen."

I'd also avoided him as much as possible. Delivered my lines and then poof! I'd run off. As the vanishing had been the result of my hard work and industrious avoidance of his person, rather than any kind of magical spell or incantation on my part, it hadn't been easy.

He grinned at me, his beautiful blue eyes warming with unconvincing tenderness. Glamour aside, he couldn't act. "Tell me all about yourself. What's going on in your life? What's your next project?"

Ah-ha. We were almost done shooting this season of *Smoky Spirits* and he didn't know if the producers had decided if the sexy Civil War ghost that he played would return for the next one or not. I could kill him—and his career—with a few taps on my keyboard.

Luke's stock in Hollywood had plummeted since our breakup. He'd made a pilot for his own show that had not been picked up.

Even Elena—who had initially adored Luke because she thought he was an excellent accessory for my career—had mentioned several times that his career was floundering.

And by *floundering* she meant his Titanic had hit an iceberg, and there was a debris field a mile long on the ocean floor.

Fortunately, I didn't have to deflect or parry his interest in my next project—my phone rang. Elena. I blurted out, "Sorry, I have to take this!" and rushed away from the set.

"Dearest, darling Sonnet, my most beloved of sisters! *Conejita*, you don't—I mean —no one has told you the news, right?"

Smiling at Elena's good mood, I moved purposefully toward the bat houses that Maverick and his hairy brother had put up to tempt the bats off our set. I had to assume they were full of flying mammals, but right now—in broad daylight— there was no sign of winged occupants.

"What's up? How are you?"

"I am unbelievably fantastic," she enthused. "And it's all thanks to you."

"Ummm—great?" It was nice to inspire happy thoughts in my siblings, but this seemed suspiciously disproportionate.

"ASK ME," she demanded. "Ask me to tell you all about it!" And then, without waiting for me to say a thing, she blurted out, "Guess whose book was optioned by a big-name Hollywood studio?"

"I give up. Who?"

"You."

I—what? I mouthed a few disbelieving, happy obscenities at a nearby innocent tree. I may have jumped up and down a few times. "Me?"

They're going to make a movie out of MY book!? Am I somnambulating? Is this an amazing dream, and I'll wake up and be crushed by disappointed hopes? I get to make my FIRST MOVIE EVER?

"The studio wants to option *Quantum Howl*!"

We both engaged in some unprofessional squealing.

This had been my breakout book. The twenty-something heroine, nerdy physicist Luna Marlowe, had not known that she was a werewolf until she unexpectedly transformed in her laboratory when the protective enchantment cast by her mother broke and exposed her to werewolf hunters.

I'd had so much fun with that book, including tormenting the lead werewolf hunter by having him fall in love with Luna. There had been family secrets too—like Luna's family being guardians of a supernatural gateway in their small town that led to a faraway planet populated by a space race of Neanderthal werewolves who had remained behind when Luna's ancestors fled a cosmic catastrophe through the gateway. The love triangle between Luna, the hunter, and the barbarian was one of my favorites.

"They want you to play Luna! You're their number one choice for Wolf Girl! AND they want you to write the screen adaptation."

"I can play the title role *and* write it?" *I'd like to thank the universe, my fairy godmother, and the goddess for this award. DO NOT WAKE UP. EVER.*

"You'll write it. They have an in-house team to help with revisions. It'll be a paranormal take on your classic caped hero, but with a girl who shapeshifts."

I stared at the nearest bat house, my brain still offline from the happy shock. "Do *they* think that I look like a superheroine? They've seen me on *Smoky Spirits*, right? I'm not all muscle-y."

"It'll be fine," Elena said. "There will be a green screen with CGI capture and a whole team doing technical stuff that I'll Google and pretend to understand. You'll shoot live-action scenes as Luna in her human form. Luna's cute and funny. People *love* her and would never believe that she turns into a hulking, muscled, dire wolf. Then you'll just do green screen for her transformations when she goes wolf. And also for the outer space stuff because obviously it would be hard to shoot on location on Pluto or wherever."

"Yes!" I yelled. Startled, an Aphrodite fritillary launched itself upward on black-and-gold wings from a nearby patch of butterfly weed. "Absolutely. Sign now. A thousand times YES!"

I had no idea how I would fit this project into my already jam-packed schedule, but for a role in a movie that I WOULD BE WRITING, I'd invent a time-turner. Give up sleep. Invest in a caffeine drip.

Before I could bring up dates and deliverables, however, Elena cut in, "And before I forget, who are you bringing to the London premiere? I need the name of your date right now."

"What?" My brain lurched from the happy-Wolf-girl train track to the less pleasant gah-I'm-a-single-girl track.

"You have to go."

My sister did have a good sense for these things but . . .

"Thom is attending with his new girlfriend."

"And?"

"And the two of you dated. He's moved on, so you want to control the narrative and make it clear that you have too. Pining is not a good look."

"We didn't date."

Elena huffed. "You did too date."

"There was no dating. I did not go out with Thom. We went rollerblading in Santa Monica, and then we went to the urgent care."

Thom had pulled a groin muscle. It had not been pretty.

"He still claims it was his best night ever."

"So not true. He explained the finer nuances of hot yoga to me for an *hour*. I was sympathy sweating."

"Well, Vlad will be there too, and the gossip sites are reporting that he's bringing his best friend's little sister. He shared a TikTok video about how he likes you still, but you're taken."

"I'm not taken," I protested. "I'm happily single. There's a difference."

"Uh-huh. Well, Benjie is also coming."

"Are you serious?" We'd been set up on a faux date for a red-carpet event, and he'd been playing the jilted lover ever since. The closest we'd got was when he'd held my hand helping me out of the car, so his drama was unwarranted. "What a bellend!"

"You might want to invest in protective warding. Between Luke, Thom, Vlad, and Benjie, that London theater will be full of your old boyfriends. Bring someone new."

I hadn't realized that defensive dating was a legitimate thing, as opposed to proof of my poor life choices, but Elena made a good point.

"Fine. You win. I'll show up with somebody new." Worst-case scenario, I'd beg Wyatt to go with me.

"Great. I'll start the travel arrangements. And congratulations." Elena's voice warmed with pride. "You are an amazing writer, and you are going to knock this *Wolf Girl* ball right out of the ballpark."

I was exhausted, but this was literally the opportunity of a lifetime. I would do it. I would prioritize.

Despite my grumpiness about having to bring a date to London, I could not stop a silly happy smile from spreading over my face. I AM DOING THIS. "Thank you for helping me make this happen. You are the best sister and manager ever."

"You know it," she said. "I love you too, *conejita*. See you in London."

Elena loved hotels and traveling, while I loved surprising her with the things she loved. I made a note in my phone app to Google fun things to do in London. Perhaps we could stay in one of those hotels that used to be a nobleman's city pad. Perhaps we could visit a supper club or a swank bar, a place where she could meet a prince or at least a duke. She deserved the best happy ending ever.

And then maybe after I wrote this book, if my first role in a movie went well, if I won the awards and broke through that glass ceiling so many other women had bumped their heads on, maybe then I could take a vacation—or a break—of my own.

* * *

Showbiz gossip traveled faster than a speed-it-up spell, and by late afternoon all of the cast and most of the crew had stopped to congratulate me about *Wolf Girl*.

The cherry on my awesome-day-sundae, however, was my date night with the hottie Professor Maverick.

I snuck back to my trailer, avoiding well-wishers and my security detail, to prepare. I had sixty minutes to make myself look amazing, and I'd borrowed the best outfit from wardrobe.

It made me feel like a goddess.

I'd paired a lacy crop top with a flirtatiously short skirt. The shirt was trimmed with black lace and had perky bows right above my assets, while the skirt was short and covered with a black fern print. The bottom was gathered up with a tiny bow on each thigh. It was playful and made me feel pretty. It also hugged my curves and made me look like a present waiting to be unwrapped.

I figured that was more subtle than jumping into Maverick's truck and yelling, *DO ME, BIG GUY. POR FAVOR!*

I made the most of my hour, taking a quick shower and then letting my hair tumble down in waves. I added some braids with ribbons threaded through them and spent way too much time lining my eyes with a sensuous eyeliner I might have purloined from the makeup team. I tucked my lucky piece of rose quartz into my pocket and laced up my boots—my mountainside location and the gravel nature of the road where I was meeting Maverick made me glad I was not a high-heels kind of gal.

Should I glamour up? I could dial my charm all the way up and wow him, but I was tired after using glamour all day. Plus, he'd liked *me* out there on the mountain, just as I (mostly) was. Still.

I took time to utter a manifestation.

I am worthy of a genuine, healthy relationship.

I am enough as I am.

There are no obstacles between me and Maverick.

It worked, too. When I opened my trailer door, the coast was clear and Luke-free. The only human in sight was Eric, the polo-shirt-and-sunglasses-wearing head of my security detail. As he was blond, had excellent personal hygiene, and liked to collect weapons, I'd nicknamed him Eric the Viking.

"Do you have a photo call?" He frowned, rifling through his mental Rolodex of Sonnet dates and coming up empty.

"Nope!" I reminded myself that technically *I* was *his* employer and walked down the stairs.

"You're not going out, are you?" He scowled. "I was not informed."

"I am not the president," I reminded him, clutching my crocheted tote bag closer. We both knew that if he "helped carry my laptop," I would go wherever he wanted. "There are no snipers or secret assassins. You do not have to sweep the hypothetical place I may be going to for dangerous persons."

"Please tell me you're not seeing Mr. Hensley," he groaned, making a pained face.

"Definitely not Luke." I tucked myself behind Eric's muscular bulk and double-checked that there were no other people lurking on set.

"Is it Zach Quick?" Zach played a wild mountain man who was a closeted werewolf.

This was Zach's first major role, and he and I got along great, but he was the adorable, fresh-faced stud type. Meaning, he had been cast in a bunch of hot young hero roles where he took off his shirt in the promo shots, and hordes of young men and women lined up to meet him outside the TV studios. Dating opportunities were plentiful for him, although to give him credit, he was sticking with his college sweetheart and had shrugged off his agent's suggestion that he do red-carpet events with other celebrities to help his career. Perhaps I should invite him to London?

"Nope. Are we playing Twenty Questions? Do I get to quiz you about your dating life?"

"My job is to keep you safe," he grumbled. I had to agree with him that dating was dangerous.

Romance on set was safe. It was scripted, and an intimacy coordinator would make sure everyone involved in the scene was comfortable.

IRL, dating was more like the Hunger Games than not. It was a revolving door of beautiful people.

Add in the constant travel, the nondisclosure agreements, and the embarrassingly public scrutiny, and most relationships came with a short expiration date.

I knew actors who had their dates sign NDAs and who kept their relationships hush-hush, but I'd never taken that route. And because my dates had been highly public, the online trolls had posted trash about how my new man was already seeing other women and how big my butt had looked in my dress.

Nothing could compensate for the constant barrage of camera flashes and being told that my celebrity boyfriend was a once-in-a-lifetime opportunity.

And they were. Except . . . wasn't *everyone* a once-in-a-lifetime opportunity? We were all just people at the end of the day. All unique and special. It was corny but I sure believed it, and I was tired of male actors who thought their job made them super-special snowflakes who deserved the VIP girlfriend treatment.

"So." Eric crossed his arms over his chest. "Do I know your date? Has he been vetted?"

"Nope. Can you walk sideways so I can get out of here unseen?"

Eric's frown deepened. He would have lines by the time he was forty. "I need to know who he is in order to provide security for you."

"It's not a problem."

"It absolutely is." He was intractable. I would have had more luck heading off a horde of his Viking ancestors rampaging across a beach. "Your dating problem is literally my job to handle. I need a name."

"He's a professor at the local community college, okay?"

"Not even close to okay."

"Do you want his social to run a background check? Should I try to steal some of his hair so you can do a full DNA analysis? He's a person. I have a date."

This was no time to explain lycanthropy. Eric was not aware that I was half Chaneque, half Fae. I had no idea, in fact, whether he believed in the supernatural. I was sure, however, that he would view it as a potential threat.

"Fine. I'll introduce you. But do not tell him who I am, and let me do all the talking."

"I need to run a background check. And he signs an NDA."

I pretended that these commands were suggestions because Eric sidestepped, covering my exit with his mountain man body, and let me slip away unseen. As soon as I was clear, he caught up to me, clearly having decided to escort me to my meeting point.

"How did you meet this guy? How do you know he's safe? He could be a crazy fan."

"He's not," I grumbled. Telling Maverick my real identity was the part of tonight that I was not looking forward to. He'd liked me for *me* and not for being the famous Sonnet Ruiz. It was wonderful.

"I'll be the judge of that." Eric scanned the trees. He seemed to be expecting a horde of aggressive wood nymphs or an ax-wielding giant. Some kind of threat. He would have had a heart attack if he'd known about the wolf thing.

When we got to the pickup point, I spotted Maverick at once. Even better, there was no sign of Ranger. Maverick pushed off the truck he'd been leaning against and flashed a smile at me. Then, he waved. I smiled and waved right back.

He was the best looking of all the many handsome men I'd dated. He wore dark blue jeans and a crisply ironed button-up shirt, the cuffs turned to reveal powerful forearms. The shirt was inky black like my favorite color, with his usual cowboy hat and . . . be still my heart . . . cowboy boots.

Sexy clothing. *Fun* sexy clothing. His buttons made me want to undo him, unbutton and unwrap, burrow underneath his layers. Bad, bad, bad. I couldn't have actual, long-term, genuine feelings. I was a dating train wreck. Even worse, he wore a pinesy, woodland-scented cologne that was all my favorite things. His skin smelled delicious. Was I allowed to lick him? To press my nose against the golden hollow of his throat? Please. Even better, I could see the outline of his biceps and muscles, shoulders, and long, lean legs underneath his clothes. No one should have a body like that. I could die of lust.

"Great," Eric muttered, drawing my attention back to him.

"What now?" Sexy butterflies swooped in my stomach.

"You like him." Three accusatory words.

I poked him in the ribs. "You do not have a speaking role in tonight's scene. You are a walk-on only."

Eric grunted with amusement. "Does he know he's got a dinner date with a celebrity actress?"

"SECRET," I whisper-hissed. "Don't make me fire you."

Eric laughed, the asshole.

Maverick's gaze bounced between my bodyguard and me, his smile polite, but just as laidback and open as always.

He made me his priority, stepping forward to drop a kiss on my cheek. The quick brush of his lips against my skin fired up my neurons.

"Hi, darling." I felt his words resonate inside me, and it made my heart tight and achy.

"Hiiiiii," I blurted out, lost in the heavenly scent of him. He smelled like all my favorite places. The here-and-then-gone scratch of his beard against my cheek sent ripples of heat through me.

Maverick set one hand possessively against me, his fingers brushing the bare skin of my back. He held the other hand out to Eric, who shook it. I suspected there was some kind of manly handshake firmness contest going on. I also suspected that—unusually—Maverick had won.

"I'm Maverick. It's nice to meet you."

Eric tipped his head in acknowledgment and looked at me. The bastard was taking my *silence is golden* fiat literally.

"This is Eric the Viking." I waved a hand at him. "We're colleagues. He needed to see for himself that you're not a psychopathically disturbed superfan."

I was hoping I could sort of slide the whole *oh sí, I have a security team* detail past Maverick. After all, he had Ranger who had made his own big deal out of protecting his older brother.

Maverick's smile grew. "I appreciate your looking out for Suzette."

Eric froze when Maverick said "Suzette." At least his sunglasses hid his expression. Eric did not surprise easily, but he had not anticipated this plot twist.

"Great. Now that we're all acquainted, we'll be going. Eric, you have a nice night now." I narrowed my eyes and jerked my head back toward the set.

"It was a pleasure," Maverick said, stepping closer still to me. His palm pressed against the bare skin of my back. It felt amazing. He was the consummate gentleman and so stinking cute.

Eric nodded, shooting a tight smile Maverick's way. He seemed to be concerned that I would chew my date up and spit him out. "You be good now," he said to me.

"You are not my father," I gritted out. "Or my brother. Or even the boss of me."

Sighing, Eric turned and strolled back toward the set. As this was the best I would get, I turned in Maverick's arms, settling into his embrace. His hazel eyes twinkled with amusement as he gazed down at me.

"I'm glad you've got someone looking out for you," Maverick said, gently steering me to the truck's passenger side.

"Oh, he's looking out." And while it was, in fact, the job I paid him to do, it still irritated me to have to run my dates past him. I did not want anyone looking into Maverick's past or asking him to sign an NDA.

Maverick opened the door, but climbing up into the truck and getting on with our night was suddenly not what I wanted. Mostly, I was being a big chicken about confessing my naming misdeeds. I might not get another chance to be this close to Maverick.

I would tell him exactly who I was. As soon as we were in his truck and finally had some quiet space, I would confess. I could not control how he would react, if he would change his mind about taking me out. I could not stop him from treating me differently.

Maybe I was greedy. And selfish. But I wanted this one last, sweet, perfect moment when we were just two strangers who'd been thrown together by life and who had a spark. I wanted to be just a girl he liked, for him to be just a guy I'd met and wanted to get to know better. We were not a witch and a werewolf, or a celebrity and the local guy.

Resting my hand against his chest, I tilted my head back, the better to drink him in. Nerves had me stumbling over my words, not sure what to say.

"I know we just met, and we've got the whole night, but I would like to . . ." Words tumbled through my head like pebbles on a streambed. I was making this weird.

He watched me with that patient, gentle expression he wore as often as he did blue jeans, but his eyes darkened as they dropped to my mouth.

Hallelujah.

My professor was having kissing thoughts; his lips parted in anticipation, his gaze growing slumbrous and hot. This was a golden moment to shut up, I decided. Action over words, and all that.

Instead of fumbling for words, I reached for him, pushing up on my tiptoes to press my lips against his.

God bless werewolf strength because Maverick wrapped his arms around me and pulled me in tight. He did not hesitate one second.

His big hands anchored me, tucking my body against his chest. Dominating me, he walked me backward until my back met the cool metal of his truck. I was good and trapped, and I loved it.

His mouth covered mine, tasting me. His lips were softer, plusher than I had imagined, his beard tickling my face. All the rest of him was deliciously hard and I ate him up. I pressed closer, kissing him back.

HE WAS A MAGICAL KISSER.

I could have kissed the man all night. It helped that my hands were fisting his amazing hair, holding him tight. He was not getting away. He was *mine*. But then instead of holding me back some more, he nipped carefully at my lower lip, his tongue easing the erotic sting, and then he STEPPED AWAY. I may have moaned.

He grinned, opening his eyes, and making a deep, happy sigh-sound that told me loud and clear just how much he'd enjoyed our kiss. His eyes were amber, but I felt safer than I ever had.

Eric the Viking was right. I liked this man. And not just because he was hot and filled out his jeans in all the best spots—although I absolutely enjoyed watching him saunter across the set toward me—and not just because he was a kissing master—though that delicious alpha strain of kissing didn't hurt any, either. He was charming yet honest. Blunt yet deep. Funny and humorous, but in a good-natured way that took no potshots or cheap shots. He was not a man who hurt others.

And he was looking at me as if I were the best ever.

Would he feel the same at the end of our date?

NINE

MAVERICK

"All fae are born with innate abilities. Most have wings or claws they can summon on command, along with various other inherited traits from the beasts of the forest. But one ability all fae share is the gift of glamour—fae can make themselves appear as anything they like."

— ELISE KOVA, *A DANCE WITH THE FAE PRINCE*

To say I enjoyed kissing Suzette was like saying a hurricane was just a bit of rain.

Or maybe it was that she was a hurricane herself. Her hands slid up my chest to my head, and she pulled me close and kissed the heck out of me. She did not hold back one bit.

A heavy pulse beat in my body, needy and hungry. A tide of red-hot hunger flooded through my body, and I knew my wolf wasn't far enough beneath my skin. He wanted out, and we both wanted Suzette. She kissed me, I kissed her back, and all I could think was, *You DO know when you've found your one and only.*

We are lucky bastards, my wolf agreed.

She tasted so good. Sweet, although she was more sass and bite when we weren't kissing. Not like strawberries or peaches. More like wild honeysuckle or the huckleberries we found in the mountains in the summer—but also her own flavor, a taste I had no name for but would never forget. Her kiss held heat and need, but also an urgency that I had never felt before.

Or maybe that urgency was all me. Maybe I was hot and hungry, impatient to get under her skin, to slip inside her and share whatever room she'd make for me. I wanted everything with this woman. She'd fallen into my life, and it was the happiest accident ever.

At first, I kept my hands on her waist so I wouldn't send them exploring elsewhere as I wanted to. Lord have mercy, but I wanted to.

Kiss the girl. Give her something to like us for.

Later, I flattened my hands on my truck because I would not thread my fingers through her hair. Would not pull her close and slide a hand up underneath her skirt with its ribbons and lace. It was too soon. I was a gentleman.

And a FOOL.

. . . But I sure did want to do all those things and more.

The strength of my response to her wasn't necessarily a surprise, but it made me rethink my relationship plan.

Should I confess that I'd sworn off casual sex? That I'd made a promise to myself to wait until marriage before I engaged in any intimacies? That I would not be putting out after tonight's date because I needed that boundary after making choices that had been wrong for me in my younger days?

Or we could just elope. Get back in the truck. Drive like hell. Have a two-thousand-mile engagement and then BOOM. Honeymoon time.

Quite a few people who cared about me would say it was too fast.

But I felt oddly certain about this woman. Yet I also knew that it was far too soon to be sharing these thoughts with her. I'd asked her out on a date, and she deserved courting.

Was I still the charmer who only knew how to flirt and kiss the girl? Was I truly a himbo, cute but relationship clueless? Had I learned anything from my indiscriminate and prolific dating past?

Hot damn, I know how to kiss a girl in the first act. Isn't that awesome? I'll just ad-lib the rest of the play! What could go wrong?

I had no idea when was the right time to discuss this stuff. When did I share my feelings and my hopes for us? When would it be too late, and the relationship boat would have sailed without me?

I forced myself to step *all* the way away from her. I took myself back to the driver's seat, got in, and waited until she was buckled up before I got us on the road.

We need a new plan. A *faster* plan. You can practice sweet-talking her when you're naked.

As we drove to Biscuits & Blessings, we engaged in surprisingly mellow social chitchat. Suzette asked me questions and I answered. I inquired about her day and the scenes that had been shot. As though we hadn't shared a heated kiss. As if my wolf wasn't threatening to punch through my skin and redirect my relationship with Suzette in a bedroom direction. Or at least a naked, hot, and sweaty direction.

We talked, but I was mostly distracted by that kiss of ours. By the time I stopped in Biscuits & Blessings' parking lot, I'd formulated a new plan. I wouldn't rush to bring up my checkered, bad-boy past and how it had led to my present-day resolution to live a celibate life until I was married. We had plenty of time—forever if I got my way—so there was no rush.

Good man, my wolf agreed.

Suzette was all but bouncing in her seat, excited about her day and a new project. I might be new to relationships, but I wasn't stupid. I stopped fretting about the future because I was missing the present.

"I got a call from my team because one of my books was optioned. They're going to make a movie out of it, and they want me to write the script. EEK!"

"You'll be amazing." I meant it with every fiber of my being. I couldn't wait to read what she wrote.

"It's about a girl who discovers she's part of a long line of powerful werewolves. She shifts one day—BOOM—and she realizes her family has been keeping secrets. She has to solve the mystery of where her people came from while fighting off werewolf hunters."

"That would definitely be a surprise," I agreed. "Do you like werewolf stories?"

My wolf chortled. **Is it a sexy movie? You could help her research!**

"I do!" She winked at me. "Although Luna's not a submissive chick. She likes being in charge, and she's good at it."

"That's great." I meant it too. "I know lots of people think wolves are all about letting an alpha take charge and boss them around, but they're wrong. Pack is about looking out for each other. You can take turns with the leadership stuff."

"Exactly. It's about having that give-and-take in your life. Luna's a girl werewolf, and she's strong in her own way, without needing to challenge or dominate other wolves. When there's a full moon, she keeps her head, and she chooses when she shifts. It's something we could all learn from."

At some point, I would have to tell her that I was a werewolf. I would need to tell her about the mating bite, too, and reassure her that I would never, ever mark her, not without her full consent and at least a yearlong relationship. It was not a conversation I had ever had, let alone with someone who mattered to me.

If you can suggest skipping a condom to your girl because you're clean and trustworthy, you can mention a little love bite.

Ouch. There had been no condoms *or* conversation with Suzette.

And no love bites, my wolf grumbled.

Slow down, I reminded him—and myself. *We're ambling down the love path. Stopping to smell the flowers and maybe have a picnic. This is not the hundred-meter dash. We can take the next step once we've been together for a while.*

This relationship moves slower than a frozen drop of water hanging off the roof.

Our date hadn't properly begun, and I was already thinking of our future life as Mr. and Mrs. Boone. She wasn't local and, for all I knew, wouldn't even want to stay on after her TV project wrapped. Just because I'd spent the last five years waiting for her didn't mean that she felt the same way.

Go wine and dine her, my wolf growled. **We gotta make her like us.**

I pulled myself together and reached for the door. It was time to get this date on the road. But she stopped me with a light touch. Her fingers curled gently around my wrist.

"I have something I need to say."

Jesus H. Christ. She's dumping us, you moron.

I sincerely hoped not, but my brain jumped on the suggestion anyhow. "I'm listening."

She bit her lower lip, her teeth worrying the tender skin. She was not happy about whatever it was she had to tell me.

"My name isn't Suzette," she blurted out.

Imma just call her Mrs. M.

It was a nice thought, but clearly I was not understanding the problem here. "It isn't?"

"No. When you asked who I was, the day we met, I wasn't super clear. You heard Suzette, but I said—" She paused and, hand on heart, I heard a drumroll or distant thunder. "Sonnet."

I didn't see the problem. Of course, maybe she'd been named for a bilious old aunt. She could be tired of bad poetry jokes. I waited for her to explain, but she just sat there.

Way to go, Mr. Charmer, calling her by the wrong name. And while I felt silly about my mix-up, I liked her new name. It seemed like the perfect name for an author and someone as whimsical as she was. "It's nice to meet you again, Sonnet."

Metaphorical tumbleweeds rolled through my truck cab.

No. Not even tumbleweeds. Tumbleweeds implied that something was happening: wind, some Wild West action, a picturesque saloon in the middle of nowhere.

We were in a truck-filled parking lot, stuck in pre-date mode.

"That's not all."

"Hit me." I was not concerned.

"You asked if I was an actress, and I said I was a writer. I wasn't lying—I did write the script for *Smoky Spirits*, but I also wrote the book the script was based on. And I act in the TV show. And I write other books. I do a lot of things." She slid me a cautious look. "I feel it's important to make sure you know this."

I nodded. Then I waited for the count of ten to make sure that there were no more revelations. "So, your name is Sonnet, and you're a super busy person. You write, you act, and you go out with me. I appreciate your time."

She looked relieved. "Thank you. I really, really appreciate your understanding. I was afraid it would—" She stopped herself, shaking her head. "I promised myself I would stop catastrophizing, so I'm not going to finish that sentence. But thank you for not being mad at me."

"Mad? For my not hearing you correctly?" I frowned at her. "You should have stopped me sooner. I called you the wrong name for over a week."

I was an inattentive asshole.

Atonement, my wolf grumbled. **We gotta make it up to her.**

I did. I got out of the truck and went around to help her down. Her skirt just skimmed the tops of her thighs, and not staring at the black bows on the hem was an act of sheer will. It was harder than not shifting into my wolf at full moon.

"I like your bows," I said, hoping she didn't think *bows* was a euphemism for *boobs*. I loved—not liked—her breasts, but that was also not something I planned on mentioning on our first date. I'd bring it up later, much later, when we were in bed. In fact, I hoped she'd wear this outfit again for me then.

"*Muchísimas gracias*." She grinned, her dimples on full display. "I borrowed it from wardrobe."

That made me laugh, and I put my hands on her waist and swung her down from the truck. Once I had her safely on the ground, I tucked her hand in mine, closed the door, and laid a course for Biscuits & Blessings.

It was the closest we got to a sit-down restaurant in Moonlight Valley. A fair number of the town's residents preferred to catch their own dinner in furry form, while the rest were bigger on BBQ than on fancy stuff. Biscuits & Blessings was where you came for birthday dinners and your big life events; they'd brought out more than one red velvet cupcake with a diamond engagement ring stuck in the frosting.

I sure hoped Sonnet would like it, and that the night would live up to my hopes and expectations.

Honestly, holding her hand was almost as good as I imagined having sex with her would be (**Not really**, my wolf interjected) but mostly I just enjoyed the closeness of it. We were two people out and about, sharing some time together, and I was proud she'd chosen me.

As irritating as Ranger was with his interference in my social life, I'd have to give him a pass. His obnoxious matchmaking had gotten me here on a date with Sonnet.

"So is this place—"

"Biscuits & Blessings."

"Yeah. Will it be crowded?"

I shrugged. "Should be fine. It's the middle of the week, and most people have work. I made a reservation."

"So, it's a local spot? And you know everyone?"

"I can't guarantee an introduction to *everyone*." I couldn't stop the smile that tugged the corners of my mouth upward. "There could be people in Moonlight Valley that I haven't met. Or that I'd prefer to forget. We even get the occasional tourist or two. Is this okay, or do you want to go somewhere else?"

Vegas, my wolf prompted. **One of those monster buffets and then a trip to the wedding chapel. It'll be great.**

Sonnet gave me a big smile and nodded. "This is great."

We went inside hand in hand, and that's when the night made a right-hand turn into Disasterville.

People didn't just look at us. They gawped. Unashamedly.

Alessandro Aymes, the local wildlife control officer, stared. The hostess, Jenny Ford, downright gawked. Her eyes went so wide that she could've been that surprise emoticon. She was all open eyes, raised eyebrows, and agape mouth.

Even though I hadn't dated in five years and people loved to gossip about us Boone brothers, the reaction seemed excessive.

I knew that most likely people had expected me and Sanye to get married someday. We'd spent a lot of time together after losing Evan, but marriage had never been part of the picture for us. We were friends and friends only.

Everyone was looking at us instead of at their steaks and shrimp. They appeared stunned, shocked, startled, and every other S-word I could think of. Were my blue jeans unbuttoned and was my banana hanging out?

I checked discreetly, but I hadn't suffered a produce mishap. Everything was where it should be.

I frown-glared at the closest table: Bennie Georgison, the local dentist, and Mike Smith, owner of Mike's Microscope Shop. They both knew better than to gawk at other people in public (in Moonlight Valley, we did our gawking discreetly from our trucks or on Instagram). I was fixing to apologize to Sonnet for their rudeness when a shriek interrupted me.

"It's you!"

Sonnet and I turned to find Evie Summers darting toward us. She was rummaging in her bag with increasing desperation. It was as if there were a kitchen fire or a person-eating dragon that necessitated an immediate 9-1-1 call, and her brain had shut down from the adrenaline surge. Her gaze was fixed on Sonnet, however.

"Oh my God. You're Sonnet Ruiz!" Evie yanked a dog-eared paperback out of her bag and waved it. "Can I take a picture? Can I have one with you? I can't believe you're here. I love all your books!"

I'd known Evie since we were both kids, but she was way too close to Sonnet. I tugged Sonnet slightly behind me.

She goes through us, my wolf agreed.

This turned out to be ambitious, however, because half the restaurant got up in a rush and converged on us. They had no idea how close I was to letting my beast out and snarling at them all, because really? Mobbing my lady? With . . .

Requests to sign books.

Napkins.

Phone cases.

A hairy, bare forearm?

It was incomprehensible. The more I watched, the stranger it all seemed. The woman I'd walked in with and the woman signing autographs were both the same but subtly different somehow. Her startled smile had transformed into something bigger and brighter.

Excellent teeth, my wolf suggested. **Very fang-like.**

She certainly flashed them more often than a wolf at full moon, but it was more than that. She seemed somehow larger and brighter, taking up more space than she had before. She quipped, delivering funny one-liners as she signed.

She's amazing. My wolf growled softly. **Sharing is overrated. You know that, right?**

My wolf wasn't wrong, but Sonnet was her own woman. An amazing woman, yes, but there was something about her in this moment, something that I couldn't quite put a finger or a paw on.

Those books she writes must be even more interesting than Wyatt's, my wolf mused. **Why don't we own any?**

We would be paying a trip to The Pink Parts tomorrow, that was for darn sure. Based on the flash mob forming in the restaurant, her books had to be as amazing and charming as she was.

One of the things I had learned from Ranger, however, was to take a deep breath and let it out. This was supposed to help me control my beast and release all the unnecessary anger and upset in my life. I started breathing like a woman in labor. *In, out, in, out, why the heck are all my neighbors rushing us? This has to stop.*

Sonnet scrawled her name on the various surfaces that were presented. She'd pulled a pink Sharpie decorated with tiny sparkles out of her bag and signed away. Some people even got little doodles after their names. Mushrooms? A fern?

Our girl's awesome, but drawing ain't her forte, my wolf observed. **You'll have to finger paint with the pups.**

This was not how I'd anticipated our date night going. People I'd known all my life surrounded us, wolves and humans, waving bits of paper and whatnot. They all wanted her attention and she seemed like she was fine with that. It was probably her Los Angeles life that had prepared her.

Worse than that, everyone had their phones out and were snapping pictures. People yelled for her to look this way and then that. It was chaos.

What in the tarnation is going on?

Finally, I tugged a book out of her hand and replaced it in the hands of its owner. Enough was enough. I leveled a stern frown at the crowd and tucked her against my chest, wrapping my arms around her.

"Enough, y'all. We're just here to have dinner, and you have no manners. There's no more napkin signing happening tonight."

The crowd around us grumbled, as though they had the right to decide how Sonnet spent her evening. There were some lower rumbles that sounded lupine too.

I narrowed my eyes, getting ready to step in, when Sonnet raised her voice and took over. "I appreciate you all reading my books and being such fans, but I do need to eat something before I sign anything else. It's been a long day on set, and I've heard so much about Biscuits & Blessings."

This was not strictly true. She hadn't known where we were headed, or so I had inferred from her asking about the name of the place.

When I looked down, she was all twinkling charm, beaming at the Moonlight Valley folks crowding around her the same way she'd beamed at me in the truck.

Weirdly enough, I could practically see an aura or halo around her now. It was like she'd turned a flashlight on inside her. People were smiling back at her and nodding, their bizarre desire for her autograph transformed just like that into an equally bizarre desire to please her.

I tucked that away to think on later. Right now, I had my girl to woo.

"I'm in town for ages." She winked at Mike, making him blush. "So y'all can hit me up later for an autograph. Right now, I want to have some of that Southern cooking I've heard so much about."

She had them all under some kind of spell. She chatted away, tugging me after her as she asked if they could just make up a picnic basket for us because she didn't want to be any trouble and she was worried that things might get out of hand and mess up business for the restaurant.

We followed the hostess from the front of the house back into the kitchen, while the diners buzzed and their phones made notification sounds. Great, we were front-page news. Maybe she was okay with that. Or used to it. Inured?

We can't ever take her hunting, my wolf groused. **There'd be no sneaking up on our prey, not with her around.**

I forbore pointing out that we were vegetarians. Soybeans did not have ears.

"Let's go somewhere where we won't be interrupted," she whispered to me as we waited for the picnic basket. Even standing on tiptoe, she had to tug my head down to breathe the words into my ear.

The kitchen staff kept sneaking peeks at Sonnet. I had a whole new sympathy for goldfish, seeing as how we were basically treading water in a fishbowl.

Eventually, the cook handed me an honest-to-God picnic basket. It had been his momma's, and he was sure she would *just love to see it in Ms. Ruiz's hands*. He itemized the many, many delicious things he'd crammed into Sonnet's basket. At length. He made other suggestions. He was real nice about having to pack up our meal, but the one thing he did not do was let go of the basket. He held on to it, Sonnet had the other end, and he just kept talking and talking.

Eventually, he remembered that I was standing in the kitchen too. He looked at me. "Didn't know you were dating again, Maverick. Haven't seen you out since we were in high school, although Wyatt's book was an eye-opener, let me tell you."

ASSHOLE.

My wolf wasn't wrong.

Ignoring the unsolicited comment on my personal life, I paid for our dinner. Angry thought bees buzzed around in my head.

My date was a stranger.

She looked up at me as we trudged back to my truck. The halo was gone. "How are you doing?" she asked, as if I'd been the one who'd been mobbed by my fellow diners.

"I'm real sorry our night did not turn out so well." I tipped my head back toward the restaurant. There were people coming out the front door now and a suspicious number of staff taking a smoke break. I could scoop her up and put her in the truck, and then we could make a run for it. Eat dinner at a nice, isolated overlook. Figure this out. "I would never have expected them to—"

"No worries. Usually, I can sort of head it off at the pass, make them go away. But I'm used to it. It happens all the time."

"It happens ALL THE TIME?"

She gave me a cautious look. "Um. Sure? I mean, not *all* the time. Only when I'm in public."

"That's awful." I opened the truck door and boosted her up, even managing to smile. *Is that normal? Do you LIKE that?* I mean, who could? It was downright horrifying.

We need to kick some ass. We can sleep outside her door and beat them off with a stick.

"But you don't do it," she said hopefully, once I'd come around the truck and gotten in. She held out her hand to me.

Before I could take it, someone tapped on her window. The chef was back. Before I could stop her, Sonnet rolled the window down.

"I told myself I'd be cool and not bug you—"

"Which was only good manners," I grumbled.

He ignored me, continuing, "But I love your books. And your TV show. And you are an amazing, talented writer and a gifted actress. And you look even more beautiful in person."

Sonnet leaned away from the window, and I watched the same golden aura sort of surround her and him. She gave him a sweet smile and thanked him for his lovely words. He ate it up.

He *loved* her.

Too bad.

While she did her act, all I could think about was letting my wolf out so I could tear him a new one. He was rude. And an asshole. I gritted my teeth, recognizing that I was losing control.

I hadn't seen this coming.

Here we were, on a dinner date, like two regular everyday people (**and a wolf**). I'd walked in there making forever plans, thinking about marriage and a home together.

And now . . .

Now she was someone I didn't recognize at all.

TEN

"The trouble with magic is that there's too much it just can't fix. When things go wrong, glimpsing junkyard faerie and crows that can turn into girls and back again doesn't help much. The useful magic's never at hand. The three wishes and the genies in bottles, seven-league boots, invisible cloaks and all. They stay in the stories, while out here in the wide world we have to muddle through as best we can on our own."

— CHARLES DE LINT

After a quick picnic in my truck, I took Sonnet to the corn maze. Mr. Allerbee planted a special cornfield each year and then charged two bucks to run through it. He picked a different shape each year: a gigantic tractor, a pinball machine, and (the year he forgot his wedding anniversary) a teddy bear with an *I love Mrs. A* message. He was real sweet on his wife even if he was bad with dates. Ranger helped him with the GPS stuff that he used to plant the corn seeds in the desired shapes in spring. Now that it was October, the corn was dry and even spookier at sunset.

People stared at us there, too, but only the ones over the age of five. Eventually, we lost Sonnet's fans in the maze, although a couple of people were waiting for her by the exit as word had got around.

After three hours of officially dating, I still did not know what to do with myself when people came up to Sonnet. They did not want my autograph or picture, and I was mostly in the way. Sonnet smiled and chatted, charming them all. She was real good at her job.

When we finally left the Allerbee farm, further evasive maneuvers were required because some of the visitors to the corn maze decided to follow us.

I stuck to mostly private roads and some off-road forays. My truck could go places that were off-limits to most people. Usually I would have enjoyed the off-roading, but tonight I was anxious. I assumed Sonnet didn't want people knowing where she was staying at night. This struck me as safer for her, and her safety was my number one priority.

Which is why we should be staying with her, my wolf grumbled. He also had not enjoyed our uninvited company.

The moon was rising, well on its way to full. The urge to shift into my wolf was a familiar itch beneath my skin.

"I'm so sorry," she said. She sounded sad and down—she hadn't said much at all since we'd gotten back into my truck, unlike our easy conversation on the way to Biscuits & Blessings. The happy glow she'd worn had faded as the night progressed.

This was bad. It made my wolf rage, wanting to do something. Nobody smiled all the time. It wasn't possible, but I still felt like something important had been leached out of Sonnet. She was sad, and I should have done more to prevent it. Told people to back off. Insisted they all leave her alone.

Everything. We do EVERYTHING for her.

I tried to figure out an actionable plan as I took a serpentine route back to Wyatt's.

I came up short.

In the end, I just reached out to squeeze her fingers gently. It was late and we'd have to call it a night on our date. But I'd got to spend time with her, I reminded myself. That was good, even if it hadn't worked out the way I'd hoped.

There's still time. Tell her you're too tired to drive home. SleeeeeepOVER!

"It's hardly your fault. You didn't interrupt our dinner or follow us around a corn maze. Did you get enough to eat? I can pick up pie."

"It's my fault our date got derailed. I should have made those people back off. I could have. I should have—"

"The people who live in Moonlight Valley are grown-ass men and women. They were raised better than that. They just took advantage of your good manners."

She made a face. "They all seemed to know you."

"It's a small town." Now I was the one making faces. "I've known those nincompoops since I was knee-high, and I had no idea they read so many books or watched so much TV."

She snorted. "I was trying not to be rude to your friends and neighbors. I want them to like me."

Something about that bothered me, but I let it go. It was late, and Sonnet looked tired. She'd been on the go since before sunrise, and now she was a bit like a burnt-out lightbulb. The glow had gone out of her.

I nodded, turning onto the road that led to Phantom Falls. "You should feel free to tell them to get lost. They don't have to like you."

I like her.

I did too.

We pulled up in front of Wyatt's place, and I cut the ignition, letting the silence wash over us. Other than some crickets and frogs—plus the usual water sounds you got with a waterfall—it was blessedly quiet. The last couple of hours had been too full of voices, most of them demanding Sonnet's attention.

"We'll go somewhere else next time. Somewhere where we can be alone." Sonnet shifted in her seat, turning toward me.

I could see her smiling in the moonlight that filtered into the cab, but I couldn't tell if it was the same brand of upbeat charm she'd hit our fellow diners with or if it was sincere.

It bothered me that I couldn't tell. I'd always been real good at reading people, which had been no end of help when I'd run with the Iron Wolves.

My bullshit radar was also excellent, or at least it was if I didn't care deeply about the people involved.

Once I cared, I went all in on trusting.

Whatever you said was gospel and that was the way it should be. You had to trust your family, your near and dear.

But where did Sonnet fit?

Silently, I got out of the truck and walked around, opening her door. She took my hand and hopped down. She didn't let go once her feet were on the ground, which I took as a good sign. She was holding on to me. I thought about that too much as I escorted her up the steps to the front door of her rented cabin, trying to decide if I should ask to come in.

HELL YEAH.

More than kissing, however, I wanted to talk. My hypothesis about how the date would go had been largely disproved, so a quantitative outcome review seemed in order. Plus, I still got that niggling feeling that I didn't know her at all, not after tonight's revelations. And that was one issue I felt that I could resolve.

So as soon as we reached her door, I gathered her into my arms, needing to hold her, and started, "Sonnet, look, I was thinking—"

This was where my thoughts stopped because the front door flew open, and a dark figure came at us. He had a gun.

I did what any wolfman would do who'd seen his date turn into a public spectacle and now had an armed threat interrupting his attempt to woo his lady with a good-night kiss and some sweet talk. I tucked her behind me to protect her, and I grabbed our assailant's wrist, forcing it up and away. I punched him hard in the face as I twisted him around and flipped him onto the ground. The man landed hard, but he was already rolling to get up.

"Stay down," I ordered. I planted my boot on his wrist for good measure. I had a knife in my boot and a gun of my own in my truck, but instead of going for either of those, I started to shift. It was the best way to keep Sonnet safe. I was fast; it would take me maybe two seconds, and then I'd have the fangs to take care of the problem.

No one hurts our girl.

"It's me," the guy groaned.

I paused, mid-shift.

"It's Eric." The voice filtered through my half-wolf, half-man brain and . . . shit-fuckdamn. This was not an intruder.

"Viking man!" Sonnet threw herself down onto the porch, patting the pieces of Eric that weren't bruised or underneath my foot.

I growled, stupidly, irrationally irritated that Eric had opened the door and put himself in the way of my fist. Admittedly, I was irritated—and jealous—that he was here at all. The fact that I'd hit first was irrelevant.

Sonnet looked up and her eyes rounded. I cursed again.

I was not myself, not completely. I was, in fact, halfway between man and wolf, and it was not a pretty look.

My face had taken on a lupine cast, the bones longer, my canines larger, and my hair more mane than not. Long claws had sprouted from my fingertips, and the rest of my wolf was a breath away from tearing through my human skin.

I winced. Sonnet now knew *I* was keeping secrets for sure. This date just got worse and worse.

There goes our good-night kiss.

Eric groaned, oblivious to the bigger issue. I shifted back before he could catch me.

Sonnet glared up at me. She knew I knew she knew that I was not entirely human. We would be having us a conversation real soon, and not just because she'd busted me.

She's not freaking out, my wolf said. **Shouldn't she be startled? Or scared? Or yelling like a banshee?**

Had Wyatt been sharing secrets with her?

Two more men—most decidedly human—appeared in the open doorway, both pointing weapons at me.

"Who are these people?" I muttered, at my limit for the night.

"Hands up," the closer of the two barked at me. "Now."

"Like hell I will."

This was clearly not the appropriate response. The second guy started toward me. What else could he do? He had a gun, and I'd refused to obey. He had to show me he was dominant.

He was about to lose that battle to me when Eric—still on the ground—tugged at the guy's pant leg.

"Spike! Cliff! Stop your roll. This is Maverick, the professor. The one I briefed you on earlier. He's just Sonnet's ride home."

My gaze lasered into each of the three guys. Pew-pew-PEW. Eric the "colleague" was a security detail. Sonnet was the kind of woman who needed three armed, burly men to keep her safe. *Three.* Men who had names like *Spike.*

We're better.

Something bitter twisted inside me. I was better at fighting and defending, but I would not be inviting myself inside tonight.

"I apologize," Eric was saying. "I heard movement out here, but I should have checked the cameras and turned on a light. That's on me."

I stared down at him, gritting my teeth, debating whether I had to move my boot off his wrist, and feeling utterly irritated and out of place. Savage too. I was a college professor. A shapeshifting wolf who had almost abandoned a lifetime of secrecy.

Yeah. We would have been in deep shit for that.

I do a lot of things. It's important to make sure you know this. Is it even possible for this woman to make space for me in her life?

Fishbowl, my wolf said glumly. **But if she knows about the wolf, then we can go all in. Love her. Bite her. Welcome her to the family?**

Maybe. But it was more than the fishbowl lifestyle. There was something mesmerizing and tantalizing about her. Attractive, yet with so much more beneath the surface. And she hadn't seemed insincere, feeding me lines about wanting to spend time with me. She felt real. Heartfelt. And then there was her warm, curvy body.

Definitely want to feel that.

I removed my boot from Eric's wrist.

"No, I apologize." I leaned down and offered him my hand. "You're gonna want to ice that shoulder. The wrist too. You two"—I pointed to the two guys who were just now holstering their weapons—"get him some ice from the freezer."

Eric took my hand with his good wrist, and I pulled him up.

"Thanks, man."

Seeing as how I was the reason he'd been injured—which was the pattern of my life—I ignored his thanks. Instead, I got out my phone and fired off a quick text to the local doc. He was just about retirement age, but he'd come out if I asked him.

I stared at the screen, ignoring Sonnet's expression of concern as she patted Eric's good arm and then applied the ice that her hired goons brought. Backsliding into my old ways and hurting people was not acceptable.

Doc texted me back, and I let Eric know that medical help was on the way.

"I'll be fine," he growled. "I've had worse."

"Yeah. I figure you will be." Sonnet gave an indignant squeak, clearly disagreeing. "But this will make Ms. Ruiz feel better."

Sometimes you had to do things to make other people happy, and this was one of those times. Eric nodded. *Message received.*

Sonnet hovered in the doorway, her gaze bouncing back and forth between the two of us, trying to read our signals. She was biting the inside of her cheek again, her fingers twisted into a complicated braid.

I rubbed the back of my neck. It was time to go.

Yeah, my wolf said. **We're done here. This date sucked.**

"Do you want to come in?" Sonnet wove around her trio of dudes and stopped in front of me.

I do a lot of things.

It seemed so overwhelming. But I was also proud of her, and amazed. She was smart and talented, and I was glad she'd found success.

Fucking greeting card right there.

"No, thank you," I said gently. I couldn't wait to leave.

I had a whole lot of unexpected emotions to sort out. It wasn't that she was sharing a place with three guys, or that she needed those guys to fend off my rude friends and neighbors. Or even that her celebrity made my neighbors lose their minds; we had no chance at all of having alone time, and I did not do audiences. It wasn't even that I now really had to have the wolf conversation with her.

Before we'd lost her, my momma had liked to dispense what she called her pearls of wisdom. As a kid, I'd decided this was code for politely pointing out ways in which future me might screw up. As a man, I knew she'd been a wise woman. She'd said that men were not big planners, not when it came to Friday date night and not for the bigger things in life, either. And for those years when I'd run wild and done what I wanted to do, making a name and a place for myself with the Iron Wolves, making our daddy proud, I hadn't planned, either.

I'd had plenty of plans for how this evening would go. I had a thing for this girl. She felt like a new beginning after five long years of living straight and making level-headed decisions.

But then we'd got out of my truck and gone into Biscuits & Blessings, and nothing had gone right.

She might not have been who I'd thought she was, but everyone else had wanted a piece of her. I hadn't fed her enough or stood up for her enough.

She'd been chased from one end of Moonlight Valley to the other, and that was not okay. If I had known how famous she was, I would've taken her somewhere private, so we could talk. So that we wouldn't have to share our time with the rest of the world.

And then we'd come back to the one place she should be safe, and I'd got into it with her security detail. I'd *shifted*.

The wolf was out of the bag.

There was no more date, no good-night kiss, no second chance.

She knew far more about me than I did about her, yet I still wanted to kiss her. But we had an audience, and I would have bet that my half shift would've scared the bejeezus out of her. And since it *hadn't*, I had questions for Wyatt.

She stared at me, like she'd forgotten her lines for once, but then she glanced at the two security guys lounging by her door. She closed her eyes and gave a bark of laughter, and not because this situation we found ourselves in was funny.

"I'm so, so sorry."

"Don't apologize." I went to reach for her, then stopped myself. How was it I was still thinking about kissing her and having sex?

Pretty woman. Five-year drought.

I turned to look at Eric because I couldn't bear to stare at Sonnet any longer.

My wolf growled unhappily. **Dude, we are FUCKED.**

True story: it was not what I had planned.

"Go on in," I said gently. "Get some rest. Check on Eric."

I turned and went down the steps. We'd have to talk about my wolf side, but that was not a conversation for tonight.

Sonnet stopped me with a soft, "Maverick?"

I stopped and turned to look at her. "Yeah?"

"You'll come by for me tomorrow morning? You'll be here?"

"If that's what you want," I said gruffly. I was out of place, off-balance, and irritated, but I was also hers. Her name might not have been Suzette, and she might be a world-famous celebrity, but she was still the woman who had tumbled down a mountainside and crash-landed in my heart.

"I'll see you tomorrow," I said as gently as I could manage.

"Good night, Maverick." Her pretty smile was gone, and there was a choked-up note in her voice that made me think she was this close to crying. That had me clenching my fists, my teeth gritting against the need to change and fix this goddamned mess for her.

I never wanted Sonnet to hurt, not ever.

Before I could bound back up the steps, sweep her into my arms, and make her promises that it was too soon to be making, she turned and went inside. A second later, I was alone in the dark, staring at the closed door.

She's safe, my wolf said. **But what a mess.**

I went to my truck, got in, and drove away.

Come up with a new plan.

I needed information, and there was one wolf I could count on for that. I'd drive to The Pink Parts and get the lowdown from Wyatt. Then I'd do some research of my own on the internet and find out what the hell I'd gotten myself into.

* * *

The Pink Parts was closed for the night when I let myself in, but I knew I would find Wyatt denned up in his office, writing. He was as nocturnal as the bats Ranger and I had rescued. Sure enough, he was tapping away at his laptop.

I dropped into the chair across from his desk. I had so many questions that I was about to explode out of my skin. The words ran together in my head, tripping over each other.

"What's up, Mav?" Wyatt closed his laptop with a grimace. "Why're you here?"

His question was a good one. I didn't advertise our business partnership, yet here I was, using my key and moving in.

"I need to know about your renter."

Amber sheeted over Wyatt's eyes, but he didn't move. "What else do you think you need to know?"

If I wanted the truth from Wyatt, I would have to come clean about my interest in Sonnet and how our date had gone south. In general, I didn't hold with sharing my personal business with anyone. I was a lone wolf.

Sure we are, but now we're making room for someone.

Suzette.

No, *Sonnet.*

This need I had to bring her into my life was unsettling. It did not sit well with me.

It had been five years since I'd let any woman get close at all. And before then, the only kind of closeness I'd allowed was the bedroom kind.

Which is a good start, my wolf prodded. **And next we mate her! And give her our bite!**

My wolf needed a mute button and some common sense.

You love me.

"I know who Sonnet is, although she didn't tell me until tonight, when we were on a date."

Wyatt's eyes flared. "You and Sonnet had a date?"

"We sure did,"

"Not just sex," he clarified, "but an actual meal and courtship stuff? Flowers?"

Shitsickles. We forgot the flowers. Go buy out the florist's shop. Or raid Mrs. Dee's rose bed. She's got a ton of them.

"A date," I confirmed. "Although dinner turned out to be more of a group activity than I had anticipated thanks to Sonnet's fans."

The sex, or lack thereof, was none of his goddamned business.

"Mav, you don't—"

"Date. Not in the last five years. I am aware."

"Just all those one-night hookups," Wyatt continued. "Meeting up for sex. Casual fun."

"I haven't done that in five years," I corrected. "And this was different, okay? I'm not saying it went perfectly well"—**or at ALL well**—"but it's okay if I'm rusty. I can practice."

"It's not like you," Wyatt said. "That's all."

Wyatt had no idea. I didn't recognize myself. And yet I liked this new me. He knew what was important.

Sonnet's important.

"It's just that Sonnet doesn't date, either. You two are as alike as two peas in a pod in that. She goes out with a guy once and then it's over."

Disappointment washed over me. Tonight had been more than a one and done. There was something fierce and genuine about Sonnet. Funny. Just a little mysterious, but with hidden depths beneath the humor she wore like armor. And it didn't feel like she thought of me as temporary. She felt . . . real. As though what I saw was what I got. And that sexy, curvy body.

"Is that what you think?" I said. "For real?"

I gave my business partner a closer look, noticing the hard line of his mouth as it curled up some. Wyatt was generally a positive guy. He was scary smart—like Ranger—but he usually was nice.

He thinks you're his competition.

I really hoped I wasn't. "You and Sonnet?"

He shook his head. "Never. Sonnet's had a hard time in the dating arena. I won't stand by while she gets hurt—*again*—because the guy she's kissing wants something different than she does."

Ouch.

"Sonnet can kiss whoever she wants, however she wants."

Sonnet wasn't a tree to pee on. She was a woman who made her own choices, and if she wanted pie, she could choose which one and how many slices she wanted.

But OUR pie is the best.

Wyatt shook his head. "Have you Googled her yet?"

I had not.

"Because don't," he continued. "You don't want to swim in that online sewer. She's a celebrity, she's got tons of money, and everybody wants to be her friend. When it comes to dating, she goes out with a ton of guys, and they're all Hollywood hotties. But it was like that back in college, too, before she wrote that first book and launched her Hollywood career. A woman like that—smart, funny, beautiful, and with depth—she could have anyone she wanted. She's one in a million. But she's also got a million Google hits and people write messed up stuff about her relationships online. They invent crap and spread rumors because a lot of them are only pretending to be her friends and just want to tear her down. She deals with a lot. But more than that, she's married to her career. In the six years I've known her, that job of hers has always come first. She works, and then she works more. She has no room in her life for relationships. She's not gonna give you anything more than superficial charm, and she's sure not gonna stay here."

She's a four-tier wedding cake. Sweet, salty, nutty—she's all the fancy flavors.

And I was plain old pie.

Awesome.

I did not feel like enough, no way, no how.

Did Sonnet think it mattered that we came from different worlds? Did I believe that it did? At any rate, she had worked hard to get where she was now. If she hung around me, my past would come up.

Plus, I still wasn't sure how she felt about my being a werewolf.

I wasn't upset that she'd dated other people. That was her past, plus she was the person who got to make decisions about her present and her future. It was her choice. But it sure sounded like she had no interest in making room for me in the future. She'd posted a NO VACANCY sign long ago, yet I was fool enough to feel badly about it.

"I all but shifted in front of her," I admitted. I didn't think the Wolf Council would find out or come down too hard on me, but it needed to be said.

Wyatt shrugged. "She already knows that you're a werewolf."

"You TOLD her?" I had visions of the Wolf Council dragging Wyatt off to live in Alaska, the way they had my daddy. They did not take kindly to wolves who threatened to out our little community. On the other hand, no wonder she hadn't seemed afraid of my shifting on her front porch. It had not come as a surprise.

"She's known since college." He crossed his arms over his chest, frowning a little now. "She's a charmer, Mav. Not a bad person, not a flirt, not someone who's untrustworthy. But she charms people, and that's something you should be asking her about. Other than that, she's a great friend even if she won't or can't stick to a relationship. Truth be told, I'm thinking you understand that almost better than anyone."

I growled. "What does that mean?"

"You inherited your daddy's charm. You were the town's bad boy. A black sheep in wolf's clothing. The ladies loved it, and you have to admit, you've broken more than your fair share of hearts in this town because you flirt and then you won't or can't commit. Instead, you move on and find someone new and start all over. You're a serial charmer. You have that in common with Sonnet, except you've shut it down these last five years—"

"And she hasn't," I finished for him.

"She hasn't, but it's more than that. This is mostly conjecture based on some damned fine observation skills on my part, but she's a *charmer*. Professional grade. She radiates charisma and likeability. It's been a big help to her in the TV business. I think it's magic," Wyatt added thoughtfully. "She's a witch or something. Yes, I know how that sounds, but surely you don't think we're the only supernatural beings in the world. Have you watched her work?"

I shrugged. I had not, unless that weird halo at Biscuits & Blessings counted.

Wyatt's frown deepened. "Let me ask you this. If you kinda look out of the corner of your eye, sneak up on her when she's got people eating out of the palm of her hand, do you see this little gold cloud around her? One that's there but not quite *there*, if you take my meaning?"

Reluctantly, I nodded. "Maybe. But I don't think these feelings I have for her are due to magic."

"Right, but you've seen it?"

I put two and two together.

"Charm."

He nodded. "Or a magic spell. Something like that."

I stared at my friend, debating the truth of his words. But it made some sense. I was not a fan of charms, however.

Was what I felt for her genuine, or was it magic induced?

Our feelings are not some kind of magical rash.

I didn't think so, but that was not the only problem here. Did Sonnet think Future

Mr. Sonnet when she saw me? Was she seeing me for real, the way I thought that I'd seen her?

Glamour's just the packaging, my wolf growled. **We're interested in her insides.**

Her heart was definitely of interest to me, but I had some thinking to do.

We should ask her. Don't do that dumbass thing and make stupid assumptions. Put some words out there. Let her tell us about the magic.

It wasn't a bad idea. It was just a hard thing to do. I couldn't quite make my peace with the possibility that she'd worked her magic on me. Not yet, at any rate.

I stood up. "Alright then. Thanks for the information."

"I'm sorry to be the bearer of bad news." Wyatt's concern warred with his desire to launch into an ad hoc pep talk. "But you're not unique and special. She charms everyone. You shouldn't feel bad about it; you didn't know."

Hearing that the woman I liked was almost certainly magically hoodwinking me into thinking I had warm feelings for her did not cheer me up any. My mood turned grimmer. But that was fine. It was long overdue payback for my misspent youth.

The karma bus beeped as it backed up over me. My ex-girlfriends cheered. *Now you know what it feels like, asshole!*

Yet, it could have been worse.

I'd had one date with Sonnet. We were not having sex, engaged, or halfway to Vegas for a quickie wedding.

D, my wolf opined. **All of the above would be fucking great.**

I'd just stay away from her, wait for these feelings of mine to abate. Like the tide. Or interest rates. I'd be just fine.

You can't forget your mate, my wolf said.

Sonnet is a part of us.

ELEVEN

SONNET

"My fairy lord, this must be done with haste, For night's swift dragons cut the clouds full fast; And yonder shines Aurora's harbinger, At whose approach, ghosts wandering here and there Troop home to churchyards."

— WILLIAM SHAKESPEARE, *A MIDSUMMER NIGHT'S DREAM*

The man who'd brought me home last night was not the man who picked me up the next morning.

The outsides were the same: brown hair, thick beard, ridiculously lush eyelashes, and a chiseled jaw. He still had kindly eyes and a dimple. He wore a new-to-me T-shirt with yet another bad biology pun: *I find this humerus*. But he gave me the same polite smile I'd seen him give the restaurant hostess, the town sheriff, and my film crew.

He was nice because that was just the kind of person he was. He directed a smile my way and asked how I was doing. My plan had been to bring up last night's spectacularly *un*romantic ending and ask if we could have a do-over. I'd written several scenes for him to pick from. Spoiler: they all ended with an amazing kiss.

I looked at the stone-faced, polite man next to me and realized I would have to rethink the kissing plan. What did it mean that he hadn't kissed me hello? Or texted me? Did he even *have* my number? I totally needed to give it to him. Except . . .

He was more closed than the FBI's files on alien visitors. He did not look at me with interest. I almost poked the space between us like a mime, just to make sure there wasn't an invisible wall there. I would not cry.

"Hey," he said, his voice as low and rumbly as ever. He gave me a hand up into his monster truck like he usually did. But instead of threading his fingers through mine and squeezing gently, he let go and shut the door as soon as my butt hit the seat.

He'd shut me out. Or in. Everything was all mixed up in my head.

I watched him stride around the truck, admiring his loose-limbed, powerful saunter, how his jeans hugged his thighs, the assurance with which he carried himself. I would not catastrophize. I would be open and not overreact. Possibly, I was allergic to vulnerability.

Vulnerable. It sounded like the Latin name for a cool flower you'd find in a cottage garden or a dark, secret part of the forest. Vulnerables would be tiny pale flowers with protective, big-ass thorns. They would only grow on glossy vines that gave people nasty rashes in unspeakable places so that no one picked *those* flowers.

I'd picked a whole bouquet of vulnerability last night and handed it to Maverick. I'd opened up. I'd invited him: *Go ahead! Hurt me!* I might have angry cried last night after he'd left me. I'd been tired too. Getting by on five hours of sleep a night for four years combined with a two-thousand-item to-do list and working every waking moment would do that to you.

Oye, I liked this man. More than I should. More than I ever had anyone. He meant something to me because I treasured the time we'd spent together, brief as it had been. He made me feel curious and special, energetic and alive. He was my favorite showtune belted out loud, a double espresso with a shot of chocolate syrup. He was my sunshine and a snack when I was starving. He was a beautiful spell voiced at the perfect moment. I was not giving him back without a fight.

"I apologize for being late," he said, swinging into his seat with easy grace. "Two of our fellow diners from Biscuits & Blessings staked out my house this morning. It took me twenty minutes to lose them." His chuckle was easy and unforced.

I laughed like that when the clerk at the grocery store made a joke.

It was polite.

Charming.

I stared at his profile while he got us on the road. Was I being weird? You bet. My heart pounded as I frantically wrote possible next lines for this scene.

Maverick cleared his throat. His hazel eyes darted to mine, then leapt away. He tipped his chin to the cupholder between us, saying conversationally, "You left your kraken cup in my truck again. I got it filled up. I grabbed you a muffin too."

"*Gracias*," I said. My heart pounded some more. I was probably about to have a heart attack, and then I'd have to say thank you again because Maverick would give me mouth-to-mouth or pound on my chest. Violate all traffic laws to get me to the nearest emergency room. He was a nice person, so he wouldn't ignore my distress.

Instead of expressing my thanks, however, I wanted to ask him: *What REALLY went wrong last night? Can we go back to the way we were before? Let's drive to Alaska and start over along the way.*

I stared at the trees as we drove. There sure were a lot of trees in Tennessee. Of course, we were in the mountains, which seemed like a tree kind of place. Fraser fir, chalk maple, sweet birch. I drank my coffee and peeked at my muffin. It was actually a cupcake.

I should have told him who I was from the beginning.

When we stopped at a light, he glanced down at the cupcake-pretending-to-be-a-muffin. "Don't you like muffins?"

"It's not a muffin," I felt compelled to point out. Apparently I was only lying about big things like my name.

"It's a breakfast item made from flour and sugar," he countered. "It came from a bakery. It tastes delicious."

I shrugged dejectedly. "But it claimed to be a muffin. It was supposed to be one thing, but it's actually another."

Silence descended on the truck's cab as I finished pitching the scene, the bump of the tires over the gravel road the only sound. It felt awkward, weird, and disappointing.

Maverick cleared his throat. He had to be uncomfortable.

I snuck a glance at him to confirm this suspicion. He'd said he understood about the name confusion. Expressed sympathy about my fan problem. Then he'd shifted into a wolf.

Now he was scowling at the innocent vegetation around us like it had dropped sap on his truck's paint job. "I think we need to talk."

Absolutely. Long overdue. Me first! "I agree."

He inhaled, but I needed to deliver the opening line in this scene, so I talked over him. "I apologize for not being completely honest about who I was from the start. When you didn't recognize me, it was awesome to be just Sonnet—or her alter ego, Suzette—instead of a celebrity TV star. Most of the time, when I meet someone, they either get all weird or act as if they already know me and we're best friends. I liked the way you were, and I like you, and I also know that none of that excuses my taking advantage of your not knowing. I'm sorry."

"We're good." The smile he gave me was reassuring. "There's no use howling over spilt sweet tea. I mean, I learned a whole lot last night, that's for sure. But I understand not wanting to be judged based on your past and wanting to be someone different."

"Because of the werewolf thing?" I embraced the elephant in the truck cab. I squeezed that sucker *hard*.

He lifted one flannel-covered shoulder. "Sure. I wish Wyatt hadn't told you, but I'm the one who shifted in front of you. That's on me."

"I'm good with it," I said, way too eagerly. God, I had no cool. "I mean, I'm not saying you should go furry right here and now, but it's just part of you, right? An important part."

"My wolf is," he said slowly. "He surely is."

"And I like all your parts," I blurted out. My stomach was turning somersaults, making a trampoline out of my kidneys. "I like you."

"I like you too." He nodded as he said this, and maybe this time his smile reached his eyes.

But . . . I waited for him to say it. To qualify his liking of me.

There was always a qualification.

An asterisk.

Could I be so lucky as to meet a guy who'd like me exactly as I was?

"But you're a busy woman, and I don't want to take up your time."

I guess I had the answer to my question after all.

"Gotcha," I breathed out.

I was being dumped.

Let down easy.

Polited to death.

This hurt more than I'd thought it would.

"Also, there's the charm thing." So, there was more. I'd assumed my celebrity fishbowl life was the biggest problem. I'd been wrong. "That thing you do. The—"

Maverick waved a hand. He expected me to help him out.

Too bad for him.

Also: too bad for Wyatt. My friend had shared secrets with the class. We would be having a conversation about that.

"Magic," Maverick finished firmly. "The magic thing you do. The one that makes people like you. I'm not comfortable with it."

Happy come-out-of-the-magical-closet day.

"I haven't used glamour on you," I protested. My glamour was like frosting a cupcake. It was still me underneath the icing, but I was just a little sweeter.

Mostly.

I fought not to squirm. Okay. So it wasn't *entirely* cosmetic, and while my intentions were the best, I wasn't being completely honest. There had been a teensy, tiny little bit of Maverick-directed glamour.

"So you think I'm acting twenty-four seven? Duping you?"

He gave me a firm look. "This is important."

Should I tell the entire truth about my glamour? Was now the time? Did I just drop it, BOOM, and then see how he handled it?

"I don't know what to say to that," I conceded. "I agree that this is important. But you also sprang the werewolf thing on me. You did not prepare me for that—you just shifted and went for my security team."

He winced.

"And I've apologized for that. It hasn't happened again and it won't. You know my secret, but you've kept your own. Total honesty, *Suzette.*"

It was my turn to wince.

Could I do this? Could I let my guard down, show him who I really was?

I thought back to our dates, to the time we'd spent together. Something in me recognized something in him. And had let him get close. He'd already seen parts of me that I had shared with no one else.

Thoughts.

Feelings.

The inside bits of me, on the outside.

Why wasn't that enough?

When I didn't answer, he continued on. I hadn't realized there would be a time limit on my answer!

"That's what I thought. So maybe we could be friends?" He sounded remote and cold. My warm-hearted, open-faced, sweet Southern gentleman was gone, replaced by an icily polite polar bear. "Or casual acquaintances, whichever you prefer."

He wanted to be "friends" with me.

Glamoured or unglamoured, it didn't make a difference, did it? I wasn't enough.

I couldn't take his friendship scraps.

I didn't know how to pull the plug on my feelings for him or how he could turn his own off so suddenly, when his previous actions led me to believe that he genuinely cared.

Apparently, those actions were as deceiving as my glamour.

"Friendly acquaintances." I swallowed too hard. The gulping sound seemed way too loud in the quiet of Maverick's truck cab. *I don't think so.*

"I can drive you each morning, seeing as how I need to check on the bat houses. But I completely understand if you want to go on your own or get one of your security guys to take you."

I curled up in my seat, staring out the window. Trees, trees, and more trees. They had an unexpected sheen of wetness, too.

My next book would be set in a desert.

I finally found my voice. "Fine. Great. I'll ask Eric to bring me. It's all good."

Maverick didn't say anything for a full sixty seconds. I counted them off in my head: *one, one thousand; two, one thousand; three, one thousand.*

Finally, he allowed, "I guess we're agreed then."

I nodded because that was the only right next line.

End scene.

"Mr. Charles Dickens was serializing his novel Oliver Twist; Mr. Draper had just taken the first photograph of the moon, freezing her pale face on cold paper; Mr. Morse had recently announced a way of transmitting messages down metal wires. Had you mentioned magic or Faerie to any of them, they would have smiled at you disdainfully, except, perhaps for Mr. Dickens, at the time a young man, and beardless. He would have looked at you wistfully."

— NEIL GAIMAN, *STARDUST*

All of Moonlight Valley was talking about my date with Sonnet.

What they didn't know, they made up.

Depending on who told the story, I'd wined her, dined her, sexed her up, bamboozled her about my bad-boy past, seduced her with the same past, given her a puppy, bought her a ring, and threatened to throw myself off the mountain if she didn't reciprocate my feelings.

The wolves also brought up the fact that Sonnet was no wolf and that interspecies dating ended poorly.

None of this eased the anger and agitation that I felt. I'd had hopes, and those hopes had been dashed. Being disappointed in love and more than a little upset, I could have done with less curiosity and more compassion.

How do you think our Sonnet is taking it?

My wolf wasn't ready to give up. He kept suggesting that we go back and have another conversation. He'd also suggested, **Kiss and make up**, and, **Boning some sense into both of you.**

Then he'd offered to go away.

In case she's not into wolves, he'd suggested. **You could be happy.**

It wasn't possible to de-wolf myself, although I guess I appreciated the offer. Was that how the glamour worked for Sonnet? Had I even asked or had I just made it all about me and how her wearing some kind of supernatural mask made me feel?

I hoped it was not my wolfishness that was standing between us.

I replayed the scene in my truck, second-guessing myself.

Had I asked the right questions? Had I respected her feelings and her boundaries?

Could I come to terms with her constant glamour, or would I always feel like I was on the outside of someplace really special, somewhere I was not welcome?

Too late now. Too fucking late, man.

I hated that my wolf was right.

By the time I made it to church, a few days after Sonnet and I had ended things in the front seat of my truck, there was no one in town who had not heard the news that, regardless of the exact sequence of date-night events, we were also through.

During the service, people looked at me sidelong. They whispered and nodded to each other.

When we sang "God Moves in a Mysterious Way," I received more looks than the highway patrol officer parked under the underpass, waiting for speeders.

I was just as unpopular, too.

Even Reverend Harris felt the need to share his observations with me when I shook his hand on my way out of the church. He was Team Sonnet all the way.

"Does she look like she does on her TV show?" he asked. "Because she just glows like an angel in front of the camera."

"She seems so sweet," his wife added, popping up by his side. "Maeve over at Biscuits & Blessings said Mike said she signed everybody's placemats! Did you get a signed placemat?"

I had to admit (although not to Reverend and Mrs. Harris) that I had not been thinking about placemats.

Hell, no. My wolf had no concern for his immortal soul.

"She is nice," I agreed. As I had just been to church and did not want to undo that good work on my soul, I refrained from pointing out that Mike and everyone else at the restaurant had been the antithesis of nice. They'd been a bunch of peckerheads.

"And?" The Reverend squeezed my hand, clearly anxious for my answer.

"Sir?" I prided myself that the word came out polite, even if my teeth gritted.

"Should I invite her over?" Mrs. Harris asked at the same time. Somehow, she'd got hold of my other hand, and now I was being pulled between the two of them. "If your momma were still with us, I just know she would have her over. I could ask Jennie Dean to make her hummingbird cake!"

Not the hummingbird cake, my wolf whined.

If you believed the people in this town, that hummingbird cake had magical properties. It could cure any ill, fix a leaking pipe, and solve the world peace problem. It had won every fair award in our fine state of Tennessee, and I had not had one birthday when that cake had not made an appearance. Everyone in Moonlight Valley bought one for their special occasions and then ran around the internet giving it ten stars.

I hated pineapple.

It made me break out in a rash.

In pure self-defense (and not at all because I was nervous about seeing Sonnet again), I shook my head stiffly. "No need for that."

Pineapple's an itchy business. Not gonna be romantic if you've got road rash on your—

Mrs. Harris huffed. Reverend Harris appeared to be contemplating next week's sermon. I suspected that the topic would be "Pride goeth before a fall."

When I didn't respond to her cake-vite, Mrs. Harris tried again. "Aren't you seeing her again? The ladies in the choir said—"

Given the hurt I'd heard in Sonnet's voice, I suspected that I would see her again when hell froze over.

She was done with me.

"Now aren't y'all supposed to be doing more singing than gossiping?" Reverend

Harris interrupted as if he didn't lead the men's Bible study group in an hour-long weekly "debrief" of town happenings.

"Please excuse me." While they started bickering at each other, I pulled my hands free and hightailed it to catch up with my brothers, who were halfway to the grass parking lot.

Seeing as how we Boones got up to trouble most weekdays, it seemed prudent for as many of us as possible to put in some time at church on Sundays. We'd carpool, then head back to the house for breakfast. Mack and Rue had already taken off, as had Ford and Alice. Knox hadn't come as he was working, as he did pretty much every minute of every day when he wasn't sleeping. *Day of rest* was not part of his vocabulary.

"Thought you weren't gonna make it," Atticus rumbled as I threw myself into the passenger seat.

"You're a popular man," Rebel said from the backseat.

It was truly downright miraculous how many Boones fit inside a Pontiac; Ranger had made us a seating chart to "optimize the available space," although mostly we just gave him shit about it.

"I thought they were supposed to be Christians," I protested.

This earned me a look from Atticus.

"Well, sure, but they're also human," he said. Then added the proviso, "More or less."

"Only Alice is a cat," I grumbled. Her shifting ability had caught us all by surprise and had taken some getting used to.

Like Sonnet's glamour?

I couldn't think about that anymore. I was a wobbly rocking chair on the front porch.

Instead, I went on the defensive. "Everyone else can stay out of my business."

Atticus pulled out of the lot, tooting the horn at a couple of passersby who had waved, and I ignored the smug smile lurking underneath his red beard. "But we're your brothers," he said. What he meant was: *so, we're not everybody.* "You should tell us what's going on."

"Alice said she and Ford were stopping by the store on the way home. He needs to pick up the fixings for chicken and waffles," Ranger answered, as though Atticus's concern had been directed toward him and his grocery list. He was piled into the backseat alongside Rebel, who was not at all concerned about our present lack of chicken and waffles. "I hope they have that soy chicken. Sometimes that fake-meat truck doesn't come on Saturdays."

"I was not talking about waffles, Ranger. I was talking about Maverick's girl." Atticus parked in front of our house in his usual spot, alongside Mack's truck; she and Rue had beat us home alright. I got out quickly, hoping to avoid further brotherly inquisition.

My luck was shit in that regard. Atticus hopped out almost as fast and followed me. "Mav, we're all dying to hear the truth about your relationship with Ms. Ruiz."

"No one is dying." Rebel pried himself out of the Pontiac. He groaned as he straightened up. "We're just about to have a conniption fit."

"You should do yoga with me." Ranger climbed out on Atticus's side. "It's excellent for your joints."

It was possible there was some truth to that, seeing as how he'd gotten out so much faster than our youngest brother, but none of us was dumb enough to tell Ranger that he was right. Then he'd never shut up.

"I'm more worried about our chicken replacement than your joints," Ranger added. "Seeing as how we still haven't had breakfast."

"Would you forget about the chicken?" Atticus hissed.

I spotted Alice's car kicking up dust as she sped up our drive. She did not like to drive slowly, and Ford liked to indulge her. Ignoring Atticus, I shut my door and laid in a course for the porch.

"I am equally concerned about our not-chicken." It was always a good idea to rankle Atticus.

Fortunately for our breakfast plans, and even more fortunately for the chicken population of Moonlight Valley, Alice parked next to Atticus's vintage Pontiac, and Ford held up a green-and-yellow box of soy chicken patties as he got out of her fancy car. We were vegetarian werewolves, as oxymoronic as it sounded.

"Chickens of the world, rejoice!" Ford intoned. "We have a replacement sacrifice."

"Thank you, baby Jesus." Ranger grabbed his chest and took a dramatic step backward. "You should have shared your location with me so I could track you on my phone. I was near to having one of my spells."

Imma spell him. My wolf sounded groggy. Except for a few unwelcome asides, he'd been napping most of the service and then in the car. He was the heathen kind of wolf.

Atticus followed me up the steps, close enough to step on my heels. I considered stopping short, but that would have just led to us tussling. "You realize you went out with a woman on the 'Top 50 Sexiest Ladies in America' list?"

"They make a list for that?" I wasn't sure how I felt about these list-making people eying up Sonnet and giving her a rank order. It felt like it might be ignoring all sorts of other qualities that she possessed, like being smart and sassy.

Plus, I didn't like other people—including my brother—judging her attractiveness.

She's number one. The best.

"They do," Atticus affirmed. He was an accountant, and he loved lists. "Sonnet is real pretty, and I think everyone can agree on that. But she has some other attributes that push her to the top spot on that list in my opinion."

Too bad we have to kill him. I can make some suggestions.

All 640 muscles in my body tightened, and I realized my canines were lengthening as Atticus explained his position on list making. He shouldn't feel so free to discuss Sonnet as if she were an ice-cream flavor or a playlist of popular songs. Of course, this kind of list making seemed to be the new hobby of just about everybody in town. Naturally, Atticus wasn't any different.

"It's like playing fantasy football," Atticus offered. "Where you pick your dream team. We're just dream dating, that's all."

"I would be careful, Atticus. I don't think Mav wants you dream dating his girl," Rebel warned, then winked at me. "Plus, sexual objectification is never acceptable behavior. Our momma would be disappointed in you."

Atticus frowned, but he shut up. Thank God and baby Jesus because I didn't feel much like explaining to him that he should keep his intimate thoughts and dreams away from my girl.

I was tired. And, if I were being honest with myself, I was down about the lack of Sonnet in my real life even though I'd been so quick to push her away.

But Atticus had inadvertently raised a fair point.

If Sonnet and I had stepped out together, I would have had to deal with a townful of Atticuses with their objectifying, unacceptable sexy fantasy lists. I'd also have had to deal with cities, states, and probably an entire world too.

Sonnet was beautiful, and people obviously liked looking at her. She'd been cast in a popular TV show, for crying out loud. All those people watching her felt like they knew her, just a little, and were entitled to a piece of her.

I held the front door for everyone, ignoring Atticus's searching glare and Ranger's frown of concern as they filed past me. I wasn't ready to go in myself, however. I stood out there, listening to the happy hubbub, and my stomach clenched.

My family would have more questions.

Questions I didn't want to answer, plus more I likely couldn't. Truth was, I didn't much feel like Sunday chicken and waffles.

Run?

You bet, I agreed. Then for the first time in a long time, I left my family and ran off on my own.

* * *

Vanity Fur Salon was closed on Sundays, but I'd checked my phone, and Sanye's contact picture showed her to be at her business, so I eventually headed there after I'd run out on my family and shifted into my wolf. I'd loped around Moonlight Valley, trying to outrun questions and feelings.

I had not been successful.

Now, hours later, I'd shifted back and remembered my responsibilities. Sunday was my day to check on Sanye and help out with whatever she needed handled.

It was very pink inside her place of business, plus Sanye had added crystal chandeliers for reasons that escaped me. Sonnet would have loved them. They sparkled and were full of feminine energy.

At Sanye's request, I'd picked up peanut butter. Not at her request, I'd driven all the way into Knoxville to do so, because if I'd gone into the Piggly Wiggly in Moonlight Valley, I would have faced an onslaught of questions about my (lack of a) dating life.

Sanye took one look at my morose face and assigned me to clean-up duty. Someone had brought in their husky after it had rolled in an entire pack of chewed-up bubblegum, and forty minutes later I was still working the peanut butter into its fur. It had been a jumbo-sized gum pack.

"Why are you here?"

I looked up from Mr. Muffin and gave her a small smile. "I'm here to spend time with my best girl."

She rolled her eyes and grabbed the spray hose. "Do you ever dial it back, Mav? Don't you get tired sometimes?"

"Tired of what?" I coaxed Mr. Muffin up into the doggy bath.

"I've known you for almost twenty-five years. You are always, always charming. You just say the nicest things."

Sanye's words—although positive on the surface—didn't feel anywhere close to being a compliment.

I laid a restraining hand on Mr. Muffin just in case he balked at his bath. This wasn't his first encounter with bubblegum, however, and he was clearly tired of smelling like strawberry Hubba Bubba, so he let Sanye wet him gently down.

"You're never not charming," Sanye accused. "You charm the pants off of everyone."

I grinned at her. "Not everyone. There are a good many people I never, ever want to see pants-less."

She rolled her eyes. "I am totally safe. This is a pants-on zone. And maybe that's why we're still friends now."

"Because you won't lose your pants for me?" I teased, before stopping to think about how that might sound.

Sanye took no shit from anyone, but I didn't want to make her uncomfortable. Or make her think that I thought about her and sex.

We were the pants-firmly-on kind of friends, no matter how many of Wyatt's romance novels people in Moonlight Valley had read where two best friends suddenly fall in love with each other.

"Don't be stupid." She sprayed me lightly with the hose and laughed. "It's not that. Maybe we're still friends because I don't fall for your charm. Because you don't have to worry about making me like you. I already like you as much as I can, and for who you are." She ran a wide-tooth comb through Mr. Muffin's fur, gently working a wad of gum out. "Don't you ever want to just be yourself and not have to act so charming?"

As I set to work on another wad of gum, I almost wished there could have been something more than friendship with Sanye. She was a great person, and Evan had been a lucky man, right up until the war accident that killed him.

Settling down with Sanye would have been easy. She fit right in here in Moonlight Valley, and everyone loved her. We all wanted her to find her happy ending, even if it couldn't be with Evan anymore. After Evan's death and my reformation, a lot of folks had expected us to get together.

Sanye gave me a small smile. "Someday, I'm gonna move on. You'll have to find something else to do with your Sundays."

"I met someone," I blurted out.

She grinned at me. "I heard."

Mr. Muffin decided to shake, which was frustrating. It was not, however, as frustrating as Sanye having heard the gossip already.

"It's over and done with."

"Are you sure?"

I nodded reluctantly. I was.

My fierce attraction to Sonnet, however, was alive and well. I'd spent far too much personal time thinking about her and how amazing she'd felt in my arms. I'd mentally planned out a dozen ways to make her feel good. To kiss her and make love to her. Worse, when I wasn't thinking about her naked, I was dreaming about introducing her to my momma. Momma would have liked her.

"She just wanted some quick fun," I admitted. "A fling. She's a firefly sparking in the night, a quick flash."

Sanye gave me an assessing look. "And what do you want, Mr. Poetic?"

Her.

"All the time in the world," I said, far more lightly than I felt. "I'm looking for forever with her and that worries me. I'm not such a good judge of character, so what if I've misread her?"

Sanye finished washing the gum out of Mr. Muffin while she chewed on that. "Darrell Boone was your father, Mav. It's normal to love him, even to hero-worship him. You were just a kid, and you had your rose-colored glasses on."

This was deeper than I cared to get on a nice Sunday afternoon. More importantly, I'd run out on my family to avoid this kind of serious discussion, so I directed an easy smile at her. "You sure didn't idolize yours."

"No, I did not." Sanye's face fell some, a shadow moving over it. "But my daddy is not charming. Not one bit. Yours, on the other hand, could give a master class in charm. He taught both you and Atticus to read people like a pro."

"I know I can read people." I grabbed a towel and set to work drying off Mr. Muffin. "They're an open book. It's downright easy—unless I need something genuine from them, some real emotion, something I can't tease or trick them into. I still haven't repaired the damage I did to my relationship with Knox. And I didn't realize I'd screwed things up with Sonnet until it was too late. Once I get involved with someone, it's like they're a black box. I can't read a goddamned thing about them."

Water gurgled in a pipe. Mr. Muffin woofed, helpfully filling in the silence for us.

Sanye knew I was right. She was picking her next words like she picked through the windfall apples looking for salvageable fruit.

I washed my hands while she thought things through. My life might be a mess, but at least I could rinse off the remnants of gum, peanut butter, and doggy bathwater.

Finally, right as she seemed about to share her thoughts with me, my phone rang. Pulling it from my back pocket, I saw that it was Ranger. Giving Sanye an apologetic smile, I answered it.

"What?"

"I need your help."

The shock of this statement about rocked me. Ranger never asked for help, so it took some time to recover. "Just tell me what."

"They called All-Purpose Animal Services down to the set; they've got an animal issue, and they need a herpetologist, ergo I need you to come help me."

I hesitated, both because his request was unusual—seeing as the twins were co-owners with Ranger in All-Purpose Animal Services and much better at general animal catching than I was—and because I might run into Sonnet if I visited the set.

"I sure can, Ranger. But why don't you ask Atticus or Ford?"

"Ford and Alice are busy making us some nieces and nephews in the woods, and obviously I can't take Atticus to the set. Plus, none of them is a bona fide snake expert."

No *obvious* reason came to mind for excluding Atticus from this animal-catching expedition, but Ranger was almost always right. I couldn't remember the last time he'd been wrong, in fact.

Still, I didn't want to chance running into Sonnet. She was my fantasy girl, so keeping some distance between us was downright prudent.

We can be a second chance romance!

Or an angry fuck.

Call it whatever you want, but our mate is our mate.

"Come on, Mav. If we see Sonnet, I'll hide you behind one of the traps."

Ranger's offer was irritating, seeing as how it just proved that he was—once again—right. He was also an expert manipulator. Even so, I capitulated. "Okay. Okay. Do you want me to stop by and get you?"

We're gonna geeeeettttt the girl!

We so were not. Unlike Ranger, my wolf was plenty wrong on a regular basis.

"You finish up with Sanye and meet me on set later. Since you've given me your solemn word to assist, you should know that this is a weeklong project. That place is just riddled with critters."

And now it'll be full of wolves.

"Gee, thanks, Ranger." I didn't question how he knew that I'd ended up at Sanye's after running off from our family breakfast date.

For reasons known only to him, Ranger had obviously decided to torture me. He did it to all of us on a regular basis. But as conniving as Ranger was, I was even better at staying out of sight.

I would not be noticeable on that set unless or until I chose to be.

"You are very welcome." Ranger sounded far too smug; I would have to do my brotherly duty and take him down a peg. "Like I said, if Sonnet comes anywhere near us, you can shift into a wolf and I'll hide you in that large dog crate we've got."

I was nowhere near stupid enough to let Ranger shut me into an animal trap and so I told him. Some mild profanity might have colored that explanation.

Ranger sighed. "But you are gun-shy about the mounting."

CHAPTER

THIRTEEN

MAVERICK

"There are no happy endings . . .There are no endings, happy or otherwise. We all have our own stories which are just part of the one Story that binds both this world and Faerie. Sometimes we step into each others stories—perhaps just for a few minutes, perhaps for years—and then we step out of them again. But all the while, the Story just goes on."

— CHARLES DE LINT, *DREAMS UNDERFOOT*

I'd spent way too many hours dreaming about what it might be like to run into Sonnet on set. I'd woken up with the sexy scenarios playing in my brain.

The reality of being on set did not match those pictures. Not in the slightest.

"Tell me again why we're doing this?" I asked. "The solution here seems obvious. Plus, I see no snakes."

The drunk seagull on the craft services table squinted its yellow eyes at me.

It was hungover on last night's beer and very unhappy about having its picnic interrupted. I didn't blame it one bit.

That poor bird had just come up to Tennessee for the winter, like a retiree headed to Florida to sit out the snow and ice. Mostly, the gulls hung out in garbage dumps and by parking lots when they were wintering, but this flock had showed up on set and now they were being asked to move on.

171

"Birdseed." Ranger held out his hand, not looking at me.

I passed him the birdseed, and he inserted it into the bird trap. He'd brought a multi-bird trap that had shade, a water pan, and now a breakfast buffet. I shifted my weight while he tweaked the tarp screen.

The gull on the table hopped closer, looking interested. Ranger would coax the birds in, and then we'd release them on the other side of the valley, near the municipal refuse center.

Or we could have poultry for dinner, my wolf suggested.

My wolf did not approve of Ranger's faux chicken and waffles.

They do *not* taste like chicken.

Neither did the seagulls, but I had no intention of demonstrating that for my wolf.

"Organic chips," Ranger barked, passing me an empty packet of low-salt nuts. Too much sodium was bad for birds, so we were using healthy bird bait only.

I gave him the chips. We'd also brought uncooked spaghetti noodles and sunflower seeds, seeing as how the gulls didn't speak English and couldn't tell Ranger what their preferred foods were. I could have been in my lab working on my article for *Science* magazine or feeding my animals. But Ranger took offense easily, and he got up to trouble when he was left alone.

Leaving him to the birds, I skirted the pile of humane bird traps in varying sizes that we'd brought with us. From the looks of things, Ranger had planned for an Alfred Hitchcock–worthy plague of ostrich-sized avians.

"Hey, Maverick. Are you helping Ranger with our angry birds?"

I glanced up from my stocktaking at the question. One of Sonnet's bodyguards, the one I'd disarmed, approached from the direction of today's set. From the number of people milling about, I deduced that they were about ready to begin.

"Hey, Eric? Right?" I held out my hand for him to shake, although I couldn't keep my eyes on him. Despite my best intentions, I was looking for her.

Eric gave my hand a firm, brisk shake, and I gave him a quick once-over. His shoulder was not in a sling, which was a good sign, and his nose was only semi-swollen.

He'll live.

Which was a good thing because killing people was a felony and wrong.

We're so reformed, my wolf said glumly. **Boooring. Fighting with other wolves is way more exciting than kicking the butts of puny humans.**

"No carbs!" Ranger barked, smacking Eric's hand as the bodyguard attempted to toss a piece of his bagel toward a gull.

Eric's eyes widened. "Right."

"Bread is nutritionally inferior," Ranger snapped. "Don't malnourish my gulls."

Eric eyed the seagull, weighing the odds of a successful bread retrieval. The seagull glared back at him.

"I didn't mean to—" he muttered.

"It's our job to protect these birds."

He nodded quickly. "Absolutely. Of course."

"So," I continued, "we're gonna remove them from your table and take them somewhere else."

"Nicely," Ranger added. "I'm not making any bird uncomfortable."

"That's great. No birds should be harmed in the making of this film." Eric nodded some more. "I get it."

My attention snagged on the activity going on behind him. Specifically, the short, curvy brunette walking toward the set.

My breath caught as she tossed her chestnut hair over her shoulder, giving her assistant a happy, sunny smile. The other woman laughed at something she said. Then Sonnet laughed. The golden sound carried easily to where I stood, staring at her like a lovestruck fool.

Eric followed my line of sight, coming to stand next to me. "Have you seen Sonnet act in person yet? On set? She's amazing. The camera can't capture her completely."

I forced myself to look away, ignoring the sour twisting in my stomach. Eric was proud of what she'd accomplished. I was glad. She deserved to be surrounded by people who cared for and supported her.

I turned to go back to the craft services table, figuring Ranger would have himself a hissy fit if I didn't return in time to admire his bird-catching skills, but Eric held up a hand. "Hang on a moment. Watch this. They're about to call action."

Without meaning to, I stopped in my tracks, entranced.

The breeze had her hair dancing, random curls making a break for it, and she laughed again. She was just enjoying being outside and the fresh air. A couple of makeup artists ran up to her, patting and tucking, and she waited patiently while they did their thing.

The set got real quiet after some hollering for everyone to shut up and turn off their cell phones, then someone called, "Standby," followed by, "Turn over." Things got busy by the cameras as the operators did some last-minute checks and started recording.

"Roll sound," someone called.

"Roll camera," came the response.

Alrighty then. Even the gulls had shut up.

If I hadn't believed in magic already, I would have then.

The director signaled and the scene began.

Sonnet had the first line. This far away, I couldn't catch what she said, which was frustrating. Listening to her voice was a pleasure. I was used to our local musical groups, where everyone was miked and the sound level about blew off the roof. These folks were speaking softly. Crew members moved around giant microphones and other pieces of equipment.

Despite my distance, I had a great view, and it was something else. She'd transformed, radiating that almost invisible aura, beaming, and drawing all eyes toward her. She was downright magical.

I had no idea what the shot was about, but it looked like she was leading a yoga class in the garden of the haunted cottage. Sonnet's character slipped from one ridiculous pose to the next; she looked like a dancing cockroach. A bulldog in a pink onesie and a matching tutu followed right along next to her. Her movements were all exaggerated, making everything seem silly. One minute she was a dying bug, and the next she was a tree whipping back and forth in gale-force winds. It was hysterical. She was hysterical.

Two production assistants were convulsed, hands over their mouths, shoulders quaking. They weren't the only ones biting back laughter.

When the director yelled, "Cut," laughter broke out, but Sonnet didn't stop.

"Alien invasion pose!" she bellowed. "Everyone try to levitate! And then we're off into imaginary pet stretch! Give your imaginary yoga-friendly animal a scratch behind the ears! Finally, we're cucumbers, folks, cucumbers! We're the coolest veggie in the yoga garden!"

She flopped dramatically onto the ground and then lay there like a log.

That cucumber's our mate, you fool. She's the best veggie in the salad.

She was.

I couldn't look away.

"I told you she was unreal," Eric said, smiling.

I could feel his eyes on me, but I wasn't done looking at Sonnet. Her humor and the show she was putting on had me riveted. I might have regrets about how we'd not-dated, but I truly did wish her the best of everything. She deserved it.

"It's amazing that she's that good at something she doesn't like doing."

I frowned at Eric. "She doesn't like acting?"

Why was I asking questions? Sonnet and I were over.

She can be a stay-at-home mate!

My wolf was a stupid optimist.

"Yeah. Well, it's not the acting. I think that's fine. But I'm pretty sure she hates the lifestyle."

I thought on that. "Then why doesn't she just quit?"

Eric shrugged. "She sort of fell into it. The TV studio optioned her book and offered her the female lead. And then it all sort of took off, so she kept doing more seasons of the show. Her success surprised a lot of people who didn't see it coming. But she's mesmerizing, you know?"

It was magic.

But WE like her for herself, my wolf said piously. He was such a toady.

I agreed with both of them. "I do know."

Sonnet had stopped doing yoga and was now talking to the director. She looked extremely interested, although I noted that she was biting her bottom lip.

"Did you know she has to burn all her trash?"

"Why's that?" Sonnet was still biting her lower lip. She was nervous about something. If she were mine, I'd kiss her. Explore that lower lip with my tongue. Coax her into kissing me back. It'd be a gentle kiss at first, not a *I-need-to-be-*

inside-you-now-please kiss. Not a *magical-tingle* kiss. Not a *horny-werewolf* kiss.

Just heartfelt affection.

Some caring.

"People go through her trash," Eric said, startling me out of my fantasy.

"What? Why?"

"To find out what she's doing, what she's like. They make up stories about it, publish pictures. She doesn't get to have any private life. She's always on display. It makes her feel vulnerable."

That's wrong.

It was. And also? What the fuck was wrong with people that they thought they had some sort of goddamned right, a hall pass, to go rummaging around in her life and share all the stuff that she'd thought was private?

"She was trying to get some privacy here in Tennessee," Eric continued. "She gets tired of all the people—and my team is people and I recognize that's a problem—but her sister convinced her to have us stay at the rental cabin with her. It's a sorry way to live, and that's the truth."

"You feel sorry for her?" I looked at him. I wasn't an idiot. He had an agenda. A goal of his own. If he didn't, he wouldn't be oversharing about his employer while he talked about how everyone *else* pried into her private life.

He was part of the problem, as was I, I realized. Because I also wanted a piece of her. I hated feeling like there were parts of her I didn't know.

"I sure do. She's a nice lady, but that doesn't stop people from trying to use her. She can't trust anyone."

"What about her sister?" This wasn't any of my business but it came out before I could stop myself.

She can trust *us*. We're real trustworthy.

Eric shrugged. "Elena wants what's best for Sonnet's career. She pushes her, guides her and stuff. But success has a price tag, right? Sonnet's the one paying the price, in her time, her life, her happiness."

"Maybe she likes working," I countered. "Maybe having a career is her choice. It's a good thing to like your work."

"Sure." Eric snorted. "But shooting a TV show isn't what Sonnet likes or wants. She doesn't need a business mentor or a life coach because achieving the next milestone on someone else's list isn't healthy for her. It's just healthy for her career."

Are you sure we can't make her our business?

My wolf was still Team Make Sonnet Our Mate, but I wasn't so sure.

At the very least, there were Sonnet's personal preferences—not to mention logistics and practicalities—that made our partnering up and pairing off together even more unlikely than polar bears in the South.

Wyatt had taken great pains to point out that Sonnet was married to her work and not looking to change that situation. She really, *really* liked what she did (unless Etic was right?) and she'd light out of Moonlight Valley once her show wrapped (which I knew but had held hopes out for a different kind of ending, one that had me wrapping her up in my arms for starters).

Her love life came a distant second, or so Wyatt claimed.

There won't be any coming at all. She's missing out or doing all the work herself.

I'd spent a whole lot of time going over what she'd said to me and then filling in the blanks where she hadn't spoken words at all. It did not look good for me and my wolf.

1. Sonnet was a TV star and Moonlight Valley was not a hotbed for that kind of work. (We'd shot our bolt with the *Smoky Spirits* gig and lightning did not strike twice.)
2. Sonnet had never, not once, indicated that she might be interested in putting down roots here. You had to set that bird free, not clip its wings.

My wolf growled plaintively. **There ain't no use hollering at a cat that don't care for conversation, but you sure could chase it. This Eric makes a good point.**

I was still trying to make sense of Eric's observation, that Sonnet *wasn't* all that happy, no matter how glamorous her life seemed from the outside. Maybe she wasn't madly, truly in love with making TV shows.

But if that was true, then I was dead wrong.

And I'd backed off my mate for no reason at all.

* * *

Atticus and Wyatt often had Mondays off. Atticus did not take clients on that day, while Wyatt maintained he needed that time free "to refill his creative well." Mostly, that meant the two of them hiked into the national park and drank beer on a blanket in the sunshine. Once a month, I joined them.

People said I was an outdoorsy scientist, but truth was, I couldn't stand being locked up inside somewhere. My wolf hated it, too.

No cages.

My dislike of forced confinement had certainly motivated my exit from the Iron Wolves.

Seeing as how Sonnet was on my mind, this particular Monday I happened to be rethinking my position on public activities.

Sure, I thought about her a lot. And sure, some of those thoughts took place in the shower.

Not the only place, my wolf complained.

He was right. I thought about her pretty much everywhere, but right now my particular focus was on her feet.

According to both the weather app on my phone and Mr. Allerbee's bones (which had a better track record than any meteorologist), the weather was shaping up to be unusually wet later this week, and I knew—because Eric had casually mentioned it when he and Ranger were lugging the trapped seagulls off set—that Sonnet didn't have the right kind of socks with her, just her fun, fluffy light ones and nothing meant to handle mountain weather.

For a man who was in the business of protecting people, Eric sure did talk a lot.

I'd run into him all over town, and each time he'd shared a new nugget of information about Sonnet. She liked to read paperbacks and always kept one in her car and in that crocheted tote bag she lugged everywhere, but she'd lost the middle two volumes of *The Spiderwick Chronicles*, and all the copies were checked out of the local library. I'd got in my truck and gone over to Knoxville, where I'd picked up a complete boxed set, plus some leaf-shaped bookmarks.

I gave them to Eric to pass on, letting him know that he shouldn't tell her they were from me.

Last Friday, after he'd told me she'd been craving mochi donuts, I'd bribed Ranger to break out his piping bag and fry up some bubble rings. They hadn't turned out any too bad, either, even if Ranger being Ranger had spent hours making each dough bubble precisely the same size. I'd put the donuts in a bakery box to disguise their homemade origins and delivered them to Eric.

I also arranged for Jennie Dean's pink unicorn Frappuccinos to be delivered to Sonnet each morning on set. Wyatt had cheaped out on the blender at his place, and it wasn't up to the job of crushing ice, or so Eric had informed me.

Yesterday Eric had mentioned that Sonnet's feet kept getting wet because they were filming riverbank shots, and she'd run out of dry socks to change into. He also told me that the wardrobe assistants had brought her some thick brown hiking socks, but they were some kind of scratchy wool and too big. Eric had asked if I had a local sock source I could recommend.

Was he subtle?

Hell, no. Of course I could see the setup.

Still, my mind was turned to the Sonnet channel. I needed to get back home, go through our sock drawers, and find her some cute, mismatched pairs. Or something fuzzy. With pom-poms. Possibly, I'd carve out time to learn how to knit.

"Penny for your thoughts, Mav."

I looked at Wyatt from where I slouched in the backseat, then stared back out the window. "You do know what inflation is, don't you?"

Wyatt muttered something about the price of mass-market paperbacks, and "had I seen how much his publisher liked to charge for an e-book?" I took that as an affirmative.

He did not offer me a penny, however.

Instead, he cleared his throat. "Have you seen Sonnet recently?"

I met his gaze in the rearview mirror with studied nonchalance. "Nope."

Nice. Simple. Accurate, my wolf approved. **Also explains our blue balls and mopey attitude.**

Atticus and Wyatt exchanged significant glances in the front seat. I ignored them.

None of their business anyhow, my wolf grumbled.

"I've texted her a few times, but she seems real busy," Wyatt said.

Then he paused, as if he were maybe waiting for me to explain the cause of all that busyness. Even though we'd left the national park, I guessed he was still hunting.

"Could be." I shrugged.

Could be NONE OF HIS BUSINESS.

It bore repeating.

She wasn't sleeping? That was Eric's business. It was possibly the business of her director, the film crew, her agent, and her sister.

It was not my business.

Not even a little bit.

Still, I worried about her not getting enough sleep. I added a Mason jar of Ranger's special sleepy-time tea to the list of items I should bring to the set.

As he pulled into our driveway, Wyatt made some growling noises, like he was irritated not to get his point across. As soon as he'd slowed to less than two miles an hour, I got the door open and bolted out on a sock mission.

I figured I'd round up the unworn socks in the house and make some selections. Ranger bought everyone ridiculous socks for every holiday, and every holiday they were shoved in drawers unworn. Dogs with ski hats and nesting puffins, penguins and corgis, turkeys and dachshunds. I tore the tags off and mismatched the pairs because Sonnet didn't like wearing two of the same. I filled up one of momma's wicker baskets and made for the stairs.

Over my load of socks, I spotted Ranger standing by the front door, turning an envelope over in his hands and scrutinizing the return address.

He startled and shoved the envelope behind his back, frowning at me.

"What's up?" I asked. "Is it another seed catalog of dubious provenance for Atticus? Do you have a secret love pen pal? Give me a hand with this stuff, and tell me what you're hiding."

"Nothing is being hidden," he grumped. His hand, however, did not come out from behind his back.

He was totally hiding something.

And I was just the Boone to pry it out of him.

"Give it up." I set down my stuff. I could tickle it out of him for sure. Ranger was painfully ticklish. Usually, I respected his quirks but now I was curious.

Ranger gritted his teeth, hard enough that his dentist would be having words with him. He was considering. Planning his response. This was concerning, seeing as how I was standing in the line of fire of whatever plan he cooked up.

Abruptly, he shoved the envelope at me. "Take it. It's yours. Give me those socks. I'll take them out to the car. You've got enough there for a consortium of octopi."

Now was not the time to point out that octopuses were more solitary than a Tennessee hermit.

I traded the socks for the letter, and Ranger stomped out of the house, talking to himself. Meanwhile, I inspected my letter. It sure seemed innocuous, until I flipped it over.

It was posted five days ago, sent from the remote region of Alaska where our father had been exiled by the Wolf Council.

Marking it RETURN TO SENDER would be smart, and honestly, what could our daddy do? He was stuck up there. I hadn't even realized he *could* shift back to his human form at all. It wasn't supposed to be possible, not according to everything I'd ever heard about mates and mating bites. He'd bitten Momma and that meant he was bonded to her for life, with no shifting back to his human form.

Of course, our daddy had never been big on fair. It should not have come as a surprise that he'd somehow figured out how to evade his just desserts, while Momma was still stuck in her wolf form. Even leaving that side, he had nothing to say to me that I needed to hear. Much like walking in on one of my brothers watching a horror movie, however, I found I couldn't look away. I had to open it.

Inside was a picture of Sonnet and me, from the night of our Biscuits & Blessings date. We stood near the hostess stand. The shot was slightly out of focus, with someone's shoulder blocking most of Sonnet, but it was clear enough that it was the two of us.

I flipped the picture over, knowing that my old man wouldn't have been able to resist adding his personal touch.

Sure enough, he'd added a message: *"You're even better than your old man at the dating game. She's got money and great tits. She can give your old man a fresh start. Think of the stories I can tell—you think those press people might be interested?"*

He's threatening us.

Maybe I could storm up there to Alaska, demand a sit-down. When he showed up I could share my feelings with him.

Challenge him. Beat him to a pulp.

I liked that option a whole lot. It would let my old man know who was in charge of our family now, who was looking after the people who mattered. I'd make my point, which was that maybe I could come to terms with his shifting back into his human form (**not really**), but I was downright rageful knowing that he was messing with my mate's life.

I was not in a relationship with Sonnet, but he didn't know that.

My wolf prowled, pushing at my skin, demanding to come out.

This is not the time for talking. DEFENSE.

My forearms itched, my wolf pelt rippling over my skin, tugging at my control. I was real close to losing control.

And defending our family.

I ran through what I knew about Darrell's exile. After he'd forcibly changed our momma into a werewolf, he'd been sent up to a remote section of Alaska by the Wolf Council. With four thousand miles between him and Momma, he should not have been able to shift out of his wolf form. Once a bonded wolf gets too far away from his mate physically, he is unable to transform. As always, however, the rules did not seem to apply to Darrell Boone. He'd always been good at circumnavigating them, mostly for his own self-aggrandizement.

The letter was a threat.

He might be coming back.

But I was damn sure that he wasn't getting his filthy paws on Sonnet.

* * *

Ranger and I met up with Rue and Rebel at the lab. We'd planned to shift and run later that evening, after they finished a series of observations they were making. I brought fresh churros, coffee, and the bad news about Darrell.

"That man has more lives than a cat," Rue growled.

Fucking cats, my wolf seethed. Alice excepted, of course. Darrell should be done for. We need to complain to the management about their handling of our daddy's situation.

Rebel paced back and forth between the lab table and the snake aquariums. "What can he possibly do from Alaska? He's stuck there. He's not allowed back here."

I was both glad and worried that he didn't understand how our daddy operated.

I did not want to be the one who disillusioned him. When I'd tried to redeem myself after the hurt and trouble I'd caused in my Iron Wolves days, he'd been the first to believe that I could have changed after Evan's death. He hadn't held my actions against me. I'd been forgiven. Welcomed home. I loved Rebel and, with him, I'd been protective in a way I regretted I hadn't been for my other brothers when we'd been growing up as Darrell Boone's boys.

Ranger frowned at Rebel, looking as if he was fixing to connect the dots for him about our daddy's refusal to follow the rules, but finally he said, "Rebel, can you take Maverick's truck and go get us all some more coffee from Jennie Dean's?"

"Maverick brought coffee and churros," Rebel protested. "This is a blatant attempt to get rid of me. You can't do that."

Rookie move.

"We sure can." I clapped my hand on his shoulder. I'd have drug him out of here by the scruff of his neck if it wouldn't have caused a fight that might damage the snake tanks. Plus, I needed to respect his independence. Up to a certain point. "You don't have the experience with this like Rue does, nor are you as conniving and Machiavellian as Ranger here."

"Plus, you know I plot best on coffee." Ranger tipped his mug at Rebel. "And Jennie Dean makes the best coffee."

"I'm not going anywhere." Rebel sat down ostentatiously on the edge of the lab table nearest our group, making the glassware rattle. "I'm not the baby of the family. You don't need to protect me."

Ranger and I exchanged glances, silently communicating our mutual unwillingness to expose Rebel to our daddy's horse pucky.

Except, even knowing what he did about our family history, Rue was of a different mind. "Let him stay. He needs to know what Darrell's capable of so he can look out for himself. Sooner or later, that man will try to pull something on Rebel."

Gotta drop the truth on the pup sometime.

I didn't like it, but the man had a point.

Plus, in my checkered past, Rue had been something of a father figure to me, even if he was all of a year younger than me. When he spoke up, I listened.

Still, to expose Rebel to Darrell? My heart said no way, we didn't need to disillusion him, but history said yes. What kind of brother would I be if I left him vulnerable to our daddy's scams?

"Alrighty then." Ranger gave in, smacking his palm on the table. "But don't test my patience unless you pour me some more of that coffee. I'm plumb out of both."

Rue bit back a smile, because sometimes you did just have to smile at Ranger's antics, but then he turned to me. "You think he's running a confidence game, one of his tricks?"

I shrugged. "It beats me. He's supposed to be stuck up there in Alaska, in his wolf form, but apparently he shifted long enough to get himself on the internet and find a post office. Might be he's just messing with me, but mostly he can't be bothered to do anything that doesn't better his own bottom line. Darrell Boone doesn't do nothing if it doesn't benefit himself. If he truly believes that Sonnet and I are together, he'll want to gain from our relationship."

Ranger smacked the table again. "I am not accepting your excuses, Maverick. You should be stepping out with that fine lady, not using our daddy as a reason to push her away. I already told you in the truck that I have him under control, lock, stock, and barrel."

"Are you planning to tell us how?" Rue asked evenly. "Or is this top-secret, need-to-know-basis only information?"

This was Ranger we were talking about. I wasn't sure he knew that the law—and the definition of "felony"—applied to him.

Rebel frowned, like he wasn't real happy with Ranger holding out on us. "You want blind trust?"

"Rebel Aldous Boone, I'm not just plumb out of patience now, I'm in negative numbers. You have made me tap my backup reserve." Ranger's tone was flat. "You owe me two cups of fancy coffee from the coffee shop for that patience-testing, ignorant observation of yours."

"That wasn't an observation. It was an accusation."

"Three cups."

"I trust Ranger," Rue said, meeting my gaze. "If he says he's got this, he's got this."

I had plenty of trust in Ranger too. He was smart and manipulative.

He'd run rings around our daddy.

Still, no one knew Darrell quite like I did. For far too long, I'd been the chip off the old block, the Boone brother who'd gone bad. Darrell did whatever was best for Darrell. He took what he wanted. I wasn't like that anymore, and I wouldn't trust anyone else with Sonnet's safety.

My wolf growled in agreement. **A mate comes first. Damn straight.**

FOURTEEN

SONNET 

"Before, I never knew how far I would go. Now I believe I have the answer. I will go as far as there is to go. I will go way too far."

— HOLLY BLACK, *THE CRUEL PRINCE*

Whenever I snatched an hour from my busy schedule to sleep, I'd lie on the bed in my fancy trailer, thoughts bouncing all over, turned on and even more down and upset.

Why had I taken up with the sexy and capable Professor Maverick? Weren't my previous experiences with Hollywood himbos educational?

Nope!

There was no getting around it. I'd invited him into my life. I'd let him get close. I'd developed feelings for him and my heart would never be the same. My new plan was to smother those feelings with an impossible workload, hence my acting, producing, promoting a show, developing a script for a new one, and signing a contract to do still *more* work for the *Wolf Girl* film. I was busy and tired—it should have been better than a sleeping spell for my sleep schedule, but nope. It wasn't enough work to drown out Maverick in my brain.

Meanwhile, instead of unproductive sleeping, I got up and wrote scenes for *Wolf Girl*.

Losing myself in the character was enough to momentarily blot out the existence of my professor's rough, rumbly voice. The way he quietly and competently looked after me.

"I don't need a man to look after me," I said out loud as I hit *Send* on an email to Elena.

Take that, to-do list!

I was independent and hardworking. I handled my own shit, made my own money, and directed my own life.

Professor Maverick could keep his cozy small-town life, his students, and the family who loved him. I had no need of his charming smile and the warm presence that made everyone in this gosh darn small town like him and invite him over for Sunday brunches, porch-fixing parties, and whatever else it was people did in small towns.

I wasn't entirely clear on that because I was always working.

No, you do NOT get to *charm your way inside my head!*

My phone buzzed ninety seconds later, and I took the call from Elena.

Elena was also a workaholic; she appreciated my breakup-inspired productivity even if she didn't actually know the cause. I hadn't told her about the fiasco of a date or Maverick's decision that he would not be joining me in my celebrity fishbowl. These did not pertain to my professional life as a writer and were on a need-to-know basis.

Elena was thrilled that I'd got so much done.

I may have preened.

"This is amazing. Did you try that *2,000 to 10,000* writing book? Are you taking a motivational class?" I heard the tapping of her nails on the keyboard as she started to go through the draft I'd sent her. "I need to know your secret!"

I meant to keep a stiff upper lip, but some of the truth leaked out.

"I can't sleep."

"*Conejita*, why not? What's wrong?" Her concern was like slipping into a warm bath. She loved my writing skills and my acting skills—but she loved *me*, too.

"Anxiety," I said. Which was true. And also: not the full story.

"Okay." I could practically hear her thinking. Elena was a fixer, and my insomnia demanded a fix-it plan, pronto. "Have you tried Mami's sleep charm? CBT? I can find you an online therapist or"—I nearly passed out at her next words—"we could scale your schedule back? Move some deadlines?"

It was official. The world had come to an end.

"A *vacation*?"

"With a snorkel." She sounded pained, but affectionate. "Would that help?"

I frowned. Honestly, the answer was no.

There was only one cure for my ills: Maverick Boone. I was addicted and I hated it.

In the two weeks since my disastrous first—and last—date with Maverick, I'd been glued to my laptop all hours of the day. The pain in my back and my hips from writing slouched over in the trailer's bed almost, but not quite, drowned out the heartache. I played the *Heartbroken* playlist on Amazon Music in a loop, and I might have daydreamed, just once or twice, about the babies I would not be having with Maverick Boone.

Pups?

I didn't know how werewolves reproduced, but our babies would have had his hazel eyes and my dimples. We would have made adorably green, fluffy, round balls of love that charmed everyone in Moonlight Valley. We could have picked out a puppy together too! Kittens! Built our dream house on the shores of Phantom Falls and hosted the family Thanksgiving dinner.

Wait. Back it up.

Darn it.

This was not me. Who was this sad, pathetic sack of a person? We'd gone on one date. This was the twenty-first century, for crying out loud.

One date, not a marriage. It was just a bad date too. Sealed with an amazing, movie-worthy kiss. You do not get to pick out names for so much as a truck together.

"I don't need to cut back on my work schedule," I said firmly. "I think I'll feel better, the more I get under my belt?"

I was an excellent liar—my sister bought it.

"Eager to get going on *Wolf Girl*, huh?" She laughed as if I'd made a funny joke. My desperation to wrap up shooting for *Smoky Spirits* was because I had a bigger, better project and not because I had a broken heart. My having non-professional feelings would have surprised her.

Imagine if she knew that werewolves REALLY existed . . .

Honestly, she would have been thrilled. And then she would have pitched a three-book deal and a film option based on my discovery.

My turning into an antisocial, workaholic hermit who slept in two-hour snatches and at random intervals was a professional boon.

"The studio wasn't expecting this until next month. They'll be thrilled."

"Woo-hoo," I deadpanned and then winced. Elena didn't deserve my bad attitude. She only wanted what was best for me.

I wanted what was best for me.

And that was not a tall, broad-shouldered, twinkly-eyed, bearded man.

It wasn't.

"We haven't finalized your plans for the London premiere." Script received, productivity accolades distributed, Elena switched to the next item on our to-do list. She was getting through all the business.

"Right. The premiere." The *stupid* premiere.

No. Stop it. That premiere was someone's work baby. Their artistic dream. A huge financial investment. I did not get to whine about it. This was a no-negativity zone, and I wouldn't throw my feelings around like moths dive-bombing a porch light. No moths would be harmed by my bad mood.

I took a deep breath and forced some cheerfulness into my voice. I was an actress. I had this! "So, about the premiere. What if I took Papi? Or our brother?"

"No. No, no, no. We've talked about this. Luke and Thom will be there, not to mention Vlad and Benjie. You need to bring someone hot. Hotly glamorous. People need to be talking about your boyfriend upgrade. There will be pictures, so we need someone who will stun on the red carpet. This is not a father-daughter dance. I could hit up the Fae court for a prince."

"No thanks." I was an *amazing* actress. I did not sound bitter or resentful at *all*.

"I can ask around, see who has a client in need of some buzz? Or we could do a love spell." Elena's power lunches with other female Hollywood types scared me.

Those ladies were terrifyingly productive. They did not need to add magic to the mix—although some of them did.

"I'll find someone," I growled. "No spell necessary."

She paused, clearly running through options. Was her head the agent equivalent of a dating app, but where the goal was publicity and orgasms were optional? What was she going to say to the ladies she lunched with? *I tried to get her to go out with a prince, but she's so fussy! She wants a bearded backwoods lumberjack!*

"You could go with Luke as friends," she suggested. "He's very pretty. People will want to know if you're back together."

Oh no.

No, no, no, no, NO.

"Absolutely not," I said firmly.

"Alright." She sighed, as if I were a toddler who refused to take a nap. "But this is time sensitive. You need to find a date soon. And please talk to someone about your sleeping issues, okay? Promise me that you'll do that."

Someone knocked on the door of my trailer. Thank you, Universe! I straightened up from my slouch. Ow. "Listen, I have to go, but thank you! I'm glad you've got the draft."

"Sure, sure. No problem," Elena said. "I'll touch base with you later. And reconsider writing that erotic serial for the phone app people."

I bit my tongue because I wanted to end our call, not rehash why I was not writing reverse harem erotica about orcs. It was easier to just hang up.

Which I did. Ugh. I was a bad person with no boundaries.

"Wardrobe," someone caroled through the door. Someone cheerful and far too happy. That was fine. If that *someone* worked in the TV industry for more than twenty minutes, they'd end up as disillusioned and bitter as me.

Positive thoughts! BE THE CHANGE YOU WANT TO SEE!

Funny. Those cute little Instagram quotes were not as good at lifting my mood as chocolate was.

Ten minutes later, I stood on the step riser in the wardrobe trailer.

While Mabel barked commands to *Turn! Lift your arm! Hop up and down!* (the last one being Mabel's weird sense of humor), I mentally rehearsed a few lines and then reprioritized my to-do list. An idea for a new *Wolf Girl* scene snuck into the back of my mind. It was business as usual. A few people wandered in and out.

My mind wandered.

Boom! I fell straight into thinking about Maverick. I might have issued a lovelorn sigh or two. Or not *love*. More like lusty appreciation and liking?

"What's up? Why the gusty exhaling?" Mabel frowned at me, loosening her tape measure around my boobs.

"Nothing." I beamed at her. Charm time!

She looked unconvinced. We weren't exactly friends, but we were friendly colleagues. We worked together, which made genuine friendship tricky, although we tried.

"Mmmhmmm." She retrieved her tape measure. "Something's up. You're stress eating. And sighing. You're distracted. OMG. You're not pregnant, are you?"

"No! No! Of course not."

Mabel shrugged. "Babies are lovely. Although it would be none of my business if you were, but it would be good to know. Strictly for wardrobe purposes."

She winked and patted my arm. A fuzzy wolf pup popped into my head. He had hazel eyes and magical powers.

No! I swallowed.

My head and my heart were Maverick-free zones. Mostly. I mean, he sort of came and went in there, wreaking havoc with my internal organs. Head, heart, *and* reproductive parts. I was in a wolfish, Maverick-induced funk, and I did not feel like de-funking. I fully intended to wallow for just a little longer. Possibly, forever.

"Tell me what's up, or I'm taking the waist in. I'll give you a twenty-four-inch waist. You'll have to wear a Victorian corset."

Mabel would do it too.

"Okay. Fine, fine. You win." I needed a brownie for courage. Or that box of See's chocolates that I'd stashed in my trailer. "I met—"

"A guy," she finished. "It's always a guy. Or a gal. Sometimes a couple of them for you energetic types. Tell me all about it."

So, I did. It was better than confessing to a priest in a confessional. I summarized. And then I elaborated a bit. There might have been some blow-by-blow recounting of our disastrous date night (although I omitted the wolfish and the magical bits). While telling her mostly all about it, I realized that Maverick and I had had shockingly little on-screen time together. We certainly hadn't spent enough time together to explain the emotions I felt.

"So, he broke up with you after he discovered you were a worldwide celebrity and a big deal? Do you think he was scared off by your accomplishments, or was it because you kicked everything off with a lie?" Mabel's observations were as sharp as her sewing scissors.

"It wasn't exactly a lie?"

Mabel snorted. "Girl, he called you Suzette for more than a week."

Okay. I had lied. That wasn't okay, and Maverick was right to be upset by it. But there was no walking back what I'd done now, and I tried to own it. "I don't think it was the wrong-name thing. I think it was being the center of all that attention. He got a glimpse of what life would be like if he dated me for real, and it scared his cute beard off, and he's not wrong. He wouldn't be able to go buy tampons and toilet paper at the Piggly Wiggly without it being front-page news somewhere, and he wasn't choosing that life. I wasn't worth that kind of effort. The end."

Mabel pursed her lips, staring off into space like all the answers were hanging around in the air above our heads, and she could just reach up and pluck out a good one. "Nah. That's not it."

"Then what?"

"Maybe he's a dickhead. Maybe he can't handle his woman making more money than him and being more successful in the eyes of some people. He'd have to be stupid to conclude that you're not worth making an effort, and he doesn't sound like he's stupid at all."

I stomped around the trailer, collecting my clothes. She was right, though. Maverick was not stupid, not one little bit.

"Ask him," she suggested.

"What?"

"Ask him why he rejected you. You're good with words. Find out what went wrong."

My brain not-helpfully staged a little scene where I asked Maverick what was wrong with me, and he explained. In detail. Then I moved the scene to Jennie

Dean's coffee shop and winced. No, thank you. I did not need to add public humiliation to my life.

Plus, it would just end up on the internet, and then I'd have global, worldwide humiliation, just for funsies.

"He's not interested in me anymore."

"You deserve to know the full reason why he's passing on your awesomeness. You deserve that respect from him. Plus, you sure are interested in him." Mabel held up her hand when I attempted to interrupt. "It's written all over your face."

She was right. I had so much interest. I had cornered the global market on Maverick interest.

"It hurts," I confessed. *¡Cágate!* Were those *tears*? I only angry cried. I didn't vulnerable cry. Not anymore.

"Oh, girl." Mabel threw her arms around me and squeezed. Somehow, in the last five minutes, we'd hurtled past the friendly-colleagues stage in our relationship and now we were friends. There *was* a silver lining, I guessed, to the Maverick cloud. "You were falling in love with him. You were starting to have feelings."

I leaned my head against her shoulder. "It was too soon for a broken heart. We hadn't had a chance to get to know each other below the surface. We were still at the outer layers, the cuticles of our mushroom feelings. We hadn't got past that mushroom skin and down to the fruit body."

Mabel shook her head. "I have no idea what you just said. But one thing's perfectly clear. You like him. Present tense, not past."

"I like his outsides," I argued. "I like the idea of him, of having someone to lean on who is actually capable of taking care of me rather than vice versa." There had been a whole lot of vice versa in my previous relationships with my Hollywood harem. "I'd heard good things about how he'd overcome his bad part, and he was such a grown-up, so strong and steady. He did what he said he was going to do. And he's hot." This last bit was not the most important item in my Maverick list, but it made Mabel grin. I mean, who didn't enjoy some thoughtful, well-made wrapping paper on her birthday gift?

"Strong and steady, huh?" She winked at me. "Does he have any older brothers?"

"Five younger ones. I'll introduce you."

She snickered. "Okay. So, your guy is a college professor. He's gorgeous and stable and he doesn't care about your fame."

"He does care. That's why he broke up with me."

That, and possibly my magic.

"You don't know that." She stepped away and started rummaging through the racks of clothing. "You can't be sure that your celebrity is a dealbreaker UNTIL YOU HAVE AN ACTUAL CONVERSATION WITH HIM. He sounds perfect, and he's burrowed through your mushroom skin and now he's in you." We both thought about that for a second. It was not a successful metaphor. At all. "Whatever. Go ask him, using actual words, what happened."

"I've never felt like that before."

She started pulling garments off the rack. "And you're worried that you'll never feel like that again."

I nodded.

"Okay, girl. I get that. But it's like when you go on vacation to a new place, right? How can anywhere else ever measure up? I went to the Maldives, and it was *magical*. White-sand beaches, blue water, all those fish. But there are other amazing beaches out there. I promise you that. You're talented, and you're amazing too. Anyone would find you magical."

She had no idea.

"So, I'm an amazing beach vacation?"

"Yeah." She snorted. "And this professor of yours, if he's half as smart as you say, will build himself a cabana on your beach, and the two of you will get busy in it. And if he's *actually* stupid, then you'll invite some else to share the beach with you."

"It's so much work meeting people," I groaned. "Simone Biles used a dating app, but she's fearless. She does somersaults on a two-inch piece of wood in a leotard."

"It's okay to want to be in a relationship. It's not okay to accept just any old relationship because of that want." She handed me a stack of clothes. "Take these. Wear some of that sparkly eyeshadow you love. Armor up! And maybe it's not just any old relationship you want. Maybe it's just your Professor Maverick."

* * *

It was wet when I woke up the next morning. The weather app on my phone promised more rain, plus fog. Our set was gray and gloomy like my mood. Where was Elena with her weather magic when you needed her?

I'd spent the night on set, shooting scenes until well after midnight only to collapse onto the bed in my trailer. I often catnapped or wrote on it, but it was not great for overnights as the trailer got cold. I needed coffee to lubricate my joints—and my brain—but I was out of pods for my Keurig.

Opening the door to my trailer, I peered out, finding Eric leaning against the side. He was wide awake and cradling a cup of hot coffee in one hand.

His other hand held a giant, gooey cinnamon roll.

My stomach growled. There was breakfast! He had a secret coffee source and had been holding out on me! I needed to get me some of that.

"Hey, Eric the Viking."

He tipped his head at me, grinning. "If it's not my fair Viking maiden."

"Where'd you get the bounty?"

"Your guy brought it. The professor."

The air whooshed out of my lungs like a sad, defective whoopee cushion. I ignored it. Who needed oxygen?

"Maverick?" Look at me, naming the elephant in the room. It felt weird, like I was working one of those spells where you visualized the person you were at odds with and then started fixing your broken shit in the spiritual realm.

Of course, after you'd done the astral work, you were supposed to go and talk to the person.

Kind of like Mabel had suggested.

Ugh. Good advice sucked.

"Yeah. He came by with his brother."

"Ranger?"

"They're good people." Eric happily inhaled his coffee. I, on the other hand, was coffee-less. And unhappy. Was Maverick still on set somewhere? Was he just the Santa Claus of coffee? Had he dropped off coffee at midnight and then magically vanished? I wasn't ready to see him. I needed to practice my lines, maybe dress up in some of the awesome outfits Mabel had loaned me.

"Why were they, uh, here? Maverick and Ranger?"

"They were on set last night and saw how late we were working, so they brought coffee this morning."

I straightened up. What? I hadn't noticed Maverick being on set. I wished I had. Partly because he was so big and sexy, and partly because I wanted to show off for him. I could admit that to myself. I was damned good at what I did, so there. Did he think about me? Did he imagine me playing sexy love scenes?

"They do the animal stuff," Eric continued. "Bat relocations, spider rehoming, bears. Birds, raccoons, a whole mess of four-legged stuff. Ranger runs that animal services company that we contracted with. He's here every day. You didn't notice?"

"No." My heart thudded foolishly. Had Maverick noticed me? Was I just oblivious? "Ranger's here all the time? Is Maverick?"

Was I freaking out over nothing?

"Sure," Eric said. "He's our snake expert, yeah?"

"We have snakes?" My voice squeaked.

"You bet. It's baby snake season, so he's on the look out for that."

"Baby snakes?" Maybe I could deal with small snakes. I didn't have to hold them on camera or anything after all.

"Yep. Copperhead season. Momma snake can have twenty-one babies." These words, delivered from somewhere behind me, made my heart bang and my spine stiffen. What the heck? Who discussed copperheads before coffee?

Did we really need venomous snakes on set?

I turned around, finding Maverick and Ranger standing a few feet away. Ranger held a basket of colorful socks, and Maverick carried two cups of what I guessed was coffee. One was a paper to-go cup, and the other was my kraken mug.

As it had been two weeks since I'd seen or talked to Maverick, I excused myself for eating him up with my eyes. He was in a flannel shirt, of course. He wore it open over a T-shirt that read *Stay positive—be like a proton!* There was a muscle competition going on underneath his clothing, his flannel and his T-shirt competing to see which could stretch the most. The green cotton brought out the green in his hazel eyes, and his beard was as thick and attractive as ever. He was like a pin-up poster for a sexy biologist lumberjack.

He didn't seem bothered by my inspection, standing there with legs braced and booted feet planted on the damp, wet ground. Rain probably rolled off him. When I lifted my eyes, his green-and-gold gaze locked with mine. He was still smiling amiably, but there was something different about him. He seemed more wolfish and predatory, less friendly and laidback. He looked hungry, and I liked it.

"Sonnet," he said, tipping his head at me.

"Hi." Did he feel it too? Had he missed this crackling sense of connection? Yes, yes, I thought he had. He was hyperfocused on me, his eyes narrowing as he looked at me.

Look away, Professor Maverick. See what you've been missing out on.

"You have delivered some mighty impressive scenes this week, Ms. Ruiz." Ranger strolled over and handed me the basket of socks. I'd been the recipient of roses, bath products, and homemade banana bread (from the fans who paid attention to my likes and dislikes), but socks were a first. "These are for you. Maverick thought you might be wet."

"We thought you might need dry socks," Maverick corrected hastily. He shot his brother a look.

"He's been thinking about ways you might get wet."

Wisely, Maverick ignored Ranger. "We were planning on dropping these off with Eric," he said, as if he felt the need to explain or excuse away his unexpected appearance at my workplace. "Didn't intend to mess up your schedule or get in your way."

"Well now, I thought you wanted to get in her. You sure did two weeks ago." Ranger beamed at me, then at Maverick. Eric snort-laughed, while I felt my face turn scarlet.

Maverick frowned, his eyes shooting murderous laser beams of you-shut-up-now at his brother. "We're leaving," he said, his voice hard. He raised the hand holding my kraken mug and said, voice softening, "You just tell me where to put this."

"Inside is good," I said, on autopilot.

He hesitated, not moving from his spot. You'd have thought his work boots had put down roots of their own.

I frowned. Was I contagious? That awful that he couldn't risk coming any closer? Would I need to walk around holding a giant Hula-Hoop around my middle to stop myself from inadvertently crossing his borders?

But then Ranger clapped a hand on Maverick's flannel-covered shoulder and gave him a friendly shove. "You heard the lady. She's holding the socks, so you be a gentleman and take that coffee inside for her." Then he turned to me and offered, "You go on in there and make sure he puts that coffee exactly where you want it."

Ranger jogged over, pushed the trailer door open, and scooted me inside. I had no idea how he'd accomplished it, but two seconds later, Maverick was deposited inside. He looked around the trailer, his gaze skipping over the signs of my insomnia and internal chaos (which was to say: my trailer was in desperate need of tidying). He should be setting down the cup and leaving, but he didn't.

He focused on me.

FIFTEEN

SONNET

"'Don't stop there. I suppose there are also, what, vampires and werewolves and zombies?'

'Of course there are. Although you mostly find zombies farther south, where the voudun priests are.'

'What about mummies? Do they only hang around Egypt?'

'Don't be ridiculous. No one believes in mummies.'"

— CASSANDRA CLARE, *CITY OF BONES*

I was unprepared for alone time with my wolf.

To be fair, he seemed equally unprepared.

He'd pivoted toward me as the door closed behind Ranger, but now he seemed turned to stone. Of course, this was my usual reaction too when my mami tried to matchmake. *Dios mío*. I needed to kill Ranger.

This wasn't working.

But it sort of was too. The delicious, pinesy warmth of Maverick filling up my trailer with his big body, his gentle smile, his thoughtful present of coffee, it's as if it had done something to me. My lungs inflated. Oxygen was restored, along with hope.

"Pine terpenes," I blurted out. "That's the source of your delicious fresh pine scent."

"You did such a great job last night," he said at the same time.

We both startled, paused, made the obligatory oh-no-you-go-first gestures. We'd come to a verbal four-way stop sign and were now out-polite-ing each other. So of course, we did it again.

"I'm a man of simple molecules and no fancy flower," he grinned.

"Have you been watching?" I asked.

And then naturally we both laughed. Well, I laughed. He smiled, a big, easy grin, his eyes trailing over me.

"I'm stealing that for my next script." I set the basket of socks down, noticing with delight that there wasn't one matching pair that I could see. I took the kraken cup from him, sliding my fingers over the spot where his had just been. Would it be weird to kiss the side? Huff it? "The random blurt-outs, the awkward staring, the talking over each other? It's comedic gold. You'll turn on your TV someday and DÉJÀ VU."

"I wasn't random." His lips quirked up. "That was all you."

I made a face and took a sip of my delicious coffee. "It's random to accuse me of being random."

"But before that I had a plan. I was very organized."

"Oh, sure." I grinned at him with my eyes over the rim of my cup. "Such a great plan. Were you flying by the seat of your pants? Was this plan newly hatched? A chick fresh out of its shell?"

Now he did laugh. "I'm a baby chicken?"

We were teasing, bantering with that easy back-and-forth that we'd had the day we first met, so of course I ad-libbed. Rather than thinking the scene out, I just spoke from the heart. "Babies are amazing. I dreamed about our babies. Roly-poly, magical fur littles."

This was what we, in the industry, called a record-scratch moment. The background music came to an abrupt halt.

Help.

I'd made things weird again. It had to be a world record in weird making. Less than thirty seconds! It was less playful and exponentially more awkward, likely because now we were both thinking about the bedroom activities baby making required.

I made a face, irritated. I needed a do-over, and I could see Maverick felt the same way.

"Maverick—" I started.

"I—" he ground out.

The door to my trailer flew open. Luke stuck his head in. The large blue plume on top of his head bobbed.

"Rimita! I need your help! Look at what they've put me in for today's shot!"

The rest of Luke's body inserted itself into my trailer. Maverick made a rough sound, his big body tensing. Oblivious, Luke twirled in a circle. I was sure Mabel had extensively researched his Civil War uniform, so it would be historically accurate.

It was, nevertheless, ridiculous.

He was ridiculous.

He wore a pair of shapeless, navy blue pants that looked like United States Post Service rejects, with a tight, lighter blue jacket that curtailed his movement and made him walk like he had a stick up you-know-where. The jacket had shiny bronze buttons; when Luke moved, they caught the light. He was a Civil War disco ball!

The moral of the story was: never, ever piss off the woman in charge of wardrobe. Mabel had had her revenge.

Sidenote side note: ask Mabel for an extra button.

"Wow," I said, trying to keep a straight face. Mabel had single-handedly demoted him to comic side bit. It was awesome. "You look great, Luke?"

He hesitated, torn between preening and outrage over his costume.

Vanity won.

"I've lost twelve ounces! You need to use the app, Rimita! It's made such a difference for me."

Es la leche. Awesome. Can I please have my sexy moment back?

"Come out to dinner with me tonight. I'll help you download it," he continued.

"She can't," Maverick rumbled grumpily. "She's having dinner at my house."

Oh. "I am," I agreed quickly. "So sorry, Luke. You'll have to mansplain the app store to me some other time."

Oblivious to the irony, Luke nodded and pranced away, probably to take selfies for his Instagram. Mabel was a genius.

A Grand Canyon–sized scowl painted Maverick's face. He was unhappy and clearly frustrated. I started to say something, but he interrupted.

"I need to go," he growled, tearing his eyes away. "I need to . . . I have things."

Was that it? Was our "dinner" together just a social lie he'd told to rescue me? I wrapped a hand around his forearm, not sure what my next line should be. It would come to me. I'd make something up. I was pretty certain I was about to blurt out my grocery list. Random lines of poetry. Embarrass myself, in other words. Make him laugh.

I would survive.

Because I made people laugh all the time. It was literally my job, and I was amazing at it.

"Don't go. Hold up a second. *Espera un segundo.*" I tightened my grip on his arm to death grip level force, but he wasn't trying to get away. He did, however, glare at my hand. Why, it might shrivel up and die from all that irritation. "I need to talk to you. I have some things I need to say."

"Like what?" His eyes were amber, his voice rough. I didn't recognize this big, irritated stranger standing in my trailer, and it had me feeling awkward and off-balance.

"I miss you," I blurted out. This was awful. What was the advantage to honesty? I stared at his ear—he had a freckle there—and gave it my speech. "I like you. You're a nice guy. You mean what you say and do what you mean. You'd be surprised at how many people just say stuff they have no intention of ever following up on. But I think I can count on you. And . . ." Going all in, I sucked in a breath and added in a rush, "And I know you said you just want to be friends and I value your friendship. But I'm lonely, but not when you're here. With me. I want more of us, driving together in the mornings, and then back home at night, but whatever. I want to tell you secrets, like about how I've got magic, and sometimes it's great and sometimes it's a pain in the ass. I should have let you in on some stuff about the glamour. But I don't know if you still want to know those things. Or any things. You can think of me as your friendly neighborhood relationship panhandler, standing by the freeway entrance with a sign that reads, *Need help—spare change?* Which means I'll take whatever you can spare me."

What I didn't mention was that I'd never felt like this before. I didn't beg people for more—or for anything, for that matter. Vulnerable was a terrible quality. Ten out of ten did not recommend. This was not a joke.

Maverick's ear said nothing. To be fair, neither did the rest of Maverick. He was silent, clearly processing what I'd just dropped on him. To be fair, it was a lot. I was asking him to take a chance on a girl he'd only just met. A *magical* girl.

SUCK IT UP!!! Pull up your big girl britches, Sonnet!

But then he surprised me by stepping forward, closing the distance between us, and sliding one big hand into my hair. His other skimmed my cheek. His palms were warm, so warm, and I turned my face into them. I was cold, he was not, and so here we were.

"Sonnet." He said my name, low and rough and so, so needy.

Maybe it was time to lose those big girl panties? Somehow, it felt okay to be less than perfect with this man. To be a little out of control.

Plus, if he kept looking at me that way, and speaking in that low, knee-trembling growl, my big girl panties would disintegrate, anyhow.

His hands tightened. Yes. *Do it,* I urged him. *Kiss me, touch me. Love me back some. It'll be enough. Probably.*

Maybe.

Something shifted in his gaze. He didn't rush, though, in-control predator that he was. He pulled me close, deliberate and slow, his gaze holding mine until he was so close that I couldn't see anything, anyone, not anymore.

"Sonnet," he whispered. "Will you—"

I sure will. I held my breath. *Whatever it is, yes.*

Was he going to propose? Were we going to have sex up against the wall of my trailer? Which was the crazier of the two?

I'd take him however I could have him.

Maverick bent his head, brushing his lips over mine. My mouth chased his, the waves on his beach, straining up to reach him. One kiss, two, a third against the corner of my mouth. He made it so good. He was my reward for being vulnerable.

When he kissed me again, we were too hungry for games. His mouth coaxed and promised, teased and devoured.

I clutched him through his flannel shirt, my fingers digging into his T-shirt, trying to get closer. The fierceness of his kiss surprised me, as did my panting response.

He turned us in a lazy, slow embrace and pressed me up against the wall. Yes! Fantasy level unlocked in the game of love! One strong, denim-covered thigh pressed between mine.

"I sure will," I gasped into his mouth.

I slid my hands down, then back up again, getting my hands beneath his clothes, desperate for his warm, muscled back. He was so wonderful.

And then his delicious mouth lifted, his hands cupping my face, holding me still so he could look at me. There was no more awesome kidding.

"I missed you too," he whispered roughly. "I did."

His gravelly, rough voice stirred me up inside, sending shivery warmth dancing through my body. He looked like a wolf, sharp-eyed, fierce, predatory. And yet he was also all Maverick. *My* Maverick.

He missed me! He's all mine! Happy dance! Happy, happy dance!

"I would love to pick you up in the mornings and take you to work." His hands slid out of my hair. He stepped away. He put a mile between us. And then another.

I nodded dumbly. He'd kissed the words right out of me. Even so, I was beaming hopefully.

He nodded, saying, "We'll be there on Monday."

And then he turned on his booted foot and left.

I . . . He . . . What?

We'll be there on Monday.

WE.

Who in the world was WE?

CHAPTER
SIXTEEN

"Isn't it enough to see that a garden is beautiful without having to believe that there are fairies at the bottom of it too?"

— DOUGLAS ADAMS

"You have let me down, Sonnet."

I looked up from the script I was reading and found Ranger Boone standing in front of me, holding a cannoli in each hand. We were in the craft services tent, which was mostly empty. Luke had flown back to LA last night for auditions. I'd taken advantage of his absence to get out of my trailer.

"Why would I be a disappointment to you?" I took a moment to lament the fact that my magical repertoire did not include a hex spell. Ranger Boone was a pain in my rear end.

He dropped down into the empty chair next to me, and I held out my hand. If I had to deal with his disappointment, he could share his fried pastry dough.

"I'm not in a sharing kind of mood." He held them away and took a bite from the strawberry one.

Now we were both disappointed. Dropping my hand, I watched him chew as he regarded me defiantly.

Maverick, being a man of his word, had picked me up this morning. It turned out that his ominous *we* had included Ranger. Were they some kind of weird hydra-headed twins? Rice grains in a sushi roll? Regardless of the reason they were stuck together, it had been Maverick, Ranger, and I riding in Maverick's truck.

Ranger had been pointedly morose and sullen for the entire drive. Worse, Maverick had switched back to being politely friendly rather than lustily friendly. Let me tell you, it was disappointing to be looking forward to some sexy heart palpitations and conversational exchange and instead get an angry Boone brother and a chaste Boone brother.

"I gave you every opportunity," Ranger accused. "Who the Sam Hill wouldn't have exploited the situation?"

"*Dios mío!* Why can't you speak clearly? You can't give me shit for not under-standing you!"

"On Friday? With the special sock delivery and the coffee? That was no accident. I arranged for it to happen." He waved his cannoli in the air.

"You are so strange." I got up and grabbed a plate of cannoli. He did not get to eat pastry in front of me. I did not offer him any.

He took a bite out of his cannoli.

"Yes. Yes, I am. But you dropped the ball. I passed and you fumbled. If we're going to get you and Maverick together, I need you to be my first string. I threw my brother at you, and you let me down."

"You were throwing Maverick at me?"

"Of course I was." He sighed dramatically and rolled his eyes. I had worked with less talented actors. "Do you want me to help you win my brother, or not?"

"Yes, absolutely, yes, please," I said quickly. "Please give me all the help."

"We need to coordinate." Ranger shoved the rest of his cannoli into his mouth.

"Awesome. You bet. Synchronized striking."

He thought for a moment. "You are officially invited to family dinner next week."

"Okay." Seducing Maverick in a room full of his brothers seemed like it would require more than mere synchronized striking, but what did I know? I was taking advice from the weirdest Boone of them all.

My phone buzzed as said Boone chewed on his cannoli. I glanced down, saw it was Elena, and sent it to voicemail.

Elena promptly called back, winning me a flinty glare from Ranger.

"You should pick up." He pointed his cannoli at my phone. "You pick that up, and I'll ponder while I finish my dessert."

Alrighty then.

I picked up.

It was probably nothing.

Or ten more things I needed to have finished yesterday.

Or feedback from the studio on my *Wolf Girl* pages?

I greeted my sister, reminding myself that I was a successful, professional, and semi-articulate adult. It would be fine news.

"What's up?"

"Where are you?"

"Craft services. On set. Why?"

"Can you go somewhere private?"

My stomach dropped. I thought of all the ways things could have gone wrong. I'd been fired. My pages were crap. The water main had broken in my Hollywood place, and there was raw sewage flowing through my living room, and the paparazzi had leapt to unfortunate conclusions about my bathroom habits. Whenever Elena had bad news and I was on set, she wouldn't tell me until I was alone.

Don't catastrophize.

"Is there a problem at home? Are Mami and Papi okay?" I'd just texted them yesterday.

"The family's fine; it isn't personal. Just go to your trailer and call me back as soon as you can."

She hung up on me. *Maldito.*

"What's wrong?" Ranger asked around a mouthful of sweet cream.

"No clue." Would a quick Google search of my name be helpful or not? Probably not. It was better *not* to know everything that was said about me. "My sister won't tell me until I'm alone."

"Excuse me?"

"She worries." I gathered up my script pages and closed my laptop. "This is her modus operandi. She's sure I'll lose my shit if she tells me something I don't want to hear, and then I'll make a scene, and there will be pictures or video online, and she'll have to do damage control."

"And do you?"

"Lose my shit?" I shrugged. "Not really? I mean, not more than most people. The last time I screamed in public there was a rat the size of a terrier running across my feet. I believe I was justified."

"Hmmm." Ranger studied me, then pushed a business card at me as he stood up. It was for All-Purpose Animal Services. "We can help with the rats. You're going to your trailer?"

Shoveling my crap into my bag, I nodded and stepped to the side as he pushed in my chair. "Yeah. Now I need to know, but she won't tell me until I'm out of sight."

"Excellent. That's excellent." He gave me a brisk nod, then jogged out of the tent.

Ranger Boone was an odd bird.

Since I didn't have time to contemplate all the ways in which he was (delightfully) odd, I darted back to my trailer. Eric fell in behind me from wherever he'd been protectively lurking and followed me. He also opened the door to my trailer and checked it quickly before he let me go in. The caution was appreciated, but my curiosity was killing me. I dumped everything on the bed and called Elena.

"Okay," I said, once I had her on the phone. "Tell me. I'm alone."

She sucked in a breath. Oh, God. This was going to be bad. "The studio doesn't think you're right to play the part of Wolf Girl. But they still want you to write the script."

What?

Ummm, EXCUSE ME?

I was literally writing it. It was my book baby and I had brought it into the world. No one knew the character of Wolf Girl better than me.

"Why not?"

Elena hesitated. "The studio's director pick thinks you're too curvy."

UGH. "He wants a skinny lead."

"No," Elena said firmly. "Well, yes. But all because you're Latina. He's worried it would be typecasting."

I reminded myself that screaming was unprofessional. Also, it would make Eric come smashing through my trailer door.

"Are you saying he doesn't want to cast me in a role about a curvy woman who discovers she has supernatural superpowers because he thinks only Latina women are hot, curvy bombshells?"

Elena snorted. "No. He knows the curvy Latina thing is a stereotype. But *because* it's a stereotype, he's getting pushback."

"That's stupid. It's entirely illogical. A brilliant, funny, curvy Latina woman not only wrote the best-selling book that the film will be based on, but she's adapting the screenplay. I have curves." I might have stomped around my trailer dramatically. "I am also more than *just* those curves. This whole thing is the perfect setup to illustrate how limiting thinking in stereotypes is."

I paced up and down my trailer. I did not kick anything. Or huff. I was a professional but this was just so wrong. When would I ever be enough exactly as I was?

"So," I continued, "the studio is worried that a television audience will get upset about a Latina woman playing a major lead role because the character is a curvy woman, never mind that I'm a talented actress. Are they also worried that I'm going to pop out babies as a sexy werewolf bombshell and have an enormous pack of wolf pups? And speak with a thick accent? Those are outdated stereotypes, Elena. This is ridiculous. The studio is taking away my chance to show that movies need and thrive with more diverse lead heroines. I was trying to give women like us a platform and a voice and now? *Nada.*"

Latina women could be anything. We were more than our Spanish last names, our appearance, or our uteruses. We were not all loud, crazy, and spicy. What I wanted, more than anything, was to make sure the characters in my scripts all had speaking parts. My women—Latina and not—spoke out. Sometimes, they even had a lot to say and did it loudly.

If I'd been a white actress, would this have been an issue? Would the director have worried that my curviness sent the wrong message about the Caucasian race? There were stereotypes about fat white women too.

This sucked.

"*Hermanita,* this isn't fair. Nothing about this industry is fair. But the good news is that they loved the last script you wrote, and they're impressed with the pages you sent for *Wolf Girl*. You'll still be involved."

I'd be involved on their terms, not mine. I'd have something, but not everything.

I curled up on the bed. What could I say?

Nothing, that's what.

Absolutely nothing.

"Sonnet? Are you there?"

"Yes."

"There will be other movie roles. We'll land you something better." She hesitated, then asked, "And you'll keep sending pages? For *Wolf Girl*?"

"Really? That's what you want me to do? Write it and let them take it over and push me out?"

"Sonnet," she said sternly. "You keep on sending those pages. Do not stop. We can spin this into something. You have *options*."

"I've got to go."

"Sonnet, listen to me—"

Nope. I was not listening to someone who was more concerned with getting her script than with how I felt about losing my part.

I hung up, turned off my phone, and wondered how long it would take me to drive to an international airport.

I had my passport. I could go somewhere else, somewhere fun. I could take that vacation I'd dreamed about.

And that was the weird thing. I wasn't seething about being called fat or losing a part because of the way I looked. Yes, I was mad. I wasn't going to be Wolf Girl because of my ethnicity and my weight. No matter how good of an actress I was, I'd been judged on my outsides rather than on my actions.

It was profoundly irritating, and yet not shooting the movie actually felt like a relief.

Someone knocked on the trailer door. I ignored it. I also ignored the second and third knocks. The knocks weren't exactly deafening, but they were firm and insistent. They would not take no for an answer.

Well, too bad!

I was not in a polite mood.

The door opened. Eric was going to give me grief for not having locked it.

"Sonnet?"

I covered my face with a cute throw pillow. Because of course my determined knocker was Maverick. I didn't need him to see me when I wasn't at my best.

He shut the door behind him and crossed to where I was burrowing into the bed. I'd thought I was okay with opening up and being vulnerable around him, but I'd been super wrong. I was dealing with a career setback and racial injustice. I was busy.

His weight settled on the bed next to me. "Hey," he said. "Are you okay?"

No.

I was not.

I was angry, I was frustrated, and I was way too close to crying.

It took a few minutes for me to get the words out, but I managed to lie eventually. "I'm fine."

Maverick settled in. His leg pressed against my hip. He was warm and nice, but I still would have preferred to have my angry cry alone.

I peered up at him, careful not to blink. That was the key to not actually crying. He was staring carefully down at me, his eyes warm and concerned. His handsomeness was almost overwhelming this close. Why was he even here?

Was he here to deliver more bad news? This was, after all, the trailer of bad news, the preeminent bad news delivery site.

So I asked, "Why are you here?"

"Ranger said you were getting bad news."

"And?"

His brow furrowed; he clearly was confused by my question. "And I was concerned about you."

His hot-and-then-cold-and-then-hot-again attitude was worse than a shower with a small hot water tank. He did not get to come here and confuse me with this niceness and sweet concern.

"So your intentions are friendly?" Shoot. I'd narrowed my eyes. The tears started trickling. I swiped them away angrily. Nothing was going right for me, not even my lacrimal glands.

Was he expressing friendly concern for an acquaintance? Like: oh, I'm so sorry some asshole rear-ended your new truck! Or: wow, it sucks that you have carpenter ants in your bathroom! I can recommend a good animal services company!

He'd kissed me like I mattered.

Then he'd walked away.

Then he'd picked me up this morning *with his brother in the backseat of the truck* —and that was not some unexpected (and unwelcome) kink.

So, no, I didn't understand why he would be concerned.

I was confused and hurt.

Should I ask him if the kissing had been a one-off, an aberration? Did he have plans to do more kissing, or were the plans only in Ranger's devious head?

While I debated these important questions, Maverick pulled his phone out of his pocket and tapped decisively at the screen. Perhaps he was launching nuclear bombs or checking on his home security system. Perhaps his house had been invaded by killer honeybees, or the raccoons were holding a dance party in his trash cans.

Whatever. I was out of fucks to give.

Unexpectedly, music played from his phone. Dramatic, soaring, very loud . . . it was opera music? I found a single, sad, solitary fuck to give.

"Why are we listening to music, and what song is that?"

Maverick's warm gaze moved over me, and he smiled. God, he had a beautiful smile. "'I Love You, Olga.'"

"You need to keep your ladies straight," I joked weakly.

I ignored my heart's pathetic little jump. It had really, really liked the first three words, alright.

The music was sweeping and happy. A tenor warbled away in a foreign language. I sighed. The singer sure seemed to have a whole lot of feelings, and he wasn't afraid to share them. Sooooo unlike my professor, who was all about hot smiles and not about words. His smile was absolutely not warm or tender.

It was not, not, not.

I would not be tricked into having any more feelings for him. Damn his beautiful music! I would not be influenced!

"It's Russian," he added, as the music swirled romantically around us.

"Oh, right," I said. Perhaps he moonlighted as a spy. Or worked for the KGB. Was that still a thing? I read paranormal romance, not the *New York Times*. Only one of those guaranteed a happy ending.

Then he held out his hand. "Dance with me?"

Ummm. What?

"Why?"

Apparently, that meant, *Yes! I enthusiastically agree!* (I had no idea how to say that in Russian, but possibly it sounded similar?) because Maverick pulled me to my feet and slid his arm around my waist. This wasn't bad, so I didn't complain.

It got even better when he tucked my body against his bigger one, one strong arm banding around my waist, while the other reached for my hand. Our bodies were flush together like pine planks on a porch or two ears of corn on a stalk. His body warmed mine with intoxicating heat, his familiar scent invading my nose. He enthralled me and soothed me at the same time.

There were hard calluses on his palms, rough spots on his hands from working hard. The friction felt delicious against the smoother skin of mine. He was so different, but it was a good different. We somehow fit together and found a rhythm that worked for both of us. So what if his hand was so big that it enveloped my smaller one? He didn't swallow me up—he wrapped me up and I felt comforted and safe.

He tethered me to him, and I loved it.

I loved him, damn it.

"Why?" I asked.

He threaded his fingers through mine and thought about it as he twirled us in slow circles to the gorgeous music. He was a great dancer. Had he taken dance lessons as a small boy? And how could he fit an entire dance number inside my small trailer?

Finally, Maverick bent his head, his lips brushing my ear. His beard tickled the bare skin of my neck. "We're dancing because you need me to hold you, but you won't ask."

HOLDING. HANDS.

We were HOLDING HANDS.

My brain yelled this out at random moments because this was an exciting and confusing plot twist I hadn't seen coming. What were we doing?

We danced around my trailer, "I Love You, Olga" on a loop, and I hung on to Maverick because I was not ready at all to let this moment go.

* * *

Sharing my bad news with Maverick did not actually make me feel instantly better. Losing the part of Wolf Girl still sucked. It was still unfair. It was still a blow for diversity in the TV industry. After we danced and I shared my bad, bad news, Maverick suggested we go for a walk in the woods. Trees were like comfort food for me, so trees plus Maverick was a five-course meal for starving me.

It turned out that he had a truckful of opossums his brothers had rescued, so we hiked into the woods on a mission. He carried the cage with the opossums in one hand, his other holding mine. We were surrounded by northern red oaks, cucumber trees, basswoods . . . so many awesome tree names. The woods were my happy place, and this one was old and beautiful. The fall colors were at their peak, all the leaves yellow and orange, red and vivid green.

He'd listened carefully to my recounting, concerned and angry on my behalf.

He was Team Sonnet. He made it clear, too, that he would have been even without the dancing and the hand-holding. What had happened was wrong, and it made him mad. He was just madder because it had happened to *me*.

When we reached a big stream, we stopped by the tree-lined bank. It was impossible not to feel better. The water rushed over the mossy rocks, chattering and singing. Maverick set the cage down, and then we let the opossums out. They were cute as heck with their little white bandit faces and black eyes.

Momma opossum waddled out of the cage carrying her little ones on her back like a bunch of furry commuters packed in a train car. She sniffed the air once and then promptly disappeared into the underbrush.

Mission accomplished.

Now here we were, sitting on a rock in the middle of the stream, our hips touching, his arm around me as we silently tossed bits of sticks into the rushing water. I was talked out, and it felt good to just sit. I snapped a few pictures for my Instagram but didn't even check to see if I had enough signal to post.

Maverick broke our easy silence. "My momma had some good advice. She used to remind me that you should never fry bacon nekkid as a jaybird."

Ouch. I snorted and looked over at him.

God, he was good-looking. Strong nose, plush lips, firm jaw. Whisker stubble where he wasn't all thick, lush beard. He was a gorgeous rock of a man.

The bacon-frying advice was spot-on. Hollywood was a kitchen full of flying, boiling-hot pig fat. In this particular case, I'd stepped into the kitchen without thinking, and I hadn't been ready for the splash back.

Sitting here with Maverick helped, though. His big shoulders and muscled arms were a welcome distraction, as were his warm fingers wrapped around mine.

Maverick was well-honed strength and power, the kind of physique that came from hours of hiking and hauling homeless opossums hither and yon. From wielding axes, collecting samples, and climbing trees and mountains.

Okay, so I wasn't *entirely* sure what Maverick did, but clearly he wasn't sitting around in a laboratory all day, and he hadn't acquired his muscles in a gym. He didn't Zumba, CrossFit, or lift. He went out and did things.

Wild, semi-civilized, genuine things.

Unlike my fellow actors who worked out in gyms with personal trainers, he used his body as a tool on a daily basis to do his job. It felt real. *He* felt real. He wasn't worried about how he would look on Instagram.

"Your momma," I said, "was a wise woman. Also, I have to ask. Was this piece of advice based on an actual episode in the Boone family kitchen?"

He laughed. "You've met Ranger, right? But no, it was more of a general observation on life."

That was so funny that I almost slid off our rock, laughing. Maverick anchored me, tucking me more firmly into his side. "Did your momma work in the film and TV business?"

Maverick's smile faded some. "No. Her bacon grease was more of the husbandly, werewolf, biker sort."

He stood up, tugging me gently after him. He waited until my feet were well planted, then started picking a path back to the streambank.

"She sounds like my mami. Mine likes to say things like, '*No puedes ponerle alas a un gato y llamarlo pájaro.*' You can't put wings on a cat and call it a bird. Usually when I'm worrying about not looking like the typical TV actress or my books not being marketable."

Maverick's smile was amused and understanding.

I was so done giving Hollywood and its unfairness room in my head. No vacancy! Find another place! So, I switched the subject and asked, "Did you always want to be a biologist?"

"No," Maverick shook his head, laughing so hard he almost fell into the stream. "I wasn't a school kind of kid growing up. I hated sitting still, following the rules, doing all that homework. I liked to run around outside and poke my nose in places I was forbidden to go. And the faster I could go, the better. I'd picked a raptor when we had to choose our favorite animal in school because they were strong and mean and went for what they wanted. Also, I wanted a dinosaur uncle or daddy." He paused for a moment. "Mostly though, I wanted to be an Iron Wolf. I wanted my own cut, to run with them, and then to lead them some day in the not-too-distant future."

Wyatt had told me this, but I got the sense that Maverick needed to let it out, to share this part of himself with me. And I had to admit, I wanted to hear the story in his words, directly from him. We'd spent too much time listening to what other people said about us, and not enough time talking face-to-face.

"Wyatt shared some things with me, but I'd love you to tell me."

I wanted to hear all his stories.

He stopped walking and let go of my hand. Folding his arms over his chest he stared out at the mountain around us. "It was a biker club, although, yeah, all the patch-wearing members were wolf shifters. I wanted to be their president, the alpha wolf." Then, quieter, he added, "It would have made my daddy proud, and running with them was all I ever wanted back then."

Maverick turned so we were face-to-face. His big shoulders blocked out the first streaks of pink sunset in the sky.

My heart beat harder.

He looked so serious.

"Evan always did the right thing. He always gave everything one hundred percent —didn't half-ass, didn't hold back. He was the good guy, the right kind of friend. I wasn't. I'd get into trouble, and so he'd come and pull my ass out of the fire. He was my own personal preacher, giving me a hand up and an earful about reforming at the same time." Maverick chuckled, remembering some long-ago scene, and shook his head. "He always saw the potential in me and didn't give me up as a lost cause, even when others did."

I could not imagine Maverick as a villain.

He was my hero.

I squeezed his hand, letting him know that I was also on his side, how I saw him right now, how he'd rescued me from my unhappy headspace.

"He was such a part of my life, and then he died. He joined the Marines. I joked that I should have been a big enough rescue job for him, but no, he had to expand his efforts to the whole world. He died on his first overseas tour. He'd always wanted to be a biologist and a teacher."

His stare became distant.

"So, you did it for him? You went to graduate school to follow his dream?"

Maverick looked at me. My easygoing, friendly man had vanished. He was a withdrawn, snarly wolf.

"I stepped up." He nodded once. "I should have been the one to die, not Evan."

"That's not true. There's no way Evan would have wanted you thinking that."

I had never met Evan, but I was certain it was true.

Good friends only wanted the best for us.

They loved us even when we were hardest to love.

And while they might push us to be better or to do more, they also held us when we needed it most.

Evan had been the best of friends.

"I was an ass. Disrespectful of my momma, rude, cocky, sure I was always right. I stole cars. I didn't hesitate to lash out—with my fists, my wolf, and my words. I once tried to make my sister the old lady of the vice president of the Iron Wolves." Maverick's lip curled. He did not like past Maverick, and I had to wonder if he liked himself now. Or was he still trying to atone? "My daddy proposed it like there could be nothing better than telling a fifteen-year-old girl that she was the property of a thirty-year-old wolf. I didn't tell him no. I did nothing to stop it. I was that sure of my daddy. Fortunately, my brother Knox stepped in and protected her. My daddy was road captain for the club, and I thought he was a big wolf. Truth was, he was only a big wolf in the eyes of the club. To the rest of the world, he was a shitty, ethic-less felon whether he was human or wolf."

Everything in me wanted to reach out and hold him. These things were awful, wrong, and fucked up. But he'd changed. He'd shown me a man who was the moral opposite of this story. He was no biker now.

"And then Evan died." Maverick's voice deepened, rough with emotion. "And I realized who I loved. It wasn't the Iron Wolves, or being a big man, or giving orders to a pack of wolves. It wasn't even my daddy. It was honor and loyalty, the family I'd chosen, belonging to them. *With* them. Because Evan had given me that chance, to be *with* the people who were important in my life, and I hadn't appreciated it. I'd tossed all that away, abandoned my brothers, for a fast bike and a patch." He frowned fiercely at the trees, remorseful and tortured. "I'd run away as fast as I could from my momma and my sister, treating them like the property the club claimed women were." He shook his head, his face full of self-loathing.

"That's not who you are now," I pointed out, needing to ease the bitterness that twisted his face. "You chose to change. You did the work that it took."

"I didn't change *me*," he said. "I was done with *me*. I became someone new. I asked myself: *what would Evan do?* And then I did that. He didn't get a chance to live the life he deserved, so I've tried to be the person he might have become. Insofar as I can."

I fisted the edges of my shirt. There was so much hurt in his voice. And pain and anger, all directed at himself. "But what about your dreams and hopes? Don't you get to do things for yourself now?"

Maverick shook his head, his smile mocking and tired. "I buried my dreams with Evan. They weren't good dreams. I wanted the wrong things."

I exhaled painfully. "I don't mean wanting to run a gang of werewolf bikers. You chose to make a new life for yourself, so why couldn't you choose some new dreams? Like a New Year's resolution or a life makeover? What do *you* want to do? If you could do anything, what would the first thing be?"

Maverick jammed his fists into his pockets. "Not hurt people."

He looked exhausted, as if he'd spent far too long rebuilding and restarting, and now he simply needed to rest.

There was no deception, no holding back, no glossing over what he'd done or not done. He'd made choices and he owned them. I'd never seen him so vulnerable. I felt like we were looking at each other, seeing pieces of each other that had always been carefully hidden away.

"Awesome! So, we can rule out dark sorcerer and vampire slayer."

I winced because my timing was awful and it wasn't the right time for jokes, but he gave a bark of laughter, the tight lines on either side of his beautiful mouth easing some. "Definitely."

Maybe I *was* enough. Maybe I didn't need to have a different sense of humor, better timing, or more empathy.

Maybe I really was enough for him.

She thought she could, so she did.

I was enough and I was done keeping secrets. I could trust him with all my pieces.

"I'm not a witch," I blurted out before he could say anything. "My sister is, but I'm half Fae, half Chaneque. The Chaneque side of my family, we're forest spirits, big on trees and being outside. We like to play a few tricks, and don't ever ask my aunties and uncles for directions, but it's not mean-spirited. The Fae half, though, is the side I get my glamour from."

"Is it magic?"

"Yes? But not a spells-and-wands kind of magic. It's just an ability that I've had from birth, to make myself seem more likeable. I smooth out my rough edges, the weird bits. I don't exactly look like this, which is something we should talk about. Also, I want to see your wolf."

"Show me?" he asked softly.

And . . . and so I did. I let the glamour go. I raised my hands up in front of my face, swept downward with my palms, dropping my hands past my forehead and my nose, from my chin to my chest. Particles of gold danced in the air like dust in the sunlight, here but not quite here.

The glamour faded and I just was.

I kept my eyes fixed on his face because I needed to know what he thought about my real face, the real me.

"Here I am. This is me."

I'd never shown my face to a lover before. My heart jackhammered against my rib cage, demanding to be let out. My stomach jumped up to meet it.

Maverick stared. "It's nice to meet you, Sonnet."

I knew what he saw. The tip of his finger traced the pointed top of my ear, eliciting a delicious shiver. They were so sensitive, those ears of mine.

"Well?" I nibbled nervously at my bottom lip, which meant he could see my sharper-than-human teeth, my pointy canines, the jagged, wickedly sharp incisors.

My ears were also sharper, rising to those delicate peaks that were so clearly visible through the tangled, curly masses of my hair. Otherwise, I was largely the same: my body just as curvy, my chin just as pointed, my height just as nonexistent. But the veins beneath my sun-kissed, golden skin were the delicate brown-green of lichens on a tree, and my eyes were the violet of pansies.

As he'd done on Friday, Maverick stepped into me, erasing the distance between us. He threaded his fingers through my hair, sending goosebumps racing over my skin. I tipped my head back.

Please kiss me. It was my turn to make him feel better about his life choices, and I took my turn seriously.

Also, my belly and my heart were leading a marching band formation in my body. Hup, two, three, four! Kiss, kiss, kiss!

Also, I just liked this dang man.

Instead of kissing me on my lips, he pressed his lips against my forehead. I exhaled in a confused *whoosh.*

"Maverick—"

"Shush," he said, his mouth against the edge of my hair. "You're beautiful, with or without the glamour. Do you know why?"

I whimper-whined something. I was . . .

I was . . .

"Because of who you are inside," he said roughly. "You don't change, Sonnet. Not who you are. And you are beautiful."

He tipped his head down, pressing our foreheads together, inhaling me. I wrapped my arms around his waist. Why was Maverick so confusing? I wasn't ready to be not-kissing. I wanted to be touching more of him, not less.

I bit back a needy demand. "What are we doing?"

"Finding comfort."

"Oh," I whispered. I smiled up at him. Seeing him from this angle was weird and unexpected and good. "You find comfort in me?"

"I do."

Mission accomplished. I could feel my smile spreading across my face, and I shut my eyes and breathed Maverick in.

What had seemed like silence without words was merely quiet. And now that I was listening, I heard all sorts of sounds that I hadn't paid attention to before. Frogs and crickets had started up. A breeze stirred up the leaves that had started falling from the trees. Something rustled, then scampered off. Maverick's heart beat steady and sure against my chest, and I felt each inhale and exhale beneath the hands I'd clasped behind his back. My own breathing slowed, matching his.

My eagerness to move on, to get going and reach the place I was headed for, faded. This stillness, this moment, being here with him, was comforting. And I didn't need more.

CHAPTER

SEVENTEEN

SONNET

". . . the fae are gracious-*ish* to our guests. Or at least we don't *slaughter* them at *dinner.*"

— C.N. CRAWFORD, *DARK KING*

L*avender for a clearing glow.*

Calm my mind and heart below.

Mint for a touch of riches.

Grant me rest and soothing . . .

I squinted at the handwritten note that had accompanied the herbs Elena had sent. Ditches? Bitches? Pitches?

Her intent was good, I thought, and I wanted to text her right now so we could laugh at my inability to follow the directions of a spell. At the knock on my trailer door, however, I tucked the sleeping herbs underneath my pillow and bellowed, "Come in!"

Mabel entered, balancing a load of garment bags. She'd told me in no uncertain terms, when I'd mentioned tonight's family dinner plan, that I was *not* to pick out my outfit.

We rummaged through the bags she'd brought, and I played dress up. I needed to strike the right note.

225

At first, I settled on a short wrap skirt that crisscrossed over my thighs and a plum-colored sweater. The sweater had a cowl that could be worn over my head like a medieval adventurer. Mabel nodded approvingly when I slipped it on.

"Does this say, 'Rip my clothes off, big guy'?" I asked dubiously. "But also 'I'm a wholesome addition to the family'?"

Mabel grimaced. Ugh. Family dinners were terra incognita. The Hollywood heroes I'd dated had been leading happy bachelor lives; they never invited me to meet their parents or siblings.

Finding comfort.

That's what we're doing.

News flash: there was nothing *comforting* about meeting five new-to-me Boones.

Plus, if I nailed family dinner, then hopefully Maverick and I would move on to lustier activities.

Screw waiting!

I mean, *screwing* was sort of the point.

Sexy screwing, bedroom activities, getting my professor out of his clothes. And screw taking things slow.

Honestly, if we took them any slower, we'd be time traveling backward. I had maybe seven weeks left in Moonlight Valley, and I wanted to spend as much of them naked as possible.

With Maverick.

Doing the aforementioned screwing.

Mabel twirled her finger, and I pirouetted obediently. "We're close. Maybe thigh-high stockings?"

"Oooh. Bringing out the big guns—I like it!" Mabel was the wardrobe expert, so I changed. Then she suggested a pair of slouchy, casual boots "because heels would say 'fuck me now' and you should appreciate his cooking first."

I drove out to Maverick's place, trailed by Eric. I'd extracted a promise from Eric that he wouldn't lurk around glowering at the Boones, but we both knew he'd lied. He'd be somewhere nearby, keeping an eye on me, but he'd also make sure that no one saw him. I wasn't entirely certain that would work, seeing as how the Boones were a bunch of werewolves with super awesome sniffers, but I had texted

Maverick a heads-up about the bonus company. He'd said that he would tell his brothers not to freak out and go all territorial, and I'd decided to interpret that as "I promise they won't eat your bodyguard." Good enough.

I hadn't been out to this part of Moonlight Valley before. Although the moon wasn't full yet, there was still plenty of light, silvery and pale. It was foggier here than it had been in Phantom Falls, which struck me as weird. The trees were larger and older, just starting to drop their leaves. The few places we passed were decorated for Halloween, with jack-o'-lanterns on their porches, along with orange string lights and a skeleton parked in an Adirondack chair. Someone had even made a giant spiderweb out of cords.

After my mountain mishaps, I was proud of myself when I successfully followed the directions on my phone and pulled into a dense alley of trees that formed a tunnel over my car. Someone had hung candles in Mason jars from the branches, and it was like driving through a fairy tunnel. Not that I'd actually ever been to the Otherland, but I had Pinterest.

The tree alley should have been my first clue, but the three-story main house was not at all what I'd expected. It was beyond grand. It was also old, sagging in few discreet spots, and impressively large. Big house, big dick? A gal could hope.

It was clear, though, that the Boones were men who were willing to put in some work because the white exterior, blue trim, and red door were all freshly painted. *I'm manifesting this, Universe. Please and thank you.*

Acres of cleared land dotted with outbuildings in various states of disrepair surrounded the house. An old carriage house—possibly it had started life as a barn?—appeared to be undergoing renovations. I hoped the work went quickly because it looked like it might fall down tomorrow. Maybe Monday.

I parked and exited the car, clutching two boxes of chocolates I'd sourced from Nashville. If dinner went badly, I had consolation at hand.

The promise of chocolate was enough to momentarily blot out my nerves at the memory of sexy Professor Maverick holding me close as we forded streams and made our way through the Tennessee wilderness. The way he'd been so capable, but also tender and concerned.

"No pressure," I said out loud. This wasn't a lie—I had the usual Fae difficulty with outright fibbing—it was a command. To myself.

This was not Little Red Riding Hood.

The big, bad wolves were not going to eat me up.

(Although I guess a girl could hope.)

Because seriously? Maverick got to have his smart, sexy job as a college professor and this amazing mansion and his brothers and sister. Plus, he shapeshifted, which seemed like it would be even more amazing than owning a Southern house with a zillion square feet. He had a sense of humor, I could count on him, *and* he wrapped these amazing qualities up in a stubbled, growly, bearded, lumberjack-sized package.

Yes, I will let you *comfort me!*

Eager to get on with the comforting, I climbed the stairs to the porch. The newly restored boards gleamed in the light; someone had turned the light on for me. Seven rocking chairs lined one side, and two wooden porch swings bookended the verandah. I refused to imagine curling up with Maverick on one of those swings and maybe kissing the heck out of him. We could make love there, and it would probably be like having sex in a very small boat.

If the boat is a-rocking, don't come a-knocking.

Inspired by that thought, I rang the bell, and less than a minute later Ranger answered.

"Hello." He wore a plaid button-up shirt, a green cashmere vest, and a tweed bowtie. He was also holding a sherry glass.

"Nice to see you, Ranger." It was hard not to like Ranger; despite our rocky beginning, he and I had become co-schemers. I had no idea why he wanted to pair Maverick with me, but I would not be looking my bow-tie-wearing, sherry-drinking gift horse in the mouth. "You're looking snazzy tonight."

"Be sure to say that loudly in front of Maverick," he whispered as he tugged me inside and shut the door behind us. "And you brought chocolate. Excellent. Mackenzie will appreciate that. She's always complaining that Knox is cutting sugar and starving the rest of us. Alice likes a good chocolate too."

"Who's Alice?" I whispered back.

"Ford's girl. Ford's the grumpy twin. Atticus is the nice one. Be careful around him though, as he'll try to charm your pants off." He offered me his sherry, like *Girl, you're gonna need a drink to get through tonight.*

I slapped a hand over my mouth to hold the laugh in. If we were sneaking up on the rest of the Boones, I didn't want to give the game away.

Ranger grinned, his hazel eyes twinkling happily. "You are remarkably pretty when you laugh. You don't need that glamour of yours one bit."

Gulp.

I guess I'd known that he knew about my magic and my half Faeness, but I hadn't expected him to bring it up in conversation. Did he mind? Did he think I was some kind of weird paranormal bad influence? But what would he complain about? *She's nice to look at, and she makes me like her, oh boo hoo!* I wanted to think it was no big deal, but the truth was that most people liked to make up their own minds.

"Ranger?" Maverick's voice came from someplace behind me, sending shivers down my spine. His voice was rough and warm at the same time, with notes of growl and spice. It was perfect. "Did you get the door?"

Ranger abruptly snagged the chocolate boxes and set them on a console table underneath an antique-looking painting that was bigger than a twin bed. It seemed to be of a log cabin set in a creepy-looking field of corn with random black birds observing from overhead. I was not an art connoisseur.

"Kitchen," Ranger whispered. "Fifteen steps north." He flipped me around with his hands on my shoulders and pointed down the painting-lined hallway. "Your man is all alone in there, baking and barefoot. You should go tell him what a delicious cook he is and how you just want to eat him up."

Ranger patted me on the shoulder and sent me down the hall.

I tromped toward the kitchen. I had anticipated flying into Maverick's arms, maybe wrapping my legs around his waist. There would have been kissing and maybe some accidental butt groping. But now that I was here, I wasn't as sure of myself. *Hello, anxiety, my old friend!* There were so many ways I could screw this up.

"No sex jokes," I reminded myself. "No weird publishing stories."

Just as I'd finished exhorting myself, Maverick popped his head out into the hallway. His glare abruptly changed into a smile, so I guessed he'd been anticipating a meeting with Ranger.

"Here I am," I said, sounding breathless. And eager. Maybe as if I'd sprinted up the mountainside on foot, only to discover that I was asthmatic. My palms were damp. I couldn't look away.

Who would want to?

Maverick had lost his flannel shirt somewhere. This was unexpected but good. Being short, I was eye-to-chest with him, and there was plenty of good reading material there. *Biology puns—they cell themselves!* I attempted to look like the kind of well-educated person who could appreciate a good biology pun. His T-shirt was stretched to the limits over his broad shoulders, and he was all muscles and biceps, corded sinew, and strong forearms. All that bare skin short-circuited my brain. He looked ready to wrestle bears. Well, except for the spatula he gripped in one hand.

Holy smokes, I'd missed him.

It hadn't been that long since I'd seen or—or, heck, known him. What was in the water on this mountain? This was weird. Probably.

"Hey," Maverick said finally, sounding hoarse. He stepped fully out of the kitchen, wiping his big hands on a towel covered with cute little kittens. He tossed the towel over one shoulder. I stared.

He was staring fiercely back at me. No way either of us moved. We were caught up in this lust magnet, sexy feedback loop, and words, words, words . . . who needed them? This felt great, so I was good.

Or bad.

I was willing to take direction as long as it ended up with my hands all over this man.

He was barefoot, which was one step closer to naked. He had beautiful feet.

Okay, I was officially super weird.

I should have practiced this scene, I realized, because the next line my brain sent to my mouth was GAH. That paltry syllable did not begin to convey the depth of my attraction.

Do not throw yourself at the man.

I had a side of dignity to go with my lust.

"I brought chocolate, and you have nice feet. Should I take my shoes off? Is this a barefoot household?"

He blinked at my torrent of words, his daze fading, and a soft smile spreading over his face. "I appreciate that."

"The chocolate or my admiration for your feet?"

"Both. I have to admit that feet have never been my favorite body part, not when there are so many other fun ones. But *shoes* are not what I would like to ask you to take off." The heat in his playful gaze did things to my insides. We would need to eat dinner quickly. His smile widened and grew teasing.

More of this, please.

I'd missed *this* smile. I'd missed how it warmed me up and made me feel special. If I were creating a list of Maverick's smiles, rank ordered, *this* would be number one. Wait. Was I cataloging Maverick's facial expressions? Was I now a Maverick librarian? Did I have *favorites*?

Yes, yes, I did.

"I'm going to need your top ten list," I teased. "Please specify all your favorite body parts. Detailed explanations of why are also welcome."

"Why tell you when I could show you?"

"Show don't tell. That *is* an important rule for us writerly types."

Maverick laughed—a deep, husky, unrestrained shout—and that made me laugh too. Holy moly. This was going so well. We weren't awkward. It was as easy as before.

I was just about to nominate myself as his live demonstration model when a buzzing from the kitchen broke the deliciously flirtatious enchantment. Cock-blocked by the oven timer! Maverick started, frowning as if he had no idea what the sound was, and then he turned said frown on me, as though my presence in his hallway confused him. Or disgruntled him. Take your pick.

"That's the chicken-fried steak," he said. Then he hesitated. "Uh, well not chicken. Or steak. It's jackfruit masquerading as a formerly living protein source. I promise you'll like my meat, though."

I was sure I would too.

He turned and strode into the kitchen to do mysterious chef things. I was not a cook. I was more of an *order takeout and live for a week on the leftovers* kind of gal. Hopefully, we could compromise.

Hope was not a familiar emotion, not when it came to my romantic relationships. My dating life had mostly engendered emotions like frustration, boredom, disbelief, and the occasional well-directed orgasm. Men in Hollywood required direction in order to achieve results. The possibility of *relating* with Maverick had me hopeful that there could be something more—and that was scary. I was not prepared for him to reject me again, and I was always prepared.

See also: this was scary.

Sidling into the kitchen (I could hear my mami's voice: *Only ghosts lurk, mija*), I discovered Maverick seated at the kitchen table. Much to my disappointment, he was in the process of pulling on his work boots over socks. I love a sexy work boot as much as the next gal, but we were now regressing in the Get Maverick Naked plan.

"Are you okay?" He raised an eyebrow questioning.

Gah, he had sexy eyebrows.

I admired them diligently from the safety of the kitchen door.

"Come on in," he offered. There was a hint of laughter in his voice, and the corner of his mouth hitched up. He was enjoying my sexual fog and confusion. "I don't bite."

Can you do a sexy werewolf bite? Can we start with nipping and work our way up? I was about to blurt out my new sexual fantasy when a loud male voice roared in the other room. Maverick definitely wasn't the only wolf on the premises.

"Nope. Not a chance. Never, ever, EVER."

"I'm begging you." This was a female voice.

"No means no." The owner of the male voice sauntered into the kitchen. He wore a scowl on his face and was rangy and muscled, built more like a runner than a lumberjack. His red hair stood out in every direction, and he had a neatly trimmed red beard. His icy blue eyes did a quick inventory of the kitchen, landing on me for a beat before he startled and then moved on, dismissing me.

I grinned, liking my odds already. I'd never been overlooked so quickly. It was awesome!

An energetic woman with brown hair twisted up in a messy bun on top of her head burst into the kitchen behind the icy-eyed guy. She was brown-eyed, freckled, and super pretty. She waved her hands, intent on making her point to the guy. "But, Ford, I wouldn't ask except Alessandro needs—"

"Like my momma used to say, keep stoats and dogcatchers at arm's length." Ford shook his head. The man had made up his mind.

The brown-haired hand-waver rolled her eyes. "Ford Montgomery Boone, don't you be rude. You know that Alessandro would be real appreciative of your assistance."

"He can take that appreciation and stuff it up his—"

"Ford Montgomery," Maverick snapped. "Company manners. Be on your best behavior."

Ford's scowl deepened. But he inhaled, exhaled ostentatiously, and then his frown lines eased up. It was a Christmas miracle in October. He held out an enormous paw of a hand to me.

"Hi. I'm Ford. One of the twins," he said flatly, as if greeting me was a chore he was checking off his chore chart. I was not a TV star; I was a prize sticker slapped on a task accomplished. It was oddly charming.

"Hi. I'm Sonnet. I'm pleased to meet you."

"This is Alice." He set a protective hand on the back of the freckled woman who'd come in with him. When he looked at her, his gaze warmed up faster than a glacier in a greenhouse. He looked downright proud and happy to have her by his side.

"I'm so excited to meet you!" Alice grabbed my hand and shook it, shooting an impish grin at me. "I feel like I know you from watching you, first on TV and then at Biscuits & Blessings. That sounds downright creepy, doesn't it? But I'm so sorry that the folks there didn't leave you and Maverick in peace to eat your dinner. Some people have no manners."

"You saw that? At the restaurant?" I didn't recognize her. On the other hand, I'd been surrounded by a crowd of napkin-waving locals. I'd been too busy charming and signing to remember faces. It had been a disappointing night.

"I was, but I hung back. I'm a citizen scientist, and we were tabulating the results from our last firefly count," she explained. "If I'd stopped, I'd have had to start all over again."

"She is an excellent scientist," Ranger announced, adding himself to the crowd in the Boone kitchen. He tipped his head at Alice. "Good evening, Ms. Aymes."

"Ranger," she returned with a small grin.

"You look absolutely lovely, Ms. Aymes," Ranger remarked.

Ford's scowl reemerged.

"You're so nice, Ranger." Alice looked like she was holding in laughter. "And may I just say that your vest is—"

"Stop right there," Ford cut in, sliding between the two of them and wrapping his arm around Alice's waist. "I know what you're up to, Ranger. There will be no matchmaking, no accidental locking of two people into a closet, no unexpected blizzards or mechanical failures. I do not need your help to kiss my girl."

Ranger widened his eyes innocently. I made a mental note to offer him tips about not overacting a scene.

"I don't know what you're insinuating, but I don't like it," he said. I was certain he did know—but didn't care. Then, turning to me, he took my hand and tugged me toward him. He leaned in and gave me a cheek-kiss. I had not expected that.

"You too look lovely, Ms. Ruiz," he declared loudly.

Someone growled close by.

"Thank you, Ranger," I said automatically, because that was usually the next line in this kind of scene. I hoped no one was about to go all furry. "You look very dashing this evening. Very lord of the manor."

"Oh, this old thing I just threw on?" he asked loudly, kissing my other cheek, then whispering, "Is Maverick watching?"

I checked. He was indeed watching and out-scowling even the grumpy Ford.

"You bet."

"Excellent." Ranger straightened up, winking. He slid an arm around my waist and tucked me against his side. I added this to tonight's list of unexpected things. "I'm pleased as punch you're here."

Maverick strode over, scowling ferociously. He gently pried me out of Ranger's embrace and tucked me up against his side. I had no complaints. "Don't you do that," he warned his brother. "Ford doesn't like it one bit. So, what makes you think I would?"

"I don't like what you're insinuating," Ranger repeated. He sounded irritated and put out. "I'm just being sociable."

"Be social somewhere else," Ford warned as yet another large, bearded man strode into the kitchen. We needed to relocate to somewhere bigger. It was like Snow White and the Seven Lumberjacks, except I guess that there were two of us playing the lead.

The new guy's hard stare took in the five of us, pausing on Maverick's hand around my waist. While he did his looking, Maverick and Ford got on Ranger's case.

"I thought you didn't want to bother her," Ranger was saying to Maverick, his hands on his hips.

The newest Boone was even taller than Maverick, and broader. Although his hair and beard were near jet-black, his eyes were bright blue, and he was Hollywood beautiful. I'd spent years looking at pretty faces up close, but this man's made me do a double take. His features were symmetrical, his bone structure photogenic. He could have given Luke a run for his money on a movie set.

And yet, despite his inordinately hot looks, he was an iceberg. He gazed around the room with icy self-containment, radiating disinterest and detachment. He lacked Maverick's ever-present charm and warmth, a genuine warmth that I'd been drawn to and couldn't seem to deprive myself of. This other guy, however, was a grade-A North Atlantic iceberg. We needed to get in the lifeboats fast, or our boat would hit him and sink.

Mr. Iceberg's eyes met mine, and they were frosty stalactites that bored straight into me. There was something fundamentally unpleasant about him that had me burrowing into Maverick's side.

"Do not talk about bothering Sonnet. And leave off kissing her as well. Keep your paws to yourself." Amber might have tinged Maverick's eyes, but his voice still held a note of amusement. Even though he was irritated by Ranger's antics, he was working hard to stay pleasant and not give in to temper.

"What in the Sam Hill is going on in here?" Yet *another* enormous Boone brother shouldered his way into the kitchen, which was starting to feel like one of those clown cars. At least this latest addition was smiling.

"Nothing," Ford and Maverick said together.

The newest redheaded addition circumvented Mr. Iceberg—who was still glaring at me with his ice-ray vision—and stepped forward.

"Well, I'll be! I know you. You're Sonnet Ruiz!"

Given the similarity between this redhead and the one wrapped around Alice, I decided this must be the missing Boone twin. "Yes. You must be Atticus."

His happy beam reminded me of Maverick's, as did his easy manner, although his charm was more excited puppy than Maverick's studly spell. Still, he was cute and enthusiastic. I gave him an answering smile.

"This is so great, meeting you. Wow. You have the dimples! If you were a vegetable, you'd be a cute-cumber!"

This made me laugh and made Maverick scowl some more, his hand planting itself on my hip. *Keep off my grass, motherfucker!* That's what Maverick's hand was saying. I suspected his middle finger might be adding some punctuation just out of my line of sight too.

Regardless, I snuggled back against his side. Kitchen time was awesome! Ranger's evil master plan was totally working.

Atticus's blue eyes shifted between Maverick and me, his smile fading some. "Hold up. Are you two . . ."

He didn't finish his sentence. Apparently, he was flummoxed by the idea of two consenting adults spending adult time together.

"Yes," Ranger, my new favorite Boone brother, announced. "Our brother Maverick has finally done right by our pack and brought home a fine woman."

Maverick grunted irritably but did not release my hip. "We're friends," he said. The Boone brothers collectively stared at us.

Alice giggled. "Real good friends."

We certainly were friends—the kind that kissed.

I filed this away for future discussion. Was he not ready to be a couple in front of his family?

"Friends is awesome," Atticus said happily. "So, it would be fine if I—"

"It would not be fine, and you can go mash the potatoes while I give Sonnet the grand tour." He spun us around with a muttered, "Sorry," and a quick kiss on my cheek. I was too busy enjoying the memory of how his beard had tickled to complain as he led me out of the kitchen and out of the house.

"I appreciate someone who's not afraid to own he was wrong," I whispered, my lips making a sneaky foray up his neck. Look at me, walking and kissing! "But that was fine. No apologies necessary. I feel like I'm getting to know your brothers."

I squeezed his waist. Could he feel my heart pounding in my chest? Because truth was, I was only *bothered* by what had happened back in the kitchen in the sexy, fun way. His steering me out of there with his arm around me was a hug, an opportunity to feel him up, or both.

Seeing as how we'd previously established the value of *showing* rather than *telling*, I swung myself in front of his ground-eating stride and wrapped myself around him like a sexy barnacle. No inch of space for us! Not being slow, he grabbed me right back and pressed me up against him. He held me tightly, big hands gripping my butt, angling us closer. He was the sexy bolt, and I was the nut grip, if you took my meaning.

"That's the carriage house." He tipped his head toward the half-restored building I'd spotted earlier. I'd rather have heard, *That's my bedroom,* or *Hey! There's a Jacuzzi tub and a discreet five-star B&B over there! Shall we check in for the night?* But such was life, and my life apparently held a distinct lack of padded horizontal surfaces.

"I've stripped it down to the drywall," he continued.

"Stripping is great," I murmured. *Hint, hint!*

He gently disentangled my limbs from his and started walking again. He was such a party pooper!

"And she's got a new roof and new siding," he continued. "I'll be done in two months, tops."

"I like a man who takes his time."

"I always do."

He moved past the carriage house, walking briskly as he steered us through a wild-flower field. Moonlight silvered the grasses and threaded through a forest thick with trees. I should have been taking pictures for my Instagram because it was truly magical. Instead, I was looking for a nice, private tree to drag my man behind. We needed to do some talking, followed by a whole lot more kissing. I had a sexy proposal to make for *Maverick + Sonnet,* the extended edition movie.

Go time.

There was no way I held in my pitch until after dinner. If he'd relocated me to the friend zone, I needed to know now. I could act my way past that kind of disappointment, but masking my hope was a challenge.

Silence on the set.

Cameras rolling . . .

"Thank you for inviting me to dinner."

He raised an eyebrow. "That was Ranger's work. He invited you, not me."

"Uh-huh." I winked at him. "So I should be thanking Ranger. Good to know."

Maverick frowned. "Ranger doesn't need your thanks. As I'm cooking, you can thank me."

"What would work best for you?" I said huskily.

We were out of sight of the house now, hidden by the thick undergrowth and all those trees.

"A few words would suffice. Maybe praise the food in front of my brothers." He smiled teasingly at me. "Let them know how much you enjoy my meat."

"But I haven't even seen your meat," I protested. "I think I should taste it first."

"Take your glamour off?" he asked, unexpectedly serious. "I want to see *you*."

Just the glamour? And not my clothes?

What was I doing wrong? I needed this man.

I slipped the glamour off as we walked, tucking it away. Like it was a sweater I didn't need. His steps slowed, and I snuck a peek at his profile, trying to read his face. His jaw was set, firmed. It did not radiate welcome. Or do much for my hopes. He uncrossed his arms and stuffed his hands into his pockets.

"This is the national park." He tipped his head toward the forest. "The house has been in the family for over a century. It's on fifteen acres. It's mine. I'm the oldest, and therefore I inherited it all, along with some other responsibilities. There's a white wolf that runs free here."

"Okay?"

"She's our momma," he said fiercely. "Our daddy bit her without her permission, forced his mating bite on her, and now she's stuck like that and I don't know if she'll ever be able to shift back. He took something real special and turned it into a nightmare. So now I—*we*—keep her as safe as we can. This is her home."

We both stared at the woods, as if the bushes choking the trees would part and the white wolf would come running out.

There was nothing but the sound of crickets and the night frogs, singing up a storm. I imagined how it would be to stand in my family home, watching for Mami and knowing she would not be coming through the door. That I would not be talking with her or hugging her or doing any of the hundreds of small things we did together. My heart broke for Maverick.

"I'm sorry for your loss," I said. Those words were entirely inadequate for what I was feeling, but I hoped he'd understand that they were a start. A down payment.

He nodded, turning. The line of his features was serious, his eyes cautious as they searched my face. "I plan to raise a whole passel of kids here in this house, on this land."

"It would be a great place for that," I said carefully. My script for this evening seemed to be missing a key page. "I grew up in the Mexican mountains. I ran all over the place, and it was wonderful."

He frowned slightly. My hopes plummeted. "I like you, Sonnet. I do." I could hear that *liking* in his voice, feel it in the tension in his body. I could also, however, hear the *but* that shivered on the tip of his tongue. "But I apologize if I misled you about my intentions or gave you the mistaken impression that I was open to a hookup while you're shooting here. I am not available for that. I don't think we're suited."

"We're not suited?" We *suited* just fine. In fact, our suitability levels were off the charts. Ten out of ten. Smoking hot. My heart ricocheted out of my chest, plummeted toward my feet like a smoke jumper spotting a forest fire from the plane, skipped upward past my ovaries (he wanted babies!), and planted itself in my throat.

"Is this because I let you believe my name was Suzette? Or the Fae thing? Because what about all the kissing—"

"No, we've talked about the name business. You explained and I accepted your apology. I understand how that happened. And being part Fae is just who you are. The problem, as I see it, is that you're young and very talented."

"This is not some kind of May-December romance," I protested. "You're only six years older than me. That's hardly a big deal."

"It's not the number. It's the difference in our life situations."

"So, you're older and what? Untalented? A failure?"

"No." He cracked a grin. "I'm not old and I'm not a failure. But you're world-famous, and I'm a wolf shifter."

"You don't want to live life in the Hollywood fishbowl."

"It is a fishbowl, and from the little I've seen, it's overwhelming. I'll be upfront about that. But that's not the problem. The real problem is that I'll never be as wildly successful at my job as you are at yours. We biologists don't get invited on

TV morning shows or have paparazzi trailing us with cameras. I like my job. I like my life here. Where I want to grow things is with my family. I want that wild success to come at home. I want to be the best-ever husband, father, brother, and uncle. That's where I want to put my time and my effort, and I can't start something, invest myself in someone who is temporary. I want a mate. I want to know that I'm with someone I could choose to give the mate bite to, and who would choose me back."

I looked away, pulling my glamour back on. "The werewolf wants forever?"

He hesitated, then nodded.

"But not with me?"

His soft gaze took me in. "With you? Yes, absolutely. At least, I'd want a chance of forever with you."

Could he be any more amazing?

Hand to God, tell me the truth. Could he be more perfect?

The werewolf wants forever.

Did I? Was I prepared to settle down here in Moonlight Valley and make wolf babies with this man? Could I take a chance on forever with him?

There was no safe answer, or at least not one I could give with one-hundred-percent certainty. Neither of us could predict the future, and yet I knew exactly what to say next.

There was only one answer, after all, that I wanted to give.

"Okay."

He nodded, looking sad. And resolute. And all sorts of reserved, solemn, and other stable sorts of things. "Okay."

He was never supposed to look sad.

"Okay," I repeated, closing the distance between us. When I reached him, I leaned up to press a kiss against his mouth. I was constitutionally unable to stop myself. His lips were plush and firm and perfect. I refrained from pressing the rest of myself up against him. We were having a conversation, but I had a weakness for him. There would be more kisses, I promised myself. We'd have ALL the kisses. "Let's do this."

He blinked. "Do what?"

"The thing." I wagged a finger between the two of us. "The not-temporary romantic relationship thing. The maybe-forever hookup. We'll be Gorilla Glue instead of painter's tape. Sharpie instead of washable marker—which we will totally, one-hundred-percent regret if we get to those wolf pups you mentioned. Your beautiful house will never be the same again once a toddler's drawn on your walls."

"What?"

I pointed to the big family home behind him. "I love your house. I'm aware that it comes with a pack of wolves, but I'll work up to loving all of them. At some point soon, yeah, I'd like a wolfy demo because I need to know just how good my imagination is. Show me around your place. If you've got a kinky toy drawer or a sex swing, a heads-up would be appreciated because I'm gonna need to start doing some yoga if our sex life comes with playground equipment, but I can totally imagine raising our hypothetical wolf pups here. But you should build a tree house because we may want to sneak away from your brothers, so we don't have to be quiet, plus tree houses are cool." I gestured toward a big yellow aspen. "Also, I must warn you that I have a big family, and at some point you might want to brush up on your Spanish. Also, you might want to invest in some of those find-my-crap tiles because my family's Chaneque, and we have a few quirks. We can talk about those after you show me your wolf."

The edges of his frown eased as I laid out our maybe future for him, his stare taking on a note of wonder. "You mean it."

"I do." I did.

"You don't know me."

"Not yet, but I will. And ditto. But we're not running off to Vegas or even buying a house together. You asked me to give a relationship with you an honest, hundred-percent shot. I'm asking for the same from you."

He put his hands on his hips. "You are a celebrity TV star with millions of fans."

"I am. And you are a biology professor who has a thing for snakes that would send most people screaming. Not to mention you go furry, and I have magic. You show me yours, and I'll show you mine. Bonus points if shifting means you get naked right here and now."

"All right," he said slowly. "Yeah."

YOU BET YOUR SWEET ASS, YEAH.

He took a couple of steps backward. I plopped down on a handy stretch of fallen tree. I was getting dinner and a show!

He gave me a stern look, so I dropped my glamour again. Fine. If he wanted a brown-and-green girlfriend, I was game.

"Your turn!" I caroled.

Maverick stripped down with the same neat efficiency he handled everything. He pulled his T-shirt over his head, folded it up, and set it on the grass.

"You could give me your clothes," I suggested hopefully. "I could hold on to them for you. That seems like a mate-ish kind of thing to do."

"Uh-huh. And what are my odds of getting them back?"

"What are the odds of you wanting them back?"

"Fair enough," he said, and handed me his shirt. Next, he bent over and shucked his boots and socks. I got to see his bare feet again, which also went in the win column.

His hands went to his belt. "I'm not sure how you all do this for a camera."

I grinned at him. "Why, Maverick Boone, are you insinuating that I've shot naked love scenes for the camera?"

"Uh—" My sweet man blushed.

"It's about the least sexy thing ever." I took pity on his embarrassment. "We have an intimacy coordinator, and we choreograph everything before the clothes come off. But you let me know if you need any help."

He muttered something profane, but then he undid his belt and slowly popped the buttons on his jeans. God bless jeans that buttoned up. The wash-worn denim cupped him in the best of places, as did the black cotton boxer briefs he wore underneath. He folded up his pants, shoved the briefs down—I had only a brief second to appreciate that Maverick was size-appropriate everywhere—and then he shifted.

BOOM. *Or more like CRACK,* my surprised brain suggested. Like the quickest pop-pop-pop of a Fourth of July firecracker on a dark night. Maverick just sort of turned inside out, his human skin going out like the tide, and his wolf fur coming in to replace it. One minute, I was ogling my man (my man!), and the next I was nose to muzzle with an enormous wolf.

I fell off my log.

The wolf yipped and nudged me. If wolves could laugh, this one was.

"Crickets and crackers." I dumped his clothes onto the ground beside me. I'd have to work on being an awesome wifey type later. "You are something unexpected."

He was unexpected, but he was also absolutely amazing. His wolf had a thick, dense pelt of brown fur, with a darker ruff around his face. His eyes were golden, his ears jet-black. He was as big as two Rottweilers, but those handsome eyes of his were still friendly and concerned. He was just watching out for me in a four-legged form. I tested that thought and decided that I liked it.

The wolf bumped against my shoulder.

It whined.

Then it licked my cheek.

Gross. I was not a fan of wolf slobber. I squealed, slapping at its shoulder with my hand. "Do not do that!"

It—*he*—laid down and put his enormous head in my lap. Warm eyes regarded me.

"Okay, so you're a handsome beast." I ran my fingers over his head. He was so soft. "In either form."

We sat like that for a while, me petting him, and he . . . I had no idea what he was doing, although when he turned his head and his muzzle brushed against my crotch, I had an idea.

"You behave yourself," I said sternly.

After that, he shifted back, and we played a little game of keep-away with his pants. I thought he should stay naked and commune with nature a while longer, while he was more concerned about unpleasant things like "chiggers in places chiggers should never, ever go."

He got his boxers on and his pants up, although I did my best to make sure he couldn't button them. While he was distracted putting himself back together again, I ran from him, waving his shirt over my head like he was one of those exotic dancers you hire for a raunchy bachelorette party.

Being a wolf at heart, bless him, he chased me.

A muscled arm locked around my waist, swinging me off my feet and up into his arms. His face laughed down at me.

"Gotcha," he growled.

"Oh, woe is me!" I threw myself back against his strong arms. He wouldn't drop me, and this was fun. "Whatever shall I do?"

Bonus: since he was bridal-carrying me, my skirt had given in to gravity and was now around my waist.

"Look! Thigh-high stockings!" I smoothed my hands down my thighs to the lacy bands. You know. Just in case the man was too much of a gentleman to look.

Fortunately for me, he wasn't. His eyes locked on my legs, his gaze growing hotter.

I win.

"And my panties match," I pointed out.

Some exciting spins and turns occurred at this junction. My wolf was either practicing a daring gymnastics floor routine or eager to get me horizontal underneath him. I was happy to help.

We ended up lying in the middle of the wildflower meadow, crushing a whole lot of aromatic but defenseless grasses beneath us. Maverick reached for me, his mouth curving in a wicked grin.

"You are a bad influence." He plucked his T-shirt from my fingers.

Resistance was futile, mostly because I was giggling too hard to put up a good fight.

"What *are* you going to do about that, Mr. Boone?" I hoped I'd find out in the next ten seconds or so. I might last an entire minute, but I was not a patient woman.

Gazing down at me, he half lowered himself over me, caging me between his arms. Yay! I approve! He planted one hand beside my head, his fingers toying with my hair. I was certain I had not-so-sexy bedhead at this point, but he'd have to take me as I was. Real-life Sonnet did not have a hair and makeup team at her disposal, and she was lazy. His other hand dipped south and smoothed over the lacy band of one stocking, his fingertips tracing small circles on my bare skin. With an achingly careful touch, he trailed them higher and then higher still until I was tense with anticipation.

"I'm going to make you mine," he growled, nipping at my green-brown jaw. "My girl, my mate."

"Nope," I countered, ducking away from his mouth. "We need to get this straight. *I'm* making *you* mine. My guy. It's part of the whole *partnership* thing."

He grinned, clearly not unhappy with my claiming. Something predatory flashed in his eyes as they dropped to my chest. Between the chase and the anticipation, my boobs were heaving in a way I'd never thought possible outside the pages of a book. "You've seen me naked, Sonnet Ruiz. If we're doing things equal, I should get to see you naked now."

I nodded. That worked for me. He groaned, capturing my mouth in a heated, searing kiss. He was not afraid of my teeth.

He *liked* me.

The hand on my thigh started drifting higher, igniting an inferno in my belly and the regions nearest his fingers. And God bless the man because he correctly interpreted my little whimpers and wriggles and moved his fingers to the front. A gentle nudge of his knee and I was spread for him, and his knuckles were rubbing back and forth over my panty-covered center. I pushed up into his touch, my hands gripping the waist of his jeans as I gasped for air.

"You're wonderful." He sounded amazed and as breathless as I felt. He took parity seriously, and I rewarded him by sending my own fingers south and under the waistband of his jeans. It would be a crime not to touch his butt.

"Behave," he growled. "I want you." His rough words were part warning, part promise. The need in his voice made me tremble. Amazing, unbelievable, out-of-this-world trembling. He made me feel so alive.

"Do you want me to behave? Really?" I asked.

His fingers pressed deeper against my front. That touch was all Maverick: sure and confident and capable. What would happen when we were finally in a bed together?

I could tell he was thinking about it too. His eyes darkened. He was this close to losing control, his breath coming harder and faster. Stopping? Not a chance.

And yet we'd agreed: forever. Or at least our best shot at that, and he'd told me that he didn't want to rush things. He wanted to take the scenic route in this relationship, slow down and savor the ride. He wanted to be as sure as he could, but here I was chipping away at those boundaries.

So I swallowed and moved my hand from his butt to his shoulders. Those were Switzerland-sized body parts, almost. I tried to ignore the hard ridge pressing against my stomach. I failed, but I tried.

"Slow," I said. "We said we were taking things slow."

Persuade me otherwise, please.

He nodded once, pressing a tiny kiss against the skin beneath my ear. Removing his fingers from my happy place, he stroked the outer edges of my thighs. He wasn't letting go, either.

Eventually, he got control of himself and lifted his head. The rasp of his beard against my neck was enough to make me rethink priorities and boundaries. Why not just leap into this?

"Penny for your thoughts?"

"Pardon?" His voice was thick and rough, as if he'd been thinking some very dirty thoughts.

"Whatever you're thinking right now, make a list. I need to know. Because when we do go to bed together, we need to do it all."

Amusement colored his eyes. "But what if it involves my drawer of adult toys?"

I pressed a quick kiss against his mouth. "Make that number one on your list."

CHAPTER

EIGHTEEN

"At least my eyes could pass for human. They're green, deep and dark."

— HOLLY BLACK, *THE STOLEN HEIR*

"You're smiling," my sister whispered, drawing my attention away from where a reglamoured Sonnet was charming Ford and Rue on our deck. She'd already charmed Atticus, Ranger, and Rebel, although she'd promised me that it was completely nonmagical charming. I believed her. "Are you two officially stepping out together now?"

Mackenzie, Rue, and Rebel had showed up while I'd been taking my extremely gratifying nature walk with Sonnet. We'd eaten my faux chicken-fried steak and potatoes out on the deck behind the house as the night was so fine. It being October in Tennessee, it was still real nice, warm enough that I wasn't entirely convinced that Sonnet had actually *needed* my flannel. I was now bare-armed, and she was wrapped up in my favorite shirt.

We gotta mark her, my wolf ordered. **Get our scent all over her so everyone KNOWS.**

I was pretty darn certain everyone here already knew. About the only thing more obvious would have been to start passing out wedding invitations.

Bet there's a late-night Kinko's open.

247

Oblivious to my wolf's demands, most everybody was slouched at one of the picnic tables, most of us itching to shift and go for a run. Knox was off by himself, seeing as how there was no room left at the already crowded tables.

Mackenzie had chased me down by the beer cooler. Mostly she just wanted to give me shit, but she was also after gossip. She should have been a cat shifter given her curiosity, but instead she turned into a silver-colored wolf.

I tried to keep a straight face, but it was no use. I was grinning like a fool. "I don't know what you're on about, Mack."

Har-de-har-har.

She snorted. My baby sister had always been the best at seeing through my bull-shit. "You are a lying liar who lies. You two keep staring at each other, and it's about to set my hair on fire. That woman is all about you."

And she hasn't even had sex with us yet, my wolf grumbled. **Then she's gonna like us even more. I promise you that.**

"Is she?" She'd told me as much, but damned if I didn't like hearing it from other people as well.

"You did good, Maverick. She's sweet on you. You've just transformed one of television's most famously independent women into a silly, rattled mess."

My smile faltered because discombobulating a woman like that seemed like the wrong thing to do. My plan was to make more of Sonnet, not less.

Gonna make her come.

Make her happy.

My wolf hesitated, then added, **Make her feel loved.**

He wasn't any more certain than I was about our ability to do feelings well, but damned if I—**we**—weren't going to try.

"Don't you ever hurt her," Mack continued fiercely. "Don't you do it."

You'd think I hadn't learned anything these past years, but I had. Hurting Sonnet—or anyone—was not on the table. But Mack had reasons for her warning, reasons I intended to respect the hell out of.

So I tucked her into my side, enjoying having her home. "You know I love you, Mack. You haven't been here in a long time, so I'm just gonna say that I have changed. I'm not the man—or wolf—I was before." I nudged her chin up, so she met my eyes. "I promised you that all those years ago, and I've kept that promise. I won't hurt anyone, ever again, and that absolutely includes Sonnet."

Mack's eyes flashed amber, likely remembering some particularly unpleasant moment back when I'd been a younger, asshole me, and then she nodded stiffly. "I do know that. You're right. I'm sorry."

I was sorry too.

Unfortunately, I could say that—and mean it—a dozen times a day, but it could never change what I'd done wrong. There was no undo button for past mistakes and selfish decisions.

"I'm sorry," I repeated. "Real sorry."

"I forgive you," she said quietly. "You know that."

I did too. It was just that I didn't deserve her forgiveness. Not yet. I needed to earn it first. "I still plan to make it up to you. You just tell me what you need, and it's yours. You need a she-shed to get away from Rue? Because I'm good with a hammer, and I can get a kit online. I'll even put a chandelier in it for you."

"Not right now." Her pretty face lit up with a smile that banished the sadness. I was grateful every day that I hadn't ruined things between us forever.

"Come on, Knox. It was a joke." The hard edge in Ford's voice drew my attention back to the rest of our family.

"Really?" Knox's voice was flat. "Because it wasn't funny at all."

"You're the only person on God's green earth who doesn't find that funny." Atticus rolled his eyes dramatically.

"Not the only person," Ranger argued. "The ladies crochet club has at least two members who also have no sense of humor. They did not enjoy the pattern I selected for our Halloween project."

"It's fine." Sonnet shrugged, apparently unbothered by Knox's surliness. "I'll work on my delivery."

"No. It's not fine." Ford scowled at Knox. "You've had a pickle up your butt since you got here. No wonder your face is so sour."

"Now *that* was funny." Rebel toasted Ford with his beer, beaming at Sonnet. "But I liked your joke too."

"I might have to steal the pickle line," Sonnet said thoughtfully.

"You steal a lot?" Knox muttered. More precisely, he articulated it at exactly the correct volume to be heard by all, but politely ignored. Screw that.

Yeah. We're gonna make him eat that pickle.

"Okay, I'm through with you. Knox Jackson Boone, stand up."

"Why?" he snapped, glaring at me.

"You heard me. Your problem is with me, and not with the lady. Don't you take your frustration out on her. You treat our guest with respect."

Knox shoved to his feet, eyes flashing amber. "What the fuck do you know about treating anyone with respect?"

I growled, my wolf pushing at my skin to be let out. I thought I'd grown accustomed to his dislike and outright hatred, but I'd been wrong. If we had been alone, I would have let it go.

Pickle or no pickle, Knox had every right to his anger. I had screwed up, screwed up bad, and worse, I'd done it on purpose. But he did not get to make Sonnet feel uncomfortable, especially not in this house that I'd offered to make her home.

His icy, bright blue eyes looked through me just like our daddy's had always done. His lip curled, fangs flashing as his control slipped.

"Don't fight." At Mack's soft plea, he snapped his mouth shut, shooting her a quick look.

Running a hand through his hair, he barked a curse; it sounded like *damned asshole*. Then he turned and stalked away without another word.

You'd think he'd pulled the lights on the party. All the fun and joy sure went out of the night. He'd as good as shut us all down. And as usual, I couldn't help but acknowledge that he had the right of it. Still, I held off on apologizing. Ranger had demanded I stop after the first year, claiming he was sick and tired of the word. It was fine. I'd just switched to showing them that I'd changed, not telling them.

Atticus was the first to break the silence. "Sorry about him, Sonnet. Knox isn't the friendliest Boone, but he's not usually such a colossal asshole, either."

Is too, my wolf snarled.

"It's fine." Sonnet flashed my brother a quick smile. "I have a big family, and we're always going at it. No family gets along all the time."

"Just how big is this family?" Ranger asked.

"And do you have any cute, single cousins?" Rebel followed up.

This made everyone laugh, mostly because we all needed a laugh. We'd hit our limit for drama.

Mack nudged me gently while Sonnet launched into a lengthy and humorous discussion of her many cousins. "You need to go after him."

I grimaced. Regret seized me. "He doesn't want to hear from me. There'll be more punches thrown than words."

"Maybe. Maybe not." She nudged me again. "But Knox once told me, 'Throw me to the wolves, and I'll return leading the pack.' He knows you've stepped up to lead this family, and you're taking us in a good direction. He may be yelling some, but he's still here, isn't he? Coming along where you lead?"

"You sound like Momma," I said. Not having Momma here was hard. Now that I'd met Sonnet and was trying with Knox, I missed her more than ever. It about killed me that she was running around in our woods, stuck in her wolf form. How could our family be whole with Momma trapped out there?

"Go find him," Mack said. "And talk, don't bite."

Now she definitely sounded like Momma.

A low chuckle behind us had us turning around, searching for the laughter. Rue stood there, contemplating his boots, but he wore a rare smile on his stern face.

"What?" Mack demanded, narrowing her eyes. I knew that look. She was fixing to wade in and yell at her man if he didn't explain himself right quick.

He shrugged, lifting his gaze to meet hers. "Maverick's got it right." There was a whole universe of affection and love in his gaze. "You sound like your momma, but blunter and bossier."

Mack considered this for longer than seemed safe, but then she threw herself at him, planting a kiss that was not fit for public viewing on my fellow professor.

You'd think he'd have pity on her brothers, but no. He kissed her back.

I averted my gaze and headed out. "Pardon me. I think I'll go check on Sonnet and make sure she's good, then I'll track down Knox."

I was halfway to the edge of the woods when I heard Rebel groan. "Get a room. This place has a dozen. Use one."

* * *

The good-natured ruckus behind me increased as I strode off into the woods looking for the belligerent wolf who was also a brother I cared about. More than cared; I loved him even when he was a rude asshole. He had every right to be upset, and most days he pretended that I didn't exist. On family birthdays and national holidays, he set aside his enmity and pretended that he didn't hate me. This was for the benefit of our siblings, of course, and I appreciated it.

In the barn, my wolf reported. **Watch out for booby traps.**

The barn had been a real popular spot with us boys when emotions had run high, and we'd been short on space. We'd all taken a turn at punching walls, shoveling horse manure, and dating girls in the barn. It made sense that Knox had headed there.

He was mucking out the stalls for the rescue ponies that Rebel had brought home last year. We had a Shetland pony, a Connemara, and a pony of no known pedigree. Their manes were gray and mottled, and their lips dropped more than an ice-cream cone in July, but they were sweeter than candy. Didn't make no sense to me that people were in such a rush to get rid of a loving animal just because it was old, and you couldn't ride it no more. Harper, Dixie, and Earl didn't even mind the scent of wolf now. We were just home.

Knox glared at me as he forked a shovelful of muck into the wheelbarrow. He might have hated me, but he wasn't going to attack me. It might have been easier if we could have sorted our differences with some fisticuffs. I got straight to the point.

"Listen, I was a shit brother to you growing up, and there's no going back and fixing that. But don't go making the same mistake I did."

"You brought a woman to our place? Honestly, Maverick?" Knox dumped his spade of manure into the wheelbarrow with more force than was strictly necessary.

He was in an ornery mood all right.

Join the club.

"I did. The others didn't mind. So what's your problem?"

It wasn't as if we'd eloped or had sex on the front lawn. It had just been dinner and some conversation.

"What about Sanye?" He turned away toward Earl the Connemara as he asked the question, but something in his tone had me frowning.

"What about her?"

He rolled his eyes. From the ensuing curses, Knox believed I was the village idiot.

When he'd calmed down some, he gritted out, "How do you imagine Sanye will feel about this?"

This did not compute. "About what?"

"About you stepping out on her with someone else, you bonehead."

I laughed. Sanye's thoughts on my dating Sonnet had not presented themselves to me as a problem. "Sanye doesn't give two hoots who I see."

Might be less than two hoots, my wolf said thoughtfully. **She's gonna be thrilled you're back on the dating horse.**

Knox glared at the wall. Earl backed up. "Are you sure?"

"Yeah. I am sure." I shot eye daggers into my brother's back. Clearly, all those hours he was putting in at work had fried his brain. He had no working brain cells left up there. He hadn't said more than a dozen words to me in ten years, yet now he was going on about Sanye Jansen-Webster.

"You visit her every Sunday, Maverick. Don't tell me it's platonic. The two of you are always stuck together." He tossed another shovelful of manure into the wheelbarrow.

"I'm her *friend*, you numbnuts. Friends hang out together. I'm just looking out for her."

"The two of you are not friends," he snarled. The ponies shifted. They were picking up on our agitation. I smoothed a hand down Dixie's side. Her coat was yellow and gray, kind of like a day that couldn't make up its mind if it wanted to be sunshine or clouds.

"We became friends when she married Evan. Just because he died doesn't mean we have to stop. Men and women are actually allowed to be friends, you know."

"Sure." He tossed the last shovelful of muck into the barrow and charged through the stall door. Harper gave him a baleful look; she was not a fan of upsets.

"Sure, what? What has you so riled up? That I have friends even though I don't deserve them? Or that Sanye counts as one of them?"

Knox started shoving the wheelbarrow toward the barn door, the wheels squeaking angrily. What the hell was wrong with him?

I was tired of his aggression and hatred. Maybe I had been thrown—or gone willingly—to the wolves, but I'd come back. I was the oldest living Boone here, and the rest of the family looked to me to lead them. Mostly this was when they didn't feel like doing it themselves, but I knew they listened to and valued my opinions. I was sort of an elected president rather than a kingly dictator.

"You know what?" I strode along behind him, irritated and just plain sick and tired of his never letting up on me. "I don't know what your problem is, but I don't have time for it. I've apologized a million times for being a shitty wolf and a worse human being growing up, and I've owned up to my mistakes with the Iron Wolves. I have *changed*. I am not the person I was, and you either accept that or you don't. Either way, I have a lady guest over—and she means a whole lot to me—so I don't have time for your hating on me. I'm real tired of it. Take your meanness somewhere else."

As I brushed by him and his load of pony shit, he reached out and caught my arm, holding on but not hurting me. I met his glare, expecting to find it filled with the usual dislike and condemnation, but instead it was unexpectedly hopeful.

What in the Sam Hill?

"You and Sanye, the two of you never ever were a couple?" The words came out muffled, like he was forcing them past some obstacle that had been choking him for half of forever.

"No. Sanye and I have never stepped out together. We haven't kissed, haven't courted. We held each other when Evan passed. I'd stay with her on the bad nights, but I slept on the couch mostly. She cried herself out, and I made sure I was there from the first night we got the news."

Knox's gaze turned inward. I had no idea what he was imagining. I never had understood him.

"But you've been . . . You haven't dated anyone. There've been no girls at the house, nobody, since Evan died."

I nodded, but my voice came out hard. I wasn't feeling nice. "I didn't date, Knox, because I made a choice not to. I had some real bad habits, habits that hurt the people around me. I treated women like dirt, like they didn't matter to me. It was a lie, but I did it, and I sure didn't like the man looking back at me in the mirror. So I made a decision to change."

Knox let go of my arm. He stood there, his eyes searching my face as if he were finally seeing me. Seeing me for real.

"I'm as far from perfect as a man can get. I made bad mistakes, I've owned them, and I will never, ever repeat them. I'm sorry."

I would repeat the words, though. My apology needed to be said over and over until Knox heard me, until he understood that I really had changed.

And even after he listened to me, *if* he listened to me, I would keep right on showing him, too.

I was not the same person.

I had changed and I was better, but I would always live with the regrets.

Knox winced and looked away, his eyes bouncing off the walls, the ponies, the damned pile of manure that stank almost as much as my past.

I had more to say. "I'm also sorrier than I can ever say that I left you to be the responsible Boone. I'm sorry our daddy beat the hell out of you instead of me. I was the oldest, and I should have stood up for you. I should have protected everyone in this house. Instead, I chose to be a crap brother. If you will let me, I'll make amends. Just tell me what to do."

We're gonna do it. Anything. Everything. He's fucking FAMILY.

CHAPTER
NINETEEN

MAVERICK

"Science is just as important as magic."

— DONNA GRANT

After Knox and I had our heart-to-heart over a wheelbarrow of pony manure, he returned to the house with me. We weren't hugging or going into business together, but we'd stopped flashing our canines at each other.

No one said anything about his stormy departure; they just welcomed us both back. I had to hand it to him too. He tried. He apologized gruffly to Sonnet for his rudeness and then made a point of laughing at all of her jokes. He'd even shared a funny story about some hijinks we'd gotten up to when we were kids.

We'd shifted, rolled in Momma's twenty-pound bag of flour, and then scared the bejeezus out of some non-shifters who had been camping in the national park. I'd forgotten how close we'd been as kids, before our teenage years when our daddy had got real bad.

Eventually, Sonnet started to yawn. She got up real early to shoot on set and admitted she pretty much turned into Cinderella's pumpkin at midnight.

I took her home in my truck, so I wouldn't have to worry about her drifting off the road because she'd closed her eyes just for a second. She didn't need to drive tired, seeing as how she had me. I'd run her rental car over tomorrow with Ranger.

257

She curled up sleepily, smiling and watching me drive. Mostly, we enjoyed a companionable silence. Neither of us had to be on or perform as just being together was enough.

"I was holding out hope for some famous Moonlight Valley parking, or maybe a sleepover at Alice and Ford's mountain love nest," Sonnet said on a sigh as soon as we pulled onto the gravel road leading to Phantom Falls.

"I could turn us around." I couldn't fight the smile on my face.

This earned me another sigh. "I've got an early flight tomorrow. I have to be at the airport at five in the morning."

I'd vaguely known she would be traveling, having overheard Eric and Spike discussing the arrangements. Luke Hensley had demanded a private jet to accommodate his fourteen suitcases. You'd have thought he was relocating to Los Angeles, not flying back for a weekend of business meetings.

"I've got studio meetings about scripts and casting. It's a there-and-back—just until Sunday night." She bit her lower lip as we pulled into Wyatt's drive. "Will you text me? Or call? While I'm away?"

"Yes." I flashed her a smile, then passed her my unlocked phone. "Add yourself to my contacts."

I walked around the truck to open her door while she added her number. She took my hands and let me swing her down to the ground, but she didn't return the phone.

"We need someplace with decent light," she said, scouting around. It was now plenty dark out, although there were stars, and the moon was rising. "Let's try the porch. I've let Eric know we're coming, so I promise there will be no assault tonight."

I let her pull me along. I was happy to do so, seeing as how my position let me admire her amazing ass and legs. The edge of her wraparound skirt barely skimmed her thighs, reminding me that her stockings ended just above those peek-aboo ruffles. I'd had my hands on her thighs. I'd touched her over her panties.

As soon as we made it to the porch, I pulled her into my arms. She tipped her head back, opening her mouth to say something, but I gently nipped her bottom lip with my teeth.

Her breath caught.

"Glamour off," I growled. She didn't ever need to hide who she was with me.

She let it go gently in a wash of gold sparks, but the prettiest color was the one washing over her face.

"Fucking beautiful."

We surprised her, my wolf growled happily. **She tastes good.**

I licked the tiny sting away, sliding an arm around her waist and cupping her butt. I should've sent her inside, said good night, walked away, but I wanted to kiss her more. Taste her.

Night's not over yet.

I certainly didn't want it to be.

I *wanted* this amazing woman. It broke all my rules, how badly I wanted her.

Lucky, that's what we are.

I agreed. So, I kissed my girl. And she pulled me into her, hanging on tightly and fitting her curvy self against me. I'd never been so turned on, and it seemed maybe she felt the same way. She moaned, eyes drifting shut as she relaxed and let me hold her up. Her tongue played with mine, teasing, inviting me in. Her amazing tits were pressed against my chest, her rounded ass in my palms. I used my grip to tug her closer, careful and sure, as my mouth consumed hers in a fiery kiss.

She wrapped her arms around my neck, her fingers playing with my hair as she arched into our kiss and my heated response.

She was the most important thing in the world to me.

She IS the world, my wolf argued before I forgot to think or plan or even worry about how much was too much. We kissed, and then kissed more.

Tugging her mouth from mine, Sonnet gasped out some words. Eventually they penetrated through the red haze of desire in my brain. Words like *bad idea, we should stop*, and *Maverick*.

I stopped.

She called the shots, and I'd honor that for the rest of our lives if she let me, but I was also encouraged by her disappointed groan. This was a *stop for now* and not a *never again*.

She was right too. It was not wise, our making out on the front porch of Wyatt Reynolds's place. Her security team was always watching, plus Sonnet was a magnet for photographers. Cameras, drones—I had no idea how the paparazzi got their shots. I made a mental note to ask Ranger; I needed to know how to protect my girl from that crap. I wrapped her up in a hug, resting my chin on the top of her head while I thought about that.

She was vulnerable and our seeing each other would make her a target.

"I want to slide my fingers under the edge of your panties." I nipped the sensitive skin beneath her ear. If I couldn't do these things just yet, I'd enjoy the thoughts. "Slide inside you."

"Your voice," she breathed out in a rush. "That drawl. It's so hot and melodic. It's like I'm hearing a slow song every time you talk. Say something else."

"What would you like me to say?"

"Whatever! Tell me a hot fantasy of yours."

"What if it's me making you hot?"

"*Sí, bueno*, then it's anything that makes you hot."

We were stuck in some circular logic here. I grinned because, damn, I was happy. I also had ideas.

All the ideas, my wolf said happily. **We're gonna be BUSY.**

"Maybe I sneak into your trailer when you're on set, and I'm waiting for you when you come back. I'll be in your bed, getting the party started without you, so I'll have to make sure you catch up real fast."

My face was still pressed against her hair, my hands holding her close, when I heard a soft click.

Danger.

I tensed, not-so-sexy adrenaline rushing through me. No one messed with a wolf and his mate. Lifting my head, I scouted the area for the source of the sound.

We'll smash the cameras. Teach those paparazzi a lesson. No one violates our girl's space.

Damn straight.

Nothing human lurked in the shadows around us. A rabbit disappeared into the underbrush, but there were no photographers, no drones overhead.

Sonnet watched me check out our surroundings, grinning mischievously. She was holding my phone out to the side, angled to take a shot of us together.

She was the photographer.

"This can be my contact photo!" She winked at me, then tapped away for a second before handing me back my phone. In the tiny circle above her contact info, the two of us kissed.

Video would have been better, my wolf volunteered. **Or one of those moving photographs like Harry Potter has. Hoo boy. I could watch that—**

I snorted softly. "You are trouble."

"You like trouble," she said saucily.

I gave her a quick kiss. "Apparently I do."

* * *

I was a biologist.

I also had a very randy wolf who was not shy to comment.

This should have given me a leg up in the business of sexy texting, but I hadn't allowed for my general lack of texting experience.

I was, as nearly as you could get, a texting virgin. I'd always figured that people who spent their days hunched over their phone screens, pecking away at an itty-bitty keyboard that was nothing but frustration, had small, frustrated lives. Missing out on the world around me would have been the mistake. Plus, if you wanted to say something to me, and you chose to say it in fifteen-point font, you didn't have the sense God gave a goose. I was not going to pay attention.

Words, I figured, were best shared face-to-face. In my brothers' case, this allowed for some important physical punctuation like a friendly punch to the shoulder, a wolfy love bite, or a slap upside the back of the head. Our family did not send greeting cards.

It took just two minutes and one text conversation with Sonnet on Saturday morning for me to see the light.

Sonnet: What are you doing?

Maverick: Building a rabbit hutch. You?

Sonnet: Thinking about you.

. . .

Uh-huh. I was an addict. I read and reread her two messages for a good five minutes, looking for subtexts. Hell, I gave them a full literary analysis. She was interested in my doings and looking to interact. And despite my boring-ass response, she was *thinking about me*. Those three words—words without even a simple subject or an adverb hinting at her sentiments . . . *madly, enthusiastically, fondly, lustily* . . . I was not particular—proved that we had an honest-to-God relationship. I was not alone in my feelings.

Three hundred and six messages and thirty-six hours later, I was in danger of a severe case of capsulitis in my thumbs, thanks to my new texting addiction. I hadn't run the risk of a repetitive strain injury since I'd discovered the joys of self-pleasuring, but I fell for the texting bait faster than a crawdad for a turkey leg. The picture of us kissing would flash across my screen, and I'd grab my phone, eager for my next hit of Sonnet. She was beautiful in that picture, but she was also just as funny and sassy via text message as she was in person.

Sonnet: If you rearrange the letters in your name, you can spell 'Vic Maker' and 'Cake Vim.'

Sonnet: Also 'Mack Vire' and 'Race Kim.' You can sound like a Scotsman or a weird cake flavor! Now I want a snack. Also, if I buy you a kilt will you stride around the mountain in it? I have a non-cake-related fantasy.

Maverick: Yours spells 'Onn Set.'

Sonnet: Close enough. Do you believe in destiny?

Sonnet: Because I do now ;)

I'd laughed out loud at that one, startling the baby squirrel I'd been feeding. What with all the momma squirrels giving birth in late summer, I'd had my hands full with well-intentioned people deciding that a solo baby meant it had been orphaned or had fallen out of a tree and needed human intervention. Sometimes, it was true. Mostly, it was not. Dwayne Junior here was almost ready to go back into the woods.

Throughout the day she'd sent me pictures of herself having Hollywood adventures. In the first one she'd posed in front of a breakfast table covered with crystal and fancy white flowers, her making a sad face, with the caption: *No pink unicorn*

Frappuccino? WUT?! She'd also sent pictures from the green room of a TV studio, a spooky film set (caption: *they have got werewolves ALL WRONG!!!*), and a long conference table with black leather chairs in front of a wall of exposed brick (caption: *chair race time!*).

We'd pretty much texted nonstop since she'd boarded her flight, sending silly stuff back and forth or just narrating our day. I knew that someone had proposed a kale smoothie for lunch (along with her unhappy thoughts on "serving salad in a glass"); she had thumbs-upped my faux chicken salad hoagie.

Maverick: What time do you land tonight?

Sonnet: Tomorrow Two a.m.

Maverick: I can come get you.

Sonnet: No. You need your beauty sleep.

Sonnet: Not that you're not already Mr. Awesomely Hot.

Sonnet: I'm gonna pitch a sexy lumberjack show. FYI. So, send shirtless pics please for my slide deck.

Maverick: Will you be in this show?

Sonnet: I hear there's gonna be a shower scene! And a nekkid sexy times scene! Let me know if you want to practice ;)

We also texted about our families. Sonnet had a huge extended family clan back in the mountains near Mexico City. She'd drawn me a family tree on a napkin with her eyeliner pencil, and there were almost too many aunties, uncles, cousins, and second cousins to fit, not to mention her mami, papi, and her brother and sister. Getting ahead of myself—again—I made plans to get to work on a much, much bigger table for our family dinners. We were gonna have to host Thanksgiving in the barn to fit everyone in. Sonnet was the adopted baby of the family after her Fae bio dad had dropped her off on the doorstep. Apparently, she was half Chaneque, and the Fae dude had been one-hundred-percent asshole. The note he'd left pinned to her onesie had read: *She's half Chaneque and all yours.* He hadn't mentioned what had happened to her bio mom, but fortunately Sonnet had been welcomed with open arms by the Ruizes. Her older sister, Elena, was her manager.

. . .

Sonnet: I need a picture of you.

Maverick: Why?

Sonnet: So I can show Elena! Can't show her us kissing!

Maverick: Nope. But here's a cute baby squirrel pic.

Sonnet: Awww. Our firstborn is darling. But I still need a pic of my baby daddy's face. Pony up.

Maverick: Earl says he's the best pony. See attached pic.

Sonnet: Nice try.

Sonnet: Photo now PLZ

Maverick: I don't do selfies

I chuckled. She'd sent me a selfie of herself making duck lips and flopped on her bed. The white duvet poofing up around her made her look like she was sinking in a cloud of marshmallow. I tried to decide if she was naked or not, but damn, there were sheets and the duvet, plus enough pillows to recreate Fort Sumter.

"Are you intending to share with the class?"

I glanced up, finding Sanye peeking at me from the door, a teasing smile on her lips.

It being Sunday, I was over at her place, checking in to make sure everything was shipshape. As was our habit, she'd invited me to stay for dinner. Also as usual, I'd accepted. I enjoyed her company, and she was an excellent cook.

"Nope." I shook my head, tucking my phone into my pocket and getting back to work on fixing the weather stripping that had come off her back door. She would have one heck of a draft whistling through her kitchen in December if it were not replaced.

She grinned at me, undeterred. "Are you texting with a certain TV star?"

I flashed her my best grumpy scowl.

Seeing as how I couldn't stop smiling like a common loon, my scowl had zero effect. "Come on, Mav. The curiosity is killing me. Ranger said she came over for dinner?"

"You two church ladies gossip about anyone else in Moonlight Valley? Or is it just me?"

"Don't you hold out on me. I'm thrilled you're dating." Sanye waved the dish towel she held in one hand. "Ranger acts like he likes her, and if he likes her, she must be amazing. He's the most particular person I know."

You could also substitute *peculiar.*

"She's amazing," I admitted. Was it too soon to check my phone again?

"Details," Sanye said impatiently. "When did you meet? How? Was your first date *really* at Biscuits & Blessings? Are you guys serious? What happens when her show wraps?"

That was a whole lot of questions, questions I had answers for right up until that last one. I didn't know what we'd do after *Smoky Spirits* finished shooting. My smile slipped. "We haven't made plans for after the show wraps, but we'll figure it out."

Run off to Vegas, my wolf prompted. **Or just den in your love nest. I recommend you get right on that, FYI. Along with the biting. Rome wasn't built in a day.**

"So, you'll keep seeing each other? This isn't a summer romance kind of thing?"

I frowned. "It's October, and I hope so."

Understatement of the year, my wolf snapped. **HELLO. Mate? We have to pursue her good and hard.**

Uh-huh.

Also do other things good and hard if you catch my meaning.

LOVE her good and hard, I corrected.

And long. Thick.

I did not need adverbial suggestions from my wolf.

"Well, I'm thrilled." The quiet sincerity in Sanye's voice had me looking up from the weather stripping. "I'm glad you're out there again, dating and falling in love. I wasn't sure you were ever going to get that houseful of pups you want."

"Hold your horses." I stood, testing the door to make sure it opened and closed cleanly. "We've barely started to get to know each other. Don't you rush to book the church just yet."

"I know you."

She's rolling her eyes, my wolf groaned. **You know she is. Your credibility is shot, I tell you. SHOT. You might as well head on over to the jeweler's right now. Two months salary, dude. At a minimum.**

"We're taking things slow," I said, both to Sanye and my wolf.

She snorted (as did my wolf). "You say that, and that just proves my point. You're serious about her because you don't want to screw this up. Bring her over for dinner. I promise I won't go super fangirl on her," she added, then muttered under her breath, "Just minorly so. I hope."

I grinned at the closed door. "Maybe it's time you tried getting out there too."

"Now you hold up a minute," she said. "I have plans. I just haven't shared them yet."

I opened and closed the door a few times, making sure it was smooth before turning to tease Sanye. "Nope. If you don't say it, it doesn't count. If I've put my heart out there, maybe you should too. We'll be adventure buddies."

Love buddies, my wolf said happily. **Although that didn't come out quite right.**

Sanye made heart eyes at me. "Well, bless my biscuits. Maverick Boone, putting his heart out there. I never thought you'd go that far."

"Ha ha." I turned around to face her, folding my arms over my chest. "Why don't you tell me all about you and Knox?"

Sanye stiffened, her smile falling.

Busted, my wolf crooned.

The idea of the two of them had been a niggle in the back of my head since Knox and I had had our confrontation, but I had not been sure. He and I had a lot to still work through, and I had plenty to atone for, and I guessed I'd thought that maybe I could help him out here.

Sticking your nose in another wolf's love life is stupid. You are not Dr. Phil.

"Why would you tell him that you and I were a thing?"

A flash of guilt and regret passed over her face, quicker than quick. Sanye was the best at hiding her feelings. She'd certainly had plenty of practice during her tumultuous and unpleasant childhood.

"I didn't tell him that," she said defensively.

"Did you strongly hint that we were interested in each other or otherwise together?" I had meant my original remark as a joke, but there was clearly some business between my brother and Sanye.

She glared at me with blue eyes that held a wealth of hurt and bad memories. I knew she'd had a rough childhood. She was Lucky Jansen's only daughter, and he was bad, bad news, not to mention the ringleader and president of the Iron Wolves, a nefarious businessman, and the asshole who had tried to blackmail and then beat up Ford. Saying he'd been a bad father would be like calling Ranger merely socially awkward. There was a wealth of intent and bad decision-making there, and Sanye had escaped the motorcycle club only by marrying Evan the day she turned eighteen.

Evan had treated her like a queen, but his gentle care could never have erased the years of abuse Lucky had subjected her to.

Turn on the charm, my wolf urged. **You know that always works.**

"Did you possibly hint to my brother, even indirectly, that we were seeing each other?"

She smiled ruefully, turning away. "I owe you an apology."

"For what?"

"For causing problems between you and Knox."

I waited for her to say something more, but she was quiet as a bear in winter.

Stubborn, my wolf said fondly. **She's good people.**

She was practically family, and I didn't like seeing her hurting. "Sanye, I don't know what all happened between you and Knox but—"

"Nothing at all," she said quickly. "Nothing recently, that's for sure. We just have a little history from before Evan. When we were teenagers."

My wolf perked up. **They were teenage lovers?**

It was news to me too.

It also made Knox's hostility in the barn all the more interesting. "Well now, you've got me feeling confused. I had no idea that something had happened between you and my brother."

Her shoulders slumped, and she shook her head. "It was ages ago, Mav. I'm sorry if my silence about my ancient love life caused you any trouble. I sure didn't mean to make things any tenser between you and Knox." She grimaced. "But I didn't deny anything when he flat out asked me."

"What business of his was it if we were seeing each other?"

"None," she said, her eyes sheeting amber. "It is none of his business."

CHAPTER
TWENTY

SONNET

> "If you do not have the courage to be yourself, what will you be?"
>
> — THE SILVER ELVES, *LIVING THE PERSONAL MYTH:*
> *MAKING THE MAGIC OF FAERIE REAL IN ONE'S OWN LIFE*

The woodchuck grinned at me.

Its cute little head poked right up out of its burrow, and it was smiling into the camera. Okay, so *smiling* was an exaggeration, but it sure looked like a very happy mammal.

Possibly this was because, in the photograph, Maverick was five feet away, holding out a fistful of wildflowers. Unlike the woodchuck, Maverick was *not* looking at the camera. He was literally giving it his back. As his back was big, broad, and wrapped in flannel, my heart gave a happy leap of its own, heat dancing through me.

He was the handsomest, hottest man of them all. At least in my eyes. Which was, really, all that mattered.

I told myself it was fine to miss him. Lying on my sun lounger, soaking in the perfect Los Angeles sunshine like a heat-loving skink, I wished he was here. Or that I was there with him in Tennessee. He was out there being a badass biologist and stomping around the woods, luring cute little woodchucks, while I was hanging poolside with cucumber slices in my Evian water.

269

. . .

Maverick: This is the only picture of myself I have on my phone.

Sonnet: Are you the only human alive who doesn't take selfies?

Maverick: Nope.

Sonnet: Are you sure? I think it's a rule of smartphone ownership. They give you a phone, you agree to take selfies and send them to your girlfriend.

Maverick: FYI, no one gives you a phone. There's this thing called money. And capitalism. If you want a picture, you can take one of me this week.

Sonnet: How do you feel about tasteful boudoir photographs?

Maverick: Is this your way of telling me you want to see me naked?

Sonnet: Is this where I pretend to be a lady?

Maverick: Only if that's what you want to be.

Sonnet: I totally want to see you naked.

"Why are you smiling like that?" Elena asked from right beside me. "And you should say thank you for all the sunshine I brought you today."

I startled, almost falling off the lounger. She'd snuck up on me while I was admiring Maverick's woodchuck, and she was reading my phone screen over my shoulder. I immediately reverted to five years old, squealed, and clutched my phone to my chest.

"This is private!"

"Why? Who is it?"

"Because I said so!" Some sisterly dynamics never change. I would need to change my phone passcode when she wasn't looking.

The look she gave me was patronizing and one-hundred-percent big sister. "You have no privacy."

Elena was referring to the incident when a particularly enterprising person had flown a drone past my window while I'd been trying on bathing suits for a hypothetical vacation that I'd never gotten to take. Various online sites had spent months debating whether a "woman of my size" had any business wearing a string bikini in public and what it would take for me to achieve a bikini body.

News flash: I had a body, and I had a bikini. Ergo, I had a bikini body.

"Just because other people have hacked into my stuff doesn't make it okay for you to look." I clutched my phone tighter to my chest. Elena was a master at tickle fights.

"You're a household name," Elena said primly. "You therefore cannot expect to have the same level of privacy as the people you meet at the grocery store. People want to know more about you. They think they *already* know you and that you all are friends."

I waited for her to round into her conclusion. We'd had this conversation approximately a billion times (only a slight exaggeration), but this was the first time she'd kicked it off by spying on my phone.

"And in order to continue at this level of success," she said, indeed bringing it home, "you have to feed the beast. And the beast demands a diet of Instagram posts. Pictures. What's in my bag. GRWM. People want to know all the things."

"Fine. But you still don't get to look at my phone. I expect better from you."

To give Elena credit, she looked mildly ashamed. "You're right. I shouldn't have looked. I apologize. Now, who are you texting?"

I decided I could work with this. Also, I was going to change my passcode just as soon as I went to the bathroom.

Too happy to consider Elena's reaction to my news, I announced, "I'm seeing someone!"

"In Tennessee?" Elena's voice held a healthy dose of skepticism.

"There are awesome people in Tennessee."

"Sure." She sounded unconvinced. Should I go to bat for the fine people in our sixteenth state? "Wait. Is it Luke? He's in Tennessee. Are you guys back together?"

"No. Absolutely not. That's the hardest hard no ever."

"Thom? That would be a great narrative for the London premiere. It could work."

"NO. He's not an actor."

"Is it Bob?"

"Who?" Did I even know any Bobs who weren't of the battery-operated boyfriend variety?

"Bob," she said impatiently. "The junior executive producer for *Wolf Girl*. He was at yesterday's casting event."

"Wow. That would be fast. And no." I'd spent every second at that event sneaking peeks at my phone to see if my sexy professor had messaged me. Which he had. Often. I'd made so many trips to the bathroom to text him back from the privacy of a stall that I suspected there would be internet rumors that I was pregnant or doing drugs. "My guy's not in the industry at all. He's a college professor."

"Who is?"

"My man. He's a biologist who teaches at the local community college in Moonlight Valley." I scrolled through my text messages until I found the picture of him and his woodchuck and showed it to my sister.

She looked at it for a long moment and started laughing. It was super cute, but I was confused. I double-checked to make sure it wasn't one of those live photos or that I hadn't overlooked some misbehavior on the part of either mammal. Nope. It was all aboveboard. It was just the woodchuck and Maverick's world's-best, flannel-covered shoulders.

"You're too much, Sonnet." Elena flopped down on the lounge chair next to me. Never mind that she was wearing a dry-clean only pantsuit. A *black* pantsuit. In eighty-degree weather. She whispered something under her breath and a cooling mist sprang up around her chair.

"I don't understand what's so funny." Usually, I loved laughter. It was literally the sound of money in the bank for me. Today, however, I was disliking it.

Elena cackled. I waited not so patiently.

"Explain it to me," I said.

My sister blinked at me, pausing, as if she thought I was halfway through the joke and there was a punchline coming. When I said nothing, she stopped laughing. "Oh my god, are you serious?" She grabbed the phone and swiped from the woodchuck photo to the kissing photo. "This has to be a joke. What is this?"

"That would be two people who have feelings for each other expressing those feelings. It's called kissing. You should try it."

"He is glued to you. Who took this?"

"I did."

"Does he have a copy? Does anyone?"

"I took it with his phone, and he air-dropped it to me."

She stared at me blankly, as if my use of technology to promote my love life did not compute. She made a little hissing sound like a shook-up can of Coke about to explode. When she did speak, her voice was flatter than day-old soda, however. "The professor has this exact same picture on his phone? Are you trying to sabotage your career? Are you so desperate for that vacation you want that you'll sabotage yourself?"

I gulped my cucumber water, stalling for time. Were my feelings for Maverick a convenient out from my career? Was I exhausted and searching for excuses?

"Sonnet?"

I mean, I was definitely tired. And desperate for a break. And yeah, I had an issue with how Elena had brought it up, as if I hadn't earned a vacation or didn't know how to ask for one. Wasn't it my life, my career, my choice?

Yes, yes it was.

"It's not sabotage," I said firmly. "And my having a personal relationship that makes me happy is not some secret time-off strategy. If I decide to take a vacation, I'll use Expedia. Maverick is one of the good guys, not a problem we have to proactively deal with."

Maverick had nothing to do with my TV career. Did he? Could I be using him, even subconsciously, to force an escape from the celebrity life I hated so much? If I was, that was the silver lining on the cape of Maverick's awesomeness.

And so what? If being in a relationship with a man I cared deeply about motivated me to make life changes that I also cared deeply about? That hurt no one. That was *good*.

"When he sells that picture to TMZ along with an erotic novel-worthy description of your torrid Tennessee love affair, don't ask me to clean it up."

I shoved my phone under the lounger cushion.

Angry heat prickled my face.

I truly didn't understand her being upset, but it made me feel embarrassed and confused. Sick to my stomach. Our relationship wasn't like that. *Defend his honor. Maverick would stick up for you—you stick up for him.* We are *partners*.

"What is WRONG with you?" I burst out.

"What is WRONG WITH ME?!! You just announced that you're dating some random biologist. From Tennessee! How do you think your fans and the studio are going to react to that?"

"I don't care what they think. It's not their business."

"It is their business. They sign your paycheck."

Since the success of my first book, I'd lived my new celebrity life with one rule: do not care.

Do not read the reviews.

Never read the comments.

It was paralyzing, the number of opinions out there about what I should or shouldn't do. What was important was that I wrote the best books and acted to the best of my ability. I did a good job, and then I went home.

But Elena did care. She read all those comments, and she took them to heart. She wanted to give people the version of Sonnet Ruiz that they asked for. And more often than I cared to admit, her caring made me reevaluate my career choices. I took on more projects because she wanted me to do so. I did or didn't do things—like take a vacation—because of the script she'd written for me. About who Sonnet Ruiz should be. I hadn't wanted to let her down, so I'd done what she needed.

But that had to stop. It wasn't just me being affected by her choices for my life anymore—it was Maverick.

"They don't know me, Elena. My life isn't a Choose Your Own Adventure book where they flip the pages. I get to make my own choices."

"That's ridiculous," she ground out.

Sunlight bounced off the pool. My hair and makeup team would be here soon to glam me up for our last event before I headed back to Tennessee.

"They call me names, Elena. I'm fat, lazy, and undisciplined—because I'm not skinny. I'm successful at exactly the size I am—in fact, my success is size-independent—and they *hate* that. They hate that I'm a woman who writes outsized, funny scripts and makes big bucks doing so. I color outside their black-and-white lines, and I don't follow their rules about how I should look or act. I'm a big, fat success, and I don't care how they define either *fat* or *success*."

Elena shot upright. She spoke over me. "You think not caring is the secret to your success? Think again. You succeed because *I* care. Because *I* push you. *I* am the reason you're taken seriously in this industry. You would be nothing without me."

I felt sick. Was this what she'd been thinking for years and years and YEARS? We weren't sisters and partners against the world? Two fat women succeeding on their own terms because fuck the people who say that fat is bad? This was all her doing and I was—what? An accessory? Was I a cute little plastic Barbie shoe?

Elena slumped backward. She smacked a hand over her face. "I'm sorry. It's my day for apologizing, apparently. That didn't come out right."

You bet your sweet ass it didn't.

Also: I disagreed.

"Pretty much every day I've come face-to-face with people who think I should be embarrassed. About my size, the way I look, how loudly I laugh, what I write about. How *dare* I not want to look the way they think I should look? I choose not to care about their opinions. Some of the crap is easy ignore, but sometimes it's hurtful or belittling. Sometimes, it's downright mean, and it's *always* ignorant. I've spent my career refusing to be ashamed of who I am, so why on earth would I be ashamed about Maverick?"

"His name is Maverick?" Her tone held a worried edge.

"Like the truck," I confirmed. "His brothers are also named after trucks. They trap animals for a living."

That was a slight exaggeration, but she deserved to imagine a bunch of fur-trapping, redneck Southerners messing up her grand plans for "our" career.

"Couldn't you at least have dated an Ivy League professor? You had to hook up with some guy from Tennessee? Does he come with a yard full of rusted-out cars and broken-down tractors?"

"He has a gorgeous home, a loving family, and a huge brain. He also has ethics. And we're not hooking up. We're falling for each other, and I'm more than halfway in love with him."

"Does he know about your magic? About the glamour?"

He sure did. I nodded.

"And you think he can keep that secret? That he won't 'accidentally' let it drop to the media or a good friend of his?"

"He won't. He wouldn't."

He actually *couldn't*, if I was being fair, because he was a werewolf. If he outed me, he risked outing his pack and all the other wolves living in Moonlight Valley, and Maverick would never force his choices on others.

It was that *don't hurt people* rule of his combined with his big, open, loving heart. He protected those he cared about and if the wolves ever did decide to do the big reveal, he'd make sure there was a unanimous vote and a safety plan. The wolves were safe.

I was safe.

Elena shook her head impatiently. "But—"

I was not going to defend my choice. I didn't *have* to defend my choice. I'd made it, and now Elena could choose to accept Maverick—or not.

I was still hoping that she would.

"We're a couple," I said firmly. "We're together."

Elena stared at me, her expression one of reluctant acceptance and conniving planning. She was spinning us, spinning our story, putting a Hollywood twist on our romance. I understood she wanted what she thought was best for me. But she was focused on my career, my bank account, my success.

There was no room in her planner for my heart.

"Alright. I guess we can discuss this later." My sister checked the time on her phone, then blew out a breath. "You have an event."

I met her gaze. We faced off. Two elephant seals rammed each other. Water splashed. The breeding site was at stake.

She looked away first. "You need to go get ready. Fight with me later."

"Fine. I'm going." I stood up, but I had one point I needed to make before I stomped into the house. "But there will be no 'discussing' anything if you can't be happy for the two of us."

TWENTY-ONE

SONNET

"'You see!' said a strained voice. Tonks was glaring at Lupin. 'She still wants to marry him, even though he's been bitten! She doesn't care!'"

—J.K. ROWLING, *HARRY POTTER AND THE HALF-BLOOD PRINCE*

Coffee? Check.

Hummingbird cupcakes? Check.

Alone time with my sexy professor in my trailer with the door locked? DOUBLE CHECK!

My call time today wasn't until 9:00 a.m., but Maverick had to help Ranger with an animal relocation before then. Today's challenge was a spotted skunk who'd been sighted marching down Smoky Spirits' Main Street. The skunk had not been impressed with Luke's glamour, and my co-star had been forced to make a hasty retreat.

At any rate, we had all of an hour before I had to share him with the rest of the world.

One of the perks of being the top name on the call sheet was that I'd got to customize my luxury trailer. I'd had it done up like a tiny farmhouse on wheels. The kitchenette had a wall of dark wood-toned cabinetry, with a stainless-steel fridge, a range, and a microwave. A wooden trestle sofa held piles of throw pillows and a chunky blanket. Potted plants filled the corners, and I'd started an air plant collection. I had several lounge chairs for curling up on and a plush rug for those days when I just needed to lie flat on my back. There was even a full bathroom and a lighted makeup area.

I pushed aside the chairs and dumped an armful of pillows onto the rug, making a cozy nest around the circular coffee table in the middle of the space.

Maverick frowned and set his own coffee and the box of cupcakes down on the countertop. "You don't need to be moving furniture around when you have me."

"Shhh. I'm not moving furniture. I'm setting the stage."

He shook his head and came over to help me adjust the table's position. "Is this a theater person thing? Is every meal going to be a three-act play?"

I patted him on the butt. "Sit, please. It's cake time."

He sat.

No. To say he *sat* was like saying Picasso doodled in the margins of his grocery list. Maverick lounged on my pillows like a Greek god reclining at table.

He set his coffee on the table and leaned back against my sofa, one arm braced on his bent leg, his other leg stretched out in front of him. Heat stole through me. How could any cake, no matter how delicious, compete with this man? Fortunately, I had cake plans. I'd do that thing I'd seen in movies. I'd—oh, so sorry— get frosting on the corner of my mouth.

Step two in the devilish icing program: Maverick would lick it off.

Step three: we'd kiss.

Step four: repeat as necessary.

Possibly, frosting would be relocated to other spots. I was also more than willing to de-frost Maverick. Never let it be said that I was not a giver.

Spoiler alert: my plan was not a secret.

Judging by the heated look in his eyes and the tension in his body, he also understood the possibilities of cake eating. Holding his eyes with mine, I took a delicate, ladylike bite. No crumbs were lost to the floor. I did not stab my nostrils or my lips with the fork. Just the teensiest smidge of frosting painted the corner of my mouth.

But then, ohmigod, life threw a curveball at my plan. The unsexiest, most surprising curveball. SWOOSH. Attention rerouted. Because hello?

The hummingbird cake was unbelievably delicious.

Unbelievably. Delicious.

Three layers of pineapple-and-banana goodness studded with dense cream cheese frosting and nuts. Delicious, salty nuts.

Unable to help myself, I moaned, "Oh my God. These are the best nuts ever."

Maverick's lips quirked up, his dimple on full display. Unlike me, the professional actress, he absolutely remembered his line. "You have something right there."

Leaning forward, he brushed the corner of my mouth with his thumb. He was ad-libbing. It was sexy. Any other time, I would have been on the man like a monkey on a tree. Right now, though, I had other priorities.

I batted his hand away and took another bite, speaking around a mouthful of pineapple-and-banana goodness. Was it enchanted? Some kind of Alice in Wonderland cake with magical properties? I guessed I'd find out. "Holy crap, this is the best thing that's ever been in my mouth."

Maverick bit back laughter. Proving that he was no fool, he did not get between me and my cake. He sprawled there, watching me devour the cupcake.

I was a woman on a mission. There may have been moaning; there was definitely licking and sucking of fingers. It would have been criminal to waste cake this good. Preoccupied as I was, I missed my cue. I was just about to lick off the last of the frosting when Maverick caught my wrist, drawing my attention to him. My protest died on my lips as he held out his plate to me.

"Aren't you hungry?"

"Not for cake," he said gently.

"But it's delicious," I teased. "So creamy and sweet. I think you'd enjoy a taste."

He shook his head. "I'm allergic to pineapple."

"Wait. What?"

"Not badly," he said. "I'm not going to keel over just because I'm near it."

"But—"

Maybe he hadn't understood my sexy frosting plans? Did this mean that there would be no kissing and heavy petting in my trailer? Had I unknowingly made a terrible choice in baked goods that would set my sex life back?

His thumb rubbed against the corner of my mouth again. "I'll bet you taste sweeter than some old pineapple anyhow."

"But then you'll be allergic to me!" I slapped my cake plate onto the table. My plan was a terrible plan.

His eyes gleamed. I could see the wolf in them, all right. "I don't think that's gonna be a problem, sweetheart."

He slid an arm around my waist. His other slid under my legs, lifting me. The world shifted. I was airborne.

In a controlled and graceful movement, he rolled me underneath him, bracing himself above my body.

I frowned up at him. "I like this view, but I'm still concerned about your pineapple allergy."

His fingers skimmed up my thigh, pushing my skirt higher, his fingertips delving between my thighs. That was a pineapple-free zone. Clear to enjoy myself, I arched up into his touch.

"Take your shirt off," he ordered.

"Why can't you—"

"If I do it, I'll rip it off."

The man makes a compelling case.

I wriggled, yanking my T-shirt upward. It got stuck for a second on my boobs, making Maverick groan. He slid a muscled thigh between mine.

As soon as my shirt had gone flying, it was time to get Maverick out of his clothes. He was wearing too many, and I wanted to appreciate his naked form. A lot. He cursed roughly, batting my groping hands away as I tried to push his stupid, awesome flannel shirt down his shoulders.

"Off," I growled. "Take it all off."

He pushed up one arm—ONE arm—and shrugged out of a sleeve. Then he did the same with the other arm. This still left him in a T-shirt that I hadn't fully appreciated earlier and that I had absolutely no intention of reading now unless it turned out to be a secret decoder ring to his favorite sexual fantasy. I settled for shoving it up and getting my hands all over his bare chest and back.

He lowered his head, making exploring his bare skin that much harder, and nuzzled the edge of my bra. It was new, it was black lace, and it was more of a boob frame than actual underwear. I decided that Maverick's hoarse groan indicated approval.

"The panties match," I panted. "And you can tear them off me."

His eyes blazed a heated trail from my bra-framed breasts, down my tummy, to the waist of my skirt. From the looks of things—and what I felt pressed against me down yonder—he liked what he saw. A lot. My skirt flew up, my panties headed in the other direction, and then he was kissing me while his fingers drove me crazy.

"You are so fucking beautiful," he growled. "No way I ever get enough of you."

He touched me, his thumb rubbing tight circles around my clit. My legs were spread wide, my hips rocking up against him. Dear God, he was amazing. So, so good. He worked his fingers up and down, which made me see stars.

That's right. *Stars.*

There might have been a supernova too.

He felt so good, I gave up on thinking and came for him.

I lost my mind a little after that, lost control of my response, definitely lost my ability to keep to an inside voice. There were some loud profanities and blasphemous invocations of deities.

I might have fisted his shirt, dragging him closer as I chanted his name. His blue jeans–covered thigh pushed between mine, pressing up against me, the best ever pony ride, and pineapple be damned, he kissed me as I came down. I was wrapped up in his strong arms, tucked against his chest. He pressed a kiss against my forehead that made me feel special and loved. I was his right then.

Maverick holding me was heaven.

A galaxy or two.

The whole damned universe.

TWENTY-TWO

MAVERICK

"What do you know? I'd caught the werewolf's eye."

— ILONA ANDREWS, *CLEAN SWEEP*

I was all in with this woman.

No.

Back that truck up.

I was with this woman in all ways. She wasn't a dating game, a hand of cards I'd resolved was good enough to win with. She was perfect and perfectly Sonnet.

My wolf hummed his approval. **That's better.**

I ran a hand up and down her bare back, over the silky sweet skin of her rounded thighs, and over her magnificently curvy backside. I owed her a pair of panties.

Better buy stock in Victoria's Secret, my wolf suggested. **Just a little investment tip.**

Destroying her things gave me some pause—**She GAVE permission, and it was SEXY destruction**, my wolf said, irritated—because breaking stuff had been something Darrell Boone had done a lot of. And sure, it had often been people, not clothing, but I resolved to think about my behavior. Later. Sonnet's satin-soft curves did very little to ease the hard situation that had popped up south of my belt. But it was a good kind of problem. It fed a different addiction.

Because right now we're snuggling our mate, my wolf said smugly. **Ain't nothing better.**

I mentally adjusted my calendar for the rest of my life. There needed to be room for doing this every day. Touching her, bringing her to release—a spectacularly loud and gratifyingly open release—calmed the beast in me even as it fed my desire for more. I wanted to do it again, and then again. Pretty much daily for forever.

"Penny for your thoughts?" she asked, settling closer and slipping her leg between mine. I pet the sweet, rounded curve of her upper thigh.

Her needing to ask surprised me.

"You." I moved my fingers higher, gently trailing the backs of my knuckles over her. She was slick and warm, and I left my hand there. Making her feel good made me feel good.

Win-win, my wolf said happily.

"I suspect," I said, pressing another kiss against her forehead, "that I'm gonna be a very hands-on boyfriend."

She rewarded me with a breathy whimper.

"How do you feel about demonstrative affection?" I stroked her gently.

"Is this a demonstration like those awesome people who hand out samples at Costco? Is public sex your thing?" She twinkled up at me. She was getting her second wind.

Round two!

"I will not be encouraging anyone to sample your goods." I tapped her clit gently and she moaned. "Nor was I planning public orgies. Unless that's something you're into, in which case I'm game to try."

I'd do anything for her. I hoped I'd made that clear.

"How about you just keep doing what you're doing right now? You do that, and I don't care if we get it on in a chilly-ass meat aisle, just as long as it's the two of us together."

We can work with that.

We sure could.

"Fuck," I groaned.

"That's the plan," she agreed happily. "You just lose your pants, big guy. I can handle the rest."

I bet she could.

I bet it would be the most amazing three minutes of my life, too, because I would not be lasting long when I finally got inside her.

Reluctantly, I removed my fingers from their happy place.

"I'm dead serious," she said. "This is me asking, with a side of lusty begging. Let's sleep together. When can we have sex, and why aren't we doing that right now?"

Woman makes a great point.

I tensed because I did like her idea a whole lot. My brain was a radio station playing sexy Sonnet thoughts twenty-four seven. My pants, however, were not the real obstacle. I didn't want to spoil what we had between us. Nourish it, yes. Feed it and make it grow, you bet. So, I had to be careful.

Our feelings aren't the only thing growing, my wolf grumbled.

Clearing my throat, I proceeded with caution. "So I'm a scientist. I study snake venom."

Sonnet nudged me gently. "FYI, your romantic talk needs work, although I sure would like to handle your trouser snake."

Sonnet joked when she felt vulnerable. Where some animals tried to match their background or used flashy body parts to deflect a bigger predator away from a vulnerable area, she used humor. *My emotions? That ain't no never mind—just enjoy this funny joke!*

I respected her need to protect herself, so I leaned back some so she could see my face. I smiled, hoping I was projecting caring and tenderness, not concern about the conversation I was launching. "As a scientist, I know for a fact that you have to be slow and methodical. You can have a great hypothesis, but then you have to prove it. You have to go through all the steps. You can't go jumping to conclusions based on a single piece of physical evidence. I believe we have something amazing between us, and I believe it can last. But we can't be making a conclusion like that based just on a chemical attraction to each other."

"You don't think sex is enough." Then she muttered into my chest, "Well, hypothesize that."

I had to laugh at the disappointment in her voice.

You could—here's a fucking order and not a suggestion—DO something, my wolf urged. **Make sweet, sweet love to her**.

"Yeah, I don't. Even if we're making enough pheromones between us to cause an entire colony of sea urchins to eject their sex cells."

"You are so weird sometimes," she said, flashing me a quick smile. "Ummm. Not to be dismissive of the sexual habits of sea urchins, but what about us becoming a sexy habit? Or we could just sleep together. Cuddle."

I brushed the hair back from her face. "Are you *hypothesizing* that we could be in a bed together and *just sleep*? Because that's a terrible hypothesis, and I have the data point to prove it."

"I feel your point," she grumbled. "But we could be strong. Think about root vegetables. Do higher order mathematics."

"There is nothing that would make me not desire you."

Another quick, happy grin lit up her face. Her dimples were out in full force. "So, I'm completely irresistible?"

I gave her the unvarnished truth. "You are."

She grinned wider, then tried to reorganize her face into solemn and serious lines. She was, indeed, up for most challenges. "I have faith in you, Maverick. I believe you can resist my charms. Actually, you *do* resist them. Draw on that werewolf strength and stop selling yourself short."

Fuck she's cute when she's laughing.

She was. I loved it when she teased me.

"I'm not," I countered. This was the part of the conversation that I had been dreading. *Confession time.*

Sonnet wasn't out of jokes, though. "I sleep in ratty sweatpants. They're holey and have weird stains from eating in bed. And I have equally ancient T-shirts. There will be no sexy lingerie, no unclothed body parts. I can get shirts that disparage biology! Or cute kitten shirts—bet your wolf wouldn't like that."

She winked at me, and both my wolf and I groaned. **This woman.**

I had to just say it. I blurted it out real fast: "I haven't slept with a woman in five years."

She paused, clearly processing my statement. Equally clearly, the concept of years-long celibacy was as unfamiliar to her as the procreative habits of sea urchins. "Excuse me?" she said finally. "Can you repeat that, please?"

She's going to think there's something wrong with you. Bad dick, bad breath, railroad tracks on the old boxers.

It was the truth that most folks didn't understand choosing *not* to have sex. You got a temporary hall pass for deep-seated trauma or religious convictions, usually along with an offer to fix what was wrong with you.

Sonnet barreled ahead. "You mean you haven't been in a relationship for five years?"

We could at least have been a monk. My wolf sounded sulky, but he and I were on the same page here, despite his teasing. After all, we were parts of the same person. Which sounded weird as fuck. I was not going there.

"That's true too. The last time I stepped out with a girl was in high school, to be honest. But what I was getting at was that I haven't had a sexual relationship with anyone in the last five years."

Don't be such a downer, my wolf grumped. **We know what we're doing. Experienced, excellent, top-shelf sex, that's us. We're high-end Tennessee whiskey, not the knock-off stuff.**

"Wow. Wow. Wowwwww." She did some inhaling and gasping that did not feel like it boded well for my future orgasms.

Abruptly, she untangled herself from me and sat up, wrapping herself in a throw blanket. I mourned the loss of naked Sonnet. "But why? Do you like sex? Do you not like sex? Are you demisexual? Sapiosexual? Oh my God, did I just violate your boundaries? Because I want to be supportive of your choices, not some kind of sexual bulldozer pushing myself in where you're uncomfortable."

"I'm not any of those." Leaning back against her sofa, I braced my arms on my knees. "I don't require an emotional bond to be attracted to someone, and I sure do have a strong desire to engage in sexual activity. I just made the choice not to have sex because I didn't want to hurt anybody, and my dating behavior was hurtful. I treated women like disposable dinnerware. They were convenient, single-use appliances, and I used them and tossed them away."

"Was it a sex addiction?"

I frowned, considering her question. "No. I don't think so. I was choosing to be out of control. I don't believe it was a compulsion. I just enjoyed being the town bad boy, and there were plenty of ladies who were happy to take me for a ride. It was part of the club lifestyle with the Iron Wolves. I don't know what you know about motorcycle clubs, but their members can have real inappropriate relationships with women. The ones in a committed relationship are old ladies, while the gals who just come to club parties and hang out with the members can be pass-arounds. The wolf clubs are sometimes even worse."

"Ugh." Sonnet glared ferociously. "I can't *even*. What the hell is wrong with people?"

"Anyhow, when I made the decision to break with the club, I also had to break all those old patterns and habits. No drinking, no messing around, no sex, no car stealing, parties, fights, lying, cheating, or conning. No uncontrolled shifting or full-moon binges. I went to school, got a job, and stayed home until I had new, better habits. I had to be able to trust myself."

"Do you drink now?"

"I have a beer once in a while. Two maybe, and then I stop." I tried to remember if I'd ever seen Sonnet have a drink.

"And you're no longer a hermit? You go out and have fun? You socialize?"

"I started socializing again a couple of years ago. But not often and nowhere I could fall back into old behaviors. I'm not a drinking-and-dancing kind of guy."

I had a picture in my head of the Hollywood lifestyle. My internet forays suggested there was a lot of fancy champagne swilling, posing on the red carpets, and raucous parties in big mansions with swimming pools. I realized now that was unfair. Some people did those things, like some people here in Moonlight Valley liked to hit the bar on Friday night. And most people didn't hurt anyone else with their choice of social activities. I just knew that after what I'd done as an Iron Wolf, I couldn't take a chance on relapsing.

Sonnet studied me from her position on the rug. "So, you are a man of moderation. You don't over-drink, over-party, or over-go-out. So why not just date in moderation too?"

"Because the drinking and the partying hurt only me. Dating requires another person, and that other person could get hurt."

"Because you weren't going to commit."

I nodded. Both my wolf and I were impressed with her insight.

"So you haven't met a single woman you could imagine yourself being in a long-term relationship with, not ever?"

I shrugged. "I've met lots of nice women, but I've never felt the urge to actually do it. It was easy to walk away from them."

Brown eyes widened. "But you can't walk away from me."

"I cannot."

"Good," she said. "I'm glad to hear that. Now tell me why." She looked worried for a moment. "It's not magic. Hand on heart, I have not tried to glamour you since the day we first met."

This should have been an easy question. I was taking too long to answer, though. I could feel it. There were so many reasons why I wanted to be with her.

Tell her, my wolf urged. **Maybe compose some freaking poetry here. You know —a brilliant play on her name. Write a sonnet. Do some rhyming shit about her awesomeness.**

I wasn't Shakespeare, but damned if she didn't deserve a poet.

I gave it my best shot.

"You're funny and smart, sassy and gorgeous. But there are smaller things too. I like learning new things about you, everyday things that aren't the epic kind of stuff you put in a greeting card. I like how you love oddities so much that you never wear a matching pair of socks. I like how you poke through every bank of ferns when we're in the woods, as if there's a treasure chest hidden there and you're gonna find it. You have a magic that sparkles in you and, boy, I didn't see that coming, but it feels right. I even enjoy the way you move all my stuff around and then pretend like it wasn't you. We talk, and that's great, but the silence is good too. It's not anything that you do. It's more that the act of being with you makes you impossible to leave or forget. We have a hundred Sonnet moments gluing us together, and I'm hoping for a million more. I'm in this for the long haul."

Rhymes, my wolf groused. **We coulda used some pizazz there, buddy. Mentioned her being our true mate. Maybe mentioned that the werewolf wants forever?**

Despite my ham-handed declaration of liking, Sonnet's cheeks pinkened. "Maverick." I sure liked the tender way she said my name. She lifted her face as though to kiss me, but I wasn't finished.

"I've got something else to say."

"There's more?" Sonnet's brown eyes widened, and she chewed on her lip. I had thoughts. Erotic, sexy thoughts. Some plans too. But first I had to tell her everything.

"Yeah." I gritted my teeth, steeling myself to lay it all out for her. "I promised myself that I wouldn't . . . That the next woman I made love to would be my wife."

Mate. We're saving it for our MATE.

Sonnet stared at me, mouth open. Apparently, I'd surprised her.

If she's good with the wolf, she's shockproof.

I wasn't so sure. I was asking her to wait for me.

"So, what was *that*?" Sonnet motioned to herself. Then she pointed lower where my hand had just been. She popped her thumb out of her fist. "A little eggplant emoji? A banana for my hot dog? A taco tango?"

I tried not to grin because she was just so stinking cute. "Getting to know each other?"

She growled, lifted herself up on her elbow, and poked me in the chest. "Well, I call it making sweet, sweet love, wolfman."

"It was sweet. But I'm talking about swinging my five wood. Making a hole in one. Using my stiff shaft." Then I winked. "A good golf game."

"Well, I'd be happy to be your *golf* partner, but I'm confused."

Capturing her hand, I pressed it against my heart. "I'm falling hard for you, Sonnet. I started to the first day I got you in my truck. I felt a connection. I was hooked. I still am, and I love it. I know my choosing to go slow in the bedroom isn't an obvious choice, but it's mine, and I have to own it. Wanting to wait doesn't mean that I don't care for or value you."

"I understand," she admitted reluctantly, her face softening. "I do. But you are such a tease, Maverick Boone, getting me all worked up and then making me wait."

Well crap. Crappity crap crap crap—

"I understand—" I scooted backward, trying to give her space. Between the sofa and the table and the general lack of space inside her trailer, I was not as successful as I should have been.

And that was before she twisted her fingers in the front of my T-shirt and yanked me toward her. "No. No, no, no. That wasn't me telling you to go. That was me making a bad joke."

"I'm not leaving," I said, my voice rough. "Not ever." I tucked her hair behind her ear, loving how her curls grabbed at my fingers. Her hair was so soft and full of sass, like the rest of her. I wanted to lean down and kiss her neck, bite her, mark her properly as mine. All the things I'd sworn I'd never do, could never dare do. Wolves mated for forever, and there was no undoing that bite. "I apologize if you feel like I misled you about my sexual availability."

"Do not apologize for being who you are." She shook her head. "I cannot say that enough. You get a choice, I get a choice, we hopefully make choices together. But none of them are *wrong*. It's just that—"

We could bite her just a little. We don't have to go full-on Darrell.

There my wolf was wrong. There was no halfway with a mating bite.

"I mean," Sonnet tried again, "if you're in a committed relationship—which is what I think we are in—I don't see the need to wait for a wedding ceremony. I admit that's not something that I understand, but I'll respect it. But given what you've shared about your past, I'm thinking that it's not me you're worried about hurting. You're worried about *yourself*. You don't trust yourself, sure, but these lines you're drawing also make sure that *you* don't get hurt. No feelings, no commitments, no worry about being heavily invested in someone who might walk away from you."

We're dating a psychotherapist. This is awkward.

I frowned. I didn't much enjoy her words, but they weren't all wrong. No. Of course they were wrong. Of course I wasn't putting the brakes on our sex life because I didn't want to end up hurt and alone. That was pure foolishness. That would make me a self-centered ass.

I hope you're not expecting introspection from me. I'm here for the sex and the biting.

But the more she stared at me, calmly challenging me, patiently waiting on my answer, the more I started to think that she was on to something. Sure, I liked to think that I could have settled down with any one of a dozen ladies in the last five years. I was charming. I had the full allowance of Boone family charm. But maybe the porch light was on, but no one was home. What woman would make long-term room in her life for me as more than a hookup quickie?

"Tell me what you're thinking."

I met her gaze, fair and square. She was strong and gorgeous, a clever woman with an amazing heart, and I made a decision: First, despite the low odds of my ever truly deserving her, I could still work my ass off every day to be the man who did. I could do my best to merit her trust, loyalty, and love. It might be a gift she'd given to me, but I would be goddamned worthy of it anyhow.

Second, life shouldn't be lived according to arbitrary lines and rules. So, I would be breaking my celibacy vow. When I was ready to make love to her—and her to me—then we would. It would be lovemaking, not just fun sex or screwing around. It might or might not include a wedding ring, but it *would* be love filled. I would take the chance on that.

"Maverick?" She frowned up at me. "I know you're thinking. Can you please share?"

"Always." I gave her a warm smile, dropping a kiss on her shoulder. "I will always share with you. Mostly, I've just concluded that we should have cake for breakfast every morning. Start our days off right, like this one."

CHAPTER

TWENTY-THREE

"She moaned and rubbed herself up against him, enjoying his big werewolf-sized body."

— GAIL CARRIGER, *SOULLESS*

"Why do I feel like I'm meeting the parents?"

Maverick slid his eyes to mine, then promptly refocused on the road. He was a very safe driver. "Sanye is not my mother. Also, she doesn't bite."

There was a pause.

And then, "Well, not in the general, socially accepted sense."

Peaches and pansies. Sanye was a werewolf too.

I glared at the cute pottery bowl of pimento cheese on my lap. The bowl was a clever disguise to hoodwink Sanye into thinking my cheese offering was home-made. Homemade was worth more points in the Who Does It Better game.

Yes. Yes, I was feeling competitive.

I was also confused.

"You have had dinner with her every Sunday for five years." Maverick had told

293

me this, and I had reconfirmed. Several times. "She is not a relative. She's your friend. A really good friend. Why wouldn't you date her?"

In Hollywood, *good friend* was code for *fuck buddy* and *secretly having sex already*.

Maverick had been offended when I'd pointed this out. I was not succeeding at being as supportive of his sexual abstention choices as I wished.

Maverick lifted an eyebrow at me. "You're making too much of this. It's dinner."

Uh-huh. It was an audition, and I was an expert on those. He was taking me to this Sanye's gorgeous, perfect house (and seeing as how Maverick had apparently been puttering around it, fixing crap for five years, it would be perfect), where Sanye would grill me and try to decide if I was Maverick worthy.

Last Tuesday, Alice, Ford's girlfriend (although Ranger was predicting an engagement ring and a relationship promotion for those two), had shown me a picture of Sanye. Alice worked at the local pet grooming place that Sanye owned. First, I'd almost peed myself laughing at the name: Vanity Fur Salon. Then, I'd wondered if it was an undercover wolf beauty salon. Nevertheless, near-urinary incontinence aside, the woman in the picture was gorgeous.

In fact, gorgeous was an understatement.

Like saying the Himalayas were tall and challenging.

Perfect territory for a short Sunday afternoon walk.

Easy-peasy, like a wolf's howl is breezy.

How on earth could Maverick spend so much time with her every Sunday, week after week, and not have feelings for her? The tall redhead was stunning. Ranger had told me she was tough and smart. Ford had praised her as super nice and thoughtful. Atticus saw an excellent businesswoman who had "real pretty eyes." Rebel believed she was an animal whisperer and could do some pretty unimaginable things with fur. He'd accompanied his high praise with an eyebrow wag.

Sidenote: Rebel was too freaking charming for his own good. End sidenote.

Knox, however, had remained stonily silent, abstaining from participating in the Sanye lovefest. I was growing accustomed to silence from him, mostly of the stormy and irritated kind.

So why hadn't Maverick made a move?

I already had a girl crush on her, and I hadn't even met her yet.

"So why not date her? Your entire family loves her. Alice loves her. She's a goddess of magical talents, endless goodness, and demonstrable beauty. Plus, she's a werewolf like you."

Maverick rolled his eyes. "Yeah, well, I know Sanye. Other than being a wolf shifter, she's just human. She has scars and flaws like everyone else. Plus, we've known each other since we were kids, and she's like another sister to me."

"Okay, fine. But I want it duly noted that I am also a goddess of magical talents and sexual attractiveness."

"I am fully aware." Maverick grinned, pulling onto a long dirt driveway that led to a small white farmhouse with a red door and window boxes. The window boxes were studded with spiky grasses and trailing lush green ivy and white climbing petunias. Matching white gourds and pumpkins lined the steps to the front porch.

Maverick parked and retrieved a pie from behind his seat, while I tried to convince the butterflies in my stomach that now would be an excellent time for a siesta. I was thinking this would be the world's quickest dinner—perhaps we could snack instead of dine—and then Maverick was helping me down out of the truck. Obviously, I was perfectly capable of getting out of his beast of a motor vehicle. I just liked having an excuse to get my hands on him.

I would nail this audition.

I would be the best woman EVAH for Maverick.

I gave myself a pep talk: *You go in there like you own this.* This being Maverick, of course. I was going to lick him like a cupcake. He would be mine, all mine. *You waltz in there and turn on the charm. You charm the freckles off her pretty face! Go! Go! Go!*

I clomped up the porch steps and made a pretense of checking out the window boxes up close while I waited for Maverick to catch up. He was cradling the pie like it was a newborn wolf pup.

God. Even her flowers were gorgeous. She also had rosemary bushes that had been trimmed into cute little animal shapes in adorable stone urns. Her porch floor was sanded and painted an immaculate black. A swing hung at the far end, tastefully stocked with throw pillows. The house looked like something out of a magazine.

"This is an amazing house." Proving I was a grown-up, I said it aloud. I mean, how could I not be impressed?

Maverick grinned proudly. "Right? I added the porch two years ago. Sanye suggested the window boxes. I painted them to match the trim."

They were Chip and Joanna Gaines. There would be a horde of TV cameras and adorable children on the other side of that door.

"You built it?"

Maverick nodded, oblivious to how his tool skills sounded to me. "I did. And the greenhouse and the she-shed out back. I do a little work on the house from time to time."

You built her an entire freaking HOUSE.

The butterflies in my stomach rioted. They launched themselves like little bomber planes up my throat. BOOM. There went my heart. BOOM, BOOM. No more brain cells.

On the one hand, Maverick was just the nicest, sweetest guy around. He built entire houses for free. On the other hand, I was dealing with some pretty intense feelings of jealousy and confusion. Why had he done this for HER? Was he just given to doing random acts of construction kindness?

And also: was it too late to develop a severe case of the plague and retreat to the truck?

Maverick rapped on the door, sliding me a glance. He looked amused. Of course, he was the prize in this scenario.

Sanye flung the door open mid-rap, almost as if she'd been staring out the peep-hole at us. Maybe she had one of those doorbell cameras?

"GREETINGS!" she bellowed at me, her very pretty eyes wide and excited.

"Uhhhhh." Shit. I should have rehearsed. Was there a polite way to say, *Excuse me, I'm feeling very insecure and would appreciate your validation of my feelings?* A quick glance at Maverick told me that he was not going to be helpful in this particular situation—his face was a polite blank slate, and he was staring fixedly at a point somewhere above Sanye's head.

"HI!" I bellowed back.

When in Rome, right?

She wrapped her arms around me in a full-frontal hug, squeezing me tight. "I AM SO, SO, SO EXCITED TO MEET YOU!!!!!"

Having set the pie baby down on an antique console table, Maverick rescued the pimento dip from my hands. It was in danger of being squeezed to death by

Sanye's python hug. Our eyes met over her shoulder. His own were shaking with laughter.

The enthusiastic squeezing continued.

Werewolves, even werewolf girls, were industrial-strength squeezers.

It was fine.

The longer she squeezed, the less time I had to talk, right?

She finally pulled away, her hands still gripping my shoulders. "I'm so sorry. I'm being super weird, aren't I? It's just that you're YOU, and I love you so much."

She slapped a hand over her mouth. Maverick shook his head.

"Oh my God. I'm the worst. I'm just so nervous. And I'm a terrible hostess. Come in." She stumbled backward into the house. Since we were still connected, I fell in after her. Sanye's cheeks were bright red. "I promised myself that I would be totally cool and not a creeper. I am not handling this well." She added this last bit under her voice.

I did some praising of the deities myself. The butterflies flew away, back to wherever it was butterflies lived. Cocoons? Bushes? Predator-deterring nests of leaves?

She was a superfan.

Sanye Jansen-Webster is a fan of Sonnet Ruiz.

It had never occurred to me that she would be a fan. I was so focused on all the ways in which she intimidated me with her amazingness that I had failed to consider that she might be equally in awe of my accomplishments.

"I promised myself I would be cool too." I grinned at her, and she blinked back. I hadn't even charmed her. She liked me for me! Well, mostly for my career accomplishments, possibly for my sexy books, and maybe for being Maverick adjacent.

"You're so cool," she said, her voice full of adoration, her eyes dazed and dreamy.

Maverick leaned down, his mouth brushing my ear. "No charms. Behave yourself."

"I am!" I said indignantly. "You heard her! I'm cool!"

I beamed back at her. Okay, whew.

"Fine, fine." Maverick grabbed my hand and towed me through a cute white living room and into the dining room. It was like a Pinterest board in here. Would it be creepy to take pictures with my phone?

"Don't be a birdbrain," he continued. "Pull yourself together, Sanye. And shut the door. We brought cheese. What's for dinner?"

* * *

Sanye wasn't exactly a goddess of magical talents, but she had aspirations in that general direction. And she could cook. Everything was Southern comfort food but with these fun twists. Homemade, pillowy buttermilk biscuits, with roasted corn and jalapeños. Oh, and she'd ground the flour herself. From organic quinoa. Just one of the crops she grew on her one-acre hobby farm.

She also made raspberry truffle butter. She picked her own raspberries and probably arm-wrestled pigs for the truffles.

For the main course, she'd made mimosa-fried chicken (which wasn't chicken at all, in deference to Maverick's vegetarian sensibilities) and a delicious white bean salad that had me rethinking my lifelong hatred for all things vegetable.

Bickering with Maverick, explaining her cooking inspirations (fortunately, I had not tried to pass the pimento cheese off as my own make after all), and my constant photographing and praise of her food seemed to snap her out of the starstruck daze. Still, more than once she stared at me and repeated (over and over) how much she loved my TV show, and how she stayed up all night reading my books, and that I had the best hair ever. But by the end of dinner, thanks to Maverick's efforts, she'd relaxed.

I had too.

"Yes, yes! Bek is the best ice planet barbarian ever." I waved my hands enthusiastically at Sanye. We were discussing paranormal space romances and, as it turned out, we shared one book-loving brain.

"Don't get me wrong. I love me a marshmallow alien like Salukh, I love a sweet man, but the grumpy ones are the best! Ruby Dixon is a genius. I mean Bek was on the redemption train! So surly! And protective! And then it was spur central!"

We both giggled, remembering the same bonus piece of alien anatomy. Sanye wiggled her thumb, miming the extra addition, launching us into renewed laughter.

Maverick reclaimed my attention, threading his fingers through mine and bringing my knuckles to his mouth for a soft kiss. His eyes twinkled at me as he mouthed, *Spur.* I felt warm and cherished.

With a quick squeeze of my hand, he got up, collected our plates, and padded into the kitchen.

"I love a man who's an animal." Sanye raised her voice, winking at me.

Maverick must've heard her all right because he yelled back, "Don't give me any grief, woman, or there will be no pie for you."

"Is it delicious pie?" she hollered.

There was no response from our werewolf waiter. Sanye looked at me.

"Is there pie? I saw no pie when y'all walked in."

There had been pie. There has also been cheese. Regardless, I decided not to point out that she'd stared at me for the first thirty minutes of our visit. Maverick could have marched a herd of elephants through her living room, and she wouldn't have noticed.

"Yes. Thanks for inviting me over."

She beamed at me, her cheeks pink with pleasure. "I think I've got the gaga thing out of my system now, so whew. I'm sorry to have acted like that. I can see you're just like the rest of us." She nodded, then added with the comedic timing of a celestial goddess, "Except you don't turn furry. Plus, you're funnier, smarter, and have better shoes."

"Sanye—"

"And with the curliest hair."

"Cease—"

"It's a sickness. Sorry."

I had to laugh. "Don't apologize."

Maverick reemerged from the kitchen. We both frowned at his pie-less hands. "You two go on out back for a walk while I heat up the pie."

He started stacking up the remaining dishes.

"I can help with that." I stood up to collect our glasses, but Maverick made a shooing motion. "Go. Scat. Get out of here. You could check out the greenhouse. I thought I might put something like that out behind our house, and I'd like your opinion."

Our house? Was that the Boone residence? Or some future love nest just for the two of us? I was so confused.

The one thing that was clear was now that Sanye had semi-conquered her case of the starstrucks, he seemed determined to throw the two of us together. He wanted us to be friends for real. It was a nice thought, but it also made my stomach tie itself into little knots. Being the approachable, likeable TV star Sonnet Ruiz was a familiar role. Even without using my glamour, I could slip that mask on whenever I needed to.

Being Sonnet Ruiz, regular human being, was much harder. Maverick made it easy to relax around him, which was one of the many reasons why I enjoyed his company. I looked from him to Sanye. She batted big, hopeful eyes at me.

"Come on," she said, grinning. "I won't bite, and I promise not to make more hair comments."

And again, just like that, my nerves vanished. "I'm only going if you *do* admire my hair."

"Deal." She turned and headed out a pair of French doors (so jealous!) that led into her amazing backyard. "But seriously, your curls are amazing. They are a frizz-free zone. What product do you use and can I buy it online?"

Maverick shot us a small, pleased smile as he turned back into the kitchen.

"I don't know where it's from. My sister sends it. She mails me boxes of products —face serums, lip masks, moisturizers—and I just use whatever's in the box. It's like makeup Christmas."

"Would you be willing to check for me? I can't find anything I like hereabouts."

"Sure. You bet." I made a mental note to have a case of the stuff sent to her because the raspberry truffle butter alone deserved a pallet of fancy hair product.

We wandered across the yard to the greenhouse. It was absolutely darling, with walls of windows, a sloping white tin roof, and a baby barn door with black hinges. He'd hung a chandelier inside, and there was a squashy velvet armchair. And plants. So, so, so many plants. African violets and late-blooming dahlias, lemon trees, and pears.

"This is amazing." I skimmed my fingertips over a geranium. How long had Maverick spent working on this greenhouse? Sanye's house was perfect, while the Boone home wasn't even half restored.

Sanye sucked in a deep breath and sank down on a cute little wicker settee. Her eyes held mine. "I'm so glad you're here."

Her flustered and bubbly enthusiasm had vanished, replaced now by a more subdued tone; her voice quiet but infused with a subtle confidence.

"We should do it again." I dropped down beside her. "I can cook next Sunday. I'm in Moonlight Valley for at least another month. I don't want to encroach on your time with Maverick but—"

"I won't be here."

"Excuse me?" Had I misunderstood? I waited for her to yell, "Surprise!"

"I won't be here," she repeated. "I bought a camper van and I'll be using it to travel around the country."

"Wow. I mean, congratulations!" That was a huge change. How would that work with her business? This is not the time to ask for career tips or to be nosy though. "Does Maverick know?"

I was almost certain he did not.

Sure enough, she shook her head. "Not yet. I'm so happy for Mav. He's found you, and that's going to make all the difference. He was all fenced in by his rules, and now you're here to teach him to color outside the lines. He's so lucky."

I wrapped my arms around my middle, feeling off-balance. *Fenced in? Coloring outside the lines?* I wasn't used to sincerity, I decided. I blamed Hollywood for that. We liked our emotions scripted and rehearsed in Tinseltown, so I had no idea what to say to Sanye.

She patted my shoulder. "No pressure, of course."

"No! It's not! In all Maverick-related matters, I welcome pressure."

She smiled softly. "Good. He deserves happiness, as do you."

And so did Sanye. I just didn't understand why she was choosing to uproot her life.

"Sanye, when did you decide to leave?"

Another smile, this one rueful. "I guess I decided on Tuesday."

"When are you telling him?"

A shrug. "I haven't figured that out. I may wait until the movers have come to put my stuff in storage and I've put a few hundred miles between us. I hate goodbyes. He knows that. And it's not as if I'll be gone forever. I'll visit and of course I'm coming back to Vanity Fur Salon. It's a *temporary* leave of absence."

"You're not . . ." I hesitated. But she'd been open with me, so that was my invitation to be candid, too, wasn't it? "I'm not the reason you're going, am I?"

"No," she said too quickly. Oh God. "Not in the way you mean. It's just that I don't actually have a reason to stay *here*. My reason left five years ago." Her gaze unfocused for a moment. "My husband died. Did Mav tell you about Evan?"

"Mav loved Evan."

"For good reason. Evan was wonderful." Her smile was sad, and she fidgeted with a geranium. Little white petals fell onto the potting table. "When we first learned that Evan wasn't coming home, I told myself that staying in Moonlight Valley was to help Evan's parents and to help Mav. I'd also be surrounded by shifters. Those felt like the right reasons to stay. But that was five years ago. I've spent five years hiding here in this pretty house, with its pretty gardens, not living." She thought for a moment, adding more cheerfully, "Which isn't to say that I'm some kind of country princess locked away in a tower. It's just that Evan's parents keep suggesting that it's time for me to move on. And now I think they're right. Although maybe I'm taking their advice a *little* literally."

We shared a smile. I thought that we understood each other, even if the poor geranium would never be the same again. Of course, the same could be said about Sanye. About Evan. Maverick.

Myself.

"I ran into someone on Tuesday," Sanye said, contemplatively. "Someone I knew long ago. We said some ugly things to each other, and afterward, after I'd walked away from him, I felt lost and upset. And then Maverick called, happy as a wolf pup, to ask if he could bring you to dinner. It seemed like a sign from the universe. I always knew I would move on when the Websters were in a good place and Mav was ready to let me go."

"Do you think Maverick will be okay?"

"He will be now that he has you." Sanye swept up the petals. "But the two of you should move in here if I may overstep. Because if you go live in that big ole Boone place, you won't have a second's privacy. You'll have all his brothers banging on your door, asking what you're doing and why, plus they only have one bathroom."

I mumbled something. My mind was paralyzed by the thought of one bathroom, six Boones, and me. Plus, it seemed awfully presumptuous of me to be thinking of moving into Maverick's house, wherever that house might be.

"Sometimes you have to go off script," Sanye said softly. "Right? Ad-lib. Change the lines to fit the scene."

TWENTY-FOUR

SONNET

"'I haven't even accepted that you're my lover, and now you want me to except [sic] that you're something off the Sci Fi Channel.'

'A werewolf.'

'Yes.'"

— SARAH MCCARTY, RUNNING WILD

Let's shack up!

Build a love nest!

Wanna be my bedroom renter?

I pulled my attention back to the tour guide. Sadie was dressed rather melodramatically from head to toe in black: black dress, black jacket, black boots. When she gestured, she fluttered. Oh, her black hat looked like something out of *Godey's Lady's Book*. A (black) scarf kept said hat from either blowing away or being snatched by mischievous ghosts.

They did not mess around with wardrobe in Crickety Creek. Even though the historic site was the tiniest pinpoint on a map and a good half hour from Moonlight Valley, I was secretly hoping for a gift shop where I could buy the entire ensemble.

"Are you nervous?" Sadie asked. Spoiler: audience participation was not required, so she kept talking. "The mill is haunted by the ghosts of the miller, his wife, and their three cats. There was an unfortunate incident with the waterwheel." She lowered her voice. "Squashed flat, the five of them were."

Maverick held up our lantern. It was pitch-black outside the circle of light. What time was it? Midnight, of course. Partly this was because midnight was a ghost-appropriate and gawking-people-free hour, but mostly it was because, like a vampire, I wasn't available during daylight hours (thanks to my filming schedule rather than any bloodsucking dietary requirements). When he'd asked to take me out tonight, I'd been expecting maybe a movie or dinner. Bowling. Cow tipping. A *classic* Southern date.

Instead, we were on a group date with ghosts.

I freaking loved it.

So far, we'd been treated to stories about two Civil War soldiers—naturally, bitter enemies who'd had opposing political views—as well as some very salacious details about a group of spinster ladies who shared a cabin, a cemetery full of specters, a Frankenstein, and a genteel gentleman who insisted on making an appearance at the full moon despite his grave having been salted.

Crickety Creek was like one of those fifty-five-and-older retirement communities, except here the criteria was being a ghost. Although it did not host any living inhabitants, it did have a tiny church with spooky wrought iron detailing and a cemetery crowded with tumbled down tombstones. Dark alleys snaked between the main street. By the old mill, a waterwheel creaked eerily as it churned up the water. We'd reached that by way of a wooden bridge that dipped and swayed as we clomped over it.

Maverick leaned down. "Are you scared?"

Since he'd whispered this in my ear—and his teeth had nipped my earlobe ever so gently—the honest answer was nope. Turned on? You bet. Quaking in my Dr. Martens? Not so much.

I patted his butt while Sadie opined dolorously about the supernatural happenings at the mill. So far, we hadn't seen any ghosts, but it'd been fun, nonetheless.

Eventually, Sadie ran out of stories and looked expectantly at us. The show was over.

Maverick slipped Sadie some discreetly folded bills, she wished us a restful death (not my favorite line in her tour guide spiel), and then she disappeared with impressive stealth. Sadie was not interested in hanging out with a famous person; she was only interested in the dead.

We'd parked by an ancient corn crib with a red tin roof. I could see straight through the wooden walls and, if I squinted, I could almost see the ghosties of mice past dancing around.

And so now, here we were, after our third date, sitting silently in his truck. I had to be up early to shoot, while Maverick had the day off.

I wasn't nearly as tired as I had been on our first and second middle-of-the-night dates. After I'd fallen asleep in the middle of the drive-in movie, I'd started taking naps in the afternoon when I had a break. Maverick didn't seem tired, either. He was preternaturally alert, his eyes scanning the darkened woods around us, constantly shifting his body as something caught his attention. He'd looked particularly tense when Sadie had insinuated that the nice ladies of Crickety Creek had held some stellar orgies in their cabins.

Sadie honked her horn and drove past us in a flutter of waving black draperies. I stared out the windshield of Maverick's truck.

We were alone in a ghost town with nowhere we needed to be for hours.

Tonight's date had been hot-hot-hot, and I was hoping it wasn't over yet. Certain parts of me were very much awake and hoping there would be a good-night kiss or six. I was also open to heavy petting and anything else Maverick might be comfortable doing.

I just didn't know what that was.

I needed a Maverick rule book.

We were definitely a couple. Heck, we were a fifty-years-married couple, except that I hadn't caught more than a glimpse of his penis naked. I would have loved to remedy that tonight. I'd tried to follow the speed limit laws in Mavericklandia; I'd come to a full stop at all stop signs, merged carefully, and hadn't tailgated. He had to set the pace in the bedroom (or his truck cab, my front porch, my trailer, and the fine Tennessee state parks) because I was the speed demon in this relationship.

FYI, I'd been having this internal debate since the Great Frosting Incident in my trailer.

"Boo," Maverick said, making me jump. He chuckled lightly, stretching an arm out behind me along the seat back. "Sorry. I'm sorry. I didn't actually mean to startle you. Are you tired?"

"Nope. Not at all." I shook my head vigorously, as though he'd accused me of cheating on my taxes rather than sleepiness.

His grin grew. "You up for doing something else?"

Who needed sleep? I'd just order up a case of energy drinks. Run an IV of espresso into my veins. Breakfast on dark chocolate.

"Absolutely!" I nodded again for emphasis. Should I say something else? But what? I *did* want to spend time with him. It was just that I *also* would like that time to be spent in a bed, both sleeping and not sleeping.

Will there be kissing?

A comfy horizontal surface? Possibly a sturdy vertical surface?

Can we DO each other?

Can I do you?

Should I download a thesaurus of romantic terms?

At this rate, I'd be declaiming the infamous "Roses Are Red" poem to him. This was embarrassing. I was a *New York Times* best-selling author!

I bit my lip to keep from offering him a blow job while he drove us to wherever this *something else* would be taking place.

Maverick studied me, his eyes narrowing, his left hand gripping the steering wheel.

"You ready?" he asked, his voice deliciously hoarse.

Yes, yes, I was.

I nodded some more. "Can't wait!"

I expected him to turn the key in the ignition, but instead he frowned. His eyes dropped to my mouth. The truck's cab warmed up faster than a greenhouse in summer. He lavished a heated look on me that almost had me combusting on the spot. I gripped the sides of the passenger seat to keep from launching myself toward him.

Breaking the moment, Maverick exhaled roughly and abruptly, tearing his gaze away from mine. His eyes flashed amber, but then he composed himself, gritting his teeth.

I stopped holding my own breath. Inhaled a lungful of Maverick's delicious, pinesy scent. What would he do next?

He started the truck.

We drove silently along the mountain roads. Silently past trees and more trees, a rock spill, and a deer that watched us from the bushes.

I expected him to maybe comment on the tour and make a joke about seeing ghosts, but he stayed silent. Focused on the road. The urge to blurt out words, to fill up the silence, grew in me.

Resist.

I had to resist.

"Did you know that ferns are a triceratops's favorite food?" I blurted out.

Maverick's eyes flickered to mine and then back to the dark road. We were driving by starlight mixed with headlight. It should have been romantic, although fern fun facts might not have been helping the mood. Still, he grinned.

"Pteridology is a sadly underrepresented field of study," I continued. "Perhaps you could consider that once you've exhausted the possibilities of snake venom."

He nodded, but his grin faded. He slowed the truck and signaled a right-hand turn.

Outside the windshield there was nothing but mountain road and trees. Lots and lots of trees. I was a big fan of botany and perennial plants with large stems, but these did not seem particularly interesting.

After three minutes of bumping down an unpaved, unmarked road like kernels in a popcorn popper, Maverick stopped. Shockingly, there were more tall trees, along with an impressive collection of inky shadows.

"This is Buzzard's Bluff. I thought we could check out the stars. We won't get any lights from town up here, and it's a clear night." Maverick proposed this plan calmly, as if he merely had some platonic celestial gazing in mind.

Nevertheless, his statement had parts of me palpitating.

My heart did some excited, anticipatory thumping.

He wants to sit around in a truck in the middle of nowhere staring at the sky.

He had to have an ulterior motive, right?

Right?

Before I could convince myself that the answer was HELL YES, Maverick had parked and stepped down. While he rummaged around in the back of the cab, I got out.

I'd dressed casually for our date: black Uggs, black leggings, and a long-sleeved, slouchy brown sweater with a patchwork crocheted scarf that my mami had made for me when I was fifteen. I loved my scarf, but it was not up to the mountain air past midnight. My wardrobe would need reinforcements if we hung out here for too long. Feeling antsy, I walked around to Maverick's side of the truck just as he tossed a squashy bundle of something into the bed of the truck.

Of course, Maverick's date-night improv included a DIY construction project. We were probably going to build birdhouses. Or a sauna.

I would love to use his tool.

I kept this to myself, however, because boundaries were important. Instead, I politely asked, "Can I help?"

Maverick nodded. "Can you hold the flashlight?"

I accepted a big bright-yellow flashlight from him and aimed it at Maverick while he tossed two more squashy fabric-wrapped blobs into the truck bed.

"Are we burying bodies?"

He flashed me a grin. "Nope."

He followed this up by striding to the back of the truck. I bobbed along behind him, dutifully beaming the flashlight at his butt. I, for one, liked what I was seeing. He lowered the tailgate and vaulted into the bed. It was nice to be a wolfman.

"Point that over here?"

I bit back an inappropriate joke about pointing and planted the flashlight on the side of the truck.

The squashy things turned out to be Japanese floor mattresses, rolled up into cute little logs. They had pillow friends and throw blanket friends as well. I stared at them and at him as he worked, the earlier palpitations increasing and moving to areas south of my belly button. He was building us a nest. To cuddle up in. So we could look at stars.

It was the best date ever.

"Are you cold?"

I blinked up at him. He was frowning at me. The cutest little crinkle of a question mark had formed between his eyebrows.

"Not yet," I promised him.

Damn it. I should have told him I was freezing. Requested that we share body heat lest I perish from hypothermia. Hypoglycemia. Hypomagnesemia? Whatever. Something that required an immediate application of his big, hot body.

He reached a hand down to help me up. Pffft. I might not be a sexy biologist who used his tools on a daily basis, but I was a sexy Hollywood television star who had a fitness app on her phone. I got myself up into the truck all on my own.

Despite my impressive truck-climbing skills and independent, can-do attitude, Maverick was right there before I could unfold myself from my frog-like crouch on the tailgate. He pulled me upright, banding an arm around my waist and offering unnecessary but still delicious support. He held my hand. He brushed his lips against mine. Then he kissed me for real.

I was pretty sure he'd gone off script, seeing as how we were neither lying down nor looking at any stars, but I always enjoyed a good ad-lib. Plus: KISSING. He dawdled, pausing each pass of his mouth with demanding nips of his teeth and consolatory licks of his tongue. His hands stopped holding me up and ventured lower, stroking and squeezing as they moved south.

"I missed you." His voice was rough, surprisingly hoarse, and gravelly; my head swam so much that I failed to point out that we'd just spent the last two hours together, so what exactly had he missed? His hands inserted themselves beneath my sweater, callused fingers stroking my sides, his thumbs taking up residence beneath the band of my bra.

Kisses were pressed against the sensitive skin of my neck.

There were tiny, erotic nibbles.

I sucked in a breath as his hands moved down and into my leggings, cupping my butt. A hard ridge pressed against my belly. I tucked my fingers inside the front pocket of his jeans and tugged gently on the fabric. There may have been accidental brushing of that intriguing ridge. I wasn't sure what the etiquette was for asking him to explain the guidelines for tonight's make-out session, but I needed to know.

"Can I touch you?"

Tug. Tug, tug, TUG. I crooked my fingers deeper inside the pocket, petting him gently through the thin fabric. He was thick and hard and so, so warm.

He hissed, tensing. I waited for the green light. Or the red light. But I was really, really hoping for green.

"Yes," he gritted out.

Wish granted!

I pulled my fingers out and wrapped my palm around him as best I could through the front of his jeans. I loved the feel of him, how he was hard and smooth, urgent and controlled. He was a man of delicious dichotomies and primitive urges, yet he kept himself under control at all times.

I tugged on his belt buckle. "Can we take this off? May I unwrap my present, please?"

He unbuckled his belt. Then said hoarsely, "Okay. Yes, please."

I pushed his jeans and his boxer briefs down his hips and dropped to my knees in front of him. God bless those Japanese futons for their pillowy protection for my kneecaps.

I reached for him, framing him between my palms. The man was a work of art. Not the marble statue kind with the tiny, disappointing dicks—more of the robust satyr variety. He was thick and long, and I leaned forward and showed him my appreciation with tender kisses, gentle laps.

"You—" He swallowed a rough sound, his hips moving.

"Me," I said happily, stopping my loving because it was just rude to talk with my mouth full. "Us. Together. *Qué linda tu pija.*"

He did indeed have a beautiful dick. I wrapped my hands around what wouldn't fit, sucking on the thick, fat head. Paired with my tight, rough strokes, I hoped he felt how much I cared about him. How much I loved being this close to him. Trusted. Safe.

He threaded his callused fingers through my hair, gathering up my curls and tucking them safely away.

"I want to see you," he whispered hoarsely. "Let me watch you, sweetheart."

I hummed a note of agreement. He groaned.

"Look at me?" He fisted my curls gently, turning my face upward.

His eyes were half amber, half hazel, all desire.

"Hi, Wolf," I whispered around him.

He growled, a low, rough sound. His wolf was happy to see me, too.

I watched him watching me take him deeper, careful of my teeth, reading his body like it was a love note written just for me.

And boy, were we on the same page here. Touching him made me feel good. The more I kissed him, dragging my lips over where he was hard and slick, licking and tasting a slow path up his length and then back down again, the more turned on I got. It was fun and I'd never felt closer to him.

"Sonnet," he murmured as I took him deep again, working him inside me. "Sonnet."

His hands in my hair tightened and his hips flexed, working. His fingers loosened, as if he were afraid he might hurt me.

"I'm going to come," he said roughly. "I should—"

He tried to pull away, but I held on. He was so big and thick, so perfect. I might have been humming a happy song when he released in my mouth with a hoarse cry.

I swallowed and then grinned up at him. I had no words. I was nothing but happy feelings and satisfaction.

From the look on his face, we were in agreement on that.

He nudged me upward. There might have been some unnecessary but totally gratifying lifting and carrying on his part. He wrapped us up in the blankets he'd brought, settling me against his chest. It felt so good, I thought I might never move.

"There was supposed to be stargazing," he mock-growled. "Someone distracted me. That someone has derailed all my nefarious plans for the night."

"I saw stars," I promised him. "Supernovas galore."

He chuckled. "A supernova?"

I winked. "Mmmhmmm. I'm just hoping it wasn't Halley's comet and therefore not due to make another appearance for a hundred years."

TWENTY-FIVE

"'My mate comes first . . . Above everything else, never doubt that.'"

— LORA LEIGH, *CROSS BREED*

"Sonnet—" I ran a hand down her back.

"Maverick." She giggled up at me.

Get in the truck. Drive to Vegas. No, wait. Book the honeymoon suite at one of those fancy-ass Strip hotels. My wolf sounded dazed. Dazed and pleased.

Me too.

I was half dressed in the back of my truck, holding my girl. I should put myself back together and then express my deep-felt appreciation. With my tongue.

And we're not just using our words, my wolf said happily.

The damned flashlight still lit up the bed of my truck. I'd been the recipient of the world's best blow job in a spotlight.

World record book, baby.

"You are amazing." I dropped a kiss against her hair. "I'm gonna need a minute to make a list of adjectives. There might be adverbs involved too. An imperative sentence or two."

"I just want to know how soon we can do this again," she said.

I groaned. "Baby, there's no place for us to be alone."

"What about my trailer and my room at Phantom Falls and—"

"Sugarplum, those places aren't private."

"Are too." She poked me in the chest. "*Sugarplum?*"

"Like the fairies in that ballet," I said. "Also, as in the sweet. You are just as round and delicious."

Good save.

She huffed.

I cuddled her closer. She'd been caught by the big, bad wolf, and now she'd have to take her medicine. "And those places aren't private enough. You're not quiet when you come. While I love your noise because it tells me I'm getting it right, I don't want to be putting on a show for the paparazzi or your starstruck fans."

She thought about that for a moment.

"So are you telling me that we're not"—she waved a hand—"*mojando el churro* because someone might hear us?"

I caught her gently and pressed a kiss against her palm. "Firstly, I'm gonna have to get me a Spanish app because the only word in there I caught was *churro*, and I'm thinking you do not have dessert foods in mind."

She laughed and pushed her index finger through the circle she'd made with her other hand. Uh-huh. A churro and a hoo-hah. I'd need to learn the Spanish words for *beautiful* and *amazing*.

"I would like what's happening between us to be just between us. I know that given your job and all, we're not gonna be private forever. I'm gonna have to share you with a million other people. But for now, I have you all to myself. We're building our relationship, and that's personal. It's private."

"So, when we weren't getting it on, it was because . . ."

When she stopped, I eased backward so I could see her face. She reached up and gently stroked my cheek like she needed that little contact.

While she thought, I explored beneath our cocoon of blankets. I slid my hands up underneath her sweater, cupping her through her bra. I loved the generous weight and plush suppleness of her breast. I tugged the cup down, reversing our positions so she was underneath me as I knelt over her, moving a knee between her thighs.

"Do you want to finish that thought?" I whispered.

"You said that waiting until you were married was important to you, and I was trying to respect that."

"Thank you." I stroked the soft curve of her breast. "But what I need is to feel close to my lover. It's not just about *mojando el churro* for me. I need to feel like we're emotionally connected. And—"

"And?" she prompted.

"And I do," I said roughly. "God help me, but I do. And I'd like to think you feel the same way. So, while I don't need the wedding ring as long as we're committed to each other, I do require a moment of privacy. Right now, though, what I'd like most of all is to touch you. Can I please taste you?"

She feels so fucking amazing.

I wanted her. Right now.

I wanted her raspy, hitching sounds, the ones she made when I kissed a spot she liked. I wanted her unrestrained, loud cries. And now that I knew she was a happy screamer, I wanted her screams too. Most important of all, though, I didn't want her holding back or hiding any of her feelings from me.

"No, wait." She twisted in my arms, sitting up.

Noooo, groaned my wolf.

"What's wrong?"

"I don't want you going downtown on me." She sounded more certain than any man ever wanted to hear.

"Why not?" I gritted out. What was wrong with reciprocating? Or was it something with my technique? Had I done something to put her off?

"Because I didn't go down on you because I wanted you to do the same for me. It was a *gift*."

I had never, not once, had a blow job as a gift. The gifts in my life had mostly been bottles of bourbon and tools.

This is so much better.

"It was a token of my esteem and affection," she continued. "Because I do have feelings for you—important, committed, three-dimensional feelings—and I need to be able to express them."

"I'd be happy to hear all about your feelings while I'm tasting you." I moved to kiss her again.

"You're not hearing what I'm saying." She shifted away.

I wasn't *understanding* what she was trying to tell me. That was for sure.

Space. I needed space.

And time.

An ice-cold shower would have helped too.

I pushed myself upright, edged to the tailgate, and jumped down. From the corner of my eye, I saw that Sonnet had also sat up and was wrapping the throw blankets around herself like a mummy. Or maybe it was armor. Fuck if I knew.

You screwed up.

"Maverick?"

I leaned back against the tailgate, glaring up at the stars.

Orion the Hunter, my wolf snarled. **Bet HE wouldn't have screwed this up.**

She shuffled over to the tailgate, swinging her legs over the edge. Her knees bumped my shoulder. "You're upset."

I thought about what I was and wasn't. "I'm not upset. I'm frustrated. I've been planning tonight for days, and instead of me making you come until you see stars, I lose control and then I don't understand what you need. I want to show you how much you mean to me. I'd *like* to fucking worship you with my body." *And with my tongue, my fingers, and a few other body parts too.*

"I get that because that's how I've been feeling for weeks. Frustrated that I can't show you how I feel. Words are good, but sometimes I need to show, not tell, *sí*? I don't want to cross a boundary, but I'm also afraid."

My sulky resentment morphed into concern. **What the hell?**

"Are you *afraid* of me? Is it the wolf?"

Hey, my wolf growled. **I'm not the dick who opened his mouth and pissed her off.**

"No, no. This isn't coming out right. I should have written this down. Practice." She flapped a hand in the air. "If you still want to enjoy my pomegranate after we talk, then I will gladly be your girl. But I do think we need to talk first."

"Then talk. Tell me what you're thinking. It doesn't have to be perfect. You never have to edit yourself for me or choose your words." I sounded gruff to my own ears. Also, possibly as if I were begging because the thought of Sonnet being afraid that I would judge her for being less than perfect made me sick to my stomach. She never, ever had to perform for me. That was the last thing I wanted.

"Alright." She inhaled, exhaled. Set a hand on her belly. The words came out in a rush. "I love you touching me. It makes me feel connected. I'd like to be able to touch you without worrying about who else might be around or hear something or see something. I'm not proposing we have sex in the produce aisle of the Piggly Wiggly, but waiting until we find ourselves in the Outer Hebrides or on a deserted island in the South Pacific isn't feasible. I also don't want to push you for more intimacy than you're comfortable with, but I'm not sure where that line is, and I'm concerned that I'm stepping over it. So, before we do any more touching, I need you to know that I'm open to anything and everything, pretty much all the time, but I'm scared that my neediness will drive you away. I do not want to lose you."

"You—" I took a moment to process what she'd shared. "You want more connection, physical connection, and you don't care if other people know we're *connecting*."

"I am not ashamed of us," she said. "We are not a secret. I don't particularly want to share our private details with the world—or even with my security team—but if someone happens to overhear or see something, I don't feel like it's the end of the world. They will deal. They will know that I am a very, very lucky woman. I also know that the celebrity thing is a pain in the ass and a lot to deal with, but I am really hoping that maybe you will deal with it. For me. I just don't want to push you away."

"I'm not going anywhere," I whispered firmly, turning around to bracket her between my arms. I trapped her in my embrace, caging her against me. "I can deal with dating a superstar. If that means sharing part of you, so be it. It may take some practice on my part, so I'll ask you to be patient with me while I come to terms with it. I am here to be your partner, though. I've got your back, and I'm supporting you, no matter what."

She sighed, her breasts pressing against my chest on the exhale. "I respect your line."

"I appreciate that, but—"

"But I may do things that come close to the line, possibly by accident. Also, possibly on purpose."

I bent my head and swept a quick kiss over her mouth. "I look forward to your playing with my line. Thank you for the heads-up. Now, let's get going."

"Ummm, excuse me?"

"Scoot back into the truck, please." I straightened up and swung her down off the tailgate. Since I had her in my arms, it was more efficient to just carry her over to her side of the truck.

"So now you don't want my pomegranate?" She frowned up at me.

I shifted her in my arms so I could open her door. "Oh, I definitely plan to eat my pomegranate. But it's cold out here, and you have a warm bed back at Phantom Falls. If I need to get used to having other people hear you when you're in the throes of having your pomegranate eaten, I might as well start tonight. Plus, I want to see all of you and it's dark out here."

Her frown deepened. I suspected it was more of a pout now. "You can't see enough when you're up close and in my business?"

I dropped a kiss on her head as I set her on the seat.

"I can see your business just fine in the bed of my truck, but I want to see your pointy teeth and those cute Fae ears of yours. I want to be looking in your violet eyes the next time you come."

* * *

I violated the speed limit, getting back to Phantom Falls in record time, and I had sweet, delicious pomegranate before going to bed.

Then I spent the night and held her.

There was more pomegranate eating before breakfast.

Tastiest. Pomegranate. Ever.

But it was more than just pleasure. Sure, it had been years since I'd had an orgasm with a woman, but this wasn't just any woman. It was Sonnet, and that made all the difference. *She* was the reason why I was so happy.

Please her, cherish her, love her, my wolf demanded. **She's worth more than just her pomegranate.**

My wolf was right.

After our stargazing post-date, I'd headed downstairs so early in the morning that it still qualified as night. Sonnet was asleep in her bed. Naked as a blue jay. **We wore her out**, my wolf said smugly. She'd be hungry when she woke up, and she'd need her coffee before she hit the set. My plan had been to head out to the Peaches and Cream Parlor, pick up hummingbird cake and caffeine before she woke up, and then spend whatever time she had left before she went to work in bed. With me and no clothes.

But the smell of fresh hazelnut coffee brewing had me stopping in my tracks as I passed the kitchen.

I glanced inside. Eric and Spike were seated at the kitchen table sharing pages of the weekly local newspaper back and forth. A hummingbird cake underneath a large glass cloche was on the counter. Odds were good that they'd heard the ruckus Sonnet had made last night. Likely, they'd heard our wee hour activities too.

Our lady is NOT quiet, my wolf said happily. **Means we're getting it right! Five-star review coming right up!**

I changed directions. Instead of heading toward my truck, I detoured into the kitchen.

"Can I liberate some of this cake? Or is it spoken for?"

Eric glanced up. His lack of surprise at seeing me confirmed that he had, indeed, heard Sonnet.

Yelling MAVERICK at the top of her lungs. Deities were mentioned too. You are keeping rarefied company.

Eric set down his paper. "Take as much as you want."

"Yeah. From the sound of things, you two burned off a lot of calories," Spike added, shooting me a knowing smile.

It wasn't a smirk.

It wasn't lascivious.

He just *knew* and he wasn't going to make a big deal out of it.

I don't mind.

Thing was, I didn't, either.

Everyone should know, my wolf agreed. **Next best thing to a wedding ring and the bite. Unless you're up for matching tattoos?**

Eric smacked Spike on the back of the head. "Where the hell are your manners?"

"What?"

"You are so rude."

"What did I say?"

"He doesn't want you talking about Sonnet like that and neither do I."

Spike tossed his newspaper pages onto the table and threw his hands up. "I didn't say a thing!"

They sounded like honorary Boone brothers. I grinned. "It's all good. Spike didn't say anything untoward."

"See? I am never untoward," Spike complained.

He's pouting.

Eric narrowed his eyes. "You need to learn some respect."

"But she was yelling the house down. No one's that loud unless the sex is the best ever. That's what my boyfriend tells me. Then he says he's starving, and since it's my fault he got so worked up and did the yelling, I have to go get Chinese. That's all I'm saying," Spike tried again. This only made Eric frown more fiercely and me laugh harder. From the look on Eric's face, he hadn't needed the details about Spike's sex life.

The front door opened, and both men stopped their bickering and turned as one. Some sort of silent communication flew back and forth between them. I took a step backward, ready to shift and defend.

No one gets to Sonnet.

"Hello?" That was Wyatt's voice in the foyer.

Asshole. People are sleeping.

"In the kitchen," Spike yelled back (**also an asshole**), dropping down into his seat. He put away his gun.

Eric's shoulders relaxed, although he was frowning up a storm. "He may own this place, but he shouldn't be letting himself in. How can I keep her safe if I can't keep people out? Why is he always dropping by?"

"He drops by?"

Eric nodded. "He used to text her invitations, but she'd pass. So now he shows up unannounced."

In the middle of the night.

"Once a week, maybe more," Spike growled. He sounded like an honorary wolf. "He says she needs to get out and have a life. Do some self-care. He worries we're not taking care of Sonnet right."

That's our job now.

It was, indeed. I crossed my arms over my chest as Wyatt appeared in the doorway to the kitchen. His eyes scanned the room, his expression thoughtful as he spotted me. He took in my bare feet, blue jeans, and no belt.

Despite coming to the correct conclusion, he asked, "What are you doing here?"

"Giving Ms. Ruiz a workout," Spike muttered too low for anyone human to hear. Of course, he didn't know that two out of three of his fellow kitchen inhabitants were shapeshifters. If he had, he would have had his gun out.

"Where's Sonnet?" Wyatt didn't bother waiting for my answer. "Is she finally getting some sleep?"

Spike started, "She's—"

"She's sleeping," I said. "She's worn out."

Wyatt's eyes widened. "She has an early call time today."

"Yep." I looked at him.

He looked back. "She hates being late."

"What's it to you?" I growled, letting him see the wolf in my eyes.

Amber flickered in Wyatt's eyes. "Someone needs to look after Sonnet."

Us. We're gonna do it so much better.

Eric cleared his throat and smacked Spike on the shoulder. "We'll be in the other room."

The two of them filed out of the room, leaving Wyatt and me swapping heated glances.

Neither of us said anything for a good minute, likely because there was nothing *to* say. We already knew the answer to each other's question. *Yes, yes, I did sleep with her,* and *No, you don't have a snowball's chance at the equator with her.*

Also: *No, I won't hurt her, and yes, I know she might hurt me.*

We've got this.

Finally, Wyatt sighed. "You didn't take my advice."

He never had been good at silences. He was too impatient, too quick to ask questions.

"I don't recall any advice." I leaned my hip against the kitchen counter.

He crossed to the coffee maker and poured himself a cup while he chewed on my answer. **If he touches the cake, we tackle him**, my wolf warned.

I agreed. That cake was Sonnet's.

"You know she's not gonna stick around Moonlight Valley, no matter what she says." Wyatt watched me over the rim of his cup. "You'll be all butt hurt when she goes."

Butt hurt did not begin to describe my future feelings.

"I am aware that her show will wrap. What happens after that is up to Sonnet." Now that I was paying attention, I could see that his mouth was curved in an unhappy grimace. He wasn't saying shit to be mean, or at least that wasn't all. He believed his words.

"She's a beautiful woman. She's funny as hell. Being near her is amazing, like cozying up to a hickory fire when you're cold." He took a sip of his coffee, thinking it over. "She and I have a long history together. We were friends before she arrived here, and we'll be friends after she goes. That's not going to change. You? You're not just her friend."

"And?" I growled.

"The thing is, she's a storyteller, and she writes great romances. She knows what her audience wants, and she delivers. So, I think this thing between the two of you is just one more script. It's a fucking great one"—he shrugged—"and as your friend, I'm hoping it's got a happy ending. But since I've been Sonnet's friend for years, I think that sooner or later your relationship will end, and she'll move on to the next project and you'll end up hurt."

He shrugged uncomfortably, his eyes filled with sympathy, as he continued, "And I'm betting it will be *sooner*. Sonnet's relationships are more short-lived than a basket of berries."

"Did you save me some coffee?"

Both Wyatt and I turned toward the door. Sonnet stood there, twisting her hair up into a knot on top of her head. She wore a floral caftan with a lace-trimmed vee that showed off her amazing breasts. As the caftan was not entirely opaque, I had a pretty good guess that she was naked beneath it.

Go kiss the girl.

Without waiting for an answer, she padded into the kitchen and made directly for me. **We're BETTER than coffee**, my wolf crowed.

When she stood in front of me, she reached up and wound her arms around my neck, pressing her body to mine and a sweet kiss to my mouth. I wound an arm around her waist, pulling her close. She sure wasn't wearing anything under that pretty caftan but skin.

Carry her back upstairs. Appreciate her.

I bit back a groan. Heading upstairs appealed. I wanted to sweep her up in my arms and carry her there, bridal style. No. Scratch that. I'd just heave her over my shoulder like a caveman. I was nothing but a barbarian where Sonnet Ruiz was concerned.

"You have the best mouth," she said with a sleepy grin, pressing her fingertips against my lips. "And the best beard." A kiss against my chin. "And the best nose." Another kiss. "And the best neck." More kisses.

Jesus Christ, please let her keep going.

I kept my eyes fixed on her, studiously ignoring Wyatt. He was gaping at us.

Sucks to be him, my wolf said happily. **We win.**

"There's coffee." I tucked her hair behind her ears and tipped her face up so I could steal a kiss. "Or we could liberate that cake over there and take it back up to bed. I have plans to feast."

"You are a genius." She planted her palms on my chest, leaning into me. One hand started sliding south. "Have I mentioned that I appreciate your woodworking skills. When we're in Hollywood, every Saturday will be wood day, okay? Can I use your tool?"

What did she mean by "when we're in Hollywood"? I felt as if I'd missed an important conversation.

Behind us, Wyatt choked.

Sonnet whipped around. "Wyatt. Crap. Wow. I didn't realize you were here. Sorry." She frowned. "No. Wait. I'm not sorry. Why are you here?"

He frowned. "I should have called first."

"Yes." She nodded, fisting my shirt. "You should have. Did the rent payment clear? Is there a plumbing emergency? *Any* kind of emergency that warrants an unannounced early morning visitation?"

"Yes." He cleared his throat. "And no. No, there isn't. I'll be going?"

"Yep," she said, then to me, "Grab the cake, and I'll meet you upstairs."

She reached up to peck me on the lips, her eyes making sexy promises. Then she turned and bounced out of the kitchen. I stood there, appreciating her full, round butt in the slinky caftan.

Jesus Christ, what a woman.

She took my breath away. She surely did.

Silence descended on the kitchen. I counted to ten, but Wyatt didn't head for the door.

"Well, I'll be." He shook his head. "Maverick Lincoln Boone, you are something else. I never thought I'd see Sonnet . . ."

"What?"

"Be serious with someone," he said thoughtfully. "She's actually serious."

"Not even with you?" The question needed asking. Wyatt and I, we had to work together. I needed to know if he was jealous, if my relationship with Sonnet was something that would come between us.

"Honestly? No. Not for real, or certainly for long. She's smart and amazing, and I'd be a fool not to switch places with you if she asked me." He grinned and then added, "But she's not inviting me to share her cake, so if she's settling and gonna tie herself down, I'm glad it's with you. You deserve each other."

"I appreciate that."

Mostly, my wolf growled. **Still think we should shift. Make a few points.**

From the images my wolf shared, those points would be made with our claws—and our teeth.

"But," I continued, "Sonnet isn't tying herself down—or settling. I'm here for her, to support her and cheer her on, and encourage her to be more. Not less, Wyatt. She doesn't ever have to be less for me."

His grin faded, skepticism warring with confusion on his face.

I chuckled. "You write all those books about love and sex, yet you don't have a clue. You'll figure it out someday." I grabbed the cake. I didn't need a plate—I'd be licking that frosting off my lady. "Now if you'll pardon me, I have a special delivery to make."

CHAPTER
TWENTY-SIX

"For some reason I thought Shifters would be like in the movies. You know. Half
man, half beast, bad breath. I'm glad I found out wrong."

— JENNIFER ASHLEY, *MATE CLAIMED*

Maverick took me pumpkin picking for our eighth date.

A sign greeted us that read, CLOSED FOR A PRIVATE EVENT. Beneath it was scrawled: *Yes, that means you,* and *Gate-crashers get toothmarks for party favors.* Maverick had reserved the entire patch just for us so I could wander without worrying about photographs or being on display.

He'd also brought hot apple cider in a thermos, and we strolled up and down the rows of pumpkins, the two of us sipping and talking. Maverick insisted on pulling the red wagon for collecting my pumpkin bounty, and it was adorable. I snapped some quick pics with my phone, wondering if I could post them on my Instagram without sparking dating rumors. My followers would love my pumpkin-picking lumberjack with his teeny, size-inappropriate red toy and his T-shirt that announced: *Blood Type: Pumpkin Spice!*

It didn't take me long to get into pumpkinpalooza. I pointed; Maverick picked. After the third pumpkin, I realized I should probably check in with him, or at least make it clear that I would be paying for my own pumpkins and not taking advantage of his generosity in the matter of gourds.

327

"Is there a pumpkin quota? I promise I'll dial back my picking."

Crouched beside me, Maverick regarded me with a wry expression as I poked around in the vines. THERE WERE TINY BABY PUMPKINS. They were nestled deep in the vines that spread everywhere, the cutest little pumpkin buds ever. Plus, being outside with my feet and fingers in the dirt made my witchy side happy.

"You can have whatever you want," he said. "I love your enthusiasm for pumpkins."

I squinted at him. Was my date making a lewd pun? It was cute and funny coming from him. Maverick's flirting was typically light and G-rated. He was respectful when he talked (and respectful in a whole different worshipping-at-the-shrine-of-Venus sort of way when we were in bed). Getting to see this side of him made me feel special, like he trusted me in ways he didn't trust other people.

"Whatever I want, huh?" My inner Chaneque squealed. This was the checkered flag to collect anything and everything.

He nodded, gently twisting a white pumpkin so it popped off the vine and into his big hands. He set it in the wagon. "As you wish."

THOSE WORDS. Those words were better than a magic spell. Just like that, I was transformed into a gorgeous blonde princess who made her humble but strong lover run all over kingdom come, pleasing her. Acts of service was Westley and Buttercup's love language. It was Maverick's too.

I wasn't sure what mine was. When it came to love, I was a pre-verbal baby, still in the early stages of language acquisition. I babbled. I made playful sounds. Sometimes, I mimicked what I heard. It had never bothered me before, but now I wished I was better at this whole *love* thing.

I love him.

Where had that thought come from? It should have been too soon to be thinking about forever feelings, but it *wasn't*. It wasn't at all.

Since Buzzard's Bluff and our fun afterward, we'd stopped keeping our relationship a secret. We weren't putting out a press release, but we were clearly a couple. He stayed at my place most nights. I stole his T-shirts because they smelled like him and apparently his wolfiness was rubbing off on me—I wanted the whole werewolf community to scent him on me.

There were kisses and hand-holding where we might have been spotted. I knew there was gossip on set about us—heck, we talked about *everyone*, so it would have been more surprising if there had been radio silence—but we'd decided not to care what people said.

We were still taking things slow, building the intimacy between us one fragile, delicious layer at a time, like the Japanese crepe cake he'd treated me to. The important thing was that we had a cake. We were a *thing*. Having sex with Maverick would just be the final layer of frosting, the cherry on top of the best relationship of my life. I'd written this book before: a whole lot of funny *no, we could never EVER work* that became *HUH maybe we* could *work* and *wow isn't he sexy*. We'd had ups and downs, downs and ups, and maybe we were headed toward happily ever after.

"You know, I still don't know all that much about what you do."

"What I do?" I yelped, startling, because my mind was on endings that were actually beginnings and absolutely not on pumpkin picking.

Stay in the moment! Don't be so future-focused that you forget to enjoy today!

I'd never been in love.

But I loved Maverick.

I love my big, sweet, slightly growly, overprotective, safe werewolf professor.

So many words for so much man.

"Yeah, your occupation," he teased. "I'm reading your books, but you never talk much about the acting side of things."

Hold up a moment.

"You bought my books." I fell over onto my butt. He was going to read my love stories? Where I wrote about sex and supernatural critters and generally poured my heart out on the page even though, naturally, I pretended it was entirely made-up fictional stuff?

Oh. God.

"Of course." He sat down next to me, crisscross applesauce, and squeezed my hand gently. "Why wouldn't I? You're amazing, and it's part of who you are."

"I'm pretty sure that if I worked at the Piggly Wiggly you wouldn't come stand at my cash register and check things out," I argued. "Or if I was, say, a neurosurgeon, you couldn't just waltz into my operating theater and pull up a chair. Hanging out at your girlfriend's place of work is something you do in high school."

He lifted a big shoulder. "Your books matter to you. They matter to me."

"Okay." Was there a way to ask for a heads-up when he got to the sex scenes? Oh GOD. Had I written a werewolf orgy in that one book? I made a mental note to check; I'd been so busy these last few years that I'd promptly moved on to the next book after finishing the last one. The details blurred. "Thanks for the dollar fifty in royalties?"

"You're welcome."

I pointed randomly to a pumpkin. He plucked it and added it to my pumpkin collection. *SAY SOMETHING.*

"You didn't Google me online?"

He shook his head. "Just in the online bookstore so I could have you on my phone. Do you not want to talk about your job?"

"It's fine. I mean, it's just kinda weird that it's never come up. People always have questions. It's usually the hot topic of conversation at the dinner table."

Or in the coffee shop line, the fast-food drive-through, the airport restroom, or the grocery store. Anywhere I went, people had questions. They all wanted to know what it was like to be a best-selling author, and they asked about my books, my TV show, my glamorous celebrity life (I edited my responses to that last one). I hadn't thought about the prominence of "Tell me about your job" in the Get To Know Sonnet question lists, but it was usually ranked number one. Sometimes, it traded places with "Have you lost weight?" and "What's your new diet?"

Yet this was the first time Maverick had explicitly asked me about it. It had come up, sort of, in his truck the day we met, when he'd misheard my name, and I'd told him I was a writer. After that, however, his questions had been about what I wished for, my opinions, my preferences. He hadn't hit me with a thousand questions about being a famous TV actress. Heck, I'd asked more questions about his snake gig—and that was *definitely* not a topic I'd embraced.

I wasn't even all that surprised that he'd bought my books. If I'd painted, he would have hung my work on his walls; if I'd been a dentist, he would have told the world that no one filled a cavity better. I could not have written a more perfect hero, and his interest in what I did for a living as an actress and a writer was only the tip of his interest iceberg.

He listened to me. He asked questions and then he listened some more. Most people were dismissive about the romance genre. They explained to me that it was just fluff or brain candy, as if it took less work or thought than literary fiction or "serious" stuff. It was love. How much more important could you get?

"Are you going to ask me where I get my ideas?"

He grinned at me. "That sounds like a trap."

"Or volunteer to be my research assistant?"

He winked. "I'm hearing you prefer to work alone."

I grinned back. "Usually, yes. But for you I might make an exception. You have no idea how many people believe I must have done every single thing described in my books."

"So, they're fantasies." His eyes were warm and playful. "That's good to know. Although I think your books have been mis-shelved."

"And why is that?"

"Because seeing as how they're your fantasies, that makes them more like recipes." He bumped my shoulder with his. "I would be putting them with the cookbooks."

"Maverick Boone, are you saying that you're going to follow along like they're a set of *directions*?"

He grinned at me. "Are they good recipes? Do I get a private cooking lesson with the chef?"

Warmth bloomed in my chest, and I couldn't stop my grin. "You are so bad."

"Mmmhmmm. And now I'm remembering one particular part." His eyes dropped to my chest, then moved lower. There was suddenly a whole lot of heat in my kitchen.

Conveniently, there was a fire extinguisher sitting right next to me.

I crawled into his lap. "Writing lesson *número uno*: show, don't tell."

* * *

We were in his truck driving back to his place after loading up our pumpkin haul, bickering amicably about the best way to decorate for Halloween, when Elena called.

Her name flashed up on my screen along with a handful of flower, poop, and unicorn emojis. Did I want to answer? Did I have to?

"What's wrong?"

331

Maverick glanced over at me, obviously concerned about the ferocity with which I was glaring at my phone screen.

"Nothing, at least not yet. It's just my sister." I ignored the call. "I'll reach out to her later."

"Your manager."

"Yeah." I hadn't told him about my argument with Elena in Los Angeles, the one where I'd drawn some Maverick-sized boundaries. Now didn't seem to be the right time to share that she saw my dating a Southern biologist as a career liability—and never mind the fact that he had a somewhat checkered and possibly criminal past. Mostly, she and I had ignored our blow up. We'd kept our texting and emails to business only, and there had been zero phone conversations where anyone could go off script.

The flower-poop-unicorn parade flashed across my screen again.

Elena wasn't giving up.

"You should take it." Maverick lifted his chin toward the phone. "She's family. It could be important."

"It never is," I grumbled. Still, I took the call. "Hi?"

"Sonnet," Elena said instead of reciprocating my greeting. She said my name like you'd greet a dog that was yapping and trying to climb your leg. *Calm down. Who's a good girl? Don't bark!*

I wasn't an actress for nothing. I imitated her tone, pitch-perfect. "Elena." *You cute little worked up thing you. YOU calm down!*

This was not the response she'd expected, and it took a moment for her to remember her next line.

"I'm reaching out about the *Wolf Girl* script and the London premiere."

I'd forgotten about the stupid London premiere. Again. *Did I even put it on my calendar? Which month is it?*

"How many pages do you have for me? The studio wants a status update. They need at least the partial."

Ugh. I hadn't written a single page since they'd un-casted me from the role of Wolf Girl.

"I don't have anything new. Not yet."

A controlled exhalation. An inhale. I imagined her puffing out her cheeks in irritation like a pufferfish that had spotted a threat. *Spines out!*

"I'm still brainstorming," I hedged.

That sounded better than admitting that it was all a big blank page where *Wolf Girl* was concerned. It wasn't like me to procrastinate, and Elena knew it. I'd let the project fall off my radar, which wasn't professional behavior at all. I needed to write the pages or officially pass on the project.

"And London? Do you want me to reach out to Luke's team?"

"Luke's team?"

Maverick shifted in his seat. His attention was fixed on the mountain road in front of us, but the set lines of his face announced that he didn't like hearing the name of my co-star.

"You need a date, and he was your last—"

"Not a chance," I interrupted her. "He's nothing to me." Then impulsively, I said, "I'll bring Maverick."

Maverick took his eyes off the road. He looked at me. *Where am I going?* his raised eyebrows said. And also: *Of course, I'll go with you, but I may need to put the address into my map app.*

Elena didn't say anything. The pufferfish had spotted a reef shark and was debating a spiny defense versus a hasty retreat into some nice, safe coral.

Finally, she asked, "Do you think that's wise?"

"I do."

Another measured inhale. Seriously: she was going to explode. "Okay, let's put aside our conversation from when you were in LA We'll just put aside my conviction that hooking up with this random Southern redneck is a terrible mistake. Put all that aside for a minute and consider this. I shouldn't have to spell it out, but: if you take the community college professor to this premiere—"

My anger rose.

I kept my voice level, however. "Maverick. His name is Maverick. Do not disparage him."

She ignored this. "Then your relationship is public knowledge. His life will change overnight. People will dig into his past. Celebrity bloggers and online fan forums will rip him apart. They'll look for reasons why he's not good enough for you, and they'll find them. Or they'll make them up. He'll be on the cover of supermarket tabloids and women's magazines; his pictures will be for sale on all the commercial websites, and they'll be downloaded and used in places he hates. People will pay attention to him, and he won't be able to go traipsing off into the mountains looking for hognose snakes without a posse of photographers trampling along behind him. Does he know that? Is that what he wants?"

And . . . the pufferfish had teeth.

It bit me.

There was blood in the water.

Flailing.

Missing body parts.

My anger deflated like a souffle hitting cold air.

"We haven't discussed it," I admitted. Crap. Maverick's accomplishments, his successes, and his good points weren't the issue here. It was the notoriety he'd gain that was. I'd been so busy playing happy couple with Maverick, living in this perfect dating bubble that we'd created, that I hadn't thought through what would happen when our solitary bubble rejoined the rest of the world.

It would pop.

Could we build a better bubble? Would he even want to?

"The premiere is in one week."

"Okay." *Fiddlesticks and flapjacks*. I had nothing.

"I'm chartering a plane."

"Great. Okay. Great."

"Do you want me to reach out to Luke's team? He can fly to London with you. You could announce that you're going as friends. Then you don't have to put Maverick out there. You'll have more time to think things through."

Think things through being code for *see things my way and end things*.

"Don't do that." No way I was spending eight hours in an enclosed space with Luke. "Let me talk it over with Maverick."

"I need an answer by tomorrow."

"Uh-huh." Technically, I was her boss. I'd never pulled that card before, but I was tempted now.

"Good night." She paused, as if she wanted to add something else, then finished up with, "You take care now."

Her tone was surprisingly gentle and affectionate. It was the tone that belonged to the sister who cared about me and not the businesslike woman who was my manager. I loved one of those and appreciated the other, and some of my anger dissipated. Unfortunately, panic moved into the newly freed up space in my heart.

We ended the call, and I sat there, silently freaking out.

I should have discussed this with Maverick before our first date.

Before agreeing we'd try for forever.

And definitely before falling in love with him.

My brain suggested a million billion ways that Maverick could get hurt. There was no way the world would dismiss him as boring and of no account. They would pry, and pry, and pry. All his secrets would come out, and while I loved this man for a reason and he was awesome, he hated his past.

"What's wrong?" he asked, rubbing my thigh gently. "Did you get more bad news? Do we need to get pie and ice cream?"

The offer of sugar and carbohydrates merited a smile, but it faded fast. I was switching gears from freaked out to practical. And practical was depressing.

I'd been selfish because I liked him so much. Despite his claim of wanting more than a quick hookup with me, he didn't understand what he was hitching his wagon to. The overly public first date and the sidelong looks we'd been getting on set were the tip of the attention iceberg.

Oh my God. He hadn't even Googled me yet.

"So, when I went back to Los Angeles, Elena saw the picture of us on my phone and she didn't like it. She was worried the photo would leak."

"I would never share it, if that's what she's worried about."

"It's not just that photo. I have to go to London next week. There's a premiere, and I need to go with someone."

"A date."

"Yeah. A date, but the right kind of date. Someone who will boost my image and create the desirable kind of buzz." I'd heard these words hundreds of times in meetings and strategy sessions and lectures (from Elena, naturally) about the ephemeral nature of my success and how we needed to leverage it before it vanished.

"I'm going to be real honest, Sonnet. I won't be happy if you date someone else, even as a one-night work thing." His tone was firm, as if he meant business, but also calm and reasonable. He was trying not to sound possessive or dictatorial. He wasn't giving orders, but he was explaining exactly how he felt.

"I don't want to go on a date with anyone but you. It would make me very unhappy."

He thought that through for a second, before asking, "So what's the problem?"

I held out my hand, and he immediately threaded the fingers of his right hand through mine.

"If you come with me to the premiere, everyone will know you're my boyfriend."

He nodded firmly. "That seems like a good thing."

"*Everyone* will know. You will have zero privacy. Strangers will dig through your trash, hack your phone and online accounts, and pop out from behind the produce displays in the grocery store to take your picture. Are you ready for that? Are you ready to be photographed with a six-pack of beer and some toilet paper, and then people will publish stories about your drinking problem and your digestive issues? Worse, they will *follow you*. And your brothers. If you shift into your wolf, they will photograph you."

Maverick shifted in his seat, amber rolling over his eyes. *Yes, dating me might mean the whole world finds out your werewolf secret.*

Could we keep our relationship a secret? Perhaps if we had been discreet, but the discretion horse was totally out of that barn. Everyone on set knew about us. It was a miracle that there were no hints on the celebrity news websites yet. *So maybe it's not too late? What happens in Moonlight Valley could stay in Moonlight Valley?*

"Yes."

I'd lost the thread of our conversation. "Yes, what?"

"Yes, I'm ready to give up my privacy and have people go through my trash. I'll need to give Ranger a heads-up, though. His personal habits are odd. Maybe I should beef up my online security. Or delete those accounts. I could move out of the family house and get a place somewhere else. I could take Sanye up on the offer to house-sit."

WHAT? I gaped at him. "You're actually considering this?"

He had mentioned her offer a few days previously, when Sanye had finally gotten around to explaining her drive-around-the-country-in-a-van plans. At the time, I had not thought he was a fan.

His warm gaze slid over my body. "There will be compensation."

I grinned despite myself and our unfortunate situation, but even his charm was no proof against reality. "You've never lived like this, Maverick. It's not just what you do now or tomorrow. It's everything in your past. Every embarrassing arrest photo, every painful, ugly moment that you thought was over and done with will be resurrected. They will talk to people who knew—or claimed to know—you, and then they'll publish that shit as the truth. You won't be moving into another place—you'll be residing in a fishbowl."

He frowned, turning my words over in his head. We drove in silence, him working things through in his head, me silently freaking out next to him.

Could we just see each other in secret? It was a time-honored rom-com trope. It could work! We'd just sneak around, love each other on the down-low. Our private life would stay private. Maybe?

"You're concerned that my past will hurt your public image," he said finally.

I flinched because he sounded hurt and accepting at the same time. He believed he didn't deserve a second chance, not after what he'd done when he'd been a teenager. "It's not that. Not at all. Nothing embarrasses me. I am impervious to embarrassment."

He pulled his hand away. "I've been arrested multiple times. There are sordid stories galore. I am not a hero, and your being seen with me would absolutely not be a good look for you."

I gaped. What. The. Hell. "Don't worry about me. Or my image."

"Would you lose more acting roles? Could you be dropped from projects?"

I opened my mouth to deny this vehemently. But the words didn't come out. Truth was, I *didn't* know what the impact would be. I hadn't given it much thought.

Interpreting my silence as agreement, Maverick cursed.

"Maverick—" I reached for him, and he backed away.

Pain pierced my chest. I couldn't breathe. I'd never seen Maverick angry and dark, closed off and ruminating. He wasn't here with me, in our moment. He was somewhere else, on the other side of a dark and scary chasm that had unexpectedly opened between us.

He looked at me from way far away on the other side. It was cold over there, and distant.

"Do you care about your career?" he asked.

I ignored that. "I care about your privacy."

We were almost to the cabin.

I tried again. "Will you come in? Stay with me?"

He shook his head.

Don't cry. You are a strong, independent woman. You are not a Maverick appendage. Or Maverick-dependent. "You promised. You promised that my being famous wouldn't make you leave me. You said I could trust you."

His eyes didn't shift from the road. "This isn't about your fame. This is about my past hurting your future. I promised not to hurt you."

And how is this NOT hurting me?

"Don't do this." I fisted my hands in my lap. He'd backed off, so there could be no touching. I would respect his boundaries. "Stay with me. Stay tonight, and we'll figure this out tomorrow. I promise you."

"Not tonight." Maverick's voice was unrecognizable, cold and stern and unyielding. "I need space."

CHAPTER

TWENTY-SEVEN

"He was sleek, dangerous, powerful. A graceful, deadly predator with wide shoulders that tapered down to slim hips, powerful thighs, and thick calves roped with muscle. The only soft thing about him was his swathe of dark hair that fell in thick waves to tease his shoulders."

— SUNNY, *MONA LISA AWAKENING*

"**S**pace." I was shocked at the steadiness with which I got the word out. "Space."

No.

WHAT. THE. HELL.

Do not push our mate away.

My wolf unleashed a blistering series of curse words.

Sonnet sat there, silent. Hurting.

The one person who'd looked at me and seen more than a man and his wolf.

Christ, I'd been a fool.

And you still are.

No. I wasn't. It didn't matter how much I'd worked to change, the time I'd devoted to becoming a better person who did better things, who was not a garbage animal

339

who took and took but never gave back. I couldn't erase my past, but I would not allow it to hurt this woman.

"You need space," she said.

You're hurting her NOW, my wolf snarled.

She did sound empty and anxious, tearful. But it was a much smaller hurt in comparison to what would happen if the world tarred her with my brush, if they looked at her and saw the beast who'd selfishly run with the Iron Wolves, stealing and lying, hurting and taking. She was better than that. She *deserved* better than that.

We pulled into the gravel driveway in front of Wyatt's place, and I slowed to a stop. My mind raced, trying to find a way out. An alternative to giving her up. Was there a way to hide what I'd been?

Ranger was good with electronics. Maybe he could figure out a way to wipe me and my arrest records from the law enforcement databases.

But even if he erased the legal records of what I'd been accused of doing, that still left all the people here in Moonlight Valley who knew exactly what Darrell Boone's firstborn son had done. They would tell stories, and they wouldn't have to lie or exaggerate. The entire, mortifying, scandalous truth would come out.

And the biggest truth of all was that I *had* done those things. I wasn't some innocent victim, and the stories wouldn't be exaggerated.

I was guilty as charged, and I deserved my punishment.

And, of course, there was my father. I still didn't understand how he'd managed to send that picture of me and Sonnet, but if he could shake his jailers and his well-deserved punishment long enough, he'd do his level best to exploit our relationship. At the very least, he'd want money.

You're even better than your old man at the dating game. She's got money and great tits. She can give your old man a fresh start. Think of the stories I can tell— you think those press people might be interested?

My chickens were coming home to roost.

He was a threat.

We'll protect her any way we can. My wolf sounded sad. He knew my plan was the safest one for Sonnet.

I would not be Darrell Boone's son, not his mini-me, and sure as hell not the chip off his old block. I would be a man who took care of his mate, saw to her needs and well-being. I would always put her first. I would not be an embarrassment or a dirty secret. Not blot her reputation. Not make her job harder. I'd done these things to my family, and I'd learned my lesson. I could never live with myself if I hurt her future.

I could not.

I would not.

"How much space?" she asked huskily. Her hands were balled up in her lap.

I shook my head. Instead of answering, I got out and walked around to open her door. I held my hand up, palm out. *Please take it. Let me help you one last time.*

She sat in my truck, glaring at me. Also, she was trying not to cry. Her solution for not tearing up seemed to mean biting her lower lip, the sharp point of her incisors worrying the tender flesh. It felt like she'd stabbed those points into me. My heart hurt, but I deserved it.

I had *hurt* her.

I TOLD you that. Let me out. I'll do the talking.

I couldn't. I just—couldn't.

"Talk to me," she ordered. "Please. You're overreacting. We don't have to make decisions right now."

Her voice cracked as she jumped down onto the gravel, slamming the door shut behind her. She grabbed my shoulders with her hands because she was not a quitter. She was trying and trying, while I—

"Maverick! We could date in secret for a while, just until—"

"Absolutely not," I growled.

I wanted to mark her. Make her mine. Be everything or nothing to her because otherwise it was too painful.

I was no longer a liar. I hated lying. I hated pretense and deception. I owned my shit—I didn't cover it up like a goddamned cat.

Sonnet flinched, her hands dropping away from my shoulders.

It wasn't so much the lying, as it was no one knowing that she was mine. She was famous and beautiful, smart, funny, and so talented. Of course, people wanted to know her or think that they did. Of course, they wanted to be around her as much as she would permit.

If being with Sonnet meant thousands, possibly millions, of people wanted a piece of her, I would deal with it. Alright. That was just how it was.

Just as long as the world knew she was mine.

And that there were pieces of her, private pieces, that I wouldn't have to share. That *she* wouldn't want to share because they were ours. My lizard brain was working overtime, and my inner caveman was bellowing. She would have given me well-deserved shit for my possessiveness, but I wasn't perfect. This was just further proof of that.

"I don't care what other people think." Her voice was small. I hated that she was making herself smaller, diminishing herself because of me. I was a liability, that was for sure.

"You should," I said. "You've worked hard to get where you are. Don't throw it away because of a few feelings for a Tennessee redneck werewolf."

I walked back to the driver's side. It felt like I was wading through molasses, but doing the right thing could be hard.

"Are you coming back?" she called after me. "Is this really it?"

"I don't know," I said honestly because I didn't want to walk away, but I refused to hurt her, and that left me with no way forward and an unpleasant past that was no one's fault but my own.

* * *

"You cleaned the bathroom."

I didn't look over my shoulder. I recognized Knox's voice. He was right. I'd scrubbed the toilet and shower, vacuumed the bath mat, and shined the faucet with Momma's baking soda, lavender, and vinegar paste. As it was going to take more than a clean bathroom to make me feel like I was in control of my life and my decisions, I'd moved on after that to the living room. And now the kitchen. After I finished up here, I aimed to clean out the garage.

When I didn't answer he said, "We have a chores schedule, Mav."

I added more hot water and soap to the sink. There was an art to handwashing crystal, and ours hadn't been washed in donkey's years.

"Mav?"

"Fuck off, Knox."

Last night, after dropping off Sonnet, I'd shifted into my wolf and run out to Lucky Jansen's place, the club headquarters for the Iron Wolves.

I'd wanted a fight.

I'd wanted to go tooth and claw at someone who deserved it and have someone go tooth and claw after me in return.

Brawling, getting drunk, causing mayhem wouldn't have felt good, but at least I would have been feeling something.

I waited for my wolf to chime in, but he'd been silent for hours.

He was in a snit about Sonnet and giving me the cold shoulder.

To quote someone near and dear to your heart: fuck off.

I'd run around Lucky's place, rubbed up against a few trees to leave my mark, and then left. I couldn't go pick the fight I wanted. I might have lost Sonnet, but I still had my brothers and sister. They also deserved better from me. I couldn't go to town on the Iron Wolves.

But I could clean the house.

Knox didn't budge from the kitchen door. "When did you build a toolshed?"

I didn't respond.

"Or are the outbuildings spontaneously reproducing like one of those fucking snakes you study?"

"Get. Lost." I rinsed a vintage wineglass in the suds.

For the record, snakes didn't spontaneously reproduce. Some of them mated, some self-fertilized, and then either laid a clutch of eggs or gave birth to live young.

Knox sighed. He stood there, judging me silently, while I took satisfaction in cleaning up Momma's favorite crystal. The glass was starting to look cloudy, so perhaps it was time for a vinegar bath.

Then a second voice spoke. "Maverick, did you clean the bathroom?"

Ranger.

I considered plunging my head into the sink of soapy water.

Ranger continued, "It wasn't your turn. It was Atticus's. How are we going to function as a unit if you go around violating the chore chart? It's like asking a raccoon to organize your garbage. It makes no sense."

"I asked him the same thing," Knox snarled. As I was ignoring him, he must have been addressing his complaint to Ranger. "And he built a shed in the backyard."

"I can hear you, you lunkhead." I set a glass on the microfiber cloth I'd laid out and glared over my shoulder, finding my brothers frowning at me. "Did you hear what I said. I'm happy to repeat—"

"Fuck off and get lost. Yes. That message came through loud and clear." Knox's tone was flat and irritated, but he didn't leave the kitchen.

Ranger raised an eyebrow. "I take it your relationship with Ms. Ruiz took a less than pleasant turn?"

And how? my wolf growled. **You are a QUITTER.**

I ground my teeth. It had been better when I'd been getting the wolfish cold shoulder. On the other hand, after I finished washing our crystalware, I would need to find something else to do. I could scratch that itch by wrestling with Ranger inside the house. He was an excellent grappler and cleaning up the mess afterward would keep me busy for the rest of the day.

As though reading my mind, Ranger stiffened. "You will not. I haven't drunk my apple cider vinegar yet, and that comes before twenty minutes of moderate physical exertion to get my blood circulating."

"Then go on and get."

Ranger grunted, looking unhappy. "If you don't tell me what happened, I'll drop by Ms. Ruiz's trailer and—"

"You will not," I barked. I set the glass down carefully and turned around.

"Then tell us what happened." Ranger held up his hands.

"What did you do to her?" Knox glared at me.

"Not a thing." I tossed the washrag onto the countertop so I wouldn't slap it against Knox's head.

Without thinking, I asked, "What'd you do to Sanye?" I wiped my hands on the edge of my T-shirt. "You obviously did something to scare her out of town and make her hate you so much."

Knox paled, and I almost regretted asking him the question.

Ranger stepped between us. "This ain't about Knox, this is about you using a year's worth of bleach for superfluous cleaning. So, you tell me, what's got you cleaning up a storm? What happened with you and Sonnet?"

Exhaustion hit me, leaving my body aching and tired. My chest hurt. "We're done."

We can't be.

But we had to be. I'd been repeating the words to myself like a refrain in a song because my past meant we had no future. And yet I didn't want to let her go.

Should we date secretly? Considering that unpalatable option had set me off on my bathroom-cleaning orgy. Like a fool, I wanted everything. I thought she'd seen somebody redeemable, somebody worth caring about.

I thought she saw somebody worth standing up for in public.

Now I was stress cleaning.

Ranger propped his hands on his hips. "Why would you be over? Did something happen while you were picking pumpkins?"

"No. Her sister called while we were driving back. Sonnet's supposed to attend a premiere in London this week for *Smoky Spirits* and she needs a date."

Ranger nodded. "And? What's the problem?"

My gaze flickered to Knox. He impersonated an iceberg, his arms crossed, his mouth grim. "I can't be her date."

Ranger *tsked* impatiently. "Why not? You have a passport. And a suitcase. Are you persona non grata in London? Did your wolf lift a leg and pee in the Beefeaters' Cheerios?"

"Because if I go, everyone will know about us. Because that means reporters digging into my past. I'm an ex-con from backwoods Appalachia. I have a GED, an arrest record, and a bad name."

"You are not an ex-con. You were never convicted."

"Tomato, tomatoh. I stole those cars, even if they could never prove it. Plus, there's the whole wolf thing. I can't have photographers following me around, poking their noses in our family business. What happens if one of them catches us shifting?"

"So, she dumped you." Ranger's eyes flashed amber.

"No." I shook my head. "I'm dumping her. I have to do it."

"You?" Knox asked abruptly. A flash of surprise disrupted his irritatingly calm stoicism. "Why would you do a dang fool thing like that?"

"Because I'm not going to be the one who hurts her," I gritted out. "Are you telling me that I should wreck her life, Knox Jackson Boone? I'm a career torpedo. A blot on her public image. You can't say you lo—"

Love, my wolf prompted. **Yeah, let's talk about love.**

You can't say you love someone and then do something like that to her.

I loved Sonnet Ruiz.

It had happened so easily, so naturally, that I hadn't stopped to think about it. I'd just gone ahead and *done* it.

It feels good, my wolf prompted. **And natural as hell. Amazing. Awesome. Well, not the blue balls part, but we're gonna work on that RIGHT?**

My wolf had no hesitation. He was already all in, even if his manners needed work.

HEY.

I loved her, and the thought of spending the rest of my days—hell, *any* of my days—without her had me panicking.

Ranger cut off my lunge for the mop. "Wait a minute. Hold your horses. What did she say?"

"It doesn't matter."

He raised an eyebrow. "What the lady wants doesn't matter?"

Poking the bear. He has a death wish.

I grabbed the mop. "She doesn't want my privacy to be invaded. And she wants us to be secret lovers. She suggested that we hide our relationship."

"How do you feel about your private time, Maverick? I know that I prefer having some me time that is not invaded or documented by y'all. Are you worried about people talking about you?"

"I don't mind them *talking*," I snarled. "They can say whatever they want about me. It's the effect that those words will have on *Sonnet* that's—"

"Got your britches in a twist," Ranger finished for me, nodding his head. "So, you *don't* care about your privacy."

"I do not."

"And she claims she doesn't care about her image." Ranger nodded. He seemed to be having a conversation with himself. "So why not just trust each other and move on?"

It's not that simple.

"There's Darrell," I pointed out. I'd shared Darrell's letter with both of them. "He's fixing to use her somehow. Do you think he wouldn't?"

"No," Knox answered. He never had been one to lie, not even in social situations where something less than bluntness might have been a kindness. "He'll use the hell out of her. I don't know how he shifted, but he'll be all over this."

Ranger waved this concern away. "Don't you worry about him. I've got him under control. You will just have to trust me on this one. You have my word."

We exchanged steely glares. How did I let it go when it was Sonnet's life at stake? But Ranger had a point. He was sneaky and devious, mean sometimes, and Machiavellian always, but he kept his word. Plus, his being mean could only help with the likes of Darrell.

"You focus on Sonnet," Ranger said. "And think on how you're going to make this right."

"I guess we could date on the down-low," I said.

Everyone should know we're a pair. We are proud of her.

"No," Knox said unexpectedly, shaking his head. "You don't want to be hiding. If you won't do it in public, don't do it at all. Hiding gets old and hurtful. You want her by your side for your moments, and she'll feel the same about you."

Knox stripped off his fancy dress shirt, hanging it neatly on the back of a kitchen chair. He took in my dirty, worked-in clothes. Then he pulled off his undershirt.

Crossing to the mop bucket, he picked it up and carried it over to the sink to start running the warm water. He handed me the vinegar spray.

"Here," he said. "Use this."

I glanced at the mop bucket and then at my brother. "What are you doing?"

He shrugged, but there was a flash of something in his eyes. It was buried real deep, here and then gone, but it sure looked like sympathy. "You scrub and I'll mop. And when we finish in here, I'll help you do the baseboards."

Don't cry, my wolf warned. **Don't you dare cry.**

I couldn't help but notice that he sounded choked up.

My voice was raspy and rough as I asked, "Why?"

"Because we're family," he said, as if it were the most obvious thing in the world. "And God, do you need help."

TWENTY-EIGHT

SONNET

"Yeah, guys like you are always spoken for.'"

— ANGELA KNIGHT, *MASTER OF WOLVES*

3:35 a.m.

Whenever I closed my eyes, my brain played a Maverick Boone highlight reel.

"What happened?" Mabel had asked the morning after our breakup when I'd shown up on set. I'd been impersonating a raccoon; I'd stayed up all night, had the dark circles under my eyes to prove it, and Wyatt's place was officially out of junk food.

Apparently, I was a groundhog, not a raccoon, however, because I'd repeated my insomnia-plus-up-all-night pattern ever since.

I was exhausted.

I couldn't sleep.

It had been days and days and (Maverick-less) days.

Hello, vicious cycle. Plus, Ranger had taken to texting me. He kept sending inspirational quotes that he'd liberated from Instagram, but he didn't tell me why.

Maverick's brother was cryptic. If I hadn't been so tired, I would have considered revenge. All I needed was a half an hour rearranging his possessions in his closet, and he'd regret his poor quote choices. Today's quote was: "Own your shit together."

I turned my pillow looking for a cool spot to rest my cheek. I was hot. And bothered. *Shit* certainly described my life at the moment. But while Ranger was a terrible therapist, he wasn't entirely wrong, either. Being an actress meant that privacy was a luxury, but so what? I could invest in a ball-cap factory, buy a gated mansion, practice writing *NO COMMENT* in washable marker on my car windows. It might work, or it might not. But either I spent the rest of my life living like a well-behaved, very lonely, sex-starved nun out of fear that anyone I let into the convent (just to continue the terrible analogy) would suffer from a lack of privacy, or I owned my shit.

I could say to the world: these are the people I choose to love.

I could draw a boundary: these are the people I will allow into my life.

And then I could throw a housewarming party and invite in the people I'd chosen.

I glanced at the photo of me and Maverick on my phone, the one I'd taken on the porch, of the two of us kissing. I'd taken it. I'd owned my shit. And . . . I loved it.

A text flashed across my screen.

Maverick: Are you awake?

I attempted to analyze his question for hidden meanings while I messaged, erased my typos, and re-messaged:

Sonnet: Yes.

Maverick: I have a proposal.

Sonnet: Ask me.

Maverick: I'll be there in five.

Was this a friendly visit? A postmortem? A new attempt to stomp on my heart? *Own your shit, Sonnet.*

. . .

Sonnet: I miss you.

Dots bounced up and down on my phone screen. My heart bounced with them. Was he writing a novel? Second-guessing his proposal? *Oh God. Please don't let it be an actual script proposal.*

Maverick: I've missed you so much. I'm sorry. Please wait for me.

Sonnet: I am out of fucks to give about my image. Please believe me. If the studios drop me, so what? We can go sit outside their gates in our lawn chairs and drink beer with a big sign that says RETIRED AND HAPPY. I'm sure I can land other, smaller, indie projects.

Nada. Why hadn't we shared our locations with each other? My abilities to stalk him in real time were severely curtailed. Should I shower? Try a finding spell? Did he mean five minutes as in three hundred seconds, or did he just mean "sometime before sunrise"? I needed a response.

Sonnet: I'm gonna fire a warning shot across the PR bow. I'm sending the picture of us kissing to TMZ.

Maverick: Wait for me please.

In the interests of motivating him to drive faster, I messaged:

Sonnet: I've got the email all cued up.

Sonnet: And I'm going to send them your name and birth date. Also your hognose snake research. They should appreciate your genius.

Sonnet: And a picture of me giving them the middle-finger salute.

Sonnet: In just my thong. I'll probably land a Swimsuit Illustrated spread out of it actually.

Maverick: Wait a second, woman. I'm almost there.

Motivated, I leapt out of bed and bolted to the landing. *Walk like a delicate ballerina! A featherweight, super stealth ninja!* Waking up my entire security team would be a mistake.

Eric was on duty, parked in front of the TV with a cooking show on mute. He looked over his shoulder as I slid into the living room.

Before he could comment on my sleepless state, I darted to the foyer. "Maverick's coming over. I'll let him in."

I paced in front of the door, staring out the window every three seconds and willing Maverick to manifest in my driveway. After two miles of walking—Wyatt might have a groove in his hardwoods now—the headlights of his truck appeared, bouncing off the windows and momentarily blinding me. Should I rush outside? Play it cool? Rustle up a trench coat and greet him Marilyn Monroe–style?

Strategy, Sonnet, strategy. If this were a script, what would you do?

I didn't want to have this conversation outside in the dark. Sitting in his truck would be awkward, plus it would be easy for him to leave.

Speed walking away from the door, I whisper-yelled to Eric, "Open the door, let him in, and send him upstairs, okay?"

I didn't wait for his answer. I was the boss of my own life.

I flew up the stairs and lurked in my room. Lounge on the bed? Wear just the sheet? Put on a full suit of clothes? Footfalls on the stairs warned that I was out of time. I hummed a few bars of "Eye of the Tiger," put my phone away, and dropped my glamour.

And then there he was, hovering in the open door to my room, my handsome, hot, amazing professor. He was dressed in a plain black T-shirt with no words, blue jeans, boots, and no belt. His hair was mussed, standing on end, and he smelled weirdly of lavender. He looked tired. He looked like he'd rushed right on over here.

My heart gave an eager thump.

"Can I come in?"

I nodded. I was too busy trying to interpret the expression in his eyes to use actual words. He looked guarded and a little lost. As if his day had not gone the way he'd expected.

"Do you want to get dressed?" he asked gruffly. "Did I catch you at a bad time?"

"For crying out loud, Maverick, it's the middle of the night. I was in bed. That's not someplace I'd wear a suit. Or clothes."

I was wearing a pair of sleep shorts and a tank top. The pattern was little holly leaves and red berries because it was never too early to wear Christmas pajamas. Of course, he hadn't seen them before because when he slept over, I'd slept naked.

"This is fine." I propped my hands on my hips and drank in the sight of him. I was a starving woman after our separation. "We can have our conversation while I'm wearing this."

His eyes heated.

Good. I wasn't going to hide how much I wanted him. No sir. I was going to serve that shit up on a platter. He'd pushed me away, and I didn't care if his reasons were noble, well-intentioned, or more fictitious than a Bigfoot sighting. He'd pushed, I'd been hurt, and all those tear-filled, sorry, sleepless days should have stood between us and yet they didn't.

Because I wasn't willing to give up on Maverick Boone.

I wasn't moving on.

This time I was staying—right here in Moonlight Valley, right here with him, right here where I wanted to be.

He was worth fighting for.

"You feel free to appreciate my outfit, though," I said. I admit, I used my sexy voice. "And you're welcome to show *or* tell."

Amber rolled over his eyes, and my breath caught because his gaze narrowed, turning sharp and predatory. He took a deliberate step inside my room.

We were doing this!

Holding my gaze, he shut the door behind him. Mentally I locked it with a dozen locks. And flipped the deadbolt. The barrel bolts! ALL the bolts!

With his signature easy confidence, he strode across the room and stopped just in front of me. I lifted my chin. *Be the change you want to see!* Ranger's inspirational quotes had not covered this moment. Here I was, alone in my bedroom with my wolfman, and I didn't know my next line. I would just have to make it up. Somehow.

His eyes dropped to my mouth. Slid along my neck. Discovered my collarbone. I was one shivery connect-the-dots of lusty goosebumps. He lifted a large hand and set it on my arm. Heat! Connection! Mirroring his action, I set my hand on his arm. His fingers brushed the strap of my tank top to one side. Tingles raced down my spine, blossomed in my stomach. My pulse raged through my body.

Staring at my bare, green-traced shoulder, Maverick said, "I love you. I'm in love with you."

Our separation had been bad for my heart health. That poor organ was beating triple time now, trying to stay afloat beneath the deluge of hope and happiness.

He loves me?

He loves me!

"Repeat that for me, please."

I needed to double-check. I needed him to tattoo the words on his skin and his heart. I needed him to carry them with him everywhere we went.

"Every day," he said. "I'll repeat it every day. I love you."

He'd skipped straight to the end of the scene. He'd stolen my lines. Those three words were mine to say. He'd beaten me to them. All the next words, the best words, the right words flew out of my head.

"You—" My lips parted, still wordless. "I—you . . ."

I had not seen this coming.

A coherent response was apparently optional. He stared at my skin where he'd uncovered me, his thumb drawing slow circles on the front of my shoulder. He seemed mesmerized. He tugged the strap down farther, his other hand mimicking the action on the other side of me, and then he had full access to my bare chest.

He leaned in, his strong fingers sliding to my back. Just that simple press of his hands and I was all happy nerve endings, folding forward so he could kiss my breasts. He licked a wet trail around one nipple, sucking me into his mouth with a groan.

No more words! No more telling!

He scooped me up and walked us toward the bed. I threaded my fingers through his hair, holding him close. Desire ignited beneath my skin, spreading through my body. He was so big and so everywhere all at once, holding me still as he devoured my skin, kissing his way over all my curves.

Own it.

I ran my hand down the front of his plain black tee, enjoying how the muscles beneath my palm tensed and stilled. Unfastening his jeans, I took what I wanted. He made a rough sound as I traced his length, cupping him through his boxer briefs.

"I love you," he repeated, but this sounded more like an observation he was making to himself. He grasped my hips in his big hands, his thumbs dipping into the elastic band of my sleep shorts. "I want to make love with you."

"Okay!" I gasped. I'd have to write him a love poem, a grand gesture, or the world's sexiest seduction scene later. Right now, I was busy feeling.

His mouth covered mine, and he kissed me gently. It was sweet, but he was holding back. I could feel the muscles in his back bunching and tensing.

"Adorable Sonnet, smart Sonnet," he growled, threading one hand through my hair, and dipping the other into my shorts and panties and easing them down my hips. "Sexy Sonnet. *My* Sonnet."

I liked the sound of that, but . . .

"Don't rush into anything. Don't do anything you'll regret."

He paused, but just for a moment, and then he was fisting my hair, pulling my head back just far enough to expose my neck. His hold made me arch, my breasts lifting.

He grazed my throat with his teeth. "Sonnet."

"Yeah?"

He groaned. "We should set some ground rules for biting."

I wanted him so badly. Yet even though his touch made me ache, my body sing, I didn't want him for a single night. Was that what this was?

He loved me.

He loved me and he was making love to me. I had what I thought I'd wanted, but now I wanted everything.

"Wait." I let go of him *down there* and gripped his shoulders.

He eased me back onto the bed, traveling lower, pressing me down. "Do you want me to stop?"

His knee spread my legs.

"No. I *want* you to keep going. But I—"

"Shush." I felt the word against my belly, his hands pulling on my tank top, shifting it so he could tongue my belly button and taste my curves.

I made a sound.

He did it again.

I had to get this right. I had to say—

"I love you too."

Ferns and fiddlesticks, I LOVE THIS MAN!!!!

And it wasn't just for this moment, for the pine-and-outdoors scent of him, the way I'd never again see a flannel shirt without remembering what his shoulders look like when they're bare, for the chiseled, muscled lines of his body braced over mine, around me, carving out a safe space for the two of us in my sometimes-crazy world. It was *everything* about him. He was epically capable, reliable, and strong inside and out. No matter what life threw at him, he had it handled. He was simply, wonderfully, always Maverick.

His hands stilled on my thighs. He froze, listening. Those four words hung there in the air between us. We were both aware of them. We had a whole conversation in the silence:

I love you. Do you love me?

YES, yes, I do.

Say it again and again and again.

Iloveyoulloveyoulloveyou. I LOVE YOU.

The heavy beat of his heart against my thigh, the harsh push of his breath on my skin, my heart pounding against my rib cage were our words.

"Forever," I said, finishing that conversation. "That's how long I'll love you. This isn't a temporary thing. And I know you made a promise to yourself, a promise that the next woman you made love to would be your lover in truth—and your wife. I'm not asking you to break that promise. I won't. But I am asking you one thing."

He ran his fingers up the backs of my legs, lifting my knees. He eased them gently over his shoulders.

"I'm asking you to be my lover," I breathed. "And let me love you as you've loved me. Because I believe, with my entire heart, that this is love."

I believed with some more southernly parts of me too. But my heart was leading the charge here. My heart knew.

Maverick nodded. And then he lowered his head and kissed me.

"Oh. God." I was done talking. Done, done, done. *We can discuss our feelings and future selves later. MUCH later.* I fisted the sheets and held on because his hot, wet, loving mouth was on me, and my body welcomed him.

He made a rough sound in response, lapping with his tongue, his fingers stroking. My breath hitched. This was so good. It drove all the thinking out of my brain and I sort of hated that. I needed to remember this. I needed pictures, video, maybe a memorial plaque for this bed. *Here in the year of our Lord something something, Maverick Boone made me see STARS.* I was coming apart before he'd even got started, my body cruising toward an orgasm like a float at a Mardi Gras parade.

Unlike our other times, he didn't draw out my climax, didn't push me to a second release. Instead, he gently rested my legs on the sheets and stood. I pried my eyes open because Maverick Boone was a beautiful man, and he deserved my appreciation. As I watched, he pulled a strip of condoms from the back pocket of his jeans and tossed all but one onto the nightstand. I loved a well-prepared man.

Holding my gaze, he shoved his jeans down his legs, tore open the packet he'd kept, and rolled on a condom. *Proceed on the runway! We are cleared for takeoff!*

"Do you want me to stop?" he asked gruffly, putting a knee on the bed.

"Do not stop," I ordered. I reached for him.

He climbed between my legs and lifted my hips with his hands, sliding himself against my sensitive center. I wrapped my arms around his back, pulling him closer still. There were impatient sounds, noises of pleasure and need. He reached down, centered himself, and slid in deep. Deeper and deeper.

He held himself still over me with teasing, disciplined control, his warm chest brushing mine, his arms banded on either side of my head. We'd waited so long for this coming together, and now we were barreling toward the finish line, his body a muscled mass over mine, his broad shoulders shutting out the world, the tense line of his jaw, the rough sounds he made as he pushed forward, making room for himself inside me.

It was everything.

His eyes were half closed, his need written on his face, but I couldn't stop watching him. The view of his bare arms and chest and stomach as he worked himself into me had me gasping, but I would not look away. This was Maverick.

This was Maverick loving me.

And me loving him back.

He made love the same way he moved through life. Like he spoke. Like he loved. With absolute sureness and a steadfast focus on making sure that the people he cared for had everything they needed. It was honest, heartfelt, and deeply erotic.

He leaned down, kissing me, his teeth scrapping my lower lip. I sucked in a breath at the delicious sting of pleasure and pain. His mouth curved up against mine.

And God bless the man, he didn't stop. We came together hot and needy, open and wild, my hands on his back and butt, my legs wrapped around his lean, strong hips so that I could pull him all the way inside me. Silently I chanted, *I love you.* There might have been words like *YES* and *Now,* because we weren't waiting any longer and it was fine. More than fine. He was warm and felt so good moving inside me. The muscles of his back tensed beneath my fingers, and he muttered something about "love" and "beautiful" and then "SONNET" because we were both coming.

I love you so much. Oh God, I'm coming now.

I knew we'd waited, and I knew we maybe should have waited more—until Maverick got his wedding ring and his public promises of forever—but when we'd finished, and he went rigid inside of me, panting roughly against my throat, I couldn't imagine anything righter than what had just happened between us.

CHAPTER

TWENTY-NINE

"The desire to run so far that he wouldn't be able to catch up played through me, but in my gut, I knew he would. And somehow, it filled me with an odd sense of safety, knowing that, no matter how far I ran, he would always be able to catch me, and I would always want him to."

— ELIZABETH MORGAN, *SHE-WOLF*

I'd eaten my dessert first.

That was not a problem. I'd have the main course now.

We lay face-to-face, our legs tangled in the sheets we'd knocked every which way with our lovemaking, our hands teasing and stroking. Sonnet was definitely going back for more.

Her body was beautiful, all luscious, swooping curves and pillowy softness. It wasn't perfect because she lived in it, and Sonnet didn't hold back when it came to life. That joy marked her skin with little lines and dimples, souvenirs of her past that I itched to kiss. I looked forward to being beside her from now on. We'd do our changing together.

Fuck yeah. Fifty years. A hundred.

My wolf was optimistic, but a hundred years wouldn't be enough. Nor would a thousand.

359

"Did you know—" she started. Then she stopped herself.

"Hey," I said, my voice rough because it was hard to go back to words after what the two of us had just done together. "You got a fern fun fact for me?"

Her eyebrows shot up. "Why would I be talking about ferns at a time like this?"

I grinned at her. "Because you always talk about ferns when you're nervous. Sometimes you talk about sedges and woodland favorites. Baby trees. I like listening to you, and it makes you happy."

Seeing as how I was now palming her breast, the lush weight overflowing my hand, I wasn't sure how much new fern knowledge I would be retaining. My hands were big, but her breasts were larger still.

So beautiful.

Sonnet's face pinkened. "Is it weird?"

I tipped her chin up, dropping a kiss on her mouth. "I love it. I love you."

"So, I can tell you stories about the large sporophyte and the tiny gametophyte getting it on to make baby ferns, and you'll be all ears?" She wrapped her leg around mine as she said this, which just felt like a challenge.

I was up for it. In all ways.

"You bet."

Gonna be some other body parts paying attention too.

"And you're not having regrets?" The tone in which she asked this was less cheery and flirtatious than her fern talk.

Fuck. Is she crying? Fix it!

Shaking my head, I tried to find the words to explain all the ways she made me feel. Truly, I had a lot of emotions right now, but none of them encompassed regret or any of its synonyms. Hearing that she loved me might have been the highlight, but what had come after (pun intended) was almost as hard to forget.

We likely needed to do it again just to make sure it was good and cemented in our memories.

Remember the plan, my wolf whined. **It's a good one.**

I studied her, wondering if it was the right time to ask her my questions. Everything had happened out of order. I'd shown up primed for conversation and sorting out our troubles. Pitching myself. Asking the question. Instead, I'd quickly been primed for something hotter and more intimate.

And while I didn't regret making love with Sonnet one bit, I still wanted to see her wearing my ring.

Barbarian, my wolf accused happily. **And our bite.**

"You made me a proposal," I said carefully. I'd practiced this speech in my head as I'd driven over, with my momma's diamond ring in my pocket and my heart in my hand. I should have asked more questions about the acting craft, I realized. Not that I was intending to pretend or say someone else's words, but I was realizing that I could use some delivery tips.

"Which proposal? Was it a dirty proposal?" She gave me a smile that was shaky.

"That we see each other secretly for a spell."

"Oh." Her fingers tapped a nervous rhythm on my stomach. "Oh?"

"Marry me," I said abruptly. I'll tell you what, I'd forgotten my lines. "We should get married."

At least she's not crying no more, my wolf observed.

He was right. Her lips had parted, and she'd made a startled whuff of air. Which was not, I couldn't help but notice, any kind of emphatic agreement with my plan for us.

"Hear me out." I tugged her closer. **Because we're never letting her go!** "You suggested that we see each other in secret—"

"I was only—"

"Hush up for me for just a minute? I hate that idea. I flat-out hate it. Some of my hate is because it feels too close to lying to folks. I'm not worried about the ones we don't know, but it feels wrong not to tell my brothers and your family our news. Mostly, though, I don't want us to be a secret because I'm selfish. I love you. I want everyone to know that. I'm yours, through and through, and they're gonna have to deal with it."

My heart was beating so hard I thought I might have a fit.

And other parts of me were also hard.

I wanted her again. I wanted her yelling out my name and losing it for me. I wanted her begging me to touch her. I wanted to be hearing her cries of pleasure, and drinking in the sight of her generous, yielding body moving under mine.

So no, I wasn't Mr. Smooth.

"So, let's meet halfway. We'll start out in secret, but only at first. I can work with someone to help lessen the blowback."

She grimaced. "Like a celebrity crisis manager or an image consultant?"

"Okay. Sure. Just whoever you think can help polish me up some so that I'm fit for public consumption, and you don't pay the price for my past sins. And I'd pay for it." I wanted to be real clear on this last point. I had plenty of money, despite some people's assumptions about Southern rednecks. My momma had come from money, and she'd left me the house and the thousand acres it sat on. Moreover, I'd inherited two million dollars. That money was just collecting dust in a bank (or digital mites or whatever it was money did these days). I'd be more than happy to use it to build a future with Sonnet.

"Maverick—"

"And I'll sign a prenup and whatever else your lawyer wants. Your money is yours, and I don't want there to be any question of that."

"I know that," she protested. "But if we're a team—"

"And we get married now," I said urgently. "Before your shooting wraps."

"Hang on—"

"And I know this probably seems overly fast to you. And maybe it doesn't make much sense, but I'm certain. I know in my heart it's the right thing to do."

"Hold up—"

"I know because *you're* in my heart. So, I want to do this right. I want to make sure you're as safe as I can make you, so we'll start out in secret and build from there."

And . . . scene. I could sense my wolf's unease. Had we done enough? Were *we* enough?

"Yes," she whispered, beaming at me. Then she threw her arms around me and about squeezed the life out of me. "Yes, yes, YES!"

It took me a moment to understand that she'd accepted. I'd mostly only heard that level of enthusiasm when I was offering orgasms, not rings. THANK YOU, JESUS. The oxygen I'd been storing up inside me rushed out roughly in a burst. My wolf was yipping and yeehawing.

"Yes?" *Say it again.*

Would it be too much to ask her to tattoo it on her lovely ass? Or we could get matching knuckle tattoos.

She nodded, grinning wildly. "Are you marrying me, Maverick Boone? Will you be my Mr. Ruiz?

"Yes," I said, grinning like a loon, beyond happy. "Yes, I will."

Wrapping her in my arms, I kissed my bride-to-be. And then I made love with her again, taking extra special care of my mate.

* * *

Sonnet had fallen asleep after we'd made love for a second time. Now, as the sun rose, I retrieved the ring from my jeans pocket.

Sunrise, my wolf snorted. **Sooooo sentimental.**

He sounded pleased, though.

I slipped the diamond onto her finger where it belonged.

We could wear a ring. Let the whole world see where WE belong.

I curled up around her as she stirred in the nest of blankets she'd drawn around herself. Her curls were headed every which way, making a break for it, and she had a crease in one cheek from the pillow. And beard burn on her throat. I brought the back of her hand to my mouth, pressing a kiss against her knuckles. She was my lady, and I was her man.

She gave me a sleepy smile, then her gaze snagged on her third finger. "What is this?" She held her hand up, turning it this way and that, mesmerized by the sparkle. "Holy shit, Maverick!"

She likes it. We should tell her there's a tiara. And a choker. And some of those tennis bracelet thingies that don't look like anything a sensible person would ever wear to play tennis.

I grinned, tucking myself tighter against her. "It comes from my momma's side of the family. It's a European-cut diamond, three carats, and graded flawless—just like you. Family tradition passed it down to the firstborn. Momma wore it, and now you do. Some day, one of our kids will pass it along."

I was allowed some cheese thanks to my being a newly betrothed man.

When Rue and Mack had got together, I'd tried to give him the ring. He'd turned me down, saying, "That's an old piece of your family history right there, and I'm new history. Your momma would have wanted you to put it on the finger of your someone special someday. She talked about the grandbabies you'd bring here, the kind of daddy you'd make. She was real proud of you."

This ring made a statement. I'd considered designing a new one—maybe one with green stones and a fern leaf pattern—but in the end I'd wanted to see Momma's ring on Sonnet's finger. My family history was not without its flaws—my behavior being one of them—but it was a long, steady history of Boones doing their best and watching out for each other. I wanted that for us, plus the ring was a good one. More than any value an appraiser had assigned, it sparkled. It demanded you look at it. Mack, when she'd been younger, had tried it on and declared it to be a piece of heaven fallen to earth. On Sonnet's finger, it did look like a star. This was a ring you gave the woman who mattered most in the world.

"You want me to have this?" Her voice cracked.

I nodded, happy she was happy. "This ring is yours."

She sniffed. "This is mine. And you're going to be my husband."

"I am." I rested my chin on her shoulder. We fit together.

Always.

THIRTY

"You're not in this alone anymore. I'm not going anywhere, and if you'll let me, I've got broad shoulders for you to lean on whenever you need me."

— LISA KESSLER, *ICE MOON*

Although I was ready to tell the world about my promotion to future Mrs. Professor Boone (and Maverick's to my Mr. Ruiz), it was surprisingly difficult to spill the beans to my near and dear. My parents had left on a visit to Easter Island and weren't due back for another day, but I called (got voicemail) and texted (left unread). Mami had already reported—via a paper postcard with a stamp starring a guy with a pompadour—that although they'd heard spectral chains in the streets at night, they had not yet encountered the ghost of Pito Pito. As he was an evil French Tahitian businessman who'd done horrible things to women, it had been a lucky break for Pito Pito. She'd have exorcised him on the spot.

Despite my previous failures, I tried texting again, but no luck. I stuck to vague remarks (Almost done shooting! Miss you!) and peppered my message with mushroom emojis. Maybe it was for the best? I could Facetime them and introduce them to my mister. He could meet my parents while sitting side by side with me. He'd charm them. There would be baby pictures. Fern jokes. Happy crying.

I wanted it to happen *now*.

I needed to share the news with someone, and they were the most important some-ones in my life pre-Maverick. I needed to hear Mami's happy curse, and then we'd both go buy the same bridal magazines and flip through them while we Facetimed. She'd ask overly personal questions about the wedding venue and my honeymoon plans, and what my thoughts were on sexy lingerie for both the bride *and* the groom, and was I pregnant right now because that would be perfect, and she couldn't wait to be the *lita* for my babies. Then she'd be horrified that she'd brought up babies when she'd promised Papi that she would never, and I'd tell her it was fine and maybe soon.

My mami had lamented, loudly and frequently, to my siblings and me that all of us were underproducing in the grandbabies arena. *So smart, so good at your jobs, and with health insurance! But where are my grandbabies?* she would ask, her eyes twinkling. *"I've got four Sterilite containers of baby clothes that I bought on sale waiting. First come, first served! And who am I going to give my Christmas village to? Hmmm? I have twelve houses, a village church, AND a train set. Those are for your children!"*

Maverick had mentioned wanting to fill up his family home with babies, a comment that was permanently incised on my ovaries. And, given his enthusiasm for baby-making activities, I suspected he'd be on board with having a family sooner rather than later.

Eric dropped me and the rest of the security team off at the private terminal for charter flights and disappeared to park the car. After checking in and meeting back up with Eric, we were ushered out to the tarmac where the jet was already waiting.

I clutched my phone in my hand the whole time, hoping my mami would pop up online before we left. She didn't, but Maverick did. That was both better and worse.

Maverick: I scheduled a virtual appointment with a PR fixer person for Monday. Anchors away!

Sonnet: I miss you. I wish you were here. I saved you a seat.

I snapped a photo of the empty seat next to me and sent it. I hated making this trip without him. I hated not having him here by my side. I also hated that we were keeping our relationship a secret, our engagement a secret. I hated that my parents were ghost hunting on a remote volcanic rock. I was a hate monster hating on everything. Mature, logical Sonnet understood the necessity of sticking to the plan, but inside I kinda just wanted to go on a charm offensive and compel everyone to fall in love with Maverick. Now *that* would have been a spell.

Maverick: We could honeymoon in London if you want.

Sonnet: I should have squashed you into my suitcase.

Maverick: An emotional-support wolf?

Sonnet: Always howling after something.

Maverick: I love you.

"Mr. Hensley, we didn't expect to see you." Eric's surprised announcement yanked my attention away from my text messages.

Luke had just stepped through the doorway of the aircraft. He had a bottle of Perrier in one hand and a cashmere throw in the other. A red Louis Vuitton micro steamer bag was slung across his chest. His assistant popped up behind him, laden with matching travel bags.

"Why are you on my plane?"

Did I want to get into it with my ex-boyfriend and colleague?

Yes, I did. Anger and upset raged inside me. I shot out of my seat. One eviction, coming up!

"Sonnet." I looked up the plane toward the cockpit, and there was Elena in her usual black sweatpants travel outfit. We hadn't seen each other since our not-so-happy Los Angeles pool party, where she'd expressed her concern about my romantic situation and I'd called her out on her anti-Maverick sentiments.

Currently, she looked *un*concerned—and not at all surprised by Luke's presence. "I invited him."

She smiled pleasantly at Luke and continued, "It's better for our carbon footprint, plus I thought the two of you could catch up. Relax. The shoot schedule has been insane, plus you've been writing. I thought this would give you some downtime."

What. The. Hell.

Downtime was beaches and spas. In what universe did confining me in a flying tin can with my ex-boyfriend for eight hours constitute *rewarding me for my hard work?*

I made horrified faces at her.

She gestured.

I had no idea what she meant. We weren't speaking the same language.

Me: I need a vacation! I need downtime!

Her: Here's eight hours of close proximity to someone you can't stand! You're welcome! Should I book you a bonus root canal?

Some of this must have been conveyed because she came over. Possibly, she sensed my imminent departure from the plane.

"Is something wrong?" She blinked at me, looking bewildered.

"I'm not flying with him. He's intolerable." I might not have entirely used my inside voice.

Her mouth tightened. "Sonnet."

Despite her excellent imitation of our mami, I was unmoved. "He gets off the plane, or I get off. Your choice."

"You can't kick him off the plane," she gritted out. "He's attending the premiere."

"Alrighty then." I turned for the door. Luke was still standing there blocking the entrance—apparently, he was confused by the lack of a marching-band-and-confetti-cannon welcome—but I was happy to go through him. "I'll see you when you get back from London."

She threw up her hands. "You are such a diva!"

No. Wait. I wasn't the diva—

I was the BOSS.

This was my plane.

I'd paid for it.

Luke was just lucky I'd decided to evict him *before* we'd taken off. I didn't think he was the flying type of Fae.

Turning to Luke, I pointed to the door. "Elena didn't have the authority to offer you a seat on my plane. I want you to leave."

Luke's gaze bounced between me and my sister. He blinked. He turned the charm up another notch. I was a duck, and it was water. It just rolled off me. Maybe he'd have better luck with the United Airlines desk inside. His face hardened, his expression turning ugly.

"Is this because of your bearded boy toy?"

Elena cursed. *Guess it won't be a secret for long.*

It was awesome being the boss. "Crickets and clovers! Could you just leave without turning this into a big scene? There are no cameras and no audience. No one cares. Just go."

He tossed his mane of platinum hair over his shoulder, flicking his assistant in the process.

I waited. *Yes, you are a pretty boy, but I'm not interested in your package. I'm in love with someone who actually understands what it means to be a partner.*

Countenance souring, he pivoted, handed the bottle to the cabin attendant, and tossed the throw around his shoulders. Oooh. It was going to be a *dramatic* exit. "You're a has-been. This guy is making a fool out of you. Everyone is laughing at you."

This was not the Luke I'd thought I knew.

Lovable, dumb puppy Luke had been replaced by Mean Guy Luke.

Anger was a volcano inside me. It was so hot that my self-control melted. The words rose up, collected, formed sentences.

"No."

Luke frowned.

"Out." My temper erupted. I pointed toward the door because Luke had always needed directions, hadn't he? "Get. OUT. Exit stage left. FYI, I write funny romances, so laughter will be totally on-brand for me."

He stomped toward the door, then paused. "You want me here, Sonnet. You and I attend that premiere together, and nobody will be talking about the bearded wonder. I'm the perfect decoy. I'll help you and your sister clean up the mess you've made."

Wow. The anger rushed out of me. Exhaustion took its place. "There's no mess, Luke, and your tone is disrespectful. Maverick is not a mess. He's a smart, caring, capable person, and he's exactly what I want. I love him."

"Even if it costs you your career?" Luke sounded baffled, as if he truly couldn't imagine a life as something other than being an actor and mega-influencer.

But all I needed was one like—from Maverick.

* * *

Elena held out until we were halfway across the Atlantic before she started speaking to me again. Usually, she gave me shit right away, but she'd been either confounded or marshaling her arguments. There had been headshaking and facial gestures while she worked through my eviction of Luke.

She looked at me. "I can't believe you kicked Luke Hensley off your plane."

"Are you ready to discuss this now? Because I can't believe you invited him after I said that I wouldn't go with him to the premiere."

Her look was disbelieving. "Sonnet, we're going to the same place. There's plenty of room in the plane. It's environmentally irresponsible to demand he take a different flight when there's room on this one."

"He can fly commercial. He can pay a carbon-offset fee. Put the DO NOT DISTURB sign on his hotel door and reuse his sheets. But he's my *ex*-boyfriend."

"And?" Elena sighed, clearly exasperated with my shenanigans.

"He is my ex. Who in her right mind would want to be confronted with her ex over and over again? You don't respect my boundaries, Elena. You don't listen. It's bad enough that I have to work with him, but then you try to tell me that he's not that bad and that I should do more."

Elena stared at me, speechless.

But I was on a roll.

I had not told her much about my relationship with Luke. We were sisters, but there were things we didn't share—and Elena had never had time for girl talk. *I* hadn't had time for girl talk.

We'd both been busy, busy bees and I regretted that.

So I took a deep breath and told her because how else would she know exactly how awful Luke was?

"We dated. It wasn't for very long, but I ended that relationship because it wasn't acceptable to me. Luke is very self-centered. I wasn't his girlfriend—I was a validation machine with a vagina. All he wanted to talk about was himself: his acting, his roles, his performance in bed, what *he* needed. I'm not in the business of directing his life, nor am I here to make things nicer or more convenient for him. Sharing plane space with him would be *in*convenient for me, as well as not nice. So, he's not welcome."

Elena frowned. "But he's so charming."

I snorted. "Well, he *is* a Fae prince. He's lovely to look at but trust me—it's all about him. And sure, we all have days when we need to hear that we're attractive and talented and fuck whoever just told us that we weren't, but a few weeks ago he suggested I use an exercise app to manage my waistline better. According to him, chubby Wolf Girls are unattractive."

Elena cursed very creatively. "Okay, yeah. I'd have introduced him to the emergency door if he were here right now. That was an asshole thing to say. There are no excuses."

I threw up my hands. "You get it!"

"Get what?"

"Get that he is no Prince Charming, no matter what antediluvian fairy court he comes from."

She smirked. "His only asset is that title. It's definitely *not* his acting skills."

It was no exaggeration to say that Luke made a wood knife block look like an award-winning thespian. He looked gorgeous on camera, but he had zero emotions other than self-satisfaction and pleased. Oh, also irate and temper-tantrumy. He didn't even have an O face!

Elena's grin faded. "But I'm still worried about you, *conejita*."

"Why?" I asked softly, happy we were really talking and not yelling or sulking in silence.

"This guy you're seeing."

"Maverick."

"Yes. Maverick. Have you done a background check? What do you know about him?"

I could not tell her about the shapeshifting.

She would shit bricks if she knew, though.

I grinned, just thinking about her reaction. "Everything. He was a car thief and a biker in one of those motorcycle club gang things."

"*Dios mío.*"

And as I *was* the little sister, the *hermanita*, I had to tease her just a little. Her horror at the optics was funny because once she met him, she'd love him. I knew she would love him.

"He was never convicted." I winked at her. "Although he's officially the town's black sheep."

Or maybe that was lone wolf? Despite his plethora of brothers and love of family time, he had run alone for the last five years.

Now he had me.

"And he gave me this ring." I held my hand out and wiggled my fingers. Shit. I should have gotten a fancy manicure. I had an explicable urge to snap fancy photos of my beringed hand and post them on all my social media.

Elena face-palmed—and peeked through her fingers. She was *so* curious. Her eyes widened and she grabbed my hand with hers. "Holy SHIT." My hand was turned in more directions than a yo-yo. "Are those real?"

Ah, my dear friend subtext. I nodded and then answered the unspoken question. "Very real. Ten-thousand-percent real."

"Which is a mathematical impossibility," she muttered, holding my hand up to the light.

"He's talking to that image consultant we used when my phone was hacked, and people were asking if I *really* believed in faeries and the Fae. We've agreed to keep our relationship secret for now, at least until she can help us come up with a plan. We're engaged. We're getting married."

Elena gently squeezed my hand and returned it—and my ring—to me. "Do Mami and Papi know? Because I don't know what to say. Does he know about—"

She mouthed FAE.

"Say you're happy for me. Say you can't wait to meet him but you already love him. Maybe threaten to rip him limb from limb if he hurts me, so I can assure you that he's the biggest, sweetest teddy bear"—*WOLF*—"ever. And yes, he knows about my family and where I come from. He's good with it."

"I *will* tear him apart if he hurts you."

"He won't."

"But you will be hurt. Your image will take a hit. You know that. He's not only off-brand, but he's also a *criminal*. Studios won't want to be associated with that."

"Which is why he wants us to not advertise our relationship for now. This is me accommodating him and agreeing. Reluctantly. Very, very reluctantly."

"It could mean your career," she persisted. "You know how Hollywood is. Maybe you'll make a comeback some day, but you'll be undoing years of hard work and for what?"

"For the man I love."

She shook her head. "But you could do so much good. You have opportunities that women like us don't get. You are representing more than just yourself."

"But what I want matters too," I said gently. "I get to live my life for me, Elena. I won't choose unhappiness and giving up the only person I've ever loved like this. Why would I not want to spend the rest of my life with him, happy and fulfilled and maybe making babies to fill up our new life together? At the end of the day, no one thinks, *OMG I wish I'd worked more hours! And not taken that vacation!* And making more money, attending more parties, or even landing more projects—no matter how awesome they are and how fortunate I am to have these choices to make—nothing could ever mean as much."

She leaned back in her seat, closing her eyes. "Fine. I'll fly back with you to Tennessee. Introduce me to this wondrous male specimen."

I grabbed her and squeezed her. Sneak attack! "Gah! You'll love him!"

I did, so how could she not?

Her eyes met mine as she wrapped her arms around me and squeezed back. "I hope so. I hope you'll be happy. Otherwise, I'll have to hire Eric to kill him, and that's both a felony and some toxic workplace shit."

"I know." I leaned back so I could see her face, and she could see mine. "I do know that. But, Elena, this is about more than just being happy. Which is amazing and wonderful, and everyone should try it. It's about the way he supports me. He takes care of me, like it's his one mission in life. And I do the same for him. We're partners."

* * *

I was used to *the looks* when I did things by myself. Want to go on an excursion to see cute little Komodo dragons? Please buy TWO tickets, Ms. Single Lady. Table for one at the restaurant? There's no one joining you? That's horrible! Let me suggest you sit with this other random solo stranger and share an awkward meal together because how can you possibly want to be ALONE.

People treated aloneness like a sexually transmitted disease.

Don't advertise it, don't show anybody the affected parts, and run and get that shit fixed as soon as possible.

Surprisingly, however, my solo appearance on the London red carpet saw no pitying looks or hmmm-I-could-introduce-her-to-my-nephew's-cousin's-dentist looks slanted my way. Not that I was actually on my own; the studio had sent a publicist to manage the press people and keep things moving. Talent traffic jams were the worst. No one wanted the carpet to pack up and have stars standing on stars (or dress trains, Louboutin heels, or tuxedo hems). My carefully cultivated image of bold, sassy, and independent meant people thought I'd chosen to make a statement.

"Sonnet!"

"Are you dating yourself?"

"Twirl for us!"

"Who are you wearing?"

"Where's Luke?"

"I heard you had frittata for breakfast! What was in it?"

"How much weight have you lost?"

Frittata? Who thought up these questions? I'd been chatted up by the red-carpet hosts (who also asked who I was wearing), posed for the entertainment TV shows, and now had moved on to the magazine crews who were shoehorned into a space the size of an 8½″ x 11″ sheet of paper. One poor reporter was slowly listing to the right in her four-inch heels, not having got the memo that sensible footwear was a must. Still, the end of the red carpet was in sight! The door to the venue had been spotted!

The hours since my arrival in London had been a blur. In those ten hours, I'd met with the producers for my next film, done media interviews, called in to a talk show, and had an editorial photo shoot for a fashion magazine where we'd done three different looks with hair and makeup. We'd squeezed in three hours of hair and makeup for the premiere, my stylist working away while I answered "What's in My Bag" interview questions and filmed a GRWM. There had been just enough time to trade a few texts with Maverick.

It had been so nonstop busy that I'd missed my parents' return phone call. As soon as I got inside the theater, I'd try calling them from the bathroom.

Moving to the end of the red carpet, I walked to the section blocked off for web media. There were more calls for my attention, but I recognized one of the reporters standing in the center. We'd worked together before, and I respected and liked her. She smiled and mouthed, *Have a minute?*

For her, I totally did. She'd also been one of the first reporters to embrace my debut novel and screen appearances, asking in-depth questions about breaking barriers as a Latina author and my experiences in television as a new actress. She never asked about my weight, my beauty regimen, or my clothes. Nor had she ever assumed that because I was Latina, I must not "be from here" or be a US citizen.

"Sonnet." Avalyn motioned with the mic she held in her left hand. I scooted in, making sure to make eye contact and stand up straight. Friendliness mattered so much. "Congratulations on the premiere! What was the most challenging aspect of bringing this season to life?"

"The Latina stereotypes." I turned on the charm for her camera. "We're not all hot-tempered, sassy lovers who work as house cleaners and have huge families. Many of us speak English as a first language, and not all of us are from Mexico. We're complex—we're not just one thing, or even a handful of things. I hope the episodes in this season show that a Latina can have any name or job or outward appearance. She can be anything, and her choice may not be at all loud, crazy, or sexy. The Latina witch lead isn't a sultry bombshell—and she doesn't want to be one."

"How do you encourage action in others?"

"Obviously, I try to encourage it by writing books and scripts where there is plenty of dialogue for women from non-white racial groups. More than nineteen percent of the population in the US is Hispanic, so we need to have a bigger and proportionate voice in Hollywood's scripts. Part of what motivates me to write is to make sure that Latina voices speak up and are heard in my projects."

"What are you writing now?"

"Uhhh." I had prepped several answers for this question, but I still wasn't sure what I wanted to say. "I am working on a script for a new paranormal project with a strong female lead."

"A source mentioned that you would also be starring in the new project?"

"That had been discussed, yes. But we haven't signed any contracts yet, so I'm focused on the script. Doing lots of werewolf research. Nailing down my setting."

Or nailing my werewolf.

The bustle behind me on the carpet warned me that we'd need to wrap this up soon. Avalyn's assistant was tapping her on the shoulder, clearly a prearranged signal that another star was approaching, and it was time to end our interview. *Luke Hensley,* the assistant mouthed to me.

Avalyn laughed, then asked, "And how is shooting in rural Tennessee? Are the locals friendly? Any gruff and growly types?"

Those questions were unexpected. Had someone tipped her off about Maverick? She was clearly wrapping things up, however, so it was likely an innocent fluff question.

"Tennessee is beautiful—I love the mountains. People have been so welcoming, but I hesitate to share the details because otherwise there will never be a slice of hummingbird cake left in my new favorite diner!"

"Beautiful!" Luke stepped up next to me, sliding his arm around my waist and kissing my cheek. "You must be talking about me!"

I tensed, scrambling for something innocuous to say. Luke's comments were as arrogant, unwelcome, and unpleasant as the Fae prince himself, self-centered and narcissistically joking. My plane eviction clearly hadn't stopped him from making the premiere.

"Absolutely," I quipped. "I was just telling Avalyn here about you and your beautiful bunnies. You know, the ones you adopted from the Moonlight Valley animal shelter?"

I had no idea if Moonlight Valley had an animal shelter or not, but All-Purpose Animal Services had rescue animals coming out of their Boone ears. Luke shot me a pissed-off glare, but his smile didn't waver. Luke hated animals, unless you counted the goats that provided the wool that had made his cashmere throw.

"You rescued bunnies?" I gave Avalyn full marks for her straight face; her assistant, on the other hand, choked.

Before Luke could answer, I cut in, "He rescued an entire litter! They were Easter basket rejects and he took them in. They sleep in his bed, and he feeds them by hand."

Smiling evilly, Luke grabbed my hand and asked, "Have you seen Sonnet's ring?"

Killing my coworker—or putting a teeny-tiny hex on him—was contractually prohibited.

My heart jumped to my throat. I gritted my teeth. I subtly tugged on my hand.

Do NOT do it, Luke.

Luke's smile widened. *Try and stop me.*

"Isn't it stunning?" He raised my right hand and waved my ring finger with its big, sparkly, wonderful diamond at Avalyn, who looked like a cat smelling chicken. "But you've put it on the wrong hand!"

For precisely one second, the press pool fell silent. Everyone stared at my beringed hand in Luke's—and then leapt to the obvious conclusion. A barrage of questions erupted.

"Sonnet, are you and Luke engaged?"

"Why didn't you arrive together?"

"When is the wedding?"

"Who designed your ring?"

Avalyn held out the mic between the two of us. "Are you guys making an announcement?"

Luke smirked at me. *I win,* his eyes said. *You can take your bunnies and stuff it!*

Don't piss off a witch! I telegraphed back. *You picked on the wrong person!*

I was mad, and I'd been mad and out of sorts for days now.

I was mad at Luke, obviously. He was an entitled Fae twit waffle.

But I was also mad at myself. If I'd brought Maverick, if I'd listened to Ranger's wise words about owning our shit and facing up to the music, then this scene would have gone very differently. I would be standing next to a man I loved and respected.

Instead, I was engaged in involuntary hand-holding with the twit waffle.

Yes, there would be ramifications. Yes, I might lose parts or contracts. There were people who would decide that I did not fit their brand, but did I want to work with those people? We had different values.

If Maverick had been standing next to me, we'd have gotten through whatever came next together. And I would have been true to myself.

For the first time in my career, I felt scared. And small. And like I'd sold out. I wasn't being me—I was being the version of me I thought other people approved of.

And I hated it.

Maverick had hated the idea of us seeing each other in secret. *I hate that idea. I flat-out hate it. Some of my hate is because it feels too close to lying to folks. I'm not worried about the ones we don't know, but it feels wrong not to tell my brothers and your family our news. Mostly, though, I don't want us to be a secret because I'm selfish. I love you. I want everyone to know that. I'm yours, through and through, and they're gonna have to deal with it.*

Those words resonated with me.

I was feeling selfish.

And I was going to put my needs first.

Not the studio's, not Elena's, and not even my fans'. This was my life; I was the one who lived it and made my choices.

Decision made, I looked Luke in the eye and flashed him my most brilliant smile. I also yanked my hand back, hard. "Why, look at that! My ring IS on the wrong hand. Thank you so much for pointing that out!"

Luke's eyes widened as I slipped Maverick's family ring—my engagement ring— off my right hand and onto my left where it belonged. Then I turned it to the crowd of cameras in front of me, holding my hand up as if I were flipping everyone off with my ring finger instead of the more conventional middle one. I was sure Luke got the message.

"I'm engaged to be married. My fiancé was unable to join me tonight. He's a herpetologist researching the use of snake venom for treating diseases when he's not rescuing bats and alpacas. Y'all will love him. His name is Maverick Boone, and he's a professor in Tennessee. We fell in love while shooting my current show, and we'll be getting married in the spring when the daffodils come out."

I grinned, my heart swelling with the rightness of the moment. From the looks of Avalyn (mouth hanging open, mic drooping in her hand), she was both stunned and out of questions. I didn't bother looking at Luke. He was chopped liver, a third wheel at a unicycle convention, the silent *k* in a knife fight. He didn't matter. His opinions didn't matter.

Because, as Maverick had said, it's good to care about what others think, but only when those people matter.

CHAPTER
THIRTY-ONE

"'I have always loved you, princess,' Robin Goodfellow promised, his green eyes shining in the darkness. 'I always will. And I'll take whatever you can give me.'"

— JULIE KAGAWA, *THE IRON QUEEN*

"Are you drinking apple cider vinegar again?"

I tried not to inhale too deeply as Ranger settled into the truck's cab beside me. The stinkfest was coming either from the paper bag he clutched or from his coffee mug.

Whatever it was, it smelled rank.

"I only drink that thirty minutes after I get up. To get my digestive system working."

I did not want to hear about Ranger's digestive system.

His wolf could eat an entire mammal, my wolf groused. **His digestive system is just rusty from being a vegetarian.**

"Then what smells so bad?"

Why couldn't he just drink Folgers like everybody else?

"Fermented tofu," Ranger said, slurping from his cup.

"How do you drink that?" He needed an intervention.

Or a steak.

"You don't," he said placidly. "You eat it. I like mine with a nice breakfast congee. It has antioxidants and lowers the blood pressure. Skunk spray also smells bad, as does durian fruit and stagnant water."

I rolled my eyes. "Why does it smell bad in *here*, you ding-dong. What's in that bag?"

"You should be more precise in your question asking," Ranger observed. "How was I to know you were initially inquiring about the contents of my bag? Which includes, thank you for asking, beard balm, hand sanitizer, a lip mask, and my personal identification. I do not want to be suffering from chapped lips or unkempt facial hair in an intimate moment. You might want to make some additions to your own bag."

Glaring out the windshield, I bit my tongue. Snapping at Ranger would only make our ride unendurable. He was being obtuse and irritating on purpose.

He's a Boone.

We'd finished up on set and were headed home, although first we needed to make a pit stop at the Piggly Wiggly. I'd dealt with the bat colony—*again*—and installed more bat mansions. I was hoping that the new habitats would convince the bats to stay off set once and for all. I was exhausted after waiting for them to leave at dusk and then installing a piece of loose screen over the entrance to their attic so that any stragglers could exit but no returnees could enter the building. Then I'd gathered some bat droppings, put up the new bat house, and sprinkled the poop around it. After being up most of the night, I'd had to collect Ranger from some mysterious task on set.

Ranger had been rude from the start. In fact, he'd been rude since spotting Momma's ring on Sonnet's finger. As it was none of his business who I betrothed myself to, and since it was still a secret, I was ignoring his petulant mood.

Ceding the paper bag battle, I rolled down my window. If Ranger thought a beard balm that smelled like three-day-old chicken and burnt tires was an aid to his love life, I figured he'd be disillusioned by the response he got from any lady friends.

Ranger sighed loudly from his seat.

I ignored him. We were almost to the store.

Another sigh.

Today's forecast is for gusty winds.

Sigh. Sigh. SIGH.

I was relieved to pull into the lot and jump out of the truck. I sped into the store, still ignoring Ranger, although I heard him get out and shut his door. There was only a handful of items on my list, but I was distracted by the display of flowers in the produce aisle.

I wanted to show her how I felt. How much I'd missed her. How much she'd changed my life. Not that pink and green daisies expressed my sentiments, but they were a start. The kind of thing a loving man would do for his woman. I suspected I could spend the rest of my life trying to show her how much I loved her.

Buy them all. Or we could go to the garden center and buy some bushes. A hydrangea. Maybe get some drip irrigation and plant her a flower garden.

"Get the *Dieffenbachia*, with the white-and-green leaves."

The helpful suggestion came from Jennie Dean, who'd popped up to stand next to me. As usual, she was in a slim, well-tailored black dress that looked to be dry-clean only. She wore taupe pumps, and her long blonde hair was pulled up in a sleek bun. She had on vintage pearls that had likely belonged to her grandmomma. She was also holding a big, dirty crate of pineapples. This equation was unbalanced: this little slip of a woman, dressed up for church or a job interview, clutching a box of tropical fruit.

I reached for the crate. Before I could help her, however, she'd set it down on the floor of the Piggly Wiggly and was reaching for a houseplant.

"Based on her TikTok channel, she loves tropical plants, so this is the one she'd like best. It's also called 'dumb cane.'" Jennie smiled up at me with her purple-pansy-colored eyes, setting the black plastic pot in my hands. "It might get as big as ten feet tall, but that would require exceptional care. And possibly a conservatory."

I made a mental note that a conservatory would make an excellent wedding present for my bride.

And after we build it, we can furnish it! Get one of those daybed things, the ones with cushions, so we can do it surrounded by a tropical jungle.

"No roses?" I turned the *Dieffenbachia* in my hands, inspecting it for damaged leaves. It was a good one, moist and fertile.

"She prefers plants with roots," Jennie volunteered. Her natural hair was an inky black, but her momma had started dying it blonde when Jennie was in high school.

Her eyes were real unusual, however, a light violet color that no one in Moonlight Valley had ever seen before. She got accused a lot of wearing colored contacts, but her eyes were uniquely pretty. They reminded me of Sonnet's eyes, when she let me see the real her and not the glamoured-up face she showed the world.

She was a striking woman, the kind who got asked to be a model and who was stared at a whole lot (and worse) by people who had no manners. Her daddy, Kip Dean, was always concerned about the amount of attention her good looks garnered, and he'd done everything he could to lock her up like Rapunzel in a tower. I'd never asked her how she felt about his protectiveness, but there also hadn't been much of a chance. She was more sheltered than a *Brugmansia* in a northern garden and twice as awkward.

Bless her heart.

I gave her a small smile. "I appreciate it."

"You're welcome." She returned my smile with interest, then bent to gather up her pineapples.

I set Sonnet's plant down in my cart and intercepted her. "Jennie Lee Dean, that crate is way too heavy for you."

She muttered something as I snatched the crate out of her grasp, and it was not appreciation for my efforts to spare her lower back strain.

"I've got it," she huffed. "I pick these up once a week. Pineapple hasn't killed me yet. A little pineapple workout is good for me."

"Those aren't pineapple-lifting shoes. You'll sprain something, and then your daddy will be all over me, asking how come I didn't help out. Where should I put these? In your car?"

"I can carry my own pineapples." She held out her hands, as if I'd concede this battle. I just looked at her, waiting. I had her pineapples, and we both knew I was bigger.

Makes you useful, my wolf said. Although you maybe should work on your delivery. I don't think Sonnet wants us carrying her pineapples, either.

Sonnet would have to get used to my wanting to help her out, I decided.

My wolf snorted. **Gonna be some FIGHTS in our house.**

Finally, Jennie huffed, made a snorting sound, and conceded defeat. It wasn't as if she could go somewhere else for her pineapple needs—there was a limited supply of tropical fruit in Moonlight Valley. "Fine. Please bring them to my car."

Temporarily parking my shopping cart by the bananas, I followed Jennie past the registers and out to her BMW. She popped the trunk, and I carefully set the crate inside.

"I could have managed. I know you have a sensitivity to pineapple."

Moonlight Valley was a small town, but I never failed to be amazed at the lack of privacy a wolf had here.

She added quickly, as if she was afraid that discussing my medical issue was inappropriate, "I'm not such a fan of pineapple myself. I don't like tropical fruit all that much. And I hate baking cakes."

Small town doesn't know everything.

This was news to me; I was certain no one else in town knew, either. Jennie Dean hating pineapples and baking was like Santa Claus turning out to be a misanthrope who would have preferred going on a tropical cruise for Christmas rather than delivering a sledful of presents.

I crossed my arms, studying her face. "Is that so?"

"Yes." She grimaced. "I've made that hummingbird cake maybe ten thousand times. It's goddamned boring. I apologize for the cussword, but cake talk gets me hot under the collar."

"No problem."

Jennie steamed on without seeming to hear. She'd got started and now she was fit to share. "I'm real good at baking cakes, but that doesn't mean it has to be my life's work. It doesn't make me happy. I'm twenty-two, and I've calculated that I could easily have to make hummingbird cake for another seventy years. That's more than twenty-five thousand cakes. I close my eyes at night, and I see cakes. At the very least, I should get to live on a pineapple plantation. Instead, I'll be ninety-two years old, still making hummingbird cake in my momma's bakery."

"So why not do something else? Publish the recipe on Instagram and inform people that hummingbird cake is now a DIY project."

Jennie frowned, a tiny wrinkle appearing between her perfectly groomed eyebrows. "I would love to have some kids. And my own house. I'd like to nest a while, stay at home with my babies and look after my partner. Or maybe I'd design wallpaper and have an Etsy business. I love wallpaper. It makes a room cozy. Someday, I'd like to see my wallpaper in *Vogue* or one of those decorating magazines."

I had never given wallpaper much thought, but Jennie clearly had.

I wondered if there was a wallpaper-making book in that Dummies series my youngest brother bought to torture Ranger.

"You should do that," I said gently. "Go make wallpaper."

I figured I shouldn't tell her to go make babies because that would sound weird.

Although it's a great choice. She'd be a wonderful mama.

Jennie's face fell. It was a slow, soft fall, like the time Ranger had been making a souffle and Knox slammed the door. It just gracefully faded from tall and proud to a confused muddle. Something I said had been the wrong thing.

Probably all of them.

She stepped toward the driver's-side door. "I appreciate your pineapple hefting. I have to get back to the bakery and work on my genome splicing."

I blinked. Somehow, we'd gotten from pineapple to baby making (**woot!**) to wallpaper to recombinant DNA technology?

"Just kidding," she said. This time her smile was smaller and more forced. "I'm not qualified to operate a spliceosome. I'm licensed for stand mixers only."

I was not qualified to handle this.

I watched her start the car, barely remembering to move out of the way.

Jennie Dean was famous in Moonlight Valley for three things: her hummingbird cake, her violet eyes, and being strange.

Shaking my head, I headed back toward the store. I had just reached the sidewalk when Jennie pulled up next to me and tapped the horn politely.

She rolled down the window and beckoned me over. "I plumb forgot to tell you! There was a whole swarm of news guys at the store when I arrived. They were looking for directions to your house."

Uh-oh.

"Do you know what they wanted?" I asked carefully. With my brothers, you never knew. We'd had the FBI come knocking once, looking for Ranger, although he'd sent them away.

She shrugged. "I don't know for certain. But if I were hazarding a guess, I'd suggest that it was related to your engagement with Sonnet Ruiz."

Secret engagement, huh? How's that working out for you?

I gaped at her. "How did you know we were engaged?"

"Everyone knows. She made an announcement on the red carpet earlier today."

* * *

"I'm engaged to be married. My fiancé was unable to join me tonight. He's a herpetologist researching the use of snake venom for treating diseases when he's not rescuing bats and alpacas. Y'all will love him. His name is Maverick Boone, and he's a professor in Tennessee. We fell in love while shooting my current show, and we'll be getting married in the spring when the daffodils come out."

Ranger paused the YouTube video and frowned. "You sound like some kind of hippy-dippy, backwoods tree hugger. Also, I'm not sure exactly which kind of *Narcissus* she's referencing. I would need to know the specific type to determine whether it's an early, midseason, or late spring bloomer."

I was regretting inviting him to my panic session in the front seat of my truck.

"Shush up, you ding-dong. Play the rest." Could I snatch his phone and finish the play job myself? Probably not. Plus, knowing Ranger, he probably had some kind of voice-activated passcode that would also fry my circuits if I tried to steal his device.

The video was an exercise in frustration. It was unedited and poor quality. The background noise threatened to drown out Sonnet's words as she talked to some lady reporter. Who knew that a movie premiere sounded like a flock of angry flamingoes dodging basketballs in a gymnasium?

It was almost midnight in London right now. I knew this because I'd added London to my weather app so I could know what time it was where Sonnet was. Plus, then I could text her loving things like, *Don't forget your umbrella—it looks like rain!*

We should deliver the umbrella. Google how to make that look sexy. Can you do a Fred Astaire number?

Ranger muttered something, glaring at his phone. I waited impatiently. He'd stomped toward my truck after I'd panic-texted him, still mad about not being the first to officially hear that Sonnet and I were betrothed.

When he started the video up again, I tried to make out more of the words while I scrolled through my text messages. And then checked my email. And my mostly unused Instagram account, which now had ten thousand followers. This was 9,994 more than this morning, when I'd been followed by no one whose last name wasn't Boone.

She wasn't answering her phone, either. It went straight to voicemail. Again.

"Y'all will love him. His name is Maverick Boone, and he's a professor in Tennessee. We fell in love while shooting my current show, and we'll be getting married in the spring when the daffodils come out."

She beamed at the interviewer on Ranger's screen, as if this was the best news ever. Obviously, I agreed with her. Beside her, Luke Hensley looked like he'd just discovered a hognose snake in his trailer.

We could make that happen, my wolf muttered.

I could but it wouldn't be fair to the poor snake.

After the announcement, reporters peppered Sonnet with questions, but the video ended before she could answer. Ranger tapped his screen and fiddled with various buttons before sliding his phone back in his pocket.

I dropped my own phone into the driver-side cupholder and gripped the steering wheel of my truck hard enough to crack it. "That was not something we discussed."

Perhaps we should have reviewed the definition of *secrecy*.

"From the sound of things, that Luke Hensley put her on the spot. He had all those folk thinking that he'd put your ring on her finger and that she and him—"

"I don't need a play-by-play, Ranger. I have eyes. And ears."

Ranger actually shut up, which just went to show that today was a day for surprises. I should stop and buy a lottery ticket. Or keep an eye out for flying pigs. The only familiar thing was Ranger's ferocious frown as he settled back in his seat, brows furrowing. He was good and irritated at me. I could read the words. They ran along the lines of *Don't let your bulldog mouth overload your humming-bird butt.*

We sat there taking up space in the Piggly Wiggly parking lot for a long time. Ranger drummed his fingers on the passenger-side door; I considered an impromptu amputation. Or duct tape. He was beating out a rhythm like a doomsday clock.

"I don't know what my next steps should be," I admitted finally. It wasn't as if Ranger would actually keep his advice to himself, and it was often spot-on.

"Although if people are trying to find me, we need to warn the others not be shifting. Should I even be talking to reporters? Could I make things worse? Is it like chatting up the cops before your lawyer shows up? I feel like I should be talking this over with Sonnet—which is what, frankly, she should have done with me."

I was feeling ever so slightly butt hurt at being cut out of our first public appearance as a couple. Hell, I hadn't even *been* there. I was just the redneck punchline.

"Why not talk to them?"

"They might be asking questions about my checkered past."

He shrugged. "Tell them the truth. Well, the truth about anything non-felonious. No one expects you to incriminate yourself."

I glared at the windshield some more because I was still irritated with Ranger. "This is not how I hoped our big reveal would go. It makes me mad. We discussed a plan, and then she went ahead and did what she wanted without paying any attention to that plan. And now the one thing I wanted to avoid—my screwing up her career—is going to happen."

"You'll have to impose some consequences." Ranger nodded sagely. "Lay down the law. Corner time."

That man has some kinky tastes.

"You need to teach her a lesson," Ranger said doggedly. "Seeing as how she's disappointed you."

I frowned. "It's not my place to punish her. In fact, it's *no one's* place. Jesus Christ. She's a grown woman. She makes her own decisions, does what she thinks best. If she spilled the beans to those reporters, then obviously . . ."

Damn it, I'd been played by my brother. He was trying to hide his smile as I worked through the obvious truth: if Sonnet had come clean about our relationship in the middle of a fancy premiere, then she had a good reason for doing so, and I would be a fool not to hear her out.

We're gonna need to practice communicating. Some kind of secret I GOT THIS DUMBASS TRUST ME sign. Like one of those football signals!

My wolf wasn't wrong. Fortunately, I planned on being an A-plus student for the next fifty to seventy years.

"You're such an asshole," I told Ranger.

He busted up laughing. "Yeah. I am."

We sat there laughing like loons for a stretch. Should I be apple pies and smiles for the press people? I could have used one of Sonnet's witchy charms about now, one of the like-me spells she was so good at. I'd be friendly yet firm, I decided. I'd chat. They could even come up and sit on the porch.

But not in the house.

Yeah. The house would be a step too far.

Be nice. Charming. My wolf sounded morose. **Kiss their butts?**

A step too far. And not maintainable.

But I *would* make them love me.

"If that man does anything to hurt you or Sonnet, I'll end him."

Ranger's casual promise of violence pulled me right out of my thoughts. His face was grim, his eyes laser focused on some internal shenanigans of his. We might make inappropriate jokes about violence, but we'd always reserved it for a measured response. We did not initiate, if you didn't count a little familiar wrestling on the porch and in the daylilies. Which I didn't.

"There will be no felonies. Who are you threatening?"

"Darrell. He won't get to you or Sonnet. Don't you pay him no mind. He knows that as long as he's in Alaska, I have ways of getting at him."

I gaped at my brother. He was . . .

Serious.

"Ranger, you're no murderer. You wouldn't actually—" I waved a hand.

He gave me a smile. A fierce, focused smile. "No murder, big brother. Just some self-defense."

What?

I had no words. I wasn't happy about Darrell, and I sure as hell wasn't tolerating his threats and insinuations—but I also did not believe in murder.

"No," I said firmly. "As the head of this family, I'm telling you that you do not get to murder our daddy. And honestly, I can't believe I have to say it, Ranger Austin Boone. You know our momma wouldn't hold with it, either."

Truth was, he didn't look repentant. **The words you're looking for are ICY DETERMINATION. Those would be an accurate description.**

I left it, though, and got us on the road. I didn't have time to address Ranger's statement right now, or whether he did, in fact, have some nefarious means of infiltrating the Wolf Council's Alaska property to get at Darrell. It seemed likely, based on Jennie's account of the earlier question asking, that I had a yard full of reporters waiting for me at the house, and I needed to be charming. That had to be my focus right now.

But just as soon as this media mess was fixed, I would bring it up again. Our daddy was a cancer, and he'd claimed more than enough of our family. I knew Ranger had suffered, like we all had. Darrell hadn't had any patience with Ranger's differences or his unusual perspective on the world. Ranger had missed out on all the regular father-son activities, but I didn't think that committing a felony now would make Ranger feel better about that lack.

I did, however, wonder what Darrell might have done that I didn't know about. I suspected that there was something in their past alright, something substantial to fuel such hatred.

Whatever it was, I still wouldn't allow my brother to kill Darrell. It was tempting, but that was how a man lost his soul—and my brother wasn't losing his too.

* * *

Being a mature, supportive partner (**In training**, my wolf sighed), I did try calling Sonnet one last time as we pulled into our driveway. I got no response.

Strange cars and people were clustered in front of the house like flea dirt on a white alpaca. Some guys held cameras, others were setting up tripods and who knew what. There were two local news vans and some unfamiliar vehicles. The dogs in the barn were going nuts, barking, and the alpacas were kicking up a storm in their stalls.

As soon as I parked, the media was on us, yelling out my name and crowding both doors. Someone started knocking on the windows, as if they could chivy us out.

Idiots.

"How on earth do they think we're gonna get out if they box us in like sheep for shearing?" Ranger locked the door, shaking his head. "What is the point of yelling and banging? Bless their hearts."

I flashed my brother my best devil-may-care smile. "You stay here and be silent. Let me do the talking."

"Stay here, be silent, let you speak for both of us," he echoed. "I believe we should add a discussion of gender roles to our next family meeting, but right now I'll acquiesce." He settled back in his seat and made a zipping motion across his mouth.

As soon as I rolled down my window, two microphones and various cameras were shoved in my face.

"Do you have a comment about Sonnet Ruiz's engagement announcement earlier today?"

"Does she know you're a felon?"

"Are your family grifters?"

"How do you afford this place? Are you sleeping with Sonnet for her money?"

Bet they'd shit themselves if they knew about the shifting.

I smiled calmly while they shouted their questions, wishing I'd watched one of those YouTube videos on how to pose. For now, I had to settle for keeping my smile easy. They wanted a bad shot, but I wouldn't make it easy for them. I wouldn't be the ogre in this play.

When they started to run out of steam, I spoke over them. "Now, you all hold up a minute. I'm happy to answer your questions, but from the front porch if that's all right with y'all. We can sit down, and I have sweet tea in the fridge. It's plenty hot out here, and I could use a cool drink."

Someone in the back muttered, *Moonshine!* But the rest of them seemed to wilt because I hadn't yelled or threatened to call the cops. Or just outright shoot them for trespassing. They shifted distrustfully away from the truck so Ranger and I could get out.

I nodded and gave them a polite smile as I walked toward the porch. "Could you bring out the sweet tea for these folks?" I asked Ranger. "And some ice. We'll be sitting on the porch."

Ranger scowled but nodded. He did not look happy about our uninvited guests. I was relieved when he disappeared inside without any further comment.

"You'll have to excuse my brother. We weren't expecting company today." Before anyone could yell out another invasive question, I turned to the reporter closest to me and held out my hand. "I'm Maverick Boone. Pleased to meet you."

THIRTY-TWO

SONNET

"Life itself is the most wonderful fairy tale."

— HANS CHRISTIAN ANDERSEN

Moonlight Valley looked the same as ever. It hadn't grown magically larger. It was the same sleepy, solitary Main Street with a handful of businesses with bad puns for names. There was the diner, the grocery store, and the hardware store. Wyatt's bookstore, The Pink Parts. Vanity Fur Salon. And yet somehow, even though I was the newest newcomer of them all (except, obviously, for Elena), it felt strangely like coming home.

It was early, not much past our usual shooting start times. We'd left right after the premiere and even before the after-party had wrapped. I'd even slept on the plane, which was a minor miracle. We'd all put our phones in airplane mode and just passed out. But now that I was so close, I just wanted to be there. *There* being in Maverick's arms. I'd missed my big guy, and I still had to tell him about my red-carpet revelation. Avalyn had mentioned dropping her footage later today, so I was short on time. Elena was twitching because she hadn't been able to get any internet service since London. It was killing her to disconnect.

We arrived with more speed than I'd dared hope for, thanks to Spike getting carsick. He'd announced this condition as Eric drove us rapidly from one mountain switchback to another. This had compelled Eric to drive even faster, as there was no place to pull off. No one wanted to witness Spike's misery firsthand, so we'd skidded into Moonlight Valley fast enough to make Sheriff Jacob frown and stroke his mustache.

Spike promptly bolted out of the SUV and began upchucking his burrito into a planter outside of The Pink Parts. The planter held a collection of ferns and flowering shade plants. Hopefully, Spike's sensitive stomach wouldn't cause *Cystopteris* carnage. The good news was that ferns were perennials. Green, leafy, and they usually came back after a hard winter—but they weren't immortal.

The rest of us climbed out with greater dignity. I slipped an arm around Elena's shoulders. She was holding her phone up and trying to get a signal.

"This place is medieval." She glared down at her phone, stabbing at it. "There is NO reception."

I glanced at the bookstore, smiling to myself. "You know, I think The Pink Parts gets reception. I might be able to give you the wi-fi password."

She looked up hopefully. "That's an unbelievably terrible name, I do *not* want to know what business that is, and yes, please."

I had just finished putting the password into her phone (WyattIsTheBest) when the door to the store opened. Bent over the screen, at first I just saw work boots and a pair of muscled, blue jeans–covered legs. I knew those thighs.

And that impressive, delicious bulge.

The T-shirt that announced, *I might be a biologist if I can make these genes fit* was new. As was the potted plant he held.

The unbuttoned flannel shirt was not. I was also best friends with the shoulders, the lush beard, the mouth curving upward in a smile, and the entire lumberjack biologist and world's best fiancé, Maverick Boone. He was grinning, and my heart did a jackrabbit impression. He was so handsome and so very, very mine.

I launched myself at him like a goof, shrieking. The potted plant was set down hastily, and then his strong arms were scooping me up, holding me tight. I wrapped my legs around his waist and buried my nose in the hollow of his throat.

I'm home.

It was part Moonlight Valley, sure, but it was more this man.

"I missed you." I came up for air just long enough to announce the obvious before I threw my arms around his neck and squeezed. I could I steal a quick kiss, right? And maybe, slightly hump him in public in front of a notoriously named bookstore? It would just give Wyatt more material for his books.

He wrapped one big hand around my ponytail, gently tipping my head back. His raspy voice and sweet Southern accent washed over me as he said, "I missed you more."

* * *

I counted it as a win that Elena didn't hex my fiancé. She was polite—which was more than she was with most people—when I introduced her to Maverick. I even dismounted from my happy Boone perch to make said introduction.

It didn't hurt that Rebel popped out of the bookstore behind Maverick, a stack of paperbacks by Elena's favorite author tucked under his arm. She'd always said that she judged a man by the books he read. He'd buttered her up by asking her for author recommendations, and she hadn't even protested when he'd squeezed into the SUV with us so they could keep up their impromptu book club meeting.

I'd wanted to ride with Maverick, but he'd followed in his truck. I'd made sad, horny faces at him all the way to the rented cabin. Maverick and Rebel had carried our bags in, taking them up the stairs and setting them just outside the bedroom doors. It was like being on a cruise ship, but with the world's sexiest porter man. A houseplant-gifting, super loving, and very horny porter man.

I followed Maverick outside and tugged him to the side. Rebel gave me a wink and wandered off to the truck. I didn't care where he went if it got me alone time with Maverick—sorry, not sorry.

"I have a confession." I wrapped my hand around his bicep in case he had the urge to flee. But also so I could feel him up. His arms were so muscular and strong. They made a deliciously sexy cage around me when he was on top of me, working himself deeper into my body. New thought: could he be convinced to play hooky from work?

He grinned at me, clearly onto my seduction ploy. "What is it that you need to tell me?"

I freaking loved his voice. It was low and raspy, a melting Southern burr that made me think about bourbon caramel and alone time with him. And a spoon. Maybe whipped cream. I needed a Maverick sundae right now!

"Sonnet, if you need me to pay attention, you have to stop thinking about me like that."

"Are you a mind reader now? Are you *sure* you know what I'm thinking?"

395

He leaned down and brushed his mouth over my ear. Whispered something. And GAH. He wasn't wrong.

"Sorry, sorry. Did I mention that I missed you?"

"You sure did. I missed you. My wolf missed you. Welcome home." His mouth was not over my ear anymore. It was, instead, kissing its way over my cheek, on a collision course with my mouth.

"Call in sick," I urged. "We evict Rebel from your truck and have truck sex. We can have lunch too. It'll be an afternoon of yumtasy."

"What?"

"Yumtasy," I repeated. "That would be something yummy that causes ecstasy. Yumtasy! Portmanteau words are the best."

He laughed, his eyes warm and happy. His mouth found mine in an achingly soft kiss. "Are you ready to confess?"

His mouth pressing tiny kisses against the corner of mine. It made me feel special. Cherished. So NO, I didn't want to admit that I'd screwed up our plan, no matter how good I believed my reasons had been. It had been *our* plan, but I'd turned it into *my* plan. I was good with the outcome, but I was not happy with my means.

I slid my arms around his waist. "Please don't get mad."

His smile was soft and patient. Instead of agreeing—or disagreeing—he simply listened and waited for me to continue.

I had thought about how to say this, but now, in Maverick's arms, I just blurted it all out in a rush. "I told everyone yesterday at the premiere that we were engaged. We should have a couple of days to come up with a contingency plan before Avalyn shares our news. I gave her an exclusive interview and—"

"I know. There's a video on YouTube."

This was bad. Very, very bad. "What? When?"

"I saw it yesterday afternoon."

I made a pained face. "Are you mad?"

"I was," he said matter-of-factly. He seemed super calm and not as if he was about to start yelling. "We made a plan together, decided what was best for us."

"Yes, but you see Luke was being—" No. That wasn't it. "Okay. He was my impetus, but I wanted to tell everyone. I hated being there without you, and I hated asking you to keep us a secret."

Maverick frowned, thinking over my words. I hated having made him mad, and even if he wasn't going off on me, he was frowning. He almost never frowned, and I'd never been on the receiving end before. I hated the hot pressure in my chest and the prickle behind my eyes—and in my conscience. I'd screwed up.

"I was wrong," I said. And that was true, but there was no walking back what I'd done. This wasn't something I could erase or fix.

He gently peeled my hand off his waist and brought it up to his mouth for a kiss. "I'll come by the set this afternoon, and we'll discuss everything then. Okay?"

It was not okay. I didn't want to wait. Not four hours, not four minutes, not even four zeptoseconds. On the other hand, now was not ideal. It was, in fact, unbelievably awkward. We were standing in the driveway in front of the cabin, with my sister, his brother, my bodyguards, and possibly some well-hidden paparazzi with long-range telephoto lenses watching us. I'd filmed kissing scenes with smaller audiences.

"Okay," I agreed reluctantly.

His mouth quirked as he studied my face. "Should I bring lunch?"

I nodded, already planning what I'd say. I had to have faith in him. In us. I had to believe that one mistake would not make him leave me. There might be yelling and disappointment, hurt feelings and regrets, but we would still be a couple. We'd just be a more experienced couple, and I wouldn't make the same mistake again (knowing me there would be a whole bunch of new and different ones).

Then he said, "Are you bringing dessert? For the yumtasy?"

His eyes held warm, teasing, playful heat, and so much interest and adoration. It was going to be okay. I hadn't screwed this up.

"So much yumtasy," I said mock-seriously. "You'll be worn out. In a yumtasy coma. It may be a very loud meal."

He raised his eyebrows and then flashed me my favorite smile. It was his happy smile and so one-hundred-percent open and Maverick that it made my knees weak, and I had to kiss him one more time before I let him go and left for the set.

* * *

"Are you going out for lunch?" Elena asked as we headed toward my trailer. "We can go together."

She smirked as she said this. She'd seen me kissing Maverick (and his enthusiastic kissing of me back) and now she'd reverted to being my big sister. She had shit to give me about my fiancé.

"I am staying in," I said, mustering up what dignity I could.

It was almost noon, and I was done shooting for the day. We were down to the last few scenes, so our filming schedule was short. I had the afternoon to myself, so long as I could convince Elena to go away.

"I'm writing." This was a sop to Elena. She was less likely to interrupt me if she believed I was making word count, not babies. "And maybe I'll take a nap. Self-care is very important."

"Uh-huh." She nudged my shoulder with her own. "Napping, is it? Would this be solo self-care napping, or does it involve your big, bearded fiancé?"

"No comment!!" I said.

She laughed evilly. "Oh my god! We should call Mami! She totally needs to meet your man, seeing as how he's about to become family. When *do* daffodils bloom?"

Elena had regained internet connectivity on her phone a few hours ago. She was still processing my bombshell red-carpet interview and the viral video of me proclaiming my undying love for Maverick Boone. Once she overcame her shock, there would be strategy meetings. PR meetings, marketing meetings, editorial meetings, wedding-planning meetings. So, SO many meetings.

"I'll see you later," I said firmly. *I'm the boss!*

She snorted, but she did leave me at the door to my trailer, so I decided to count our conversation as a victory. I gave Eric a stern heads-up to let *no one* but Maverick inside my trailer. He had my permission to go all ninja assassin predator dragon on any unbearded person who tried to open my door.

I'd brought along my silk caftan, the one with the suggestive peony flowers and the plunging neckline. Maverick had expressed his admiration for my caftan, and I was of the mind that it was a costume that announced: YUMTASY INSIDE. UNWRAP AT YOUR VIRTUE'S PERIL! I stripped down to my birthday suit and slipped on the caftan. Was Maverick striding up my path, looking manly and resolute and adorably in love? No. No, he was not. Ugh. I wandered around the trailer, rearranged a few pillows, and threw myself on the sofa. An idea came to me for the *Wolf Girl* script, so I flipped open my laptop and got to work.

When I looked up (thanks to my bladder's insistence that a bathroom break was urgently needed), I'd lost two hours. On the plus side, I'd written twenty pages, and they were awesome. On the downside, yumtasy was in short supply. I rubbed my eyes, stood up, and did some stretches that Elena swore would extend my ability to type into my nineties.

Focused on rapid bathroom access, I was surprised to discover Maverick parked at my kitchen table. He had a beverage in a to-go cup that he was sipping through a straw, and he was flipping through a binder and scrolling on his phone.

Maverick did not understand the definition of *yumtasy.*

He looked up as I flew past him. His warm, teasing smile lit up his face. "Sonnet—"

"Hi! I'll be right back! Nature calls! Prepare ye for yumtasy galore!!"

It was not my suavest, sexiest moment ever. We both needed yumtasy practice.

When I emerged from the bathroom, he scrawled a few lines in his binder, flipped it shut, and smiled at me. "Hey, baby. Are you all done? Word count made?"

"Close enough. How long have you been here?"

He checked his phone. "About an hour?"

"You should have interrupted me!" My family gave me shit about being in the zone when I wrote, but they knew they could poke me, and I'd snap out of it. I loved Maverick's respect for my job and my writing, but right now I wanted less respect and more loving. I'd been promised yumtasy, and who passed that up in favor of working *more*?

"How should I have interrupted you?" He had his legs stretched out in front of him, and he'd set his hat on the table. His flannel was unbuttoned, and his hair was mussed. He was my strong, capable, adorable man, and now I was thinking about having dessert before I had my lunch.

But we needed to talk first. We really, really did. If we went straight to the yumtastic sex, it would be like putting the roof on the house but skipping the essentials like a good foundation. Or the AC. If you tried to live in the South without a good, strong, capable AC unit (or so I believed), you'd end up miserable, hot, and bothered. It was the same for talking and relationships.

Nevertheless, I straddled his lap, linking my hands behind his neck. My caftan rucked up around my thighs. "Hi, gorgeous. Next time, interrupt me, please."

His eyes heated as they swept down my body and lingered on my bare thighs. "With pleasure."

I grinned at him. "You answered your own question."

We sat like that for a moment, mutually ogling each other. Who knew you could have yumtasy without actually kissing? Just by riding your man like a horse? (Actually, I knew that one.)

Heat and pleasure and utter and complete awareness rushed through me as I leaned into him. He was so completely amazing. *Please don't let me screw this up.*

Thus, I blurted out, "I'm so, so sorry."

His amused eyes cut to mine. "What are you sorry for?" I didn't miss the note of fond exasperation in his voice.

"Because we had come up with a plan and I said I bought into it ten thousand percent and then I just went ahead and did something else in the heat of the moment. I didn't stop to think about the consequences, and I'm sorry."

"Wrong turn, right place." Maverick shrugged. His big hands cupped my hips and pulled me closer.

I had agonized over my confession.

I had felt guilty.

I had been sure it was the end of the road for us, a bad, bad turn on the road of our relationship. At the very least, it had *mattered.*

So how could he be so laissez-faire about it?

Did he now think we both got to run around, ignoring the other's wishes? My stupid selfishness was not his license to be a dick.

"Wrong turn, right place?" My voice rose slightly.

Okay. A lot.

He nodded, a smile teasing the corners of his mouth. "You bet. You learned something. The windshield's bigger than the rearview mirror. Wrong turn, yes? But now you're in the right place."

"I'm sitting on your lap."

"You are." He brushed a kiss over my mouth. "I'm definitely thinking *right place.*"

"And it's all good, just like that?" I snapped.

I would not be disarmed by kisses.

He nodded once. Slowly. The man was totally aggravating. "Yes."

"Enlighten me, oh professorial one."

His fingers had discovered by diligent stroking of my hip bones that I was not wearing underwear. He gave me an amused yet exasperated look.

"We make plans together," he started.

"So far, so good."

"And then we stick to the plan."

"Okay. Yes. That's where I jumped ship."

"So, if one of us wants to change the plan, we discuss it."

"Agreed."

"Good," he said firmly, as if we'd just worked out the master plan for achieving world peace and could now rest on our tranquil laurels. "So now I have a confession."

Plot twist.

"You do?"

"I do. Yesterday, after I saw the viral video of your red-carpet interview, I did try to call you. There were reporters camped out at my house."

Crickets and clovers.

"Was there bloodshed? Was Ranger there? Should I call Elena and have her get a team on it? What did you all do?"

"I invited the reporters up onto the front porch. We had a sit-down and some sweet tea. I answered some of their questions."

He probably thought I'd thrown him into a snake pit. He was an actor in one of those Indiana Jones movies with all the snakes, asking himself, *WHY AM I HERE*, each time a reporter snake snapped at him.

"Was it awful?"

He shrugged. "It could have been worse. They didn't know about my wolf, and that's the most important thing. That would have been hard to explain. But they did know about my teenage years, and the car-thieving, and my arrest record. They particularly wanted to know how I thought TV audiences would react to learning that America's sweetheart was hooking up with a redneck ex-con. I pointed out the need for greater accuracy in their reporting, seeing as how I'd never been convicted of a crime and therefore was neither a felon nor an ex-convict and would be likely to sue them for slander if they published that untruth. Other than that, however, our chat was largely nice."

"Okay." I could call Elena. Hire a team. A large, battalion-sized team of people. Their mission would be to look after Maverick like a rabid badger. "We're okay."

His hands stroked my back, anchoring me. "This is the beginning. This week may be a challenge, so you have to let me help you. You need to talk with me, tell me when something comes up. There will be all sorts of stories, things coming out—not because I was keeping secrets but because we haven't had enough time together yet for me to tell you everything. Not when we keep getting distracted by bedroom matters. Ask me whatever you want. I won't get mad. My wolf won't get upset, either. We're in this together."

"We are." *We're in this together.* I didn't have to do this alone. Maverick would be right there beside me. I guessed we could hold each other up. We'd never let each other go. That was the deal we'd made. We had our mini galaxy of wonderful. That galaxy might undergo a few cosmic events, but we would be love astronauts, overcoming all.

It would be Maverick Boone and Sonnet Ruiz—teammates, partners, lovers, and best friends—standing together. What we'd done in our pasts, the labels people gave us, those things didn't matter. They weren't what was important. He'd found me in the woods on the day we met, lost and ass over teakettle. And I'd found him back. Our love was all that mattered.

Mostly.

Almost entirely, except, you know, for our families. What the Ruiz clan thought counted for a great deal with me. I'd always listen to them, even if in the end I disagreed. It might even be polite disagreement.

What Maverick's family thought also mattered, but they'd already made it clear that what made Maverick happy made them happy as well. I was good with them.

Maverick's thoughts mattered.

My thoughts mattered.

Everyone else? Bless their hearts. They didn't get a vote.

"I love you, Maverick Lincoln Boone." I reached for the bottom of my caftan, pulling it upward. "Fair warning. I plan to drive you wild, tempt that wolf of yours, fill your house with our part-Fae, part-shifter babies, and write a sexy memoir about it all because I want the whole world to know just how amazing you are."

He grinned down at me, his smile part amused, part devilish delight. His large, strong hands slid down my sides, curving inward to cup me. I loved how he touched me, how he cherished me exactly as I was.

"I love you, Sonnet Ruiz." His voice was low and smoky as he brushed a kiss over my mouth. "You are happiness and joy, sunshine and sparkle, but you're more than that. You're the best kind of puzzle, a maverick, and a treasure hunted. But," he whispered gruffly, "it's not my house. It's ours. Our place, our life, our family."

And then talking time was over. It was time for yumtasy. Love. And thanking the universe for the wrong turn down a mountain that had landed me here in the arms of the right man.

About the Author

Sign up for a newsletter 1-4 times a month with book factoids, cats, and behind-the-scenes glimpses of author life (which mostly involves more cats and wondering just how flexible Harlequin deadlines and word counts are): **https://anne-marsh.com/newsletter/**

New York Times bestselling author Anne Marsh lives in rural North Carolina full of neighbors who will pull you out of a ditch, bring you a truck of mulch, or fix your car just because they can. Who said heroes don't exist in real life?

* * *

Website: https://anne-marsh.com/
Newsletter: https://anne-marsh.com/newsletter/
Twitter: https://twitter.com/anne_marsh
Instagram: https://www.instagram.com/author_anne_marsh/
Facebook: https://www.facebook.com/annemarshauthor/
Pinterest: https://www.pinterest.com/annemarshauthor/

Find Smartypants Romance online:
Website: www.smartypantsromance.com
Facebook: www.facebook.com/smartypantsromance/
Goodreads: www.goodreads.com/smartypantsromance
Twitter: @smartypantsrom
Instagram: @smartypantsromance

Also by Anne Marsh

The Awesome Agency

Bet Me, Mr. Billionaire

Cute Guys with Cuter Dogs (Angel Cay)

The Player

The Beach Baby

The Heartbreaker

Really Funny Harlequins

Have Me

Hold Me

Her Intern

Hot Boss

Hookup

Inked

Royally Hung

Ruled

The Inheritance Test

The True Love Experiment

Lumberjack Men with Hoses (Mister Hotshot)

Hung

The Big One

Swagger

Wolves on Bikes! (The Breed MC)

Wolf's Heart

Wolf's Property

<u>Wolf's Claim</u>

<u>Lone Wolf</u>

<u>Bad Wolf</u>

ALSO BY SMARTYPANTS ROMANCE

<u>Green Valley Chronicles</u>

<u>The Love at First Sight Series</u>

<u>Baking Me Crazy by Karla Sorensen (#1)</u>

<u>Batter of Wits by Karla Sorensen (#2)</u>

<u>Steal My Magnolia by Karla Sorensen (#3)</u>

<u>Worth the Wait by Karla Sorensen (#4)</u>

<u>Fighting For Love Series</u>

<u>Stud Muffin by Jiffy Kate (#1)</u>

<u>Beef Cake by Jiffy Kate (#2)</u>

<u>Eye Candy by Jiffy Kate (#3)</u>

<u>Knock Out by Jiffy Kate (#4)</u>

<u>The Donner Bakery Series</u>

<u>No Whisk, No Reward by Ellie Kay (#1)</u>

<u>Dough You Love Me? By Stacy Travis (#2)</u>

<u>Tough Cookie by Talia Hunter (#3)</u>

<u>Muffin But Trouble by Talia Hunter (#4)</u>

<u>Oh Brother! Series</u>

<u>Crime and Periodicals by Nora Everly (#1)</u>

<u>Carpentry and Cocktails by Nora Everly (#2)</u>

<u>Hotshot and Hospitality by Nora Everly (#3)</u>

<u>Architecture and Artistry by Nora Everly (#4)</u>

<u>Small Town Silver Fox Series</u>

<u>Love in Due Time by L.B. Dunbar (#1)</u>

<u>Love in Deed by L.B. Dunbar (#2)</u>

<u>Love in a Pickle by L.B. Dunbar (#3)</u>

<u>***The Teachers' Lounge Series***</u>
<u>Passing Notes by Nora Everly (#1)</u>
<u>Band Together by Piper Sheldon (#2)</u>
<u>Ex Marks the Spot by Hazel James (#3)</u>
<u>Past Tents by Stacy Travis (#4)</u>

<u>Story of Us Collection</u>
<u>My Story of Us: Zach by Chris Brinkley (#1)</u>
<u>My Story of Us: Thomas by Chris Brinkley (#2)</u>
<u>My Story of Us: Grayson by Chris Brinkley (#3)</u>

<u>Seduction in the City</u>
<u>Cipher Security Series</u>
<u>Code of Conduct by April White (#1)</u>
<u>Code of Honor by April White (#2)</u>
<u>Code of Matrimony by April White (#2.5)</u>
<u>Code of Ethics by April White (#3)</u>

<u>Cipher Office Series</u>
<u>Weight Expectations by M.E. Carter (#1)</u>
<u>Sticking to the Script by Stella Weaver (#2)</u>
<u>Cutie and the Beast by M.E. Carter (#3)</u>
<u>Weights of Wrath by M.E. Carter (#4)</u>

<u>Common Threads Series</u>
<u>Mad About Ewe by Susannah Nix (#1)</u>
<u>Give Love a Chai by Nanxi Wen (#2)</u>
<u>Key Change by Heidi Hutchinson (#3)</u>
<u>Not Since Ewe by Susannah Nix (#4)</u>
<u>Lost Track by Heidi Hutchinson (#5)</u>
<u>Ewe Complete Me by Susannah Nix (#6)</u>
<u>Meet Your Matcha by Nanxi Wen (#7)</u>
<u>All Mixed Up by Heidi Hutchinson (#8)</u>
<u>Write or Wrong by Heidi Hutchinson (#9)</u>